Once Upon
a
Crossroad

R. M. Gibson

BookLocker

ISBN: 978-1-63263-237-1

Published by BookLocker.com, Inc., St. Petersburg, Florida.

Printed on acid-free paper.

The characters and events in this book are fictitious. Any similarity to real persons, living or dead, is coincidental and not intended by the author.

BookLocker.com, Inc.
2019

First Edition

Dedication

To Sandra for her encouragement and enduring support

Chapter One

It was a weary Erich Maurer who stirred when the cabin lights were turned on aboard American's Flight 18, an overnight 707 from San Francisco to New York's JFK, and the final leg of a long trip. A few minutes later a warm, friendly voice came through the overhead speakers.

"Good morning, folks. This is your captain speaking. Sorry about the late departure last night, but as you heard before we left the Bay Area there were connecting flights we had to wait for. At American, we don't want to leave anybody behind. And along with the delay, Mother Nature's tailwinds haven't been very helpful, so we haven't made up much time. We're figuring on being at the gate at, uhh, about eight o'clock. If we have to wait for a place to park, it'll be a few minutes after that. The weather in New York is overcast, breezy, and a chilly forty degrees. We don't have far to go now, so just sit back, relax, and enjoy that tasty breakfast your cabin crew is serving. We hope you got a little sleep, had a good flight, and that you'll come back and see us again real soon."

As Erich ate, he reflected on the events of the past few days. He'd left Sydney on Friday morning, spent a night in Hong Kong, then another in Tokyo before stopping in San Francisco to see Roxane Bouchard. They'd been lovers for a year, and she was ready to marry. Erich wasn't. A recent divorce, his second, had left its mark and taught him that he should take whatever time he needed to sort out his feelings. Roxane had grown impatient, but she was sure that his reason for arranging the stopover was to propose. After nearly three hours together, and he hadn't popped the question she expected to hear, she told Erich they were through, left him at the airport, and walked out of his life, indifferent to the fact that he had a wait of nearly eleven hours for his ongoing flight into JFK. The day they'd planned on spending together came to a sudden end, and their affair died with it on the first Sunday of November 1969. Now that it was over, Erich had few regrets. But his two teenage sons needed stable maternal support, especially Rudi, the younger of them, who'd already been into barbiturates. Both he, and older brother, Kurt, thought Roxane might one day become their surrogate mom. It was not to be.

As they were making their descent into JFK, a polite young stewardess said, "Sir. Excuse me. We're about to land. You'll need to bring your seatback into the full upright position."

"Sure. Been busy reminiscing."

The later arrival wasn't a problem for Erich. He could put in part of a day at the office before going up to Grand Central and taking an afternoon train home to suburban Seaford, Connecticut. He'd be at the station by five o'clock, a time he'd already given the new woman in his life, Brenna Walsh. Once back in his office, he'd call her to confirm that he'd be in as planned. He wasn't up to working any later than midafternoon.

When the cab driver dropped Erich off at his downtown building, 4 New York Plaza, his office partner, perky auburn haired Katie Dunne, was shocked to see him come through the door.

"Erich! Good grief, what are you doing here? You look wiped out. I didn't expect to see you until at least Wednesday. Anyhow, glad you're back safe and sound."

"I'm mostly okay . . . just look like death warmed over. Anyway, it's not life threatening, and I'm better off here and busy for a while. The nine-hour time change is a bitch, so it'll take a few days to get turned around. From the looks of what's on my desk, I'll need to do that sooner rather than later. And after I'm home I've got some catching up to do, too, you know. Be best if my internal clock is reset to Eastern Time."

Katie understood what he meant and smiled faintly. "The only personal call you had while you were gone was from Brenna. Another one, Erich? You sure do keep busy. Maybe someday it'll be my turn. Whatever, she said on Friday that if you wanted to come out earlier, she could still pick you up. Sounds like she has a special welcome home event in mind. You up to it?"

"Shouldn't take long to find out. But before we get on to other things, there's some news I think you'll find interesting. You were right about Roxane. She's history. You remember I was to meet her in San Francisco. We kept our date yesterday, took time to get reacquainted, and then all of a sudden she pulled the plug. It's over. Odd thing is, it really doesn't matter all that much. A while back, I got the feeling she'd walk if I didn't propose fairly soon, so what she decided wasn't exactly a surprise. And Lara's getting so wrapped up in her businesses that after a year of being close she's beginning to drift. Maybe I'm wrong, but that's the way it looks. So with the love of my life, Tina, having moved to Washington I'm fallin' on hard times. Brenna and I are close, but she's not the marrying kind. We just enjoy each other's company and let it go at that. No commitments. Anyway, glad she called, but I may stick with what we agreed on a couple of weeks ago."

"I told you last spring what I thought about Roxane, so she did just about what I expected. But if times are tough, there's always me, you know."

"Katie, you're a sweetheart, and I love you dearly, but I've said it before. There isn't any way we can work side-by-side Monday through Friday and then sleep together on weekends. Still, I'm pleased you think I'm someone you'd like to snuggle with. Good for my ego. Could be I'd look at it differently if one of us leaves the company and you get around to dumping your Danny."

"When he's gone, you'll be the first to know. Then I'll name the day, the time, the place, and hope you'll turn up and let me show you what kind of partner *I* can be."

"Easy. You're way ahead of me when it comes to the subject of us."

"In that case, I'll be patient and then pounce on you when you're least expecting it."

"You're hopeless. Let it be. On a less stimulating subject, I started writing my trip report over Indonesia and finished it on the flight into Tokyo. If you can get it done fairly soon, one of us will deliver it to the boss before I go. As I remember, his name is Henning."

Katie chuckled. "No change. Still the same livewire. And about your report, I'll get to it right away."

"Speak of the devil, look who just walked in. Hi, Joel."

"Mornin', Erich. Surprised to see you here, but since you are how'd it go?"

"Good. It was a busy week. Only got in about an hour of sightseeing, and maybe half that to do a little shopping."

"I've heard from Malcolm, and he's pleased with what you were able to do for various parts of IMCO-Australasia. And I'm sure you know about this from him directly, but while you were on your way back he confirmed that he wants you to help with their search for a new personnel head. I said yes, of course. The evaluation process begins on December 15. That's firm now. It's a Monday, so he suggested that this time you might want to come in a couple of days earlier. Since it's a busy time of year, you should probably get your reservations started before you head home."

"Good idea. And if you can stand it, my trip report's done; one of us will get it to you before I leave. Whenever that is."

"You're unbelievable. Always trying to stay one step ahead of me, and you're doing it. Says something about your dedication."

"Thanks. Just trying to do a good job. You pay me well."

"Okay. See you on Wednesday, maybe. Have a good rest."

"Thanks, boss."

When Erich finally got to his desk, he phoned Brenna.

"Hi, babe. How're you?"

"*Erich*. Good to hear your voice. I've really missed you. Especially after dark."

"That'll change. Katie gave me your message. I thought on my way in from Kennedy that I'd wait until the four-something train we talked about. Then it dawned on me that I'd be spending the better part of a full day in the office. Truth be known, I ain't up to it."

"Then you'll like my news. I'll still be able to pick you up because I'm taking the afternoon off. The people I work with are beginning to wonder what's going on. I'll let 'em guess. Can't wait to see you."

"Ditto. That's my kind of good news. What I'll do now is wait until my report's finished and then get myself on a train that leaves at about midday. I'm really glad you have the afternoon off. It'll give us more time to get caught up. And if you were able to make arrangements for the overnight, that'll be even better. I'm ready for a big bear hug."

"Mmm. I hear you. The overnight's set, and all day tomorrow, too. It's the way you wanted me to work it out if I could, and I've been able to do it."

"Great! What I'm setting aside is to pick up Kurt and Rudi. But it's probably best if they stay with the Engels until after we've had our reunion and I get my circadian clock running on Seaford time."

"Good we did some planning before you left. Now that you're back, I'm going to get you cornered and then keep you all to myself for a couple of days. It's called being selfish. Or maybe greedy is a better word."

"Ahhh, cornered is it? The southwest corner of number 710 is where I usually get horizontal. Is that what you have in mind?"

"Now *you* need to take it easy."

"Okay. It's just that I'm really looking forward to spending the next two days with you. Gives us time to enjoy each other's company. We're overdue."

"Sure are. But I've got to get back at it. See you at about one."

"I'm really pleased with all your news. Hope I survive the sluggish train ride out. Bye, babe." He smiled at Brenna's latest surprises and her afternoon off.

Then Erich phoned Clayton Zorn, his good friend and former boss at Essex Steel, to confirm their Friday afternoon date.

"Hey, Erich. Good to know you're back. You're on my calendar. I want to hear all about your trip, but I'm off to a meeting and gotta run. I've found a new place, The Bodega. See you there at about five thirty." He gave Erich the address and added that they might have one too many.

His trip report finished, signed, and delivered, Erich listened to Katie's summary about the status of their various projects. When she'd finished, he decided he'd given IMCO management all they had a right to expect at the end of his long trip. He gathered up all his stuff, said goodbye to Katie, and hailed a cruising taxi for the ride up to Grand Central.

On the train ride out, Erich's eyes took in the bleak cityscape. He found it drab compared to Australia's delightful spring weather, and his lids grew heavy from looking at too many familiar scenes. Drowsy as he was, though, he couldn't take his mind off Lara Renzo. By chance, their paths had crossed in the laundry room of his building almost a year ago. It was shortly after he'd met Roxane at a conference in Las Vegas. Taken with Erich, she'd come east to spend several days with him and had flown back to Vegas on Monday, Veteran's Day. It was the following Saturday afternoon that he and Lara met. Other than the various machines in the room, they were alone and she'd made a brazen comment about his messy sheets. They'd shared a chuckle, talked some, and then taken with her charm, Erich had invited her up to his place while their clothes were washing. They'd shared glasses of potent homemade Italian red wine. Later that afternoon, their defenses lowered, they'd bedded and found paradise. Since then, they'd been lovers and constant companions. But Lara's focus was different now, and Erich was beginning to think their romance had about run its course. Unlike his reaction to the end of his affair with Roxane, he'd hurt some if his relationship with Lara came to an end. Worn out from his travels, and by the thought of what might be, he dozed. It was only from force of habit that he awakened in time to get off the train at Seaford Station. Years of conditioning. Pavlov would've been proud.

Shuffling off the old coach, Erich and Brenna spotted each other at about the same time. She waved. He smiled. Then she greeted her returning road warrior with a warm hug. It felt especially good.

Raven-haired, attractive and well-built, Erich's eyes liked what they saw. "No need to ask how you are," he said. "You-look-absolutely-great!"

"Good to know the clothes I picked out and the extra time I took getting ready this morning were worth it. The other part of it is that I'm also showing you how glad I am that you're back."

9

"It's interesting to think about what I've just done, but it's also good to be home again—and to see you. But the news is I'll be going back to Australia in about six weeks. More about that later."

"Not much doubt that you've had a long trip. It shows. Best thing I can do is get you home so you can relax before we go out for dinner, assuming you're up to it. Maybe you can take a nap. I'll keep you company. After all this time, it'll feel good to be close."

"I like your idea, but I shouldn't nap. Except for the morning I got to Sydney, I haven't done that during the day since I was about three months old. Mother likes to say, 'You were such a pill'. I need to stay up. Otherwise it'll take forever for me to get on local time.

"Well, I'm yours for the next forty-plus hours, right up to Wednesday morning. "

Glad you could work out having tomorrow off, too. You really are making my homecoming special."

"When you look back on it in a few days, you'll be able to confirm it. But if we get friendly too soon, we might never get to dinner." Her mischievous smile was priceless.

Brenna pulled into a visitor's parking space at 17 Mianus Ridge, and then the two of them made their way up to Erich's apartment, number 710. They were both glad to be back in his comfy nest and its familiar walls.

Erich shed his blazer and pants, badly wrinkled from the long hours on flights all the way from Tokyo. His aim was to put on something casual. But as he was undressing, and despite what Brenna had said, so was she. What followed was driven by passion.

Fatigue had set in, so Erich was far from his best. But they loved, and both soon reached a place that took the edge off their having been deprived. Then, for only the second time in more than thirty-nine years, Erich napped. He slept for nearly two hours. Brenna watched him, fascinated with his face and the lively mind, now mostly at rest, which was hidden beneath his head of disheveled hair. What was he dreaming about that made him smile slightly? Then, thinking about their relationship, she had to admit that she was fond of Erich and also taken with all he'd done during the past two weeks. She cared about this man, someone who'd almost certainly never be her husband, but she always felt a special kind of warmth when he held her close. It was good seeing him at peace. But she wondered about their future and where their paths would take them. Probably in different directions since the lives they led were different.

Later, rested some and showered, Erich suggested they go out for an early dinner. Brenna agreed. Before they left, he told her about his meeting with Roxane, at least some parts of it, during his stopover in San Francisco.

"She's gone, just like Katie and Tina, my secretary at Essex Steel, said she'd be. They'd both met her and were sure she wouldn't wait more than a year. By coincidence, maybe, it was exactly one year—plus a few days. It was Tina who said that most women would hang on until the end, and maybe beyond, so she couldn't understand how Roxane might have the will to shut off her feelings, her affection, like a light switch. But she did it. And know what? I really don't much care. Part of it, I guess, is that I found out she's sixteen years younger than me, not eight like she said. I'm certain that being married to her wouldn't have lasted, and there was no way my psyche could handle another divorce. And Lara? I think we're headed in the same direction. Difference is, she matters. Another couple of weeks, and we'll have known each other for a year. That seems to be the magic number, and it explains why I need to be patient. It'll take a year, maybe longer, for me to know if a relationship feels right and it has a good chance of working out."

"I can relate to that. But, two things. First, you can expect Brenna Walsh to be around for more than a year. Second, don't count on me being the permanent squeak in your bed. I told you pretty much the same thing when we first met. I'll be your companion, but there probably isn't a ring, or another altar, in my future. I like you, Erich, maybe more than I should, but I want to keep things between us just about the way they are. And another thing. Since you and I have gotten close, I'll have to decide if I should keep helping Lara out at her shop on weekends, assuming she asks. Could be that seeing our long friendship fall apart is the price I'll pay for taking over her place in your life."

"It'll be something for the two of you to work out. Why don't you just cool it and see what happens. And how you feel about us is fine. It means we don't have to spend much time thinking about romance, or trying to figure out where our relationship is headed. Now, dear heart, I'm not just tired, I'm hungry, too. How 'bout some dinner?"

Erich decided his Mustang could probably use some exercise, so he drove to a restaurant they liked: The Ingleside.

"We're in a rut, kind of," Erich said later. "Let's go someplace else tomorrow night. Problem is, Tina's shadow is in lots of the other restaurants. Same thing with coming back here if someday we decide we've had enough of each other. It's because we ate here the night we met, so it'll always be our place. I said that at the time. There'd forever be an image of you sitting at one of the tables. Guess I'm a hopeless romantic."

"I know. It's one of the reasons I like you. But you were going to give me a rundown on your trip, and the other one coming up."

Erich went into more detail than was necessary, but Brenna seemed interested in every bit of it. He talked about the stops along the way, including Athens, Tehran, New Delhi, Hong Kong, Manila, and also his business in Sydney. Then there were the stopovers in Hong Kong, Tokyo, and San Francisco on the way home. By the time he'd finished, they'd long since finished dinner.

Over an amaretto, Erich said, "The reason I'm going back to Sydney in December is that the head man down there, Harry Malcolm, wants me to interview candidates for his personnel director's job. The current guy is retiring, and they need to find a replacement. Yesterday. The search should've been started sooner, but that was out of my hands. Before I left at noon, we tried to work out another round the world trip, but there were sectors, as they're sometimes called, that were sold out. Not important. Malcolm said I should travel smarter anyway. What he meant was that I should fly west, straight down and back, but make a stopover in the Fiji Islands. So, I'm doing that. I leave here on December 9 and get home on Christmas Eve. But once I'm back, I don't suppose we'll see much of each other over the holidays."

"It's still a ways off, but we'll work something out. I'll be busy during the holidays themselves, but we should be okay otherwise."

"I'm taking time off starting the morning I'm back. With both Christmas and New Year's Day on Thursday, my five vacation days turn into almost two weeks off. So if you're free, there'll be time to do whatever."

"Good to have your schedule. Family comes first during the holidays, but I'll work around them. Count on me fitting into your days off. On second thought, I shouldn't get to be too much a part of your vacation, or your life. I might get to like it too much, in spite of what I said earlier."

"Before we find out if I have enough energy left for nocturnal delights, I have a little something for you."

Erich dug into a pocket of his jacket and pulled up a small box. Smiling, he handed it to Brenna.

After a brief pause, she opened it. Inside was a magnificent black opal from Australia's Lightning Ridge area that he'd brought back from Sydney.

Brenna's radiant blue eyes came alive. "Ohhh, Erich. It's stunning. How can I ever thank you?"

"Just keep on being the Brenna Walsh I've gotten to know. Call it an early Christmas present. I didn't know your ring size, so I couldn't have it set. Anyway, there wasn't time. If we can get to a jeweler during the holidays, you can pick out the ring. It's part of the deal that I couldn't get done in Sydney. But don't think of it as an engagement ring. I just wanted to do this because you're important. Another way to say it is that I think you're special."

"I don't get misty-eyed very often, but you've almost gotten to me with this. It's elegant."

"Now, let's go back to number 710, do some cuddling, and then see if I have any oomph left."

"I'd like us to try. If it doesn't work out, I'll understand. You've had a rough seventy-two hours, so I won't worry about it since we have tomorrow. I like the idea of sleeping late on a Tuesday. I owe Sis. You remember Colleen. She's a sweetie."

When they were home, Erich burned what little energy he had left to do what Brenna had in mind. Contented, she snuggled up to Erich as their loving, and their day, came to an end. He badly needed rest and sleep came instantly. Feeling at peace, Brenna smiled amiably before she slept.

On Tuesday, Erich's body clock was so disoriented that he felt worse than when they went to bed. So he squandered much of the morning trying to decide if there was any chance he'd live. It was a lot like the Sunday morning in Sydney when he went down and slept for almost sixteen hours. "I don't know about international travel," he groused. "It's debilitating."

"You'll be fine. Just take it easy. I promise not to put a move on you. At least not until later."

A quiet day, a very dry Gibson over ice, a high protein dinner, and Erich did feel better by the time they got home. So much so that he was nearly his virile self later in the evening.

Brenna purred afterwards. "You're almost back to normal."

On Wednesday morning, the two of them slept later than usual. Didn't matter. Brenna would most likely get to her job at the Metro Agency on time. As office manager, she had some small perks, like being a little bit late. When they finally started their day, Erich walked Brenna to her car. They both savored their affectionate hug and gentle goodbye kiss. Then, into the garage, Erich brought his Mustang to life and headed toward the parking lot across from Seaford Station. Brenna was at work by nine o'clock. Erich was more than an hour late.

When he got to the office, Katie smiled brightly and greeted him with her always cheerful, "*Good* morning," and then added, "I thought maybe you were taking the day off."

"No, I waited until Brenna was ready to leave. She works for the biggest insurance agency in Seaford and doesn't have to be in until around nine. But I could've used another day. The turnaround hasn't been easy."

"Especially when you have someone to look after."

"It took some effort, but I managed." There was a hint of envy in Katie's thin smile.

"You had a call from Lara at a little after nine. Since she called here, I guess she doesn't know you're back. Anyway, her message was that they just found out that an uncle who lives up in Worcester, Massachusetts has lung cancer, so she and her mother are going up to see him over the weekend. She said you'd know that her shop is closed on Mondays, and with Veteran's Day coming up the day after, she's taking a four-day weekend and will call you when they're back. I took everything down. Here are my notes."

"That's really sad news. He's been like a father to her after her dad was killed in a rail yards accident several years ago. She and this uncle have been really close. Why do these things happen to such good people? Makes you wonder if the Lord hasn't abandoned her Uncle Gino."

"Do you want me to get her on the phone?"

"No. It may not be the right thing to do, but we weren't to talk until Friday. She has enough on her mind, so I'll let it be and call her then. We were going to spend the weekend together."

"Her being away ruins your plans, but her trip has priority."

"Lara will need lots of support when she gets back, and I'll be there for her. She's certainly has been for me when I needed it. I know what she's going through. The man is special to her. But it's best not to dwell on it further until she has a better idea about where things stand. Now, what's on our schedule this morning?"

"First item is an update on your trip back to Sydney. You got confirmation from the travel department late yesterday that your reservations are all set. Your December 9 departure is on BOAC's Flight 591 and it's been confirmed. It leaves at 3:00 p.m. The return flight gets you into JFK just before eight on the morning of the twenty-fourth. Not much time for Christmas shopping."

"I'll do it en route—and in Sydney if there's time. I'm stopping in Fiji, as you probably saw. I'll have two days there going down, and about twenty-four hours on my way back."

"Travel also said that on your return you'll have about a seven hour layover in Los Angeles before you fly overnight into Kennedy. BOAC will put you up at a hotel near the airport. It's their Flight 592 from Sydney to New York, including your stopover in Fiji and theirs in Los Angeles. Here's the itinerary."

"Not ideal, but I guess that's it. Okay, it'll give me part of another day to get turned around. Christmas will probably be a train wreck. May sleep through it. So, what else is on our plate?"

"The usual requests for support, and a workup that I've started for a trip to Chicago on the sixteenth that Joel wants you to make. These are the notes I took while he was talking about it. Looks like another get acquainted trip more than anything else. Then he wants you to start thinking about a trip to London in April to visit IMCO Ltd. Here's what he scribbled out. He'd have talked to you about it himself, but he had to make a quick trip to Detroit. Something came up, and he left on Monday evening. It's way early, but while it was on his mind he wanted you to have his ideas about what he thinks your agenda should be."

Erich and Katie busied themselves with the more important items first, then tackled less critical requests. Not much work was needed on the Chicago trip as it really did look as if he'd be going out to meet with his contemporaries. The London trip was far enough off that it'd keep until after he was back from Sydney.

Before he went to lunch on Friday, Erich phoned Lara to find out how she was doing and to see what her plans were.

"Hi babe, I'm back. Katie gave me your bad news. You're still leaving today?"

"Good to hear your voice. Feels like you've been gone forever. Yeah, we'll be on our way around four. Sorry I can't keep our date, but you already know that this is the uncle I told you about last Thanksgiving. He's my favorite and the father I haven't had since we lost Dad. It's a trip we have to make. And it looks like I won't be able to see you at Christmas either. I know you'd planned on it, but it'll be for the same reason. We really don't have any choice."

"I understand. It's important to be with family at a time like this. Just let me know when you think we might be able to get together."

"Maybe the following weekend."

"Not ideal. I'm going out to Chicago on Sunday, the sixteenth, but maybe you could stay over the night before."

"Been a while since I've seen you. I'd like to come over, even if it's only for one evening. That's better than not seeing you at all."

"I'm going to Sydney again in early December and won't be back until the morning of Christmas Eve. But I imagine you'll have already left for Worcester by then. So, see you a week from tomorrow. After that, we'll have to figure out what's doable."

"It could always be a week night. With our schedules, we'll have to be flexible. I'd like that. You're still important to me."

"And you are, too. So I'll plan on your staying over on Saturday night next week."

"It's a date. I'll try to get away at midafternoon. Now that I have some help, it's easier for me to do that, and it'll give us a little more time together."

"Good. See you then. And drive carefully.

Chapter Two

After Erich got back from lunch, he checked the address Clayton had given him for the new guy-gal pub he'd found. The name he'd written down was The Bodega. Looking at it more closely, he realized that it was in the same neighborhood he knew well from the days the two of them had worked for Essex, now a part of Luxembourg's ARBED Steel, S.A. No need for a map to find it.

Late in the afternoon, Clayton and Erich got to the pub at about the same time. It was the start of the weekend and busy. So after looking around, they spotted each other through a break in the crowd. They shook hands and then found a small opening at the bar right next to a couple of rather nice looking young ladies.

Clayton, in his typical engaging form, asked, "Is this the space reserved for my handsome friend here from New York Plaza?"

The girls smiled politely and the taller of them said, "Not much choice."

"Sorry we're late," Clayton added facetiously, and aimed a thumb in Erich's direction. "It's his fault. He's just back from Australia and is still on Sydney time. Aren't you impressed?"

"Guess so. That explains why he isn't pale like the rest of us."

"I didn't lose my voice Down Under," Erich said, "so may I join the party? I'm Erich, and this good-looking guy is my ex-boss, Clayton."

"I'm Joanna. And my dear friend here is Linda."

Hellos done, they ordered drinks. The girls were at least one up on them.

"We'd ask you join us at a table, but there aren't any," Clayton said. "Looks like this little space is it."

Linda spoke up. "Not important. We have other plans and will be leaving shortly."

"Sorry to hear that. I thought we might make an evening of it."

"I think not," Joanna said. "And just so you know, we're not into dating, live together, and value our caring relationship."

Clayton replied, "I have business friends, men mostly, who're similarly oriented, and I understand."

As the gals got ready to leave, Erich spotted a table nearby that was free. Before they sat, both wished the girls a pleasant evening.

Clayton surveyed the people in the place and observed, "It's a fair guess that at least some of tonight's customers are gay."

"Having grown up on in Ohio farm country, we never had anybody like that around, so they and their lifestyle are foreign to me. Guess I have a problem understanding their way of life."

"I suppose gays are more likely to be city residents; that is, compared to rural areas. But they're good people, many of them are very sharp, and some have key corporate jobs. But on to other things. Tell me about your trip Down Under."

"They kept me busy. I had a close look at the policies of our Australasian subsidiary, mostly focusing on how they manage their human resources. My mission was to see if they, other of our affiliates, and New York corporate, could improve our results if we had like procedures. We're not that far apart, so it's doable."

"Sounds as if you're into a new province, international, one that's broader than what you did at Essex. Sounds interesting."

"It is that. And I'll be going back to Sydney in December to help find a new personnel director. But how're you doing?"

"I still have a demanding job, but the day may be coming when I'll want to see what else is out there. At this stage, I'm able to take on almost any kind of role at the personnel management level. And since there aren't many people who have a skill set as wide-ranging as mine, I'm marketable at pretty good money.'

"Well, I'm sure you'll keep me posted."

"I'll do it. Now, I've got a couple of errands to run. My treat this evening. Your turn next time. We'll get together soon just so we can stay current. Great seeing you, Erich."

"You too, Clayton. G'night."

Erich caught one of his later commuter trains and was home at a little before eight. He went about fixing himself a bite to eat. Then with no one at home, and completely alone for a change, he decided to have another drink and then go to bed. Turned out to be a good idea, because it was the best night's rest he'd had since getting back from Sydney.

Next morning, the first thing on his agenda was to call the Engels, the family Kurt and Rudi had stayed with while he was away. Young Chris answered. "Hey, XM. How ya doin'?"

The story behind the "XM" was that the vanity plate on Erich's Mustang had just those two letters on it. It stuck with Chris, and that's how he addressed Kurt and Rudi's dad. Didn't matter; there was no disrespect involved. He was a great kid and full of life.

"I'm home and figure it's time to pick up my guys."

"You probably don't have to do that. Dad has to go over to the plant, so he can maybe drop 'em off on the way. Okay?"

"I've got shopping to do and can come up if it isn't convenient."

"Let me make sure."

Erich was able to hear Chris's dad, Matt, say that it wasn't a problem.

"No, it's all right. He's leaving in a few minutes, so they should be home by about two. What'd you bring me from Australia?"

"I'll never tell. Well, okay, it's a hot chick."

"Groovy! When can I get delivery? Gotta keep up with Kurt."

"I'll let that subject be. Maybe I should've said something else, like I brought you a roll of Australian toilet paper. It's metric size, you know." Chris thought that was funny and worth a chuckle.

"If your dad can come up, I'll give him what I brought back."

"I'll tell him. Thanks, XM."

"Appreciate your putting up with the guys."

"No sweat. We had a ball."

"Take care, Chris."

"See ya, XM."

Matt Engel delivered Kurt and Rudi, and all their dirty laundry, at just about the time Chris had guessed. Erich hugged his sons before they went to dump everything in their bedroom.

"Can't stay, Erich. There's a problem at the plant I have to fix. But I'd like to come back and talk to you one of these days."

"Sure, Matt. I've got a crazy schedule, but you're welcome to stop in whenever I'm here. By the way, since I was gone a little longer than I expected, here's some extra money to cover the additional cost for food."

"You don't need to do that. We like having them around, and the three guys always have a great time." Still, he took the money.

"The latest news is, I have to go back to Sydney in about five weeks and won't be back until the morning of Christmas Eve. Could I lean on you and Cynthia to take them again until maybe the nineteenth? School vacation begins that afternoon, and I'm hoping my ex, Dawn, will help me out. She's done it before. Thing is, she's been pretty quiet lately, so I'll need to find out if having them for a few days won't interfere with whatever plans she might have."

"You know it isn't a problem. We feel like they're part of the family."

"I'll see that you have money to feed 'em. They sure know how put it away."

"So can Chris. Not much difference in appetites when they're teenagers and full of piss and vinegar."

"Appreciate it, Matt. You've been a tremendous help. Don't know how I'd manage otherwise."

"Glad to help out. But, I've got to go. The problem at the plant won't wait much longer."

"Call me when you want to talk."

"I'll do it. I've got a load on my mind and need to get it out in the open."

"I understand. You're not alone. But my concerns are probably different. Oh, nearly forgot. Meant to give you this when you got here. It's a neat T-shirt for Chris that I brought back from Sydney."

"Thanks, Erich. I'll give it to him when I get back to the house."

After Matt left, Erich said, "Hey, guys. Time to see what I brought you and then get all your stuff washed."

They grumbled about having to start doing chores but loved the T-shirts with "Australia" and the image of a koala on them.

"Thanks, Dad. Guess we have to start helping out again, huh?" Kurt asked.

"Yep. That's what it means. You've got a ton of dirty clothes, and so do I. Now, I've got to go find food, or we'll have to start eating dirt. And over dinner, I'll tell you about my trip."

Shopping and laundry done, the three Mauer guys sat down to dinner. And as promised, Erich told them about Australia, plus the long trip down and back. Then the boys brought him up to date on what they'd been doing.

Afterwards, Rudi asked, "What's happened to Lara?"

"Wish I had a good answer. She seems to be marrying her business. I'm not that important anymore. At least that's the way it looks. What she's doing is opening more stores, working longer hours. I don't know. It happens, and it's one of the reasons I'm taking time to decide who I think is right for me and the two of you. If we'd gotten married, it wouldn't be any good because she wouldn't be here to look after you, or bake those cookies we've talked about. You know what I mean. And Roxane's gone now. I saw her in San Francisco on the way back, and it's over. I told you a long time ago that I had a feeling she wouldn't hang around while I made up my mind about us. And that's what's happened. She's in a hurry. I'm not. And Brenna isn't interested in a husband. She has her own house, two boys, lots of friends, and a life she's happy with. We're just people she likes. So, we'll have dinner, go to movies, and maybe spend a weekend together. But it's not serious, so she won't be your new mom."

"Doesn't matter that much," Kurt said. "In another couple of years I'm done with school, and then I'll be out on my own."

"Sure, but it'd be nice to have a woman around, someone who cares about you, don't you think?"

"Yeah, but I can live without one. You're doing all right, and if that's the way it's gotta be, we'll get along. You can have your friends, I have mine, and we'll make out." Kurt grinned. "That came out wrong, but you know what I mean. We'll be okay."

"Not me!" Rudi said. He had tears welling up and started to leave the table. Lara was important to him and very much on his mind.

"Rudi. Sit for a minute. Please?"

He wiped his eyes and sat down.

"What I haven't told you is that Lara was going to be here this weekend, but she has an uncle, a favorite of hers, who has cancer. He lives in Worcester, a city up in Massachusetts that's not that far from our building lots at Bass Lake. She and her mother have gone up to see him. I have to go to Chicago a week from tomorrow, but we're planning on her being here next Saturday evening before I leave. Maybe she'll stay with you until Monday morning. Ask her to explain what's going on. Maybe you'll understand better why things don't seem to be working out for us."

"I will because I really like her."

"She's gotten to be like a mom, so I understand. But I might meet someone new that you'll like, too."

"But I'd miss Lara," Rudi said. "I sure hope she can be here next weekend."

"That's the plan. So I guess you want her to be at your birthday dinners."

Both boys said they'd like that.

"You'll have to ask about that, too. It'll mean more to her if you do. She's really busy."

"We won't take no for an answer," Rudi said.

Chapter Three

The following week Erich called Clayton if for no other reason than to chat for a few minutes. As often happened, they talked about the women in their lives. Since Clayton had met Lara the previous December, he asked about her.

"It's been a year since we met, and you know about the life cycle of a romance. At least mine. The fire isn't as hot now. Says she still cares, but she's fallen in love with her business. There are a couple of new stores in the works, has plans for more, a bank to back her, and seems intent on being Seaford's woman of the year, I guess. Along with her being awfully busy, her favorite uncle is dying of cancer. Lots on her mind. She may stay over before I go out to Chicago on Sunday afternoon. If not, it'll be on Kurt's birthday next week and then maybe the weekend of the twenty-second. But the end is near, I think. Another name to add to my collection of busted romances: Roxane, Tina, something you didn't know about, and probably Lara before much longer."

"I had a hunch about you and Tina. You took it way too hard when she left Essex. Glad you confessed. You've got to tell me all about it the next time we get together."

"It's left its mark. But the other news is that I met a friend of Lara's at the end of September. It was when she was in the hospital. You may remember that she had a bad scare from an internal lady thing. The friend and I were there visiting her on the same evening. Name's Brenna Walsh. We've seen each other since then, but she's not part of the women's lib parade and resisted getting friendlier after dark. Took a while. It was just before I left for Sydney. Worth the wait. I'll also tell you about her when we bend an elbow."

"You've got all kinds of news."

"Yeah. And at that I may have missed something."

"You said on Friday that you're going back to Sydney. When's that?"

"December 9. I'll give you the details when we have our drink. How does a week from Friday look?"

"I'm on vacation all of Thanksgiving week and will be on my way up to the Cape on the twenty-first. You remember that my folks have a house out on Long Pond. If the fifth will work for you, let's do it then."

"It's a ways off, but I'll put it on my calendar. If you would, have your secretary call me earlier in the day to confirm that we're still on. And in case we don't talk again before then, have a great Thanksgiving."

"You too, Erich. Take care."

Katie heard some of her partner's conversation about the women in his life. Although she couldn't help but smile, she clearly envied them. "New love, Erich?"

"Eavesdropper. Not really."

"Here I was going to attack you at the Christmas party, but you're not even going to be back by then. I just realized that over the weekend. How am I ever going to know what I'm missing?"

"I guess you'll just have to wonder. But I've told you before that I won't give your fantasies any thought until one or the other of us doesn't work here any longer and that you and your Danny have untied the knot."

"I know. I know."

"How about we get some work done before Joel throws both of us out into New York Plaza."

"Well, that would satisfy half of your rules."

"Give it up, girl."

"Not while there's the slimmest chance."

"Katie, we have things to do. Part of it is to finish up the Chicago trip file. I shouldn't have to remind you that I fly on Sunday."

"Glad you mentioned it. Your flight's been changed. You're going out of LaGuardia at 4:30 and coming back on the nineteenth at 2:15. Flight time is about two hours. You'll get home in time to have some fun."

"In time to get dinner ready. Not exactly fun after a full day in Chicago, the flight back, and the limo ride out to Seaford. But it's all got to be done. Nobody to help me out. Kurt's birthday is on Thursday, the day after; we'll have dinner out then."

"I take back my smart aleck comment. My day will be easier than that, even if I do have to go home and cook for a stranger I've known nearly all my life. But I won't bore you with my story. Let me bring you the Chicago file. After you've gone over it, tell me what you think."

At midday, Lara called to say she was back and wanted to know if she could spend the night. Her uncle, she said, was in a bad way. "I know it's mid-week, but I've been there when you wanted support. Now I need yours."

"You don't have to ask. I'll finish up here so I can be at home by about a quarter after six. If you're going to leave the shop early, I'll let the boys know you're coming. You still plan on spending Saturday night with us?"

"Definitely. I really need to do that, and I'll stay over until Monday morning."

"Wonderful. My flight's been moved down to half past four, so maybe I can talk you into taking me down to LaGuardia."

"I'd like to do that, too. Kind of like old times. But you also know that I like driving your Mustang. It'll lift my spirits some."

"And it shouldn't surprise you that both Kurt and Rudi want you come to dinner with us on their birthdays. Kurt's is just eight days off, and Rudi's is on a Saturday night, so maybe I can talk you into spending the rest of the weekend with us."

"I'll plan on it. And you're making me feel better because both evenings should be fun. I'm overdue to spend some time with healthy people."

"You've been busy, so I wasn't sure. I'm sorry about your uncle, but we've sorta been left to ourselves lately."

"Not much choice." Lara voice was unsteady. "You're still important, but I'm really caught up with everything that's going on. It's hard."

"Well, if you and I are to eventually come unglued, let's do it in style and leave each other with some pleasant memories."

That did it. Lara choked up and wasn't able to say anything other than, "See you around six." Erich wished he hadn't said what he did. He'd not meant to confront her this way about how unclear their future looked, especially with her uncle so bad off. He wasn't at all happy with himself. He'd hurt Lara. "Dammit!" he said.

Later in the day, he rang Kurt and told him Lara might show up before he got home. "She's spending the night with us. With her uncle so sick, she'll need our support. I told her we'd be there for her, but I made a stupid comment that hurt. Anyway, I'll be home by a little after six. Hold the fort, will you?"

"Sure, Dad. It'll be good to see her. Been a while."

"Yep, it has. Thanks Kurt. See you later."

Lara had come up earlier and was there when Erich got home. Kurt and Rudi were with her, but when he came in Lara went to the foyer and held him tightly. Then she broke down. And like their dad, the boys found it hard to be a part of such a painful moment. Erich knew he had to be her pillar because she needed comfort, and he gave her all the support he could with soft words and by just holding on. He was still in his coat.

After several minutes of tears, Lara let go, gave Erich a gentle kiss and said softly, "Thank you."

Erich put a curled finger under Lara's chin, tilted her wet face up just a bit, and asked, "Feeling a little better now?"

"Some. I'll manage. It's times like this when I think maybe we shouldn't try to be a permanent part of each other's lives. You have your work, I've got my business plans and, well, you understand."

Tears welled up, and she needed holding again. It didn't last long. Erich gave her his hankie and asked if he might take off his coat. Lara smiled weakly. "She's mending," he thought.

After he got out of his coat, Erich asked her, "Could I interest you in a glass of very good Chianti?"

"Yes, please. But I have to be careful, though. For two reasons. One is that I'm out of practice. The other is that too much of it will make me depressed, and I'll be back into tears. You let me have my cry, and I've gotten some of the hurt out of my system. I'm a little better now."

Erich poured wine, Cokes for the guys, and a dry Gibson on the rocks for himself.

"We haven't talked for three weeks," Lara said. "Tell me about your trip."

"The first thing that may interest you is that Roxane's gone. She drove down from her mother's place in Sacramento and met my incoming flight from Tokyo. The idea was to spend the day together. But after about three hours, and it became obvious I wasn't going to propose, she said, 'I'm going home', and that's what she did. No hug, no kiss, and when she walked away, she never even looked back. Pretty outside, all granite inside."

"You've said all along that you thought it wouldn't last."

"When she was here in May, I felt there were big question marks hanging over our heads. It's just as well that I saw her on the way back. She settled it all. And you know that on Saturday, it'll be a year since you and I met. With Roxane it was exactly a year—plus a few days. Could that mean we're all done on Sunday? That'll be a year and a day."

"Erich! It doesn't mean anything of the kind. We'll be together on Kurt's birthday, and there's a chance I'll be able to stay over on the Monday before Thanksgiving. Like last year, we'll be with family. Mom thinks we have to do this while everyone's still alive. Uncle Gino's her brother, and his cancer has brought it home. She said we're going back to Worcester to give him support and to see how he's doing. I have permanent help now, so we'll be leaving right before Thanksgiving and coming back the Monday after. I've also hired an accountant, and he's doing all my year-end books, the ones I did myself last November. Remember that? Much easier on me this year. With my expansion plans, I'll need that kind of professional help."

"While you were talking, I was thinking about that Saturday we met in the laundry room, how much fun it'd be to relive that day and those that followed. They were light and happy. We were new friends, and I enjoy thinking about the lovers we became. What a difference a year makes. We've been through a lot, and the future is so uncertain. There are rumblings that IMCO may revert to their earlier management philosophy. If that happens, most of us probably won't survive their return to decentralized operations. The company will be downsizing, so I may need you to prop me up again. We'll lean on each other. But I'm going back to Sydney on the ninth and don't get into JFK until Christmas Eve. Ahhh, my mind's gone soft. I told you about that already. You'll be in Worcester, so we may spend the holiday alone. But with the time change I won't be worth much. I found that out after this last trip."

"I hope you aren't by yourself on Christmas. That'd be terrible. Makes me sad to think about it."

"The boys will be here, but we won't be able to have a tree. Maybe Dawn would have us. We've not heard from her in a while, so I'll get Kurt to ask."

"Like I said, we're back on the Monday after Thanksgiving, the first, and I'd like to spend that night with you, too. The rest of the week is out, and I go into New York on Friday afternoon to meet with possible suppliers for things I'll need to stock the new outlets. I'm adding to my product lines, and there are distributors in during that weekend. I really need to go."

"Buy you a drink before I leave the city? It's the fifth we're talking about. Clayton and I already have plans to meet, but I could see you afterwards."

"It's sweet of you to suggest it, but I'm going straight to the exhibition from Grand Central. Fun idea. But I have to do what I'm there to get done."

"Then we're into the new decade. But we have tonight, part of the weekend, Kurt's birthday, and the first, if I've got it all sorted out. Maybe I could talk you into adding either the Monday before Thanksgiving that you mentioned, or the night before I leave, or both, to our hectic calendars."

"Looks like you're trying to make up for lost time. Makes me feel good. And speaking of that…."

"Best we set that aside until later. So, until then, tonight's menu features mother's very fine chili soup."

"You know how much I like it, and treats like that also help me deal with the all things that are keeping me awake at night. But you've usually been able to do that."

"So have you, dear heart. I won't ever forget how you've been there for us when we needed a lifeline."

After they ate, the boys wanted time with Lara, and they had every right to it. She meant a lot to both of them, especially Rudi. It'd been weeks since they'd had dinner together, and it was good to have her back, even if only for one evening. When they'd had a visit that satisfied them, they gave her a hug and went off to bed.

"I guess that leaves you and me to pick up where we left off," Erich said. "It was something you said about feeling good."

"On the way up, I was thinking about being here tonight and wondered if my fire had gone out. When you're not around, I have no interest in a man, or loving. It hardly enters my mind. It's like it doesn't exist. Really strange. Then we get together, and that's all it takes. The wanting is there again. It's like you're the only one who can turn me on. In lots of ways, that isn't right. I've said something like that before. But I'm here, and I want you to make me feel like that whole woman again."

"You've come to the right place. No waiting for service. Whenever you're hot to trot…."

"How 'bout now?" She showed him a genuinely impish smile.

It had been weeks, if not months, that Erich felt sure Lara was totally entranced by the highs they'd reached—and then what they ultimately shared. They returned to the same oasis of pleasure that had been part of their lives during those first weeks after they'd met a year ago. Afterwards, they kissed and held each other close.

Minutes later, Lara said, "Maybe it is possible we could have a marriage that'd work. I keep thinking about my expansion plans and then you. When you're not around, they win. Tonight, it's all different. It's you that matters."

"The thought of that isn't ever very far from my mind. During the daylight hours your passion has another outlet. After dark, and when we're together, we have this. Five or ten years from now, which passion would be the survivor?"

"I know. Over time, things change. Not as much fire. We've seen that happen in only a year. Except for tonight. But then, it's been weeks, and that makes a difference. Had I not been here tonight, my needs would have been ignored. Or suppressed. I come back to what I said before. When I'm close to you, the woman inside and the desire come alive. It's confusing. It was a long time between my divorce and last November, and you were the only man who ever got to me. I've said before that when you came through the laundry room door, I was yours if you wanted me. Didn't take long for it to happen. And since then you've always left me contented." Unseen to each other, they both smiled at the memories.

"I don't know. Like you, I wonder if we could make it work. I have the feeling that I'm not ready, at least yet, to make a lifetime commitment."

"That says that you want to keep searching, that I'm not the answer."

"Those are unkind words, Lara, and not true. I just want to be sure. Come spring, I might propose, maybe you'd say yes, and we'd have a good life together. I'd give up corporate life and become your bikini specialist."

They laughed, and it defused the disquiet they were beginning to feel.

"No, I wouldn't want you to be that close to a woman's nearly nude body. I'd have you in charge of hats or jewelry, something less stimulating." They found humor in that, too.

"Hate to be a killjoy, but it's getting late. There's an early morning train, and a very full day tomorrow."

"But coming up, there's also part of a weekend. I'll be ready for it, and Kurt's birthday dinner."

"Me too," Erich said. "G'night, dear heart. Sweet dreams."

"Night, guy."

When Erich and Lara burrowed in for the night, they turned, fitted themselves together like two spoons and were soon sound asleep.

The following morning, Erich went on his way, and Lara got the boys off to school, just as she had many times before. It was obvious they were pleased to have her there to help them start their day. When they left, Erich's two sons showed their affection by giving her a hug. Lara had blurry eyes after Kurt and Rudi were gone. This was something she'd surely miss if she and Erich couldn't make their relationship work.

The remaining two days of the week went by quickly and then on Friday afternoon, Katie handed Erich his tickets to O'Hare.

"Thanks, ma'am. See you on Thursday. It's Kurt's birthday, and what'll make it special is that Lara's said she'll be having dinner with us. He's pleased."

"Guess I'm glad to know you're still seeing each other—even though I'd like to be in her shoes. Sounds like she still matters."

Ignoring most of Katie's remarks, Erich gathered up his gear and wished her a good weekend.

When Erich got home, he called Brenna.

"Hi, dear heart. How're you doing?"

"Hello, stranger. Now that you've called, much, much better. I thought you'd forgotten all about me."

"Not a chance. You know I'm leaving on Sunday and will be in Chicago next week, but I was wondering if you'd have any interest in staying over next Friday and Saturday nights."

"I can't do Friday, but Jordie has the boys starting at noon on Saturday until late Sunday afternoon. Would that do?"

"Sure enough. Don't bring any clothes. You won't need 'em."

Brenna laughed. "You're bad. Sounds like you have big plans."

"Enough to keep us occupied; for sure when the lights are out. But otherwise it'll be the usual quiet weekend. Be good to have you around to hug when the urge surfaces."

"Sounds good. I've missed you. Never thought I'd say that."

"What are you doing for Thanksgiving?"

"I'm the one who sets the table, so I have family coming in from all directions. It means I'll be covered up right through that Sunday evening."

"Maybe you'd like to plan on a repeat visit the night of the sixth. Any chance you could do that?"

"I'll work it out. Somehow. You'll be gone for most of December, so I'll be kinda lost. Maybe you'd invite me over for the Saturday after Christmas."

"Long way off, but you're on. After three weeks, I'll be ready to give you a gigantic bear hug."

"I'd like that. Nice to have plans and stuff I can look forward to. At least you didn't forget about your good friend, Brenna."

Chapter Four

Lara spent Saturday evening with the Mauer guys. After bedding down, she shed her business persona and showed Erich that he was still the only man who could reawaken her sensual appetite. It was a return to the beginning of their affair a year ago and the feelings they'd rekindled on Wednesday night.

"Happy anniversary, Lara. We met exactly a year ago today, and it's an afternoon we'll most likely never forget."

"Not ever. And we still have lots of passion left. Now, hold me." And he did. For nearly the entire night.

On Sunday morning, Erich remarked, "We seem to have salvaged some of what we had a year ago. Maybe the break had something to do with it."

"Could be. But if we were living together, we couldn't take a month off to keep my fire from going out. When you're not around, mine sure does."

"That wouldn't be any way to live. And if all we had were embers when we were together every night, that wouldn't do either. Dilemma, isn't it?"

"I'm having a good visit, and ready for Kurt's birthday, so let's just enjoy ourselves. You found the woman inside, and I feel good."

"OK. I'll let it be."

Erich finished packing at a little after two on Sunday, and they were on their way shortly afterwards. Erich said goodbye to the boys, and then had something to say that he thought would make them happy.

"Lara going to stay with you right through Tuesday morning. Mr. Radford is coming in until I'm back on Wednesday evening. Then it's the four of us, and your birthday dinner on Thursday, Kurt. How do you like what's in the works?" The boys were happy that they'd have time to spend with Lara. Especially Rudi.

Erich drove to LaGuardia, and they talked about Rudi's birthday coming up on the sixth.

"You'll be in New York with suppliers," Erich said, "so I'll have to break it to him that you won't be around."

"It may be I can say something. But you asked about the eighth, just before you leave for Australia. I'll make sure I can stay over that night and will suggest to Rudi that maybe we could have his birthday dinner then. Okay?"

"Good. He'll understand better if you tell him what's going on. I'd have questions I couldn't answer. I'll leave it with you."

"Why don't I keep the Mustang after I get back to Seaford, come get you on Wednesday, and then stay over. I can be in charge of things one night early if you'd like."

"I'd like. Sure. I get in at 2:15 on American. Even so, traffic will be getting messy by then, but it's another good idea. Looks like your business smarts have begun to trickle into your personal life."

"Could be."

At LaGuardia Erich said, "This has been a pretty good weekend. Short, but quality time. Seems like we've managed to turn the clock back a little."

"Yeah. And until Tuesday morning, I'm going to pretend I'm a member of the family. Lots of good memories there; it'll be easy."

"Enjoy yourself while I'm off in the Windy City."

They chuckled, and then shared a goodbye hug.

"See you sometime around two thirty on Wednesday."

"I'll be here."

Erich smiled and then boarded.

Meetings in Chicago were less than stimulating, and Erich began to wonder if his life as a corporate animal was beginning to lose the keen edge that had always been there. The Chicago facility was close enough to New York that its policies, and their way of managing people, should be similar. The main difference was that IMCO-Chicago employed mainly blue-collar workers for their manufacturing operations. The parent company at 4 New York Plaza was anything but that. Even the mail boys dressed pretty well. Erich felt the presence of "shop mentality" among the management people he met. Different from the aerospace and steel companies he'd been a part of for over a dozen years. But he expected that with such a high percentage of their people turning out finished products, it was to be expected. After all, it was the company's bread and butter, and what allowed him to enjoy the amenities of stock options, bonuses, extra vacation time, and other benefits.

Erich was staying at The Palmer House and had enjoyable and expensive dinners at The Blackhawk and Henrici's restaurants with members of their administrative staff. But it surfaced over desert on the second evening that the company might be reverting to centralized operations. He prayed it was only a rumor. If not, "How could Chicago be better informed than the corporate executives who run the company from our building on New York Plaza?" He'd talk with Joel about it later in the week. Another job hunt had absolutely no appeal. If what Erich had heard was in the works, he'd be back in the same boat he was in at Essex Steel about ten months ago. He shivered at the thought.

At mid-afternoon on Wednesday, Erich was glad to be back on the ground in New York and to see a smiling Lara Renzo waiting for him.

"Hi, babe. How're you doing?" They shared a brief hug, and then merged with the flow before they got run over by other passengers.

"Good. Fun meeting you like this. Makes a difference in the way I feel about my shops and expansion plans. I'm almost human again instead of a Seaford business machine. And the news of the afternoon is that traffic's a mess, just like you thought. But I'm worried about Rudi, though. He may have gotten into a downer on Monday night. But he was okay yesterday morning. I know you worked with Nate Kaplan at Juvenile when Rudi first got into drugs. I thought about calling him. If it had been more serious, I would've. But it wasn't, and since I'm not Rudi's mother, I didn't."

"What was the problem?"

"Lethargic, slurred words. He might have gotten into your booze, but I couldn't smell anything. He ate dinner okay but sure was wound down."

"I'll hit him over the head to get his attention, and the club I'll use will be his birthday party. You'll be the heavy. He'll understand that if you think he's in trouble again you're not sure about wanting to eat with us."

"I don't want you to do that. You'd be talking for me, and I've already said I'd be there if we can do it on the eighth. Anyway, there has to be a better way to reach him. Maybe you should call Nate and ask what his spies have turned up. Could be there's a new supply of stuff on the street."

"Your idea is better than mine. It's a more levelheaded approach than to go for the jugular. I'll call Nate."

For the trip home, Lara offered to drive. Erich agreed. Caught in heavy traffic, she shared her thoughts about the past several days.

"This has been a good week. I'm feeling more at ease because you seem to like having me around. My attitude is better. Mom saw it right away, and she knew why. But one of these days, I could be like Roxane. We're either going to have a life together, or I'm going to shut you out of it and focus entirely on my business plans. Exclusively. I can't have it both ways. If it's you, then the business will be secondary. If you're not a permanent fixture, then I won't have you as a part-time lover in my life."

"Those are harsh words, Miss Lara. Are you the same person who picked me up at LaGuardia?"

"You're changing the subject, kind of. Yes, I'm still the person who met you at LaGuardia."

"Going back to what you said, is your good week over? You once said you'd give me time to sort out my feelings. Has that changed, too?"

"Not really, but my good week will depend on a number of things. And, no, the rules haven't changed. I just want you to consider how things could turn out. Looks like I got your attention."

"Not nice, babe. You're tampering with the positive feelings I've had since you came over last Wednesday wanting support. Don't do 'em in. Okay?"

"Now I'm feeling ungrateful and apologize. You were there when I needed your help, and I've shot myself in the foot."

"Okay. But it's time we sorted out where we go from here."

"In some ways we're back to where we were last year. Maybe we could try keeping it alive."

After Lara pulled into the garage at Mianus Ridge, and just before they got out of the car, Erich leaned across the console and gave her a kiss.

"Mmm. Can we jump in the back seat before we go up?"

"I think not. This is a public place. And the boys are probably starved. But it seems like at least a part of my old Lara's back."

"Be fun to do something impulsive, but we don't have anywhere to hide. So I guess we wait."

"Yep. No choice. We wait."

The boys were glad to see Lara—and their dad, too. It was about time to eat, so the two of them got busy and put dinner together. Afterwards, Erich unpacked and trotted out a pair of T-shirts. Then they visited until nearly ten o'clock. The boys went off to bed, and the lovers followed shortly afterwards. Under the covers, they soon gave each other a full measure of contentment.

Minutes later, Lara said, "I'd like it, maybe, if we could figure out how we might stay together, one that we've talked about lots of times. You make me happy, and my hours with you are the special moments every woman wants. I don't mean just at times like this. But I've said it before. You understand. Would you just hug me?"

They rolled over so Erich could hold her. They kissed once tenderly, and then slept like two embracing logs.

Early morning began with a hug and a smile.

"I'd like to go for a morning encore," Erich said, "but you'll have to accept a rain check. I've got to get out of here before somebody, meaning Joel Henning, thinks I'm shirking my duty."

When Erich got to the office, Katie's practiced eye assessed her partner's disposition and offered, "You look healthy and in good spirits this morning. Who was it this time?"

"Lara. She felt deprived, so I spent time fixing her up." He couldn't help but chuckle at the envious look on Katie's face.

"Some women have it all. Maybe I'll start hating her."

"Katie, if you don't like my answers, then you shouldn't ask those kinds of questions."

"I know. Okay. I'm ready to get back to work so I don't have to think about it. Sorry you won't be here for the Christmas party."

"Is Joel in? I need to see him for a few minutes. And here's the Chicago report. Hope you can read my writing."

"Usually isn't a problem, but it's gotten worse. Could be your after-hours social life has something to do with it."

"Thought you were going to concentrate on work."

"I am. You're work; my hard work." She giggled at what she was trying to turn into a double meaning.

There wasn't much that needed to be said about Erich's trip to Chicago, so Katie finished up his report quickly. When it was done, he hand delivered it to the boss so they could talk about the subject that had come up over dessert on Tuesday evening.

"Joel, I heard a troubling rumor out in Chicago. Seems that some of their admin people feel that management's approach is going to return to what it was before I got here. It caught me off guard since it looks like they know more about what's going on than we do here at corporate."

"Their administrative people should keep their mouths shut. Too much booze turns their brains into jelly. I can guess who it is you're talking about. But the story is that the Board has retained a consultant to see what we've accomplished over the past seven or eight months. Some of the locations are pleased with our hands-on support. Those you've visited are in that camp. You've either helped bring them aboard or reinforced the idea that the contributions we can make are helpful. Others want to be left alone and are resisting interference from New York, as they call it. Their view is that we can't possibly understand their situation well enough to implement policies they can live with. Questions remain. Are they any better off, and in the aggregate are we a better-run, more efficient company if we're centralized? That's what the consulting firm is trying to determine. Problem is, we have a long history of letting the operating units run themselves without any of us spending much time trying to create a close-knit family.

We have practically no track record as a vertically integrated company, and it's way too soon to make comparisons. Two or three years from now an assessment would have some validity. The pressure is coming from the senior people out there, and I pretty much know who's mixed up in this. What's important is that there are key people upstairs who're listening. Chicago is by far our biggest profit center, so they have plenty of clout. I'm not happy about any of what's going on, but unfortunately my views expressed at Board level don't carry as much weight as I'd like them to."

Erich sat quietly, stared at his hands for a moment, and then volunteered, "Consultants: people who borrow your watch so they can tell you what time it is. I know how this is going to wind up. Feel it in my gut, and it sure takes the edge off my Sydney trip. If it ends up the way I see it, all the good people you brought in will be history. Like you suggested, it'll be a flawed study. There isn't enough empirical data available at this stage to conclude that our centralized approach to management is right or wrong."

"First, I'm a little annoyed by your attitude. Second, Australasia needs the new personnel director no matter which way the study turns out. Third, you have a job to do. Be the consummate professional you've been since day one. Don't let any of this damage your record or color your judgment, because as long as you work for me, I expect your best. You show me something less, and you're gone. In the seven months you've been here, you've moved to the head of my class. Nobody else has gotten a raise. Don't muck it up, Erich."

"I get the message. Guess I need the reminders. This is my third company, and acquisitions of the first two forced me into the market. I've been lucky, but how many times will I be able to land on both feet?"

"You haven't been lucky. You're qualified, capable. But just between us, I think your opinion is probably right. If so, we're all at risk. And if that's the way it goes, I'll give you all the support I can. Now, that's the end of it. We'll not discuss it further until we know which way the wind is blowing. In the meantime, keep what you know under your hat. I don't need a palace upheaval on my hands."

"You've got my word. And you don't need to worry about me because I'll continue to deliver the best product I can. Too much pride to do anything else."

"Thanks. That's the Erich Mauer I've gotten to know."

Erich spent part of the day wondering about his future, so he didn't accomplish much. Joel wouldn't have given him very high marks for productivity. The timing was unfortunate because today was Kurt's birthday, and he needed to make sure he was up for his dinner party tonight. At the same time, he had to think about how he'd deal with the months ahead. It was vital to have a game plan in place so he could put the matter behind him and get on with the projects management expected him to complete successfully. By late afternoon, he'd mostly adjusted to the news he'd gotten earlier in the day.

It felt good to come home to a smile from Lara and a cheerful welcome from the boys. The magic of Lara's presence was obvious. Could it be that the apparition in dreams he'd had recently given him the right guidance when it urged him to think further about his relationships? He'd been in and out of the subject so many times, both with Lara and in quiet moments alone, that he was nearly bored to death with it. But this was a tranquil setting, so it wasn't possible to miss what was at work, and working.

"Kurt, I'll bet you thought we'd forgotten your birthday."

"Well, I didn't see any presents, other than the ten dollars Mother sent me."

"There wasn't time, so let's open presents."

Gifts came out of Erich's bedroom closet, and Kurt was wide-eyed. His presents had gone from games and sports equipment to clothes and personal accessories. He was happy with the new shirts and pants and the gift certificate Lara gave him to buy shoes.

"Thanks a lot. I like everything you gave me, but you probably won't think much of the cool shoes I want."

"I'll make a guess they wouldn't be a hit on New York Plaza, but I don't have to wear 'em."

Wrapping paper scattered about, the foursome left the mess behind, drove off to a favorite restaurant, Rubino's, and enjoyed their evening together. When the boys went off to the restroom, Lara told Erich that she hadn't gotten around to saying anything to Rudi yet about his birthday dinner. "I decided after we first talked about it that it would be better if we did it together. Maybe we can do it when we get home."

Dinner finished, and after another thank you from Kurt, they went up the hill to 17 Mianus Ridge. When they were comfortable, Lara turned to Rudi and brought up the subject of his birthday party. "I thought you should know that I can't be here because I have business to see about in New York. So your dad and I thought maybe we could all eat together two days later. Best I can do. Will that be all right?"

"S'pose so. Be better on my birthday, but if you have things to do it'll be okay." Erich and Lara glanced at each other since neither of them thought he'd accept her suggestion that quickly. "Wait a minute," Rudi said. "We'll already be at the Engels."

Erich explained what was going on, knowing that Rudi would ask him for all the details. "No, our plans have changed. You're not going to their house until you're done with classes on that Tuesday, the ninth. You'll need to have your gear ready, so you can ride home with Chris. Lara will come by the afternoon before and stay overnight. We'll be here to see you off to school, and then I leave that afternoon. You already know about that and also that I don't get back until the day before Christmas. It's kinda crazy, but it'll all work out. Kurt, did you ask Dawn about Christmas Day?"

"Yeah, but I forgot to tell you that she's glad we'd like to come over because they didn't like the idea of opening gifts and eating dinner alone. She's on vacation all that week and will pick us up at Chris's house the Saturday before Christmas. Sounded to me like she's lonely. Anyway, we'll be there when you come back. We can talk about the rest of it later."

"Okay. That's it, then. Hope I can keep it all sorted out. Now, off to bed, guys. Lara and I have some things to talk about. The boys gave her a hug and Kurt thanked her again for the gift certificate. After goodnights all around, they disappeared.

"Well babe, since I won't see you over the weekend, I guess tonight's it. Be nice having you here the night before I leave. The sad part is that we may be strangers by the time you're back on January 4. It'll be four weeks."

"By then I'll either be a raging inferno or will have forgotten all about you."

"Considering how things have gone lately, I'm surprised to hear that. If what we've shared will turn into frost in four weeks, then I don't see that we have much hope."

"I was just trying to put everything in perspective."

"Hasn't the last week or so shown you that what we have might still work?"

"Oh, I'm not saying things very good. Just hold me." And he did. "You should know you're important and won't be forgotten. I didn't mean to hurt you and hoped you wouldn't take it the wrong way. Sorry."

"Not your fault. It's just that I got some bad news today. A good guess is that my job could be wiped out by spring or early summer. I'm overreacting."

"Not again. Maybe I will put you in charge of hats or jewelry. But that means you'd have to be mine and vice versa." Lara smiled.

Seeing the concern in Lara eyes, Erich felt better. He'd gotten prickly again. Not the way to insure that the two of them enjoyed their last night together for nearly two weeks. He smiled to let her know he was okay and then added a hug and a kiss.

"Time we turned this into something memorable."

In bed, they did what they set out to do. Neither was left wanting.

"Will you remember who I am by January?" Erich asked.

"Don't worry about it. You won't be forgotten."

Next morning, Erich went on his way and Lara stayed at number 710 until the boys left. Both of them made sure they'd wished her a good Thanksgiving, as Erich had done, and that she knew they'd be glad to see her again in a few days. Hugs and the door closed, Lara had tears welling up. "I really do care about these guys." But now there were complications, so she had doubts that their relationship would survive—in spite of the improved rapport she and Erich had shared recently.

Brenna arrived early on Saturday afternoon and, as always, they enjoyed their time together. It was a relaxing visit. The boys' feelings we're clear. Lara was their favorite, but they liked Brenna, too. She was a real mom. But not to be missed was the opportunity Erich and Brenna had to share their evening. She continued to be animated, just as she'd been since the first time they'd loved before his October trip to Australia. Still, there were moments when Lara was in his thoughts. A small part of it was that he assumed Brenna wouldn't be interested in marriage, something he felt could make Lara a happy woman. But his reluctance to make a commitment was still there.

Before Brenna went home on Sunday afternoon, she confirmed that she'd been able to work out arrangements to stay over on the Saturday night before Erich left for Sydney.

"I'll be ready to give you a good sendoff. Then I'll welcome you back after Christmas. It'll be my present to you, and yours to me. So don't go giving away any of your gifts to someone else."

"There you go talking naughty again."

"You do that to me, you animal. It must be your scent. Whatever it is, it agrees with me."

"We'll talk between now and the sixth. After a few days, I'll want to hear your voice."

On Sunday evening, Erich had a call from Matt Engel. He wanted to know if he could stop by next Saturday afternoon.

"Sure. What's a good time for you?"

"How 'bout three o'clock? It'll be before I make my regular checkup over at the plant."

"Suits me. See you then."

"Thanks, Erich."

The office routine during the two-plus days leading up to Thanksgiving was just that. Not a whole lot got done. In fact, there wasn't even very much left for Erich to do in preparation for his trip back to Sydney in less than two weeks. For a change, Erich would be getting a little turkey and all the trimmings ready. And there'd be football galore, so the guys would be busy during their holiday break. They were ready for it.

Chapter Five

At two o'clock on Thanksgiving Eve, Erich wished anyone who was still around a happy holiday and a good weekend. He also made a special point of seeing the boss before he left if only to show him that he was in better spirits. Joel appreciated it. Then as Erich passed Katie's desk, he gave her a hug. She felt awfully good, so he decided that he shouldn't do that very often because he might get to like it. With the last of his holiday wishes behind him, he walked out of 4 New York Plaza with his colleague, Warren Lambros. They shook hands, wished each other a happy Thanksgiving, and then went their separate ways: Erich to Grand Central and Connecticut; Warren to Penn Station and New Jersey.

Into the holiday, the Macy's Thanksgiving Day parade and football filled the space before and around dinner—which the guys said was good. Erich was glad it didn't turn out to be a catastrophe.

Then right at three on Saturday afternoon, Matt Engel buzzed at the main entrance to 17 Mianus Ridge. Erich couldn't imagine what was on his mind unless it concerned the boys and maybe some bad behavior during their stay last month. When he got to number 710, Erich greeted him cordially. Matt was a big, muscular man with a handsome face, not unlike that of Rock Hudson's. But his physical attributes probably weren't important prerequisites for his job as warehouse manager with a cosmetics company based in Seaford.

"Have a seat, Matt. What's on your mind? Hope it doesn't have anything to do with my guys."

"Not at all. They're well behaved when they're over. If things get out of hand, I sit on 'em. It's personal, Erich. I don't expect you can help all that much. It's just that I've got to talk to somebody or I'll explode. You didn't grow up here, don't know many local people, so I think you can be counted on to keep quiet." Erich was certain he knew what was coming.

"Sounds like you mostly want me to listen."

"You're not a priest, and I don't want you to try to be like one, but I don't dare go to confession. What it's all about is that you know where I work and the kinds of people we hire because of our product lines. Most of them are women. All ages. And that's the beginning of how I got into trouble back in late spring. We don't see many good looking ones in the warehouse, but one of my foremen hired this cute gal, and we hit it right off. We thought we were just good friends until a bunch of us went out one Friday night, had a few beers, and the next thing I knew I was at her place, and we ended up in bed. If I have a problem, it's that I attract women, but I can usually keep 'em at a distance. This one was different. I really wanted her. What's worse is that I've kept on seeing her. She's ten years younger and really turns me on. Cynthia's been a wonderful wife, and what I've done is terribly wrong. Thing is, I don't know how to end it. My guilt, and what she might do to my marriage, is about to eat me alive. It's close to driving me nuts."

"Whew! Not a very big corner you've painted yourself into, and there aren't many simple solutions. But I guess if she isn't madly in love with you, then what I'd probably try to do is maneuver some handsome young stud into her line of vision. Let him put a move on her and hope that he'll take you out of the picture. I don't have many ideas, Matt. In the meantime, you'll have to refuse her invitations to bed down. Work up a list of excuses, some of them having to do with family. Breaking the cycle is up to you. She may feel good for a few minutes, but alimony, and child support, and visitation schedules are crummy alternatives to some delights after work. I'd offer to help, but I'm a little older, shorter, and don't have your looks. The other part of it is that I have enough going on. I'd need an eight day week if I were to get involved with your gal, assuming *she* was interested."

"You may have an idea about finding someone else for her bed. I hate to give her up, but you're right. I'll have to find enough grit to put an end to it. If it gets messy, there'll be no place to hide, and I'll have to face the music."

"Let me tell you a somewhat similar story," Erich said. "The difference is, I don't have a wife any longer, as you know. I'll try to keep it short."

Erich told Matt about the brief involvement he'd had with Tina, his secretary at Essex Steel, just before the company was acquired. He also explained why they'd shared the decision not to look back, but how the end of their affair was utter heartbreak for both of them. "The rationale was fairly simple. Tina's fifteen years younger, wanted children I can no longer father, and was worried about maybe being a young widow. I could never have been her long-term partner unless she thought differently about what she saw as complications. Yet the feelings were there, and still are, so I'm not sure how either one of us found the strength to turn our backs on what we had. That she moved to the Washington area didn't help heal my wounds any faster. Never in my nearly forty years had I cared so much about a woman as I did her. She's still in my dreams, and sometimes I've made love to her when I'm with someone else."

"We male animals sure do like to take on punishment for ourselves. Wife or not, you've had a painful road this year, too."

"But we survive. Like an open wound, we eventually heal."

"I appreciate your listening to my story. I feel better, but whichever way things go, I'll face some tough decisions and, like you, probably hurt some. I'll have to see how it plays out."

"Not sure I'll have any other ideas, but if you want me to be a sounding board, let me know. You know where we live."

"Thanks again, Erich."

After having gotten his affair out in the open, Matt Engel wasn't quite the same friend he'd been before he came through the door at number 710 on that Saturday afternoon. And Erich would never understand, until later, why it turned out that way.

On Sunday afternoon, now the last day of November, Erich got his affairs in order so there'd be no loose ends that had to be dealt with while he was away. After his bills were paid, it was obvious that he'd have to ease up some on the use of his new Visa card that Chase Manhattan would like him to keep busy. A budget might be a good new year's resolution for him to make—and follow. One other matter that he'd forgotten to nail down was whether or not Dawn would let the guys stay over on Thursday night.

"Kurt? Did you ask Dawn about staying over on Thursday?"

"I called, and she said it wasn't a problem. Then I mentioned that on Friday you were going to see your old boss from Essex and would probably be late. When I told her that, she said if she had to feed us we might as well stay over to Saturday morning."

"She sure is being cooperative. Wonder why?"

"The last time we stayed there, she said you couldn't live together but she thinks you can be friends, kind of. Ryan and Greg like having us over, and we always have a good time. She's been a lot better mother since we moved out. It was almost like she didn't really didn't care about us when we lived over on Hogan Avenue. I don't understand much about it, but maybe that helps."

"It does. And thanks for helping with my social calendar. I'm pleased to hear about Friday night. That means Clayton and I don't have to do all of our catching up in forty-five minutes. You and Rudi know that Lara will be back tomorrow and is staying over."

"We don't forget things like that," Rudi said from the living room. "And Monday night, too, right?"

"Yep. See, you can remember things when you want to."

Again, from the living room, "Anything about her is easy."

Erich was beginning to worry about his son's affection for a surrogate mom who might not be there much longer. His fear was that in the absence of Lara's maternal sway, Rudi would turn away from the nearly drug-free path he'd been on for the past year.

Monday's routine went well, in part because Katie was full of efficiency. "You must have had a good weekend."

"I did. Would've been even better if you'd been involved."

"Let it be, Katie. We've been over this how many times? If you have somebody looking after you now, then I won't have to deal with your fantasies any longer."

"Don't you believe it. Someday you'll see things my way."

"Let's get back at it, or maybe I'll start thinking you'd be better off in some other department."

"I get the picture."

With their weekly ritual behind them, they got busy dealing with problems and questions that seemed to come in just about every day. Erich was glad when it got to be five o'clock. A lot of what they'd worked on was kinda dull. As he was getting ready to leave, Katie asked him a question.

"Sure you wouldn't like me to come home with you?"

"Get a little crowded. Lara's back from her trip up to Worcester. You remember that her Uncle Gino has cancer. She'll need lots of support. It's been awfully hard on her."

"That's more important. Given her situation, my question is out of place. Sorry. See you tomorrow."

"G'night."

Erich was right about Lara. She looked gaunt. It was as hard for her as he'd guessed it would be. She asked him to hold her close, just as she had nearly three weeks earlier.

"He looks so bad. A big, beautiful man, a wonderful human being, just wasting away." Then she broke down.

Erich wanted to be as consoling as he could, but there wasn't much he could say. Her uncle couldn't last much longer. Lara had no interest in loving this night. Her mind was elsewhere, and it was possible that the events of recent days might change how she saw the road ahead and any lasting relationship with a man, specifically Erich Mauer. The hope that Lara had expressed one night nearly two weeks earlier, that of maybe sharing a life together, was at considerable risk of becoming irrelevant. And it would follow that her good week would then be reduced to little more than a collection of fond memories. December was off to a bad start for Lara and her family. Longer term, it would likely alter the direction of Erich's life. He was certain of his feelings.

"Would you like a drink?" Erich asked.

"Thanks. No. As soon as my eyes are fit to be seen in public, I'm going home. Mom needs me more than you do."

"I'd say it's about equal. But you know you can count on me to be the same kind of pillar you were for me when I was going through hell. I showed you that three weeks ago."

"You don't understand. I have to get myself together and then go give my mother support. Gino's my uncle, but you remember he's her brother. And spending the night is the last thing on my mind. It won't happen."

"I know that. There are too many other things we have to deal with. If you just want me to hold you, then I'm here." She was in tears again but recovered quickly.

"Sorry. You're being nice, and I'm treating you like dirt."

"Not so. I know what you're going through, and you have to decide what you think is best. That you'd put your mother first is the right thing to do."

"You do understand, then?"

"Of course. Only question I do have is what can I tell Rudi about his birthday dinner?"

"Wish I had an answer. Could be that my New York trip is off. Time's running out. We may have to go back up to Worcester at a moment's notice. Whatever happens, you know we'll be going back at Christmas."

"Then let's leave it this way. Should you need me, all you have to do is tell me that you think a hug would help, or you want to talk, or if you'd prefer that I leave you alone."

"I don't want you to do that, but if I had to go through something like this with you I couldn't handle it. I'd be destroyed, and I'm scared stiff that it would come about. Can you understand that?"

"Not really, because you can't live in fear of what *might* happen. What's out there isn't for any of us to see with any certainty. In the end, though, it has to be your decision."

"I'd like to have that glass of wine, stay the night, and have you hold me, but I'm needed at home. This is about as hard on Mom as it was losing my dad. In some ways, harder. The rail yard accident and his death were quick. This is like watching the same thing in slow motion. It's terribly, terribly painful. But it's time I went home. I told Mom I'd be back. She was of two minds about it, but I know she was glad to hear me say that I'd be there for her. She assumes that you and I may have our day. If I can keep our dinner date with Rudi, I'll do it and maybe feel different about our night together. I thought when we left for Massachusetts that I'd be ready for some of you when we got back, but it just isn't there."

"Let me say it one more time, Lara. I understand. Don't worry about it. As to the birthday dinner, I'll talk to Rudi. It's just as well he hasn't heard any of this. He'll be disappointed because he cares a lot about you."

"Ohh, Erich. Like always, you're helping me cope, and now I'm feeling guilty about backing out on you."

"Lara, stop it! You're doing what's right. I'll be here tomorrow, the rest of the week, and after Christmas when I'm back from Sydney. If next Monday works out, you'll make three guys happy. However things go, our prayers will be with you and your mother."

"That means so much to me." Tears welled up. Erich hugged her gently.

"Now, get going. Let us know how things are. Call when you can. I'll want to hear your voice whenever it's possible."

"Thank you. I will call. You're a big part of my support system, you know."

"Give your mother our love, and let her know that she's in our thoughts, just as you'll be."

"Night. Say good night to the boys. I couldn't deal with that just now."

"What-am-I-doing? I was about to say good night and let you go to your car by yourself. Unbelievable! Let me get a jacket."

Erich went down to the visitor's lot, saw that Lara was safely on her way to the Sound. Before she left, Erich gave her a firm, compassionate hug and said good night with a tender kiss. It confirmed that she mattered. To hang on, she clenched her teeth.

Back in number 710, Erich got a soup and sandwich meal together and then later on told the boys what he knew. They were concerned and even Rudi, much as he cared about Lara, understood that she might not be able to have dinner with them.

"I hope she can make it," Rudi said, "so I'd like to wait until next Monday. If she can't, then we can go to Rubino's and pretend like she's there." That got to Erich. He was having a hard time with all this himself. It was a difficult evening and his emotions were also a bit frayed.

During the early morning hours, Erich had another of his unusual dreams. The apparition and the voice he'd heard in the past had returned, but it was less adamant about having him re-examine his feelings. The key word he heard was patience. Wait for the woman with beauty within. It may take time, it suggested. Then his Bass Lake building lots came into view, as did the face of the young woman he'd seen before. Erich awakened and sat up. He still didn't know what to make of it all. Was this another of his sporadic visions that gave him a tiny glimpse into the future? Unlike the others, this one was uncommonly personal. When he slept again, he was completely at peace and rested well. The future would take care of itself a later dream assured him. At the beginning of the new day, Erich decided he'd give the prophecies and counsel a chance, no matter how illogical the idea might seem. In time, he might find them to be at least somewhat accurate.

Chapter Six

Back at work, Erich was barely inside the door when Katie said, "Looks like you didn't go home last night. That's the same suit you wore yesterday."

"Not at all what you think. But a guy can't do that?"

"You haven't, unless you've had a busy evening."

"Well, okay, I went trolling last night and came across a fiery blonde who needed to have her fire put out. But all the while, you were in my mind."

"You wicked, nasty man!" Katie threw a pencil at him. That he caught it upset her even more. "That hurts, Erich Mauer. Just for that, I'm going to find a man, get pregnant, and blame it on you."

"Wouldn't work, Katie. I was decommissioned a long time ago. Besides, getting us fired won't further your cause. Remember, I'm the guy who got you a good promotion and big raise last spring."

Katie got back to business, but she was really upset with her partner. Fortunately, Erich had meetings off their floor much of the day, so they didn't see each other again until nearly five o'clock. By then she'd cooled down and apologized.

"Sorry about this morning, but you didn't have to say what you did. You know how I feel about you, so it wasn't fair that you took advantage of it."

"My fault. Next time, if I say that, we will have gotten involved."

Katie smiled. "There's hope. You've made my weekend."

"Don't spend a whole lotta time thinking about it. You know my ground rules."

"Oh, I nearly forgot. Lara called, said her uncle is fairly stable, so she's coming into the expo and should also be able to keep her date to have dinner with you on Monday. And Mr. Zorn's secretary also called. She said to remind you that he'd meet you at The Watering Hole at five thirty."

"Thanks. Rudi's birthday is tomorrow, but we'll party when Lara can be there, too. That's what Monday is all about. But I've got to scoot, or I'll be late. Have a good weekend."

"You too, Erich."

It was a pleasure for the two former Essex managers to spend part of their evening together. It'd been a month, and they had some catching up to do. Drinks ordered, Clayton went straight into his social life. He told Erich that after a year he was still seeing Judy Haynes. In the meantime, he'd met a woman named Nicole when he was on vacation in Massachusetts. Recent news was that she'd be moving to New York fairly soon. Clayton added that it was too early to know how this new relationship might wind up. But from the expression Erich saw as he talked about her, it was obvious that Clayton thought she was special. Without realizing it, he might already be hooked. On the job front, working in retailing wasn't what he'd hoped it would be, and he was looking at the possibility of joining the national magazine, *The Week's News*. He expected them to make an offer soon. Martinis gone, they ordered another.

"So, what's new in your world?" Clayton asked.

"First item on the agenda is a reminder that I'm on my way back to Australia on Tuesday. Be gone until the morning of Christmas Eve. The new woman in my life is a friend of Lara's. Name's Brenna Walsh. She's the gal I mentioned to you on the phone a while back. Met her in September, and we went out a few times before my first trip Down Under in late October. She'll never be a bride, but I enjoy her company."

Erich took a sip of his extra dry Gibson and then played with the tart little onions for a few seconds.

"Lara? Lots of things tell me we're winding down. She's marrying her business, has an uncle dying of cancer, says she couldn't deal with that if it happened to me, and so on. I like her, but the end is near, I think, in spite of the fact that things have been pretty good lately. And for the first time since Tina left New York, I'm sorry to see a relationship come to an end if that's the way it turns out."

"I promised myself to ask you about Tina. No one except me had any reason to think the two of you were involved. I thought I read your feelings pretty well. Part of it was that you looked just plain awful right before the Essex takeover was completed."

Erich finally told Clayton the entire story. How it began, their three-plus months as lovers, and how it ended. When he'd finished, Clayton's face wore an expression of genuine sorrow.

"That's right out of a soap opera, and what you've told me is genuinely touching. I'm truly sorry. It would've been a wonderful union. She's a fine young woman. You must have had some very painful days after she left."

"Absolute agony. I've never been through anything like it. It was awful. But Essex was winding down, and I had to get myself up to do what IMCO expected of me. The job change helped. If I'd been on the street trying to find a job, an interviewer would probably have suggested that I look elsewhere. Now, having confessed, it's about time for me to be on my way.

Nobody at home tonight, so I can do whatever. Brenna will be over tomorrow evening, and it'll be good to see her. Been a while."

"I'm at loose ends, too. Why don't we go have a bite?"

"Sure. Beats feeding myself at this hour."

Erich and Clayton found a small restaurant nearby and had a light meal. They continued their reminiscing and talking about a favorite subject: the women in their lives—both past and present. As they were waiting to pay the check, Erich mentioned the unusual dreams he'd had about a spirit, a young woman with a delightful smile, who'd offered guidance about his future.

"Either your mind is gone or you're onto something. If the stock market comes up, and your apparition gives you a tip, let me know." They had to chuckle about the possibility that one or the other of Clayton's suppositions might be accurate.

Their bill paid, Erich saw that he could easily make the 9:57. They'd had a pleasant evening and agreed that it was something they should do on a regular basis. He and Clayton shook hands, wished each other a good holiday season, and then went their separate ways.

Erich got home to an empty and silent apartment. Suddenly he felt terribly alone, and there was more to it than the fact that the one of his companions, or the boys, weren't around. There was a dank chill. He wasn't sure what it meant. A bit disconcerted, he poured himself a stiff scotch, drank it down, and went straight to bed.

At a little after eight on Saturday morning, Lara called. She was in New York. Erich expected bad news, but she said her uncle was holding his own, and she was fairly certain that their Monday night date was still on. That assumed there'd be no change over the weekend.

"I got Katie's message, and I'm pleased for you. And Rudi, too. He'll be thrilled. I'll let him know when the guys get home."

"They've been away?"

"Yeah, they were at Dawn's last night."

"Where were you?

"Here. Like I mentioned, Clayton and I had a drink, and then we decided to have a bite. I got home at a little after eleven. It was *verrry* quiet."

"My mistake not to have told you where I'm staying. We could've had an unplanned night together. But if you'll have me on Monday, I'd like to stay over. I've decided that one more night with you would be the right thing to do."

"I've missed you, but I accept what is. Pretty hard to get worked up when there are a lot of uncertainties."

When the boys got home, Erich told them about Lara's call. "Keep your fingers crossed. Things could change. And in exchange for the good news, maybe you'd be willing to help with the laundry while I go get some shopping done. Brenna will be here tonight but not tomorrow. Usual stuff. How's Dawn?"

"Okay. Told us she's glad we're going to be there for Christmas. And she said that if you wanted to come over after you're back, you could sleep there. I guess she means with her."

"We've slept together before, as I recall." They all snickered. "So I may do just that. We both know that I'll be wiped out because of the nine-hour time difference. When you get there, tell her that I appreciate the invitation. Being at home alone on Christmas Eve would be sad. Anyway, let's get going. Make sure everything you need for the next three weeks starts out clean. I don't want you getting to the Engels saying you have laundry to do. Oh, before we do anything else, Rudi, happy birthday! Here's a card, but you have to decide if you want to open your gifts this evening or when Lara's here on Monday afternoon."

"I want to wait until Lara's here. It'll mean more." Rudi opened his birthday card and said, "Wow! Twenty bucks. Thanks, Dad."

"You're welcome. More gifts to come on Monday evening before we go to Rubino's. So, one more time, happy birthday."

The boys were a big help, and Erich got shopping done to cover their needs for the weekend and the days following Christmas. No need to overdo it. He'd be on vacation for nearly two weeks after he got back and could pick up whatever else they needed then.

Brenna was at the main entry door at midafternoon and buzzed number 710 to be let in.

"Yes?"

"It's me."

"Sorry. We gave at the office."

"Let me in, hotshot. I've got a big smooch for you."

"In that case, come right in."

Erich could hear over the intercom that she was chuckling.

Brenna turned left out of the elevator and could see at the end of the corridor that Erich's apartment door was open. Not having looked in both directions, she didn't see Erich pressed against the wall to the right of the elevator door. When Brenna started walking toward number 710, Erich sneaked up behind and grabbed her. She let out a squeal, but then turned around and gave him the kiss she'd promised.

"You clown. A hotshot executive like you playing games. Shame on you." Then she grinned and added, "But that was fun. Glad you're not uptight about your trip."

"Nope. You said you'd get me prepared. My motto is, Semper Paratus!"

"Sounds like Latin. Always something?"

"Always wound up. Or always ready, and I am you luscious thing you."

"You're in rare form. We ought to have a good roll in the hay later on."

"I'm counting on it. And again three weeks from tonight when you look after all of my stored up energy."

"Energy? Not exactly what I'd call it."

"Best we change the subject."

Finally inside the door, the boys gave Brenna a quick hug. Then she handed Rudi a birthday card. This one had seven dollars in it.

"Thank you. But you didn't have to give me anything."

"Don't be silly. It's your birthday. That's fifty cents for every year. Just don't go out and spend it on anything dumb. You know what I mean by that. Right?"

"Yeah, I know what you mean. I won't. Promise."

When it got close to dinnertime, Brenna had a request. "Could you do your mother's chili soup? I love it. It's really cold out and a perfect night for something with a little fire in it."

Erich turned around and stared at Brenna. He grinned and asked, "Are you referring to me, by any chance?"

"If the shoe fits...."

"They both do, but the hamburger's frozen. Well, maybe not. It hasn't been in the freezer all that long. Let me check."

Brenna was in luck. Before the night was out, she had two servings of something "with a little fire in it". One at the table, and the other much later in the evening. She found the second serving equally robust.

"Don't you go giving away any of that until you're back," Brenna said. "I told you before that I'll be the welcome back party on the twenty-seventh."

Dawn's invitation to stay over on Christmas Eve crossed Erich's mind. He had a pretty good idea what to expect.

"I understand your meaning. But why don't we concentrate on tonight in the meantime."

Brenna couldn't spend much of her day with Erich and the boys, but at least they had some time together. She was always enjoyable company. Romance and future plans didn't get in the way, so the time they shared often led to a lively give and take. Having her around was fun. One thing about it, she didn't take guff from any of them. Years of being a mother had sharpened that edge. She could dish it out when she had to. But it was always light. Different from the other women in Erich's life, both past and present.

Before Brenna left, she asked if it would be okay to feed Kurt and Rudi some evening while Dad was away. She said they could bring their friend, Chris, and she'd see that they got back to the Engels afterwards. Kurt and Rudi jumped on that instantly. Brenna suggested that a Saturday night would be best and that it would have to be the thirteenth. The following weekend she'd be getting ready for all the family coming in for Christmas. She and the boys worked out the details and it was a done thing.

When Brenna was ready to leave, she said goodbye to the boys, gave them a hug, and said she'd see them next week. Erich went with her to the parking lot to say a warm, cold weather goodbye.

"You know, Erich Mauer, I've gotten so I really like being around you. I'm not supposed to feel like this, but I do. I always leave here feeling good. It's going to be three weeks this time, and I already know that I'm going to miss you. Even with what's going on at Christmas, you'll be on my mind. But I don't want you to think I'm in love. At least that's what I keep telling myself." Erich held her tightly and felt a shudder. No tears. Just a shiver.

"I'll miss you, too. But, call me on Tuesday morning. I'll want to say goodbye before I fly. Don't make it any later than eleven. I'll have some stuff to go over with Katie, plus some loose ends that'll keep me busy until I leave."

Brenna gave Erich a hug and an affectionate kiss before she started home. Driving away, she waved and then mumbled to herself, "I hope what I'm feeling isn't love."

Erich and the boys had dinner and then spent a quiet evening with the NFL. It was a game that didn't much interest any of them. So, he left the guys with it and went to get his bag from their storage room. He decided that it was time to start packing.

The game over and with his bag partly the way he wanted it, Erich said good night to the boys.

As he was getting ready for bed, the phone rang. It was Lara.

"I'm home, Erich. How're you doing?"

"Okay. I'm beginning to think about my trip. Finally brought my bag up and threw some things in it this evening. But how are you doing, dear heart?"

"Better, thanks. But you just started packing? If I was making the kind of trip you are, I'd have started ten days ago." Erich chuckled.

"I've gotten ready for long trips going back nearly fifteen years. Gets to be routine after a while. How'd you make out at the show?"

"Fine. I turned up some good suppliers, made a few buys, and am glad I was able to go. It'll help me stock items I'll need for my new shops. But you don't want to hear about that, at least not at this hour. If it wasn't late, I'd come over and spend the night."

"You're welcome to, if you want. It isn't all that late."

"I'm *sooo* tired. I was on the run day and night. Much as I want to, I'm not up to it. But I think I'll come over anyway. I haven't been there overnight in how long? Two weeks?"

"About that . . . the night of Kurt's birthday. I'll come down and meet you in the parking lot in about twenty minutes?"

"That'll be about right. See you shortly."

That gave Erich enough time to change the sheets on his bed.

When Lara got out of her car, he could tell that she was tired. Since she'd be with him until Tuesday morning, she brought an overnight bag. It was cold out, so he saved his welcome until they were in the elevator.

"Good to see you again, Miss Lara." Erich gave her a hug. "But I have to say that these past three weeks have taken their toll. It shows. You remember having said the same thing to me nearly a year ago?"

"I'll look better in the morning. I'm just worn out."

Into number 710, Erich asked Lara if she'd like a drink.

"As a matter of fact, I would. Maybe a half glass of red. The plan I had on the way over was to get friendly. Won't happen. Be best if we wait until tomorrow night.

They each had a little bit of wine and then went to bed. It was rare that being together as they were, with the lights out, that it didn't lead to something further. But theirs was now a settled relationship, one that no longer needed an amorous ending to their day to sustain it—or do it in.

Come morning, Lara slept through the alarm and Erich let her snooze. She looked at peace, and he didn't have the heart to disturb her. After he'd dressed, and was getting breakfast ready, she wandered into the kitchen.

The boys were at the table and shocked to see her. Rudi got up immediately and gave her a hug. Lara, for some reason, grimaced slightly.

"I didn't know you were going to be here," he said.

"Your dad said I could come over. It was late, and I said no. But then I did anyway, and slept really good. Thanks for letting me stay in bed, Erich. Last thing I remember is you were holding me."

"You look much better than you did at eleven fifteen last night. Are you going to the shop later?"

"After the boys leave, I'll go back to bed for a while. You won't mind?"

"Nope. The place is yours until I leave tomorrow morning."

"Then I may not go in at all. I'm closed today but I'm open the next two Mondays. Just like last year. I can do what I have to from here. My briefcase is down in the car. Thing is, I'll need a key to get back in."

"You can have mine," Rudi said.

"Thank you. And happy birthday. Sorry I couldn't be here on Saturday. It was the business in New York we talked about."

"But you're here now, and I'm real glad. Neat surprise. Didn't expect it."

"If it hadn't been for your dad, it wouldn't have happened."

"Time for me to go," Erich said. He gave Lara a hug, said goodbye to the boys and added, "See you at a fourteenth birthday dinner tonight."

Lara said she'd be there, and the boys cheered softly. Both were all smiles. "A good way to leave them," Erich thought.

The last full day before Erich left for Sydney was busier than he wanted it to be. There were requests for support from everywhere it seemed. He asked himself: "How can the company return to decentralized operations? Lots of staff people have discovered they don't know much. They're always knocking on our door for help. Even with basic things. It may not be fair to Katie, but I'm glad to be gone for the next four weeks or so."

People at their various subsidiaries had questions, so Erich spent time with Katie getting her ready to deal with the range of issues that had come up. "If you get into a jam, you'll have to lean on Joel for answers, but I hope I've given you what you need so you won't have to bother him too much."

When they'd finished, Erich spotted a note he'd written to himself over two weeks ago to call Nate Kaplan at Connecticut Juvenile. "Damn!" he said aloud. It was about Rudi the night Lara thought he was into something. Angry with himself about the oversight, he picked up the phone and dialed Kaplan immediately.

"Nate. Erich Mauer."

"Erich. This is a surprise. What's up? Got a problem with our young man?"

"Not sure. I was out in Chicago, and Lara was staying with the guys. She was certain that Rudi got into what I'd call a downer. He was fine the next morning, and has been ever since. I promised her I'd call you. That was over two weeks ago. I'm on my way back to Australia tomorrow, and in the meantime I've had a lot on my plate. I just now spotted the note I wrote to myself."

"Might've been better if you'd called right away, but I'm familiar with heavy workloads. Ours has grown, too. Anyway, what can I do for you?"

"Just answer a question or two, I guess. Lara and I wondered if there was a new supply of junk on the streets, or what your moles are saying."

"The supply is about what it's always been. No big increase in it for months now. My guess is, Rudi took advantage of your absence and that it was a one-time thing. You'll need to keep an eye on him. If you're going to be away, ask Kurt to do it for you. He's dependable, despite the fact that he likes his beer we've learned."

"Yep, I know about that, too. I just hope I don't have another son with a problem that I'll eventually have to deal with."

"It isn't that yet. We'll all know if it gets to be one."

"At some point, I'll say something to him about it."

"Good idea. Let him know that we know. But what arrangements have you made for the boys while you're gone?"

"They'll be at the Engels until the weekend before Christmas, and then Dawn will have them until I get back the morning of Christmas Eve. She's settled down and is being the mother, or stepmother, that she wasn't when we were married. And the four boys have a great time together."

"I know what you're saying about Dawn. Positive stuff. And the Engels are good people. Matt and I haven't had much reason to be in touch lately, but he's a good father and their boy is rock solid."

"We agree. He's a neat kid." Erich was surprised that he knew Chris. Maybe he shouldn't have been. Could be he's one of Nate's covert sources.

"Since you mentioned Lara, how're the two of you doing?"

"I have to be honest with you, Nate. We've been okay recently, but I'm convinced we're winding down. She has an uncle dying of cancer, plus all kinds of expansion plans, a bank to back her, and is about to turn her businesses into a lover. At least that's the way it looks. I might be wrong, and I hope I am. It'll be hard on Rudi if she takes herself out of the picture. I'll need to keep an eye on him."

"Thanks for the tip, Erich. Keep me posted if you will. I'm sorry your personal news isn't better. I've known Lara since high school, and I'm betting she could help stabilize your situation."

"Good guess. Whatever, I'll bring you up to date if there's any change. Thanks for all you've done. Nothing personal, but I'd be just as happy if I didn't have any reason to call you again."

"I know what you're saying, and we're on the same page."

"Happy holidays, Nate."

"You too."

After Erich got off the phone, Katie returned to her favorite subject, that of openly trying to promote herself to her partner. She expressed her regrets, again, that he wasn't going to be around for the office party just before Christmas. Erich mostly ignored her.

"I'll be here the morning of Christmas Eve to give you my trip report and drop off anything I won't need over the holidays. You remember that I'll be off until January 5. It's your domain for almost four weeks while I get caught up on all the personal stuff I'll have missed while I was away. That's the vacation part of it."

"There you go being nasty again. But one of these days...."

"Could be, Katie. Could be. Now, I've got to go home and pack. See you in the morning."

"I assume someone will give you a proper sendoff."

"Only three of 'em. They're spaced about two hours apart. I recuperate well."

Katie stuck her tongue out and said curtly, "See you tomorrow."

Even though the close bond that Erich and Lara knew a year ago had been at least partly restored, he sensed that their relationship had undergone a fundamental change. It was still pleasant enough to have Lara meet him at the door, just as she'd always done. But the atmosphere and her temperament weren't the same. For some vague reason, and it bothered him, he had the feeling that this would be the last time it'd happen. The possibility that his insight was correct troubled him more than he wanted it to.

"Hi, babe. Have a good day at your office in number 710?"

"It's amazing what you can get done in a place this quiet. I put a week's work behind me in about five hours. Maybe I should have a desk in the bedroom and operate from here."

"Wouldn't work, gal. You're too much hands-on and have to be in the thick of things. With the move out of your shop coming up, opening new ones, hiring and training qualified people, keeping bankers happy, ordering stock, managing day-to-day operations, running back and forth between your stores, and whatever else I've missed, you won't have time for lunch, let alone me."

Lara had no reply, and her silence pretty much confirmed what Erich felt shortly after he'd walked through the door.

"At first I thought it sounded like a good idea. You'd have had the chance to at least look at my back while I was here." They tried to chuckle about her comment. It didn't happen.

"What's a guy got to do to get a drink around this place? Booze, woman!" That did get a thin smile from Lara.

"It's ready and in the fridge. With your carrying on about my workload, I nearly forgot about it. And I'm having a glass of red, also poured."

They toasted, and then settled down to a gentler exchange, including details about Erich's trip, his return, Christmas dinner with Dawn, and Lara's trip back to Worcester. After they'd had their drink, Erich suggested they go to dinner.

"I've got a little more packing to do. After that I'd like you to join me in bed for some serious cuddling. If we stay with it long enough, maybe we'll come up with some other ideas. What do you say to that?"

"Thought about it since I finished up this afternoon. Doesn't enter my mind otherwise."

"Thought maybe you'd sworn off evening delights."

"I have except when you're around. So we'll see about later on."

"Hey, guys. Let's party," Erich said.

They all had a delicious meal at Rubino's. The mood was light, and the birthday celebration was a success. Rudi got his presents, mostly all clothes. They were two days late, but it didn't seem to matter. He was pleased with everything and happy that Lara could be there, too. It was important. He loved his part-time, surrogate mom.

"Glad you could come with us," he told Lara, and then he gave her a hug.

For the first time ever, Erich saw ambivalence written all over Lara's face. The message her expression conveyed, and what was going through her mind, were both clear, he thought. She'd now convinced herself that she couldn't live two lives—as she'd suggested recently. It was either Erich and his sons, and their love, or a total commitment to running her expanding businesses. They'd talked about it before, and he was done pressing her on what the choice would be. No need to now. He'd just seen the answer. A growing obsession with managing her businesses had won. That same immersion would also help her escape the torment of watching someone close to her die. What seemed to be her apparent decision was a bitter pill for Erich to swallow.

Their night in bed was physically satisfying for both of them, but the highs they'd known were absent. Erich knew that robust passion diminished over time. What made this peculiar was that it had happened so abruptly. It was another indicator that Lara was about to go into hibernation. At the same time, he was sure that she couldn't help thinking about her dying uncle, so he'd give her the benefit of any doubt. But with him leaving, he guessed that she felt it was optimal timing to end their affair.

During the night, Erich had an intriguing dream. He and Lara were standing before a minister, and when Lara was asked if she'd take Erich to be her lawfully wedded husband, she answered, "No". Erich didn't fight it. He accepted it as truth. His dreams of a week ago had given him peace of mind and the resolve to be patient.

Morning loving was perfunctory, but they had other things on their minds. Lara was getting back to business in earnest and also worrying about her uncle Gino. Erich was facing his long trip to Sydney and still had to finish packing. Before they got out of bed, Erich remarked, "We've done better."

Lara's unemotional, detached response was, "Yeah, I know."

After breakfast, Erich stayed at home just long enough to give the boys a hug and see them off to school. He reminded them that they were to go to the Engels at the end of the day and then stay with Dawn from the weekend of the twentieth.

"We know what to do, Dad," Kurt said.

"Okay, then. I'll see you sometime on the twenty-fourth."

Both boys hugged their dad, and a fairly impassive Lara, wished him a good trip, and then left for school.

When Erich was ready to go, Lara reminded him that she'd promised to drive him down to the station.

On their way, Erich said, "I'm not sure what's left to say. We've been through a good many emotional highs and lows over the past month. I guess it began with your uncle. But back in mid-November, we had a good renewal of our relationship. For those few pleasant days, I thought the future, ours, showed promise. We were back to what we meant to each other a year ago. But then…."

"Three weeks ago, when I met you at LaGuardia and welcomed you back, I was upbeat. And the days we shared after that were special. A high point. Just like in the beginning. But there's been Uncle Gino's inoperable cancer, and I started to think that someday it was possible I'd have to go through the same thing with you. I've already said that. So how do I feel about what we've had these last few weeks? I don't know. Maybe it's like a light bulb that flashes bright just before it burns out. It's been painful enough with my uncle, but there isn't any way I could watch you die, Erich. You're too much a part of me. And now, almost overnight, it's grown into a real fear of losing you and all the ways it could happen. Much as I want to hang on to what we have, the future we've both talked about, frightens me. So since all my worries about what might come about don't leave me with many options, I think it's best if I let go."

"You've known for a year how much you mean to me, but I won't plead my case any further. You understand what's in your heart and what you feel you have to do—for the all reasons you've explained. The best I can hope for is that I'll be able to see you after we're both home. But it's your call."

"Let's see how things go. Okay, travelin' man, here we are."

"Appreciate the lift. Look after yourself, Lara."

Erich held her tightly for a moment, and then they shared a gentle kiss.

"Bye, dear heart."

"Bye, Erich. Have a good trip."

Erich got his luggage, and before he disappeared behind the station door, he turned and waved. She didn't return it. Lara then pulled into an empty parking space facing away from the station. She leaned forward, put her head on the steering wheel, and in a trembling voice said quietly: "Goodbye, Erich Mauer. Thank you for all the wonderful memories. Thank you for having been a part of my life. I've loved every minute of it."

Then, without restraint or shame, she cried.

Chapter Seven

Off the train at Grand Central, and into a taxi, Erich got to the office about an hour late. He'd just stashed his bag when the phone rang.

It was Brenna. "Hi, dear heart. Sorry I wasn't available before this, but there have been all kinds of calls this morning. Mostly from charming young ladies calling to wish me a good trip."

She hung up on him.

Erich turned back to some new requests that he needed to go over with Katie, and then he smiled. "She'll call back." Within a few minutes, she did.

"Who? Are you sure you've got the right Erich?" Katie knew they wanted to talk, so she left and closed the door.

"Erich Mauer, at times you can be a real pain you know where. I don't like being a bitch, so please don't do things like that. I like you too much. What you did hurt a little. No, more than that."

"You've said right from the start that you didn't want another romance, and certainly not another husband. We were to just enjoy each other's company. Probably, deep down inside, I was testing your resolve. It wasn't fair. I agree, and I apologize. Forgive me?"

"Maybe. When I left on Sunday afternoon, I felt all warm and tingly inside. You know what I said to myself when I was driving home? 'I hope what I'm feeling isn't love'. It isn't exactly that, I think, but it's right next door to it. When I see you on the twenty-seventh, I'll have had time to think about it and will try to explain what's been going on inside my head."

"Fair enough. But you also know that I care about you. More than I should, considering what we keep saying we want our relationship to be. What I said earlier was all bull. It's possible that I do see someone else once in a while, but you're important. What works against us is that the kind of relationship we have won't ever go anywhere—much as I might like it to. Anyway, Lara's gone, I think. I'd bet money on it. If you're working for her while I'm away, she may get into it. Like I said some time ago, I'll miss her. But that's another hit I may have to deal with."

"We can't talk about things like this over the phone, especially with me being at work and you leaving. I've got a tiny lump in my throat and that's not good. All the people I work with are nearby."

"I didn't mean to get into any of this. It's a subject we might have talked about on Saturday evening, but we didn't. What we need is an overnight away somewhere. It'd give us a chance to find out more about who we are, what we mean to each other, and maybe what's out there for us. That's heavyweight stuff to think about at this hour of the day, but I have to say it."

"I know. For now, just let me love you at night and don't ask me to love you all day, every day for the rest my life. Not sure what I'm trying to say, but we'll get into it when you're back. I like the idea of going away with you overnight. Something to think about."

"What you want will be up to you. I'm not good at forcing anyone into something they don't want. Lara is a good example."

"The lump in my throat is still there. What is it about you that gets to me? I've got to go, Erich. After you're home, let's go find a ring for the opal you brought back last time. I look at it just about every day. It's just gorgeous. So many vibrant colors."

"Sure. I was hoping you'd want me to go with you. I'm off until the fifth, so maybe on a Saturday, or some evening, we can work it in. Pick a jeweler you think will do a good job."

"I will. But since I'm on vacation then, too, we'll have plenty of time for it, and other things—assuming you're interested."

"Sounds as if I'm on your holiday schedule. I'll try to be ready."

"We sure got off on the wrong foot. I blame you for that. The reason for my call was to hear that voice of yours I like so much and also to wish you a good trip. See you on the twenty-seventh, but I'll be thinking about you until then. Every day."

"Pretty hard to avoid; that is, thinking about each other. You'll be on my mind, too. Maybe I'll have an inspiration and can find you something for Valentine's Day. Christmas is already covered."

"You don't have to do that. Just come back alive and well. Now, I really do have to go. See you after Christmas. Happy landings."

"Look after yourself while I'm away. Bye, dear heart."

Erich finished giving Katie the last set of instructions he wanted her to have, had lunch, and then got ready to head for JFK. Before he left, he gave Katie her Christmas gift, a small bottle of L'air du Temps. She opened it.

"Oooh, Erich. This is good stuff. It's an older fragrance, but I love it. Thank you so much."

"I like the pigeon on top." He chuckled.

"That's not a pigeon, silly. It's a dove."

"Oh, okay. I don't know much about perfume birds."

"Your gift will be on your desk when you come back. I forgot to bring it in with me this morning."

"That means I can push Christmas over into the new decade if you forget it until I'm back from vacation. Be fun. But it's time to go, partner. The limo's here. I'll see you on the twenty-fourth."

Katie came over to Erich and gave him a hug and a quick kiss on his cheek. Brief as their exchange was, there was no mistaking how she felt about her partner. He was also reminded, again, how good she felt.

"That's for good luck. Have a wonderful trip. Sorry I can't go with you."

"I'd never get any work done with you around." Erich chuckled all the way into the foyer. Katie smiled warmly, and then her eyes followed him until he was on an elevator and gone.

Erich took the limo straight to JFK. No more helicopter rides off the top of the Pan Am Building since that service had ended almost two years earlier. His flight from Kennedy was on BOAC's Flight 591, and he'd be going all the way to the Fiji Islands with them. He'd never flown on a Vickers VC-10 before and was interested in finding out if the glowing reports he'd read were accurate or if maybe some of them were written under the influence of too many martinis. Comfort was going to be important. The trip to Nadi was just short of eight thousand miles.

Check in was easy and boarding, at least for First Class passengers, couldn't have been smoother. It was Erich's first exposure to British friendliness and efficiency. He was impressed.

Takeoff was on schedule, and as the flight reached cruising altitude, Erich was struck by how quiet the VC-10 was. The comments he'd read were right. He'd fly with BOAC, and on this aircraft, anytime he could.

After a stop in Los Angeles, and they were on their way to Honolulu at just after seven o'clock Pacific Time, he asked a steward if he might have a look inside the flight deck. When asked, the Captain said he'd gladly show a "Colonist" what his front office looked like. Once there, Erich remarked that it was very efficiently designed and that it appeared to have a better instruments arrangement than the 707. The Captain's response? "Of course. It's British built." They shared a healthy chuckle.

After more drinks and then food, Erich's New York body clock said it was long past time for some rest. Honolulu was behind them now, and, with the flight still nearly three thousand miles out from the Fiji Islands, it was a chance to rest for a few hours. Considering that they'd left Hawaii at midnight local time, sleep came quickly and a tired body welcomed it.

Before landing, breakfast was served and passengers were given a certificate declaring that they were now "Equatorial Voyagers". He'd crossed the equator twice before without any fanfare, so to have it acknowledged was kind of a neat thing for BOAC to do.

At just about 4 a.m., now Thursday morning, Flight 591 made a smooth landing at the international airport at Nadi, pronounced Nandi, according to IMCO-Australasia's managing director, Harry Malcolm. The mid-seventy degree temperature was most agreeable when compared to New York's cold December weather. And after eight thousand miles in the same seat, he was ready for the break.

Erich had done a little bit of research on the main island, Viti Levu, and had decided on flying around to the capital, Suva. It would get him away from the airport and into a city, small as it was. Checking with Fiji Airways, Erich found that their first morning departure, Flight 122, left at exactly 6:00 a.m., so he bought a round-trip ticket and hoped he could find decent accommodations somewhere on the southeastern part of the island. While killing time until the flight was called for boarding, he spent a few minutes at the currency exchange window buying Fijian dollars. Afterwards, he had a bite to eat and then simply roamed the terminal building. His body welcomed the exercise.

The aircraft to Suva was a DC-3, and the forty-five minute flight followed the southerly face of the island, also known as the Coral Coast. Their destination was Nausori, the town nearest the airport that served the capital city. Along the way, Erich could see from his window seat that there were islands absolutely everywhere. It was a fascinating introduction to a part of the world totally unfamiliar to someone who'd grown up on a small farm in northwest Ohio.

Once at the airport in Nausori, Erich went out toward the taxi queue. He never quite got there. With no tan, he stood out in the crowd and was approached by a pleasant young man who asked, "Taxi, sir? I drive cheap."

Erich had to chuckle at his approach. "If you mean it, sure. Thing is, I don't have a room, so maybe you can recommend a hotel. Something clean and reasonably priced. Can you help me out?"

"Oh, yes," the young man said with a friendly smile. "I have lived here nearly all of my life, and I know everything."

Erich returned his smile and said, "I like your style. What do you suggest?"

"I know a very nice place at what is called the Bay of Islands. It is right on the water with a wonderful view. And the price is very good. Then when you want to go into the city, I will be your driver. How long will you be here?"

"Just two nights. Until Saturday. Then I go on to Sydney."

"Are you American? You speak like one."

"I just came in from New York."

"Oh. Welcome to Fiji, sir. My name is a long one, Ravinandan, so just call me Ravi. I will look after you while you are here."

"Well, Ravi, my name is Erich, and it looks like I'm fortunate to have found you, or for you to have found me."

"Mr. Erich, whatever you want to do, just tell me. I can help."

Luggage stowed, Ravi invited Erich to sit in the front seat with him. As they made their way from Nausori to the hotel, he told Ravi that he was interested in buying a good 35mm camera at a fair price. "There must be stores in Suva that sell them."

"You have found the right man. A member of our family owns camera shops in town. I will take you there tomorrow and help you save money, too."

"What good luck. You're just the man I need."

"Oh, no, Mr. Erich. It is not luck. It is fate. I am certain of it."

Ravi pulled up in front of a nice-looking two-story hotel, The Southern Cross, which was situated in a quiet area. It faced the water and there were boats tied up at their dock.

"It's perfect," Erich said. "You do know everything. Now, how much do I owe you?"

When Ravi gave him the amount, just a few Fijian dollars, Erich could hardly believe it. Tokyo fares had been much the same when he was there at the end of October. Considering that the Fijian dollar was worth almost 90 percent of its U.S. counterpart, it was a whole lot of service for very little money. It would have been impossible for Erich to go anywhere in Manhattan for what Ravi had just quoted for roughly a twelve mile trip from the airport. He decided that because he'd lived in and around New York as long as he had, he knew very little about the cost of services in other places. That included many parts of the U.S. For all of Ravi's help, he decided to give him a little something extra.

"How much to be my driver until after lunch on Saturday?" Erich asked.

"Would thirty-five Fijian be too much?"

"No. But why don't we make it forty? That way you can help me find a good deal on a camera. I'm mostly interested in the Yashica Electro 35G that came out about a year ago. I'll bet you know where we can find one."

"Oh, yes. As I mentioned before, there are shops owned by a member of our family. We will do that tomorrow after you have had your morning meal. And I thank you for the offer of extra money."

"You're welcome. If you can help me out, it'll be worth it. Now, I've had a long trip and may sleep late. Do you think you could pick me up at around ten tomorrow morning?"

"Of course, Mr. Erich. I will be here by ten o'clock. Now, let me help you with your luggage."

Settled in, Erich had a second story view of the marina, and of narrow earth knolls that stood up in the bay. They were odd-looking things with grass, and shrubs, and small trees on them. They couldn't have been more than forty or fifty feet across, so he wondered why they didn't get washed away or fall over. He also had a great view of a trimaran flying a New Zealand flag that had pulled in near the seawall and anchored. What got his attention were the attractive girls in bikinis that were part of the crew. With all the trim, well-tanned young men on deck, he got the picture. Envious, he had the impulse to volunteer his help but laughed it off as pure fantasy on the part of a guy who was an overly keen admirer of womanhood.

Unlike his earlier trip to Sydney, Erich felt as if he was doing much better this time. Flying west *was* the answer. Tired, but not absolutely drained, he kept going and spent the day walking around the general neighborhood, having lunch, and resting some. At a little after five, he found the bar and had a beer. The weather was delightful and perfectly suited to trying the local product. It was called, very simply, "Fiji". Erich took a sip and said to no one in particular, "This is good." He generally didn't drink much beer during the winter months, but in the Southern Hemisphere it was the season for it, and he was also looking forward to having more good brews when he got to Sydney. He'd discovered when he was down in October that both Foster's and Swan were certainly tasty.

With the seven-hour time change beginning to set in, Erich went off to the dining room to have dinner. A little early for the locals, maybe, but way too late in New York to eat, he thought. Now, was it the same day, or tomorrow, on New York Plaza? He'd try to figure it out over a dry martini and some food.

Erich ordered mahi-mahi. It was excellent. Another martini just about put out his lights, and he never did figure out if it was today, or yesterday, or tomorrow in New York now that he was west of the International Date Line. It wasn't high on his list of things to untangle, so he went to bed.

With open windows that let Erich hear the sound of water slapping against the seawall, he was asleep in a matter of minutes. But during the night, he had another of his curious dreams, one with unusual clarity that was also pleasantly serene. The setting was his building lots in Massachusetts; a long way from the Fiji Islands. A cottage was going up, and the nameless young woman with long hair that he'd seen in a dream late last year, and then again just days ago, was inside looking it over. The man she came with was his real estate broker, Owen Laird. What was the connection? It was basically the same dream he'd had less than two weeks earlier, and for them to have now gone to episode three was indeed puzzling.

Up at a reasonable hour, Erich was still puzzled by his dream, but he also felt well rested. After a good breakfast, he was ready to have his tour of Suva, maybe buy a camera, and then see the countryside. Ravi was in the lobby by ten o'clock, as promised. They greeted each other in Fijian, "Mbula", meaning hello, shook hands, and then went on their way. It was a delightful morning and one of those times, Erich thought, when it felt good to be alive.

"I've been in Fiji only about thirty hours, but I'm very taken with what I've seen so far. What a place to call home if it were possible to make a living here. You must be happy with all of this, Ravi."

"It is a beautiful place, Mr. Erich. The climate is good and all of us in our family like it very much. When we are done with the camera, I will take you out into the country and show you what things grow here."

"Ahh, if we're going to go for a drive, then that adds another ten Fijian to your fee."

"Oh, no. That is not necessary. I enjoy your company. Also, I don't see many Americans so it is a good opportunity to study one." Erich had a good chuckle over that.

"I don't know that I'm especially typical. Maybe I am. But if you had fifty Americans in your taxi next year, you'd find that we'd all be different, just like members of your family and people you know. We come in all shapes and sizes and each of us has a different way of looking at things. But I'll let you study this American as much as you'd like. I won't charge you a thing."

Ravi laughed softly. "I like you, Mr. Erich. You would be happy in Fiji, and it would be good for you. I would also be pleased to have you as a friend."

"Those are kind words, Ravi. Thank you. I'll remember you, and what you just said, long after I've made the trip back across your Pacific and gone home to New York."

Ravi drove into Suva and parked. "We are going to see my cousin in his shop. It is right over there on the corner. He will make the best deal for you anywhere in the city or on Viti Levu. I have already told him about you. His name is Sanjay."

And Ravi was right. On his last trip, Erich had priced the Yashica camera he was hooked on in both Hong Kong and Tokyo, and Ravi's cousin did have a better price.

"It's a deal," he told Ravi's cousin. "Do you accept credit cards, or would you prefer U.S. dollars?"

"The dollars would be much better, if you please."

Erich bought film, lots of it, two filters, and a lens hood before he escaped Sanjay's shop. It was obvious he was pleased that Ravi had brought him a good customer. When their business was done, they shook hands and said thank you. It was a good deal for both of them, and Erich was certainly happy with his end of the transaction.

"Now," Ravi said, "I am going to drive you out into the country so that you can see what you cannot see from the air."

And drive he did. Erich quickly scanned the manual, then loaded his new camera and took pictures of just about everything in sight. There were fields and forests and mountains, all covered with lush green foliage. Thinking about the gray northeast U.S. at this time of year, the contrast was striking.

After their long drive, Erich thanked Ravi for the time he'd taken to show him more of the island than he ever expected to see.

"It has been my pleasure. But before I return you to your hotel, I will take you to my home. We have been fasting, but this is the first day that we can eat again. I want you to share a part of our meal."

"I don't want to impose, Ravi. You've been very kind, but it sounds like a special family day so I shouldn't intrude."

"No, no. You will be my honored guest. Please join us."

Ravi lived in a small house with his parents and a younger sister. From the street, they walked straight into the living room. It was probably twelve feet on a side and obvious that it was where the family gathered and also where they entertained guests. Erich was welcomed and asked to sit down.

The family was curious about this man Ravi had talked about, and they asked him questions, some of them a bit awkward considering what was going on in Vietnam. That subject might have caused him to bristle, but not wanting to portray himself as an ugly American, he made a determined effort to be courteous. At the end of the discussion, the parents smiled and offered him a bowl of something akin to yellow custard, but it was more liquid than solid, and rice was its principal ingredient. He'd obviously met with their approval.

Then, when it became clear that their visit was at an end, Erich thanked his hosts, and Ravi drove him back to The Southern Cross. It had been a very interesting day. The only problem was that he never did get the name of whatever it was he'd been served. After asking a second time, he decided not to embarrass his hosts, or himself, and let the subject die. As Ravi was dropping him off, Erich said he'd have to be at the airport in Nausori by around three o'clock tomorrow.

"I will be here, Mr. Erich. When you said yesterday, 'after lunch', I was sure you meant that you would be on the 3:30 flight to Nadi. It is as I told you. I know everything."

Erich chuckled. Then on an impulse, he gave Ravi a quick hug. It was evident that he was both surprised and pleased.

"See you tomorrow. Oh, here's half of the money I owe you. I'll give you the rest in Nausori. Don't spend it all in one place."

"I will be sure not to. Thank you."

Erich went to his room and made an attempt to organize his bag a little, mainly separating clean clothes from the laundry he'd need to have picked up on Monday. Then it was back to the bar. He ordered a beer, and from his ringside seat he watched the beautiful young people on the New Zealand trimaran. He envied the guys. They sure knew how to pick 'em. There wasn't a marginal looking female in the entire lot. Oh well, he'd be home in less than two weeks, and on arrival he'd most likely be attacked by Dawn. There wasn't any reason to resist. She'd always been a lively partner.

Finished with his beer, and having had enough of merely being a spectator, enjoyable as it was, Erich gave it up and went off to the dining room. He ordered his martini and settled on grilled swordfish with all the trimmings. The waiter pointed out that the fish was fresh, and not "line caught". He explained that a fish harvested that way might be dead for hours before it was "collected", as he called it. Erich loved swordfish, and he made a mental note to always ask which it was. But he bet that in New York not one waiter in ten would have any idea what it meant—or even care to know the difference. Dinner finished, he stopped by the little gift shop and bought a half-dozen postcards. He'd send one to his mother, Brenna, Lara, and, just for the fun of it, Roxane. He saved two and would give them to the boys when he got back. No point in mailing them. Deliveries were stopped, so they wouldn't see them until he got home. On second thought, he'd send them one anyway.

Saturday morning dawned bright and warm. It was the rainy season, but if there was any precipitation around, Suva had escaped it. Erich skipped breakfast, had a good lunch, repacked, checked out, and waited for Ravi. With a few minutes to spare, he bought stamps, stuck them on the cards, and asked the man at the desk to put them in the outgoing pouch that was ready for pickup. He hoped that, unlike those he dropped off in New Delhi last October, these cards would get to the post office, be sent on, and eventually delivered to the U.S. addressees.

Ravi showed up right on time, and they made the relatively short trip to the airport adjacent Nausori. On the way, the two of them chatted. They'd become friends and would remain so if Erich ever came through again. His instincts told him that this would be his last trip to Australia. He spared Ravi his reasons for thinking so. Then at the airport, Erich paid his young friend the balance in U.S. dollars. By doing that, it would amount to about a 12 percent bonus. Ravi couldn't argue—and he didn't.

"You are a generous man, Mr. Erich. I am very grateful, and I will always remember you as a friend of mine and my family."

"And you're someone I'll not likely forget, the man who knows everything." Ravi smiled amiably. "Thank you for all you've done, and please remember me to your family. I'd like them to know that I appreciated their hospitality."

As they shook hands, Ravi's face showed Erich a look of sincere friendship.

"Goodbye, Mr. Erich. And bless you."

"Thank you, Ravi. All the best."

Chapter Eight

The aircraft for the return flight to Nadi was a Hawker Siddeley. It was faster, so the westbound trip took but thirty-five minutes. Sitting on the right side of the cabin, Erich had a good view of the mountainous part of the island. It was all a lush green, and he was falling in love with this British colony, which in the coming months would most likely gain its independence. Everyone he'd met was outgoing and pleasant, and he looked forward to his one-day stopover on the way home in about ten days.

Erich had only forty-five minutes on the ground in Nadi, so the connection time couldn't have been better even if he'd made up the schedule himself. Then aboard a Qantas V-Jet, Flight 575, the four-plus hour trip would put him at Sydney's Kingsford Smith Airport right at 7:00 p.m. local time. Since it was only six miles out, he guessed that he'd be checked in and having a Foster's by eight o'clock. And he figured it just about right. Knowing the Wentworth Hotel layout, and how to find the lower level pub facing Bligh Street, was helpful.

Erich had his beer, a good dinner and then went back to his room to relax. It had been a long ride, almost ten thousand miles, but the break in Fiji had really helped. He'd be ready for Harry Malcolm, and IMCO-Australasia, on Monday morning. Now that he'd learned how to make the trip easier, it probably wouldn't matter. The handwriting was on the wall, he thought, and it was likely he'd be on the street job-hunting again sometime next year.

Then he thought about Lara. Given that he was on something of a high, he didn't want the memories of her to dampen his spirit. But he was convinced they'd spent their last night together, shared a final kiss, and that there'd be no more words of affection. "Damn shame," Erich thought. "But if that's the way it is, I'll need to get over it and move on. That's callous, maybe, but Lara knows what she wants, doesn't want, and what she fears. Her business is personal, but impersonal. It might die, but it isn't the same as flesh and blood. Over her thirty-five and a half years," he reflected, "it's been a rough road at times. Her husband broke her heart. She suffered badly when her father was killed and is going through the same trauma with her Uncle Gino. One day soon it'll be her mother. But she's not emotionally equipped to watch a husband die. The answer? She'll avoid that by not having another one."

For all the emotional insulation Erich was trying to preserve, his recollections about Lara got to him. Too many fond memories that began last year on a Saturday afternoon in November when they'd met in his laundry room. He vividly recalled the first time they'd loved that same afternoon and all of what had happened since. Now alone, everything came back to him. He'd miss her and would forever remember all they'd shared, brief as it was. "But she's most likely gone," Erich had to admit. "I'm truly sorry, Lara. If it is over, you'll have left me with some very fond memories."

Late on Sunday morning, Erich got a call from Malcolm welcoming him back to Sydney. He offered to come by the hotel at about nine o'clock tomorrow, and they'd walk over to IMCO's offices together. That little bit of business done, Erich had some lunch and went for a long walk around Sydney. He'd also brought his Land camera just in case he couldn't find a good buy on the Yashica. It was a pleasant day, so it gave him a chance to take lots of pictures. At the same time, he could use up the last of the Polaroid film that had been sitting around his office for several months. By the time he got back to the pub to enjoy a cold Foster's, he'd taken a good many photos that would preserve memories of what he assumed would be his last trip Down Under. Then, as he was coming into the hotel, he noticed some unusual items in the gift shop window. He had to have a closer look. They were figures of dancing women, and the product line was called "Bushcraft", something created by a George Fernley. Their bodies were formed by branches taken from "Australian natural timbers" and they really did look like people, complete with a full head of hair. He was captivated and bought two. Very different, to be sure.

On Monday, the process of helping IMCO-Australasia find a new personnel director got underway in earnest. Malcolm was at the hotel just before nine o'clock, and as they walked to the office he laid out Erich's schedule for the coming week.

"There's a meeting with principals at Harpole Associates this afternoon. First screening interviews will begin tomorrow morning. Then you're to fly down to Melbourne late in the afternoon to interview candidates there. You'll have to be back by Wednesday evening so you can see the last of the prospects here on Thursday. That evening, Nigel Forsyth, head of the Sydney office, is having a "Happy Chrissie" party at his house. It's for close friends and his best clients. You'll be his special guest. Only curb is that you'll have to take it easy on the booze because Joel wants an on-site report and will be calling you there. On Friday, you and I will debrief, come up with a short list, and then talk about the people on it. Hopefully, there'll be at least three that we can agree on. You'll have input, but I'll make the final decision right after the holidays. You'll have Friday evening and Saturday free, but on Sunday afternoon, one of Nigel's clients, and a personal friend, Myles Edwards, has offered to take you out on his boat that's docked at Spit Bridge Marina. He and his sweetheart have invited a lovely young lady to be your companion for the afternoon. It'll give you a chance to unwind and to get a different view of the harbor, Bondi Beach, and the city. Your companion, by the way, is from an old family that's well known in Australia. They've made their fortune from sheep and exporting, specifically wool. That's your agenda, right down to the date on Edwards's big boat come Sunday."

"Holy cow," Erich chuckled. "I'm already exhausted."

"You're here to help me out, Erich. I need it, and with Christmas coming up, our schedule is probably tighter than either of us would like. You don't get home until Christmas Eve, I understand. Hardly fair, but that's life in the fast lane."

"Don't worry about it, Harry. I'm at your disposal until next Monday when I start back. I was just kidding about being pooped. Your suggestion to break the trip in Fiji was good advice. I feel great, but I couldn't say that in October."

"I know. No disrespect, but you looked like you were about two steps away from the morgue when you walked in that first morning. At that, you did some really helpful work for us."

When Erich and Malcolm got to the office, they continued their discussion about the week ahead. It would be a busy five days.

Doubling up on his schedule, Erich met with unit heads in the personnel department to answer any questions they had. These were some of the same people who sent up telex messages when he was in New York. After having dealt with any loose ends, he and Malcolm had lunch in the executive dining room and talked about all kinds of things—but not business.

The afternoon meeting with the Harpole people went very well. This was a search firm that knew what it was doing. Chances were high that the candidates they submitted for consideration would be excellent prospects. And Erich hit it off well with Nigel Forsyth. It was a pleasure to work with another professional.

Erich spent the remainder of the afternoon going over the candidates' files and making notes about anything that needed clarification. There were some well-qualified people in the group, but it would come down to the chemistry between Harry Malcolm and those on the short list.

Tuesday was a long day. There were four people to see and Erich was pleased that he had ample time to dig into each candidate's background. As one part of the process, he tried to determine if the prospect and Malcolm could work together well. If it wasn't clear-cut, he chose to err on the side of prudence. And in the interviews, he found that two of the applicants were stronger in a couple of areas, and weaker in others. His self-imposed mandate was to find a professionally balanced manager. Two fit the bill. He was inclined to reject those who, like himself, had expertise in only one or two fields. In Erich's case, he was oriented toward recruitment and placement and wasn't all that interested in working elsewhere in personnel. As such, he could easily spot that in others.

At the end of the day, he finished up his notes on the interviews and then went out to Kingsford Smith for the ninety-minute flight to Melbourne. For some reason, his hotel was located in the central business district, not at the airport. That didn't seem to make much sense since it was probably less convenient for the candidates.

On Wednesday morning, there was no reason to rush because of the three applicants he was to see one of them had just accepted another job. Forsyth had left a message for Erich that was given to him at check-in. That meant he had a 10:00 a.m. appointment and another after lunch. An easy day, relatively speaking, so he spent his spare time talking a short walk and then later on putting all of the candidate's profiles side by side to see what he had. He and Malcolm would be going over all the prospects, and his supporting notes, so he had to feel comfortable with his choices and be fully prepared to defend his recommendations.

The morning candidate, Trevor Hughes, had excellent balance. He'd worked in the personnel departments of two major companies, had gained broad experience, and during his tenure was promoted to supervisory roles in labor relations, employee benefits, staffing, and compensation. Interestingly enough, he and Erich were born on the same day. When Hughes was about to leave, he remarked, "We may have arrived on the same afternoon of the same day, but you have to remember, I'm older than you." His reference was to the time difference, and the fact that Hughes had already been delivered while Erich was awaiting his turn to put in an appearance at the little county hospital in northwestern Ohio. It gave them a way to end a fairly rigorous interview session with genial smiles.

Erich's final interview went well, but he got the impression that the prospect was mostly shopping around and consequently less committed to making a change than others he'd seen. The man was well qualified, so it was a shame that he'd essentially taken himself out of the running.

After the second of the Harpole referrals had left, Erich finished his notes, went to the airport and caught an earlier Ansett flight back to Sydney. When he got to his room, he took a closer look at all of his earlier notes, and also reviewed the resumes of the last two candidates. One was scheduled at 10 o'clock and the other right after lunch. Much like today's schedule. That would give him the balance of the afternoon to write a summary report for Malcolm, and then get ready to party at Forsyth's house at a place north of Sydney called St. Ives.

Thursday's candidates, to Erich's surprise, were clearly off the mark, so his recommendations were set—at least to his satisfaction. But he and Malcolm would go over the details on each applicant starting at 9 a.m. tomorrow. It would likely take much of the morning. Finishing up the last of the reviews, Erich went back to the Wentworth to change into something more casual and then wait for Forsyth's call. It came at about six o'clock, and he said Erich should be at the Phillip Street entrance in about a half-hour.

While Erich was waiting, he looked down the street and saw a face that bore a marked resemblance to someone from his past. Erich's heart skipped a beat. "Amazing likeness," he thought. "I wonder. No. Impossible. Forget it." As he was moving forward to get a better look, Forsyth drove up. Since he was headed in the opposite direction, he had no choice but to let it remain a question that couldn't be answered.

"Nigel. Good evening. I appreciate your invitation to share in the fun, but Harry says I shouldn't drink too much. Joel is supposed to be calling sometime this evening."

"We'll look after you. My guess is, he'll ring you at around nine o'clock, maybe a bit after. That's before breakfast in New York. He'll have to be fair, though, and let you get a little bit of a buzz on. He hired us, you know. It was when we met him in your New York office during our last trip. A good man. Tough, but solid, we think."

"You're right about that. He's straightened me up on a couple of occasions. You know it when you're on the receiving end."

"What did you think of our candidates?"

"Excellent. But the two you scheduled today weren't up to par. To be honest, they were something of a shock. No, a better word would be disappointment. It was almost as if they were an afterthought or warm bodies just to fill out the schedule."

"Good to have your assessment. You won't much like this, but we regarded it as an endeavor to see how well you know your way around the interviewing and assessment processes."

"You're right, Nigel. I don't much like it. Not one bit. No one has *ever* raised questions about my abilities or my understanding of the placement process quite like that. I've been at this a few years, and I damn well know what I'm doing. That's dirty pool, as we used to call it in rural Ohio."

"It wasn't our idea, and it hit us wrong, too, so I'm pleased that you saw through it."

"Then the mousetrap was designed by someone I know. In that case, I'll let it be."

"No, the likelihood is that you don't know who was behind it."

"How about a good guess? The consulting firm that the Board has hired. If so, theirs is an unprofessional way to get answers." Erich toyed with the idea of telling Nigel that he'd mention all this to Joel, but then he thought better of it.

As they drove, Nigel Forsyth's silence confirmed that Erich's guess was right. Then, for sure, he'd let Joel know what had happened. The underlying reason might be that Erich had gotten crossways with someone in executive management recently. "Ought to be an interesting phone call later this evening," Erich thought.

By the time they got to Forsyth's house, Erich had apologized for having bristled. Nigel waved it off. He fully understood.

The Forsyth family did very well for themselves. It was an elegant home in a lovely setting. And Erich said so.

"We sit near wooded areas, so it's 'bushy', as we say. It's a bit far out, but we value the serenity."

"Peace and quiet is it? Sorry, but I hear laughter. Sounds like there's a party going on." They chuckled. The unpleasant subject was behind them.

And a festive event it was. A good many people had been invited. The area at the rear of the house had been decorated with hanging lanterns and other touches, so there was the allusion of Christmas all about.

"This is our annual Christmas party, Erich. Thursday night isn't ideal, but a good many people are leaving for at least a fortnight beginning tomorrow afternoon. This is the best we could do, so it's a compromise, if you will. Fact remains, the holiday is just a week off. Sorry we don't have any snow, but I should imagine you'll find some of that when you're home next week."

Erich was introduced around, and Nigel made a particular point of having him meet another Erich Mauer.

"That makes two unusual coincidences in the last two days. Don't these things usually run in threes? If they do, I wonder what's next. About the earlier one, you wouldn't have any reason to know it, but your candidate, Trevor Hughes, and I were born on the same day. By the way, I rank him number one."

"So do we, but you and I aren't making the ultimate decision. Enough about business. Another beer, Erich?"

"Sure, and I want to try some of those shrimp off the barbie, as I think you call it."

"Make yourself at home. There's plenty of food and beverage. And, here's my wife. I'd like you to meet my Winifred. We've been married since primary school." They all chuckled.

"I'm very happy to meet you, Mrs. Forsyth. And I have to tell you that I think you have a lovely home. Being an apartment dweller, I envy you."

"Thank you, Erich. It's wonderful that you could make our little affair. I've heard a great deal about you, so I'm pleased that we could meet." She didn't invite him to soften his "Mrs. Forsyth" to something less formal.

While the party was well underway, Joel kept his promise and called just after nine o'clock local time. Nigel's prediction about the timing of it was about right. And Erich had followed his own advice and taken it easy. He ate more and drank less.

"Morning, Joel. If I've got it figured right, it's pretty early in the day. You have to be calling from home."

"You're right. It's still very dark out, but I brewed up some coffee and am ready to do business. Are you able to talk?"

"Meaning am I'm cockeyed, or do I have some privacy? If it's the latter, I'm in Forsyth's office at home, and I've nursed two beers since I got here at a little after six thirty. But watch out after I'm off the phone."

Joel laughed softly. "Sounds as if you're doing all right. But what about the candidates?"

Erich went through the list of people, gave him a sketch on each of them, and said he was ready to debrief in the morning. "I hope we don't have too many conflicts on the three people I'm prepared to recommend. I'll send you a telex after we've had our meeting."

Then Erich told Joel about the trap involving the two unqualified candidates, how Nigel said it wasn't their idea, and how he didn't reply to Erich's guess that the consulting firm was behind it.

Joel went ballistic. Erich thought he was going to blow a fuse. "I've had enough of this! When we hang up I'm headed straight for the office, and as soon as the president is free I'm going to let him know in no uncertain terms that I don't want anybody messing around with my staff. Particularly you. You're among the best, and your qualifications have never been subject to question. That impugns your integrity, my integrity, and I *cannot* believe what you're telling me. I'm absolutely livid. To my mind, these people have confirmed that they don't know what the hell they're doing. But if I find out it's Malcolm, and not the consultants, I'll have his job. I'm not going to sit idle on this, Erich. I'm glad you told me about it."

"Appreciate the support. Nigel said he was pleased that I saw through it. Now, boss, may I go get quietly and politely smushed?"

"You're entitled. Have one for me. No, make it two."

"On second thought, I have to keep things under control. Harry and I will be going over the candidates in the morning, so I'll need a clear head."

"A better idea. But you know what your limits are."

"Yep. I do. And, by the way, if we're on time, I'll be on the ground at Kennedy at around eight next Wednesday morning and will drop off my trip summary, see if there's anything that needs attention, and then go home. I'm spending a day in Fiji on the way back, plan on having a beer or two and will write my report while I'm in the midst of enjoying the refreshments and the therapeutic sunshine."

"You're going to be dead on your feet. If you want to take a cab out to Seaford, I'll approve it. You've given Malcolm and me everything we wanted. It's the least I can do. Call it a Christmas present for having put up with what you did earlier in the day. I'm off next week, but when you're back I'll let you know how management reacts to what I'll have to say later this morning."

"Thanks, Joel. Now, I'm headed back to food and beverage. Have a good Christmas."

"You too, Erich. Any special plans over the holidays?"

"I'll see if I can't find someone who'll rub my back, sew on any missing buttons, and also provide some recuperative therapy. I'll probably need it."

Joel chuckled. "I hope it works out exactly the way you want it to. Got to go, Erich. I'm on the warpath and impatient to get some dialogue started. Have a good trip back. See you next year."

"Thanks, Joel. I'll be back in the office on the fifth. G'night. Or rather, good morning."

Erich went back to a party that had thinned a little, but there was still a good crowd. He had more food and drink, and when Nigel asked him to tell him when he was ready to go, Erich said it was about time to start back.

"Big meeting tomorrow. Harry and I are to talk about your candidates." Erich told him who his three selections were, and they agreed entirely on the short list. "See, I'm not such a bad placement guy after all."

"No, in fact if you were here, I'd offer you a job. We could use someone like you. But if you're ready, I'll take you back. At this hour of the night, and it being a Thursday, it won't take long."

Erich slept well, and dreamed about going home. He was looking ahead to his Monday flight out, the stopover in Fiji, freezing cold at JFK, and then feeling like death warmed over again by the time he got to the office at an early hour on Wednesday.

When morning came, he felt fine. Plenty of food and not too much booze was the right balance. His meeting with Malcolm wouldn't be torture. He was ready for him, too.

Erich walked into Harry Malcolm's office right at nine thirty and after having said good morning, they settled down to tackle the only item on their agenda. After a review of Erich's notes, and his conclusions, they agreed on two of the candidates, but they differed on the third choice. Erich went into great detail about his reasons for selecting him and made every effort to overwhelm Harry with the facts. He finally caved in but decided he'd meet with just the two they initially agreed on. Difference was they were also at odds on who was number one. Erich and Nigel Forsyth saw eye to eye. Malcolm didn't, and no amount of support for Trevor Hughes in Melbourne had any influence on how Harry was thinking. The final interviews might change his mind.

Erich finished his day at IMCO-Australasia, and then went back to Malcolm's office to say goodbye. "I won't see you between now and the time I leave on Monday," Erich said, "so I want to say thanks for all you've done to make this a productive trip. I'll be interested in finding out who it is you pick. I imagine you'll let Joel know when you've made your decision. All three candidates are top quality, and my view is that it's about a tossup. It'll come down to chemistry, and that's personal."

"I can't thank you enough, Erich. If I had a place on my staff that could make use of what you do well, I'd sure as hell like to have you work for me. Joel's fortunate. You do good work."

"You're making me blush, Harry. But before I go, best wishes for a Merry Christmas. If there's anything I can do for you after I'm back in New York, just shout. It's been good seeing you again. Look after yourself."

"You too. A good Christmas and a happy and healthy New Year. Thanks again for your support and all you've done for us."

"You're welcome. See you in New York one of these days?"

"Always a possibility. Have a good trip home."

They shook hands, and then Erich started back to the Wentworth Hotel to begin the process of unwinding.

Chapter Nine

Back in his room, Erich dropped off his attaché case, freshened up a bit, and then headed down to the lower level pub for a cold Foster's. It was a good day for one. As he passed by the newsstand, he stopped to look at the headlines on the various newspapers from around the world.

And then something absolutely unimaginable happened. Within a matter of seconds, one word would change the direction of his life.

"*Erich?*"

He recognized the voice. Instantly. The face he'd seen at a distance last night was familiar, and the third coincidence he'd mentioned at Nigel's party had become reality. He froze. After a few seconds, he looked up and then turned slowly. His eyes confirmed what his auditory senses already knew.

It *was* his Tina that he'd seen. "My God!" he whispered. The memory of their brief but fervent love affair came flooding back. All of what they'd shared, and then discarded, still made him ache at times. He wondered how much more damage this chance meeting might do to his mending psyche.

Erich was facing her now. She looked radiant, and that captivating smile, the one that had stolen his heart, was aglow. He stood in awed silence and couldn't move. She reached out, walked toward him slowly, and for a moment took his hands in hers. Then they held each other tightly as if their tearful goodbye at Penn Station nine months earlier had never taken place.

"*Ohhh,* Tina. This isn't possible. But what on earth are you doing down here?

"Company business."

"Well, these things never, ever happen—not even in the movies."

"I know, love, and I'm as shocked as you are. To meet you like this, to see you here, is . . . is beyond words. But it's meant to be, I think."

"I'm totally dumbstruck and don't know what to say other than you look absolutely fabulous."

"It's not like you to be out of words, so let me help. A one in a million reunion calls for a celebration, and I think you should invite me down to the pub for a drink." Tina smiled affectionately.

"I can't think, so I'm glad you're doing it for me." He chuckled softly. "You have the best idea I've heard in nearly a year."

Holding hands as they walked, they were finally able to find a small table in a reasonably quiet corner of a busy place. It was, after all, the start of the weekend, and a long Christmas holiday for many. Voice levels were up but not overpowering.

Seated, and drinks served, Erich said, "You can't know how much I've missed you. There's never a day when you don't cross my mind."

"It's so good to see you, to touch you. In all these months, there hasn't been anyone else who's mattered to me. You did; you still do." Tina reached across their little table and took Erich's hands in hers. The expression on her face confirmed that her words were sincere. "I couldn't help making comparisons. No one else has come close. I've learned that the way I feel is both good and bad, but it says something about what's in my heart. I never stopped caring, and my love for you is as alive and full of meaning today as it was at the end of March. I can still see us saying goodbye. Not healthy, maybe, but I can't help it. You and those last heartbreaking minutes we shared at Penn Station are burned into my memory."

"Why did we do this to each other? The Monday after you left I shut the door to your little office and never opened it again. There wasn't any way I could deal with the reality that it was empty, that there was no longer a smiling face sitting behind your desk. Then the message you left behind nearly did me in. After I read what you wrote, I had my door closed all that morning. If it had been possible to open a window, I might've been tempted to jump. Never in my life had I felt such intense pain."

"I'm sorry, Erich. It wasn't what I intended. I just wanted to say thank you for all you'd meant to me. You remember the words?"

"You have to be kidding. How could I forget them? I saved your memo, of course, but it's put away so that when I'm eighty-something I'll be able to reread it and remember what it was we had. Our unbelievable meeting here will add a footnote to it. Is this good for us? For a few hours, maybe. But longer term? Almost certainly not unless we do something about your concerns. If we don't, then we're back to weeks, maybe months, of trying to put today's memories behind us. But, what the hell. We probably go through life just this once, so if we get it mostly right the first time then we don't have to come back and do it over. Not sure that makes any sense at all. But if there is another life, I'll want us to share it. All of it."

"Well in this one, you know were going to spend the next two nights together. It's only a question of whose bed we mess up." They finally had a chance to smile again and then laugh gently.

"Mine," Erich suggested. "Housekeeping won't think much about that kind of thing going on in a man's room."

"I can't tell you what it feels like to be sitting here with you. I've missed my Erich so much."

"After we finish our drinks, we're going off somewhere and have dinner. Not in the hotel. We need a romantic place, dimly lighted and intimate. Before we go, I thought you might be interested in knowing that Roxane is history, just like you thought she'd be. And it *was* a year—plus one day. Your prediction was off by twenty-four hours." Erich smiled. "I was down here in October and went back through San Francisco at the beginning of November. She said it was over, walked away and never looked back. Pretty outside. All steely inside when she wanted to be. And, Lara's gone, too, the way it looks. Her favorite uncle is dying, and she sees some kind of link to me in that. Some of her last words before I left were that she cares too much to watch me die. Her business is growing, so she's going to marry it, I guess. But I do have a local gal I see. Just friends. Nothing more. I've learned patience, though. Like I said before, you cross my mind every day and that's sufficient. The memory of you, and us, is the ember that keeps me going."

"You know how deep inside that touches me? Not fair, Erich." Tears welled up but went no further.

"Let's go find dinner. You have to tell me about your new life. I still can't believe that our paths have crossed halfway around the globe. Long way to go for a weekend together." He smiled warmly. "No complaints, though, until we get on different flights. But let's enjoy what we have while we have it. Didn't one of us say about the same thing back in January?"

"We both did at different times. So, yes. Please. Let's do make the best of what little time we've been given. I start back to Washington late on Sunday morning, but until then I'm not letting you out of my sight."

"And you know that I'll go with you to the airport and see you off. A repeat of Penn Station, kind of?" Erich suggested.

"Maybe. But let's suppose that these next two days are maybe the start of something new and to see what we can do to build a lasting foundation."

"Our paths won't ever cross like this again, and give us that chance, so amen to that."

Erich and Tina found a small restaurant they were told had been part of a jail many decades earlier. It was the kind of place they had in mind. Great ambiance. Perfect. Even though it was busy, they were seated quickly and their drinks arrived soon afterwards.

As they sipped their cocktails, Tina talked at length about how pleased she was that she'd had the opportunity to move up from her executive secretary role when she worked for Erich at Essex Steel. She was happy with her new administrative job, felt at ease with her growing responsibilities, and liked the fact that she was pretty well paid. Seen as a rising star, she'd been sent to Sydney in August for orientation. It was their mid-winter, but it didn't matter because she enjoyed traveling, especially to Australia. She was back this time for further training. The road ahead looked promising.

Tina paused as their meals were served. The break gave Erich a chance to comment, "None of what you've said surprises me. Had Essex remained intact, you'd have outgrown your secretarial job with me before long. I could see that day coming, so the acquisition was a blessing in disguise. I'm proud of you."

Continuing, Tina said her job was the positive side of it. Her personal life, adjusting to a new community, and all that came with it, left something to be desired. There seemed to be plenty of men around. Some were single and interested in her, but the strict way she'd been raised was still a hindrance. "If you want to know the truth," she added, "I thought maybe I could find someone like Erich Mauer, but there's only one of him. And you don't know how happy I am to be sitting across from the only one there is." She smiled affectionately, then took one of Erich's hands and squeezed it gently.

"I know about that. All along, I've felt the same way. There's only one Tina. But we're forced to think about our future again. And it's odd, because I had a dream not long ago that's stuck with me. In it, a voice was telling me not to worry, and to just be patient. I have to wonder if this was what I was being told to wait for."

"We can talk it about it tomorrow. Tonight I just want to look at you and soak up all of what it feels like to be close again. What we're sharing at the moment could never be any better."

"This'll set your search for a husband back maybe another year, you know."

"Could be I've already found him. Again."

"Like you suggested, let's talk about it tomorrow. But, none of this would be happening if you'd seen me and just kept walking."

"There wasn't any way I could've done that. I'd have given up my life first. It would've meant turning my back on the chance to hold you and to have you love me again. Not possible."

"Then I guess neither one of us was serious when we said what we did at Penn Station last March; that is, about it being the end of the road for us."

"This is different. After the Essex takeover was underway, and we'd left, I knew how to reach you both at home and at work. We decided then that I shouldn't call or write because it was over. But when you were just a few feet away from me this afternoon, you couldn't have expected me to walk away from you. We meant too much to each other during the two years we worked together, and then the three months we were lovers. I'd have had to be less than human, someone with iffy feelings, to do that."

"Like Roxane?"

"Like Roxane."

"I have to tell you that just for the fun of it I sent her a card from Fiji last Friday. I haven't heard from her since she left me at airport in San Francisco the first Sunday in November, and won't ever, but I couldn't resist the temptation. And it's interesting. When she turned and walked away I didn't try to call her back, didn't even have a lump in my throat. It was so very different from how it was when you left. My reaction to what she decided was sort of, well, that's it. But Lara was in the picture, and in spirit you were still with me."

"We seem to have the same problem, it sounds like. More on that later, too, because if you're finished I want you to take me back to the hotel and love me."

When they got to Erich's room, clothes were left where they were tossed. There were no preliminaries, even though Erich had secretly wanted to start from the beginning and relive what they'd discovered about each other when their love was new almost a year ago. But with their pent-up needs setting the pace, it wasn't long before they shared a magnificent finale.

Resting, Tina said, "You haven't forgotten how to make me feel truly happy. Only thing I'm sorry about is that there isn't a little one in any of it."

"For the first time, I have to confess that I feel the same way. It's something else for our agenda tomorrow. I looked into it."

They talked on for a while. Then, at peace, they held each other close and stayed that way throughout the night.

When Erich awakened, he saw that same lovable face he'd gotten to know so well. There was the trace of a smile, but he had no doubt at all about what was in her dreams.

At a little after eight, Tina opened her sleepy eyes, smiled and said, "Good morning, sweetheart. You can't know how good it is to have you next to me and feeling perfectly contented. I'm expecting to live now."

"That was the general idea. We may not have done it all just yet, but we're off to a pretty good start." He chuckled softly.

"I'm lucky that you recover so quickly."

"That's directly related to who the companion is. We'd most likely have a good love life for decades. It would probably slow down some, but the feelings would always be there. To see your sweet face each morning would remind me how much I care about you, and how much I need you, both emotionally and physically."

"You're making a good case, mister. A night with you is part of it. I'd like to attack you, but I'm not sure there's anything left."

"We have time for encores, so maybe we should refuel first."

"I like the sound of that. I'm starved."

"If we go like this, we'd get plenty of attention." They laughed. It felt good—and to care so much about someone.

"I think not. I'll shower first, or would you like to join me?"

"You know I would." He showed her a naughty smirk.

Erich and Tina were amused at the way they'd left their clothes strewn about. "Colorful," he remarked, "and decorative." After they'd showered and dressed, they went down to breakfast.

When they were seated, Erich said, "I hope housekeeping will give us another set of sheets we can mess up." Tina grinned. "But why is it," he asked, "that you're the one person who makes me feel so good about myself? And what is it the two of us have that's so unique? I haven't felt like this since I finally recognized a year ago how much you meant to me. It's easy to laugh when you're around, but it's just as easy for me to hurt when you aren't. It confirms, again, how much you matter. Yet, it may be that I can't have you."

"I'm a lot less certain about that now, mostly because all of the love I felt for you then is still there. But one thing is going to change. You'll know where I live, and you'll have my phone number. We've come a long, painful way since March, and no matter what paths our lives take, I think we can handle letters, and calls, and spending weekends together. Our love has strengthened since last spring. I can feel it. The mistake we made, and I'm sure of it, was what we decided about not looking back. There's no question that it made life harder for both of us. It would've been so much easier if we hadn't turned our backs on what we had."

Tina sipped her orange juice. Erich waited.

"But we made the decision," she continued, "and those last few days together were so hard to deal with because of it. We were all hung up on what we'd decided—as if it was the *only* solution. It's important to me that I stay in touch with you now. It'll make life happier. At least mine. I think we can manage it. One thing's obvious. The nine months of separation didn't change how we feel. Like I suggested, our bond is stronger. So it's possible that by this time tomorrow I might decide to accept the proposal you haven't made. But if not, and we keep in touch, I may come to terms next week, or next month, with what I think is best for us, call you and say let's celebrate your fortieth with a wedding. I have no reason to think you'll have married someone else by then."

"Funny. I almost proposed in the pub last night. You know it's there, and the choice is yours. We've both survived a test and have matured, I think, since you left New York. So you were right when you said that we didn't solve a damn thing by creating an artificial barrier. The proof of it, as you pointed out, is that what we meant to each other then hasn't changed. Roxane and I would never have seen this happen. And Lara? She thinks that anyone she really cares about dies. I can't change that. But about a wedding on my fortieth, it's a weekday, I believe, so that wouldn't do. Yeah, it is. I remember now. Clayton promised to buy me a drink to celebrate my coming of age."

"We can work it out if and when that day comes."

"But if we do stay in touch, the unkindest cut would be the day you call and say I've found another Erich Mauer, and we're going to marry. I'd need some kind of safety net in place; otherwise, I'd be right back at March 29 and Penn Station emotionally."

"We could still have our little meetings somehow. Maybe when I'd come up to New York to visit family."

"Ordinarily I'd be dead set against something like that," Erich said, "but it's you, and I'd have absolutely no scruples. I *would* meet you and love you, just like always. Until you're expecting. Then that would be the end of it. Forever. On the other hand, if I were married by then, I wouldn't be a party to a rendezvous. That's just the way it would have to be because I'd be committed and monogamous. But you don't have to worry. There isn't anyone but you that I'd consider marrying this afternoon, or tomorrow, or next June. Should we go pick out your ring?"

"Sounds like you're serious."

"Yep. Seems that way."

"Well, I guess we could look. What else are we doing today?" Tina asked.

"Being out in the fresh air, walking along the Botanical Gardens, having lunch, and picking out a ring," Erich felt good about what was happening and smiled in a way that expressed how he felt. Tina joined him. "So let's start our 'walkabout' as I've heard people here call it."

"You're being more persuasive about us than you were at Essex," Tina commented.

"It's the Foster's beer. Makes a man out of you."

"Remind me not to drink any. I like things just the way they are."

"Me too." Erich gave her an affectionate hug.

"What we might do is call our shopping exploratory," Tina suggested. "But I have to admit, it's kind of exciting to think about looking at rings, and then maybe getting serious about one. I wouldn't do this with anybody but you. I think you know that."

"I hope you wouldn't. Otherwise, I'd be terribly jealous. Tell you what. We'll just window shop so that we don't get carried away and actually buy one. If you decided on your trip back to the States that all of this was just fun and fantasy, I'd have to hock it in New York. That wouldn't do either because I'd lose my shirt on it."

"Sounds like you're already backing away from the idea of giving me a ring. That didn't last very long."

"Not at all. I'll do it. Gladly. But only if you'll think seriously about marrying me someday. I've just proposed. Sort of."

"Ohhh. In that case, I better start paying attention. Could I think about my answer until I see what size diamond you're willing to give me? It'll tell me how much you love me."

"You've learned how to be something of a gold digger," Erich said. "And I suppose you're only mercenary when it comes to money." They laughed. "Small diamond, but lots of love. I'm mostly poor and live from hand to mouth, you understand."

"Well, I don't know. Let me sleep on it."

"Only if it's with me," Erich said.

"Wouldn't have it any other way. That's how it's always been."

"We're being loose as a goose. And goofy. I don't think we're taking ourselves seriously about any of this."

Tina put her arm around Erich's waist and asked, "Do you have any idea how much I love you, mister?"

Erich scowled. "Not all that much if you're turning down my proposal."

"This has been light and good fun. Let's keep it that way. If you're going to get serious and grumpy, I won't give you my phone number."

"Police. Help. Blackmail."

They laughed themselves into keeping it light. It matched the beautiful weather on this last day of spring in Australia.

As Erich and Tina walked, they talked about all of the things that had happened since late March. And he had to mention Katie.

"After you left New York, my Katie said you'd called and told her about my likes and dislikes. It was sweet of you, but having to deal with things like that would bring up the image of my Tina, and I'd wind up in a blue funk. Then Lara wanted to go to Mazza's Restaurant, the place you took us, and I vetoed that in a New York minute. I couldn't deal with another ghost. You didn't ever let go of my head. You still haven't. But our chance meeting is exactly what I've needed to get you, and me, and us sorted out. I'll be at peace when I start back on Monday evening. And on that subject, you haven't asked about my return schedule, but I'll tell you about it anyway. After I leave here, I'm spending a day in Fiji to write my trip report, and I get home the morning before Christmas."

Erich and Tina had the time, so as they walked they stopped for a couple of minutes to admire some beautiful yellow roses that were in full bloom. Their fragrance was delightful.

As they continued their walk, Erich said, "I want to come back to Katie for a minute. If you're ever in New York on a weekday, I'd like you to meet her. She married her high school sweetheart back in the spring. It was when I was in Guatemala. I guess the bachelor in him resurfaced not long after that and the thing is already in deep doo-doo. She has serious designs on getting me into bed and makes suggestive comments nearly every day. I tease her a lot, and the last time I put her on she threw a pencil at me, which I caught. And then just before I left, she stuck her tongue out at me because of something I said. Yeah, I remember. She asked me about a proper sendoff, and I said I had three women going to do that two hours apart. She wanted to be part of the fantasy. And she's devastated that I wasn't around to attack at the Christmas party. Katie's a sweet gal, but she needs a good man in her life, a guy who can look after her needs. She and I obviously have a good working relationship, and she's terrific when it comes to supporting what I do. Back in May, I arranged to have her promoted. A big salary bump came with it. She's extremely capable, but she also wants a piece of Erich Mauer. Won't happen."

"I do get into New York during the week sometimes. Maybe the daydream I mentioned will be turned into something real before long. It's what I mentioned last night, the one where I walk in and say I want to be a part of your life. It does have lots of appeal. We'd be good together. Always have been. Anyway, I'd like to meet Katie. More important is that I'd get to see you."

"After I get back, about the only thing on my agenda is a trip to London sometime in April. At least that's the way it looks. Like to come along?"

"I'd love to, but my boss wouldn't agree to anything like that. Anyway, before we get to April, I'll be in New York over the holidays and will want to see you if only for a day, or a night, or whatever we can arrange. Think we can work something out?"

"It's a must. Be great. I'm doing my only open dates from memory, December 29 and then January 3, but overnights would give us at least a little time together. I'd like to have you at home with the guys and me. They're still in love with you, too."

"That's so special, Erich. Now I just have to come back to Mianus Ridge. But if it's the third, you'd have to get me down to Penn Station on the afternoon of the fourth."

"Ahhh, I'd rather not see you off there again if it can be avoided. The last time we did that it nearly took me apart. I'll drive you down to LaGuardia and put you on a flight, even if I have to pay for it myself."

"I know how you feel. But if your memory is as good as I remember it, why not plan on both nights? There isn't anything else I'd rather do. Be the high point of my vacation."

"I'll look at my schedule when we get back to the hotel, but I think the dates are right. Lots of social stuff going on, and the guys will be around, so I have to keep an eye on them over the holidays. I'm worried about Rudi. There are some signs that he's back on something once in a while, but my real concern now is how he's going to handle Lara's having apparently taken herself out of the picture. She's been his stand-in mom for over a year and loves her as if she'd delivered him. The news that she's gone, if that's the way it turns out, will be as hard on him as it was on me when you left for Washington last spring. His emotions are on the fragile side, and he may decide that the only way to deal with the hurt is to take a big step beyond good reason. Maybe mainline stuff. He likes you, so I will want your number. You may be able to help stabilize things. I don't want to saddle you with my troubles, but at minimum you might want to know how he's doing."

"Sounds to me like you still have your hands full. But I'm not sure how much help I can be from Georgetown. More important, would I be able to help Rudi? He's a neat kid, but I can't replace Lara. No one can. And you're getting into a subject that's starting to take the edge off our day together. If you don't mind, could we set it aside until we're all together in Seaford?"

"You're right. Sure.

"A change of subject is that I was supposed to have reservations at a different hotel, but there was some kind of mix-up, and I wound up at the Wentworth. I'm *so* glad. Then I was the one who saw you, and not the other way around."

"All it took was one word. I recognized your voice and froze."

"I know. I saw it. I was there, too. Remember? When I knew you knew, I wasn't sure what you were going to do next. That's why I put my hands out toward you. More than anything else, I wanted you to hold me. I needed you to do that in the worst way. You'll never know. I'd have died if you'd seen me and then walked away. God! I don't even want to think about the possibility that you might've done that."

"We seem to be so right for each other. I can't imagine that any one man and any one woman have what we do. Yet there is still that one obstacle."

"You were going to tell me about it. From your expression, I guess it isn't good news."

"The surgical procedure to put a man out of business is intended to be permanent. There have been some successful reversals, but the percentage is pretty small. The other part of it is that it's been almost fifteen years, so I'm not a good candidate to have it come out the way we'd want it to. Anyway, the chances that you'd get pregnant are close to zero. Crummy odds, Tina. I've come around to thinking that I'd be willing to start over again. But only with you. It says everything about how much I care about you, about us, and the nameless new life that would be the product of our love. I would like that, but I really am out of business. At the end of the discussion I had with the urologist, he told me not to waste my money. Because you were on my mind so much, I did find out what you wanted to know—never dreaming that we'd ever see each other again. But if we did...."

"Oh, Erich. I don't know what to say. You tried, and you were willing to meet me more than half way. So, again, whatever happens next is on my shoulders. But I'm not going to think about it today. I don't want this to be anything less than a perfect day. Just you and me, without a care in the world. Should we look at rings in the window across the street?"

The balance of their day together was perfect, just as Tina wanted it. They walked with their arms around each other, or hand in hand, window-shopped for rings, saw parts of the Botanical Gardens, had lunch, saw some of the city, and savored the warmth of their love. They also talked about what brought them to Sydney. Late in the afternoon, they had a drink at a sidewalk café and then went back to Erich's room and loved fervently. They couldn't get enough of each other, of kisses, of holding on. They were starved for affection and their needs were infinite.

As they were getting ready for dinner, Tina handed Erich a sheet of hotel stationery. "Here's my address and phone number. Right below it is the company I work for, and their address and number. I'll give you my business card tomorrow before I leave. We're not hidden from each other any longer. We're going to be in touch. I want us to have it that way."

"I'm happy with your decision, at least this one. We agree. For the first time in months, I feel like I'm a whole human being again."

Over dinner, Erich told Tina about having met Clayton for a drink recently and how he'd finally told him about their involvement. "Clayton said he thought there was more to it than just our being a good team in the office. It seemed to him at the time that I took your leaving much too hard for it to have been just a boss-secretary relationship. He wasn't at all cross with me, or surprised. Apparently I looked terrible, and he was worried about both my physical and mental health. I told him it was devastating, but that it was good I had a demanding job to go to and could avoid walking the streets looking for one. Nobody would've hired me in the state I was in. And since you'd called Katie, she had to know the story. She's a livewire and always upbeat, so that helped, too. And I imagine your move, and the new job, helped you as well."

"It was the only thing that kept me going, even though it was a distant second to staying in New York just so I could be near you. At that, there were days when I was tempted to come back. But it was a good opportunity for me, and still is, so I stuck it out. If I hadn't, I wouldn't be sitting across from you now. I'll never get over the fact that we met here. It's totally mind boggling."

"I'll be seeing Clayton sometime after the holidays. He'll be flabbergasted by my story about our having met here."

"I'd love to see him. Where is he now?"

"He's personnel director at a retailing chain, but he's not happy. *The Weekly News* magazine, TWN, is after him, and I suspect he'll make a move soon. I'll give him your best. He'll like that."

"When I make one of my trips up to New York, maybe we could have an early dinner with him."

"Sounds like you've been in and out of Manhattan and never called."

"That's what we agreed on, Erich. If you'd had my number, I'll bet you'd have crumbled and called me."

"No question about it. I would've. Oh, and while we're on the subject, I brought my calendar. The twenty-ninth, thirtieth, and the third are all good. Come out early so we can have lunch. That'll give us more time together. I'm really looking forward to having you at home with us again."

"That sounds so good. I'm really excited about it. We didn't buy a ring, but I still have some thinking to do. How my parents feel and our age difference isn't important now. With people in your family living into their nineties, or nearly so, it would be silly to worry about your longevity. It comes down to you or babies. Guess I can't have it both ways. If I didn't have the kinds of maternal urges I do, it'd be easy—like it's been for Lara, and Roxane. A career doesn't mean the same thing to me as it does to them. What's important is that we'll be in touch. It'll give me time to sort it all out."

"There's still something missing, though. Like I said, if we start seeing each other again, it'll surely put a damper on your finding a Mauer replica, assuming that's what you still want to do. If so, and your search goes on, I'm sort of on the outside looking in. A spectator. Then when someone who'll do eventually comes along, and you've kept my hopes alive, I'm going to be shredded wheat again. Now that I think about it, I'm not sure how much emotional whiplash you can expect me to handle. Roxane felt like her future was in my hands, and in fact it was, but I feel like mine's in yours. I'm on the other side of the question now, and I know how she felt. I've already brought this up, so you get the picture."

"So far, I really haven't been serious about finding someone to replace you. It can't be done anyway. But I understand what you're saying, and I guess it isn't fair to make you feel like you're a puppet I can manipulate. I'm not sure how we compromise. If I give up the idea of having a family, then we have the answer. It's that simple. Anyway, I had hoped that the end of this wonderful day wouldn't include what we've just talked about. On the other hand, I do have to face the issue. Again. But I want you to know this, Erich. I love you deeply, and, looking back, I probably have since the spring of sixty-seven when you were new to me as my boss at Essex. I've never confessed to you that it went that far back. When your marriage was in trouble, I couldn't put a move on you then, much as I wanted to, because of any possible legal consequences. And I was also engaged at the time. That was a mistake, I found out. You showed me something so different, and I wouldn't have ever been happy with Anthony."

"Then we might say we've already been engaged for more than two years." Erich smiled at that. "I don't know. Maybe it's better that I don't have your number. If we stop talking, then I'll know it's over and family comes first. Erich, like an Avis rental, will also be number two."

"No. Not so. And let's get out of this downward spiral we're in. Think about all we've had today. The beauty of it. Two people who care about each other. I want you to have my number and to call. Anytime. All the time."

"Okay. You win," Erich said. "Now, let's go back, love the night away, forget about all this, and make it the end of the perfect day we both want."

Tina showed signs of tears, but kept them in check, smiled instead, and said simply, "I love you, Erich. Take me to your room; I'll show you how much I mean it, and what you mean to me."

And she did exactly that. At no time during Erich's adult life was so much affection so clearly expressed as it was in the way his Tina loved him on this night. And never in the years immediately ahead would he know the same depth of feeling. With her in his thoughts, he hoped they could find a way to live out their years together. They were far more than just physically attuned. They also had a fusion of hearts, of minds, and of souls.

Then at first light, they loved again. Tina sighed from the feeling of extreme contentment that swept over her. Erich then joined her in the celebration of their love. It was the conclusion of their totally unexpected two nights together and a union that ended with a feeling of total fulfillment.

"How can we ever walk away from an expression of love like that?" Erich asked a few minutes later.

"We haven't. Think of it as beginning again. My heart has never belonged to anyone but you. We'll have time together. It may not be often, but no matter what happens there will always be us and our memories for the rest of our lives. I've said that before, and it's still true. These two days proved that our love is as strong as it's ever been. Now, hold me close."

They held on to each other until it was time for Tina to go back to her room and pack. After they'd showered and dressed, Erich went along to help and then to bring her luggage back to his room. After they'd finished their late breakfast, they picked up all of Tina's paraphernalia and made the trip to Kingsford Smith at a little after ten o'clock. Her Qantas flight didn't leave until eleven thirty, so she was checked in well ahead of boarding time. It gave them nearly a half-hour to have a coffee and also share their thoughts about what had happened since Friday afternoon.

"These two days we've had together are the happiest I've ever known," Tina said. "What I'm feeling inside is so new, so different. For want of a better word, I'll call it serenity. You've made it all possible. I'm grateful that, once more, you've given my personal life meaning, something that hasn't been there since March. And you've brought back the memories of all the things we've shared. It feels wonderful to have them come alive again."

"We both feel the same way; it's a shame we can't spend some time together in Fiji. You'd enjoy it, and it would be wonderful having you there. But you already know I'm flying late tomorrow afternoon. And since mine is a more direct route I won't be that many hours behind you."

"My itinerary is the reverse of your October trip and the long way home."

"It is that. But, two other things. I'll have a little Christmas gift for you. It'll just be four days late because I haven't decided on it yet. You've been with me every minute since Friday. The other is trivia. Today is the summer solstice, in case you hadn't thought about it. It means we're having a second longest day this year. You get cheated a little, but I'm here all day."

"What's most important is the beautiful day we had yesterday. If I live to be a hundred," Tina said, "I'll never forget it, even if you didn't buy me a ring." They both smiled at her words. That they could do so just minutes before she boarded confirmed how much their relationship had matured. "So, what are you doing later on?"

"I'm going trolling to see if I can't find a hot chick to look after me tonight. I got used to having company in my bed."

Under the table, Tina kicked him gently and said, "You're a rascal. Are you the same guy I spent the last two nights with? I can't imagine that you'd have anything left for someone else."

"I don't. Anyway, I only have eyes for you. And you can probably guess that you're leaving behind a guy who'll miss you."

"I do. But this time it isn't the end. It's like I said: a new beginning."

"I like the positive sound of that. Now, back to your question about this afternoon, I've been invited out on a boat to cruise Sydney Harbor. The guy who owns it is a client of the search firm we've been using here. He's head of marketing for a big chemicals outfit and apparently does pretty well for himself. The boat's supposed to be a fairly big one. Whatever, it'll be a chance to get a little more sun. I'm to be picked up at one o'clock, but I'll wait until you're airborne before I go back to the hotel.

"Sounds like a fun afternoon. Sorry I can't go with you. You'll come back with even more tan than you have now. You look healthy, and like maybe you're a little bit in love, too."

"I am that, ma'am. But, it's time for you to board. Now that I think about it, why aren't you flying into New York?"

"Too much trip stuff to carry. Just as important, I need to get rid of my lighter clothes and make sure I'm dressed for winter."

"I keep forgetting that I'll probably freeze to death when I come in early Wednesday morning. But about the time you roll out of bed on Tuesday, I'll be landing in Fiji. Track me as I fly. I'm going to follow your trip and know where you are. That's another way of saying that I'll be with you all the way to Dulles. Just make believe that I'm sitting next to you."

"You're such a love. I will. Now, it's time to go, my sweet."

"Before you run off and leave me," Erich said, "there's something I've been wanting to ask ever since we were sitting at dinner on Friday evening. But every time I'd think about it, our conversation would change direction and it would slip my mind."

"Should I apologize?"

Erich chuckled. "Certainly not, because talking about you, and me, and us was much more important."

"Now I'm curious. What was it?"

"Your ID bracelet. When I put it on your wrist the night before you left for D.C., I thought you might eventually get tired of it and take it off. I'm pleased to see that you're still wearing it."

"Oh, Erich. You know how much it meant to me at the time, and it still does. I've never taken it off. It's a part of you that went with me and was a special thing you did. I look at it every day."

"What I had Tiffany's engrave on the back expressed how I felt about you. May I read what's etched on it?"

Tina held out her left arm. Erich turned the silver bracelet over, and in a soft, loving voice read: *"Forever yours. Erich. 3.29.69"*.

"That's the first time you've said those words. It brings them to life. They have as much meaning today as they did in March. Maybe even more so. And just so you'll know, I don't ever plan to take the bracelet off.

Especially now that you've read the inscription. It was beautiful, and I'm touched."

"You know it was a sincere thought then. It still is. Now all you have to do is figure out what you're going to do with this guy living up the tracks in Seaford."

"We'll talk about that when I'm up on the twenty-ninth. I'm so looking forward to being at home with you again. It's been such a long time."

"The guys and I will be ready."

"I hate to put an end to something that's making me feel all tingly inside, but I really should board."

Erich walked Tina to the gate. They hugged tightly and then kissed with deep feeling. "See you a week from tomorrow," Erich said. "Try to be on the train at a little after ten. If you can make it, we'll have the whole afternoon together. Call me before you leave. And just wait till I tell the guys about us and that you're coming out. They'll go bananas."

"Love to be there and see their reaction."

"I'll give you a replay."

"Hate to go, Erich. This has been absolutely wonderful."

"I feel the same way, but today isn't March and Penn Station, and there are no tears or heartache. It's just plain old everyday unadulterated happiness."

"Glad there's none of what we went through before. Once in a lifetime is enough. And we have next week to look forward to. I'm delighted about it. But I have to go. Bye, my love."

"Bye, sweetheart. Have a good trip home."

"You too. See you in eight days."

A quick hug and Tina was on her way to the Qantas 707 V-Jet that would begin her long westward trip back via London. As she was about to disappear from view, she turned, waved, and gave Erich that million-dollar smile. He showed her one in return and blew a kiss her way.

Pushback was right on schedule. As Erich had promised, he waited until Tina's flight was airborne and she was on her way home. And with her departure, he had the hollow feeling inside that he knew so well. They'd had two perfectly idyllic days together, so he hated to see them come to an end. Erich watched Qantas Flight 763 until it became a speck in the western sky. Before he turned to leave, he said quietly, "God bless, Tina."

Chapter Ten

Myles Edwards arrived at the Wentworth pretty much on time. Forsyth had told Erich to watch for a good-looking guy in a dark blue Holden Brougham, and that was what had just pulled up at the main entrance.

"Might you be Erich Mauer?" the driver asked.

"I was early this morning. But now that my honey is on her way back to Washington, I'll need to double-check."

They shook hands. "I'm Myles Edwards. Nigel's told me quite a bit about you. Thinks you're top shelf. My kind of guy. Climb aboard. We've got a splendid day for a little cruising. By the way, the lady who'll keep you company will be at the marina by the time we get there. Name's Simone Dekker. Family's in the wool business and loaded. Might be a chance to ensure a soft landing when you retire, but it sounds like you're looked after."

"Man's an idiot if he turns his back on an opportunity to feather his nest—or his bed."

"Clever to have options."

"I'm not among the needy, but someone once commented about my being able to recover quickly. In fact, it was Tina who left just before midday."

"How do you know somebody down here?"

"If you have a few minutes, I'll tell you whole the story. At that, it's probably more than you need."

"I'm always interested in listening to stories about how things come about. Have at it."

Erich went back to their relationship at Essex Steel, the change of jobs, the separation, and the unbelievable chance meeting late on Friday afternoon. "We made good use of our time." Erich chuckled. Edwards joined him.

"Delightful tale. No moss on you, mate."

"Tell me about my boat date."

"Well, Simone is fun, but I'm not sure how far you can go with her. Not much time. Nigel said you're leaving tomorrow."

"Yep, at 18:00 hours. I'm stopping in Fiji for a day to write my trip report so I won't have to screw around with it while I'm on vacation. I'll be on the ground in New York early on Wednesday morning, Christmas Eve. Plan is to drop by the office, leave the report with my gal, and check to see if there are any crises brewing. If there are, tough. They'll keep until the fifth."

"I like the way you do things. Maybe you ought to come back and work for me. You could get to know Simone, settle down someplace up in North Sydney, have some kiddies, and live the good life."

"Nice idea, but I've had my family and have since then been put out of business. It's the major issue, in fact the only issue, between Tina and me. She wants little ones. Crowding forty, I'm not keen on starting over, but would with her if it could be done. It can't."

"You're nearing forty? What are you on? I wouldn't guess that you're any older than mid-thirties. You're well preserved."

"Marinating is a better word. In New York, we call 'em martinis. I'm what you might call pickling."

"You just clinched it. I would like you to work for me. Know anything about the chemicals business?"

"Not the first thing. But I do know good music when I hear it. Who's that you've got on? She's terrific."

"Nana Mouskouri. Greek, but she sings in at least three or four languages. Charming bird."

"Got to have that tape. When you pop it out, let me have a look at it."

"Sure thing. We can take it with us and listen to her on the boat. Okay, here we are. And there's Simone."

"Decent. I like what I see. Maybe she'll have dinner with me this evening. Last chance to do that, or whatever else I might propose. On the other hand, I'm in no real need, so I'll be the exemplary gentleman."

"You're on your own. She was Nigel's idea. I don't know her all that well, but good luck. She's older than you might guess, by the way. Looks to me like you could be made for each other."

Myles first introduced Simone to Erich, and then his girlfriend, Belinda Rosewall, to both of them.

"There was to have been another couple, but they got into a row and decided they wouldn't be fit company for a friendly outing like this. Their loss. It's a magnificent day."

Out on Sydney's harbor, Erich made good use of his new camera. He took pictures of sailboats, the North Head, the South Head, not as impressive, views of the city, the opera house under construction, and anything else that caught his eye, which included Simone Dekker.

"Tell me about you," Simone said, finally.

"Well, I'm an American. How's that?" She chuckled amiably.

"I know that, witty man. No, I want you to tell me things I don't know."

"Problem is, I don't know what you know. Dark secrets then?" He smiled.

"You're being mischievous. It's fun, but I really do want to know more about you. Nigel thinks you're serious minded. You're not showing me any part of that."

"It's leisure time, and I can't be too serious when I'm in the presence of a pretty lady. But, okay, if you fall asleep I'll know my life isn't very interesting or that I've gone on too long."

"If it turns out that way, I'll let you know early on."

Erich gave Simone a thumbnail sketch, leaving out divorces, sons, and what he felt were non-essential parts of his life. He didn't go on too long, and she didn't fall asleep. As they cruised around the harbor, Erich and Simone sipped Australian wine and got to know each other better from all their small talk. She was a university graduate, and had been working with her family in the wool export business. She had a fair number of suitors, it seemed, but a serious relationship wasn't of interest, or one simply hadn't developed. Simone wasn't what Erich would call stunning, but she was sweet, good company, and certainly wasn't carried away with the fact that her family was well off. She was very much down to earth, and her affluence certainly wasn't obvious.

"We should have dinner tonight, assuming you're not busy," Erich suggested. "It'll be my last night Down Under, and it would leave me with another pleasant memory."

"I'd love to. I don't see that many Americans, and I'm really pleased that Nigel put us together. Dinner it is, then. You wouldn't know the neighborhood places, so I'll choose one."

"Something small and intimate with thick ambiance would suit me just fine."

"Exactly what I had in mind. Leave it with me."

At the end of the afternoon, Erich thanked Myles for his hospitality, a great ride around the harbor, and for the name of the Nana Mouskouri tape, *Over and Over*. Simone dropped Erich off at the Wentworth and said she'd be back at seven to collect him. After a shower to get all the salt spray off exposed skin, he did a little bit of packing and then got ready to go out.

Simone arrived at the appointed hour, and they went off to a place called the Argyle Tavern, a small restaurant situated in "The Colony", that was perfect. They had a good meal, more Australian wine that Erich decided he liked, and far more conversation than they were able to carry on while they were aboard a cruising boat with big engines.

"You ought to come to New York," Erich suggested. "I could show you around, and we'd have a great time. If you wanted, you could stay with me. But I suppose I'm being presumptuous by suggesting something like that."

"Sounds tempting, and I'd love to make the trip. But, no, you're not being too audacious. In fact, I'd like to spend a little time with you later on. Only difficulty is that my interests and my calendar aren't cooperating with each other. I'm quite sorry about that."

"Well then, you *must* to come to New York. I'd really like to see you again."

"You will. Tomorrow. Something I'd like to do is see you off, and I'll take you down to the airport if you don't mind."

"Not at all. I'd love it. My flight leaves at 18:00, so I guess we ought to be on our way an hour or so before that."

"If you promise to behave yourself, I'll come up to your room at about midafternoon."

"Well, if I understand what you just said, we know what we *aren't* going to do so there's no reason to worry about it. If you won't come to New York, I'll just have to come back."

"You're one of the few men I've met that I'd like to know better. Most of the blokes who say they're interested in me really have their eyes on the fact that our family is well off. That doesn't seem to have a place on your list of priorities if it's on it at all."

"Not important. What comes first is a truly caring relationship. To me, that means you have to appreciate how your partner feels about things. All things. Then you've got to be able to deal with whatever give and take there'll be. A union won't work if there isn't understanding and a willingness to compromise. And you need to see the beauty inside the other person. If two people don't have these basic things going for them, then all the money in the world won't put it right. End of my short philosophical overview."

"You're an uncommon man, Erich Mauer. I wish we'd met when you first got here. I'd have wanted to spend more time with you. No one among the people I know thinks quite the way you do. It's refreshing. I share your thoughts, and you've touched me."

"I've been married before and have finally discovered what's important. It comes the hard way."

"You've learned, and I admire you for it. Now, I hate to put an end to a delightfully pleasant evening, but it's getting late. You'll probably want to get some rest, so I'll drop you off."

"You mean you're not making me walk back to the hotel?" Erich grinned.

"It'd be a hike. No, I'll drive you back. After a fine dinner and wonderful company, it's the least I can do." Simone showed Erich an engaging smile.

At the hotel, Erich thanked Simone for having dinner with him, gave her a soft kiss, which she returned, said good night, and then went up to his room.

It was Monday morning and Erich was up at a reasonable hour. He had two opals and maybe some other things to buy before Simone showed up. As luck would have it, there was a shop not too far from the Wentworth that specialized in semi-precious stones. After looking at so many black opals that he lost track of what he'd seen, he picked one that he thought would get an "*oooh*" from Tina. Opal in hand, there was some other shopping Erich wanted to do, but in the end decided that he'd see what he could find in Fiji. Then back at the hotel, he spotted sweatshirts in the gift shop window, so he bought one for each of his guys, and did the same for Dawn's Ryan and Greg. Since it wasn't the season in Australia for anything that heavy, they were marked down to what amounted to a steal.

Up in his room, Erich stuffed the sweatshirts at the bottom of his bag and then rearranged it so that what he needed in Fiji was on top. Having seen the current forecast for New York, his London Fog topcoat, in the next layer down, wouldn't come anywhere close to protecting him against their now below freezing temperatures. Suddenly, he dreaded going home. Too many rich memories would be left behind in Sydney, and he also figured that the weather at Kennedy would frost his delicate assets and maybe set his love life back several days.

At midafternoon, Simone knocked at Erich's door. When he let her in, she looked scrumptious.

"Hi, girl. Ahhh, you shouldn't wear a short skirt like that."

"I'm being calculating. It's my way of luring you back when I could be more obliging."

"Not what I'd call playing fair. A trip from New York isn't exactly like flying in from Melbourne. So there isn't any way we can get to know each other better in the meantime?"

"Afraid not, even though the thought is inviting."

They chatted while Erich got the rest of his packing done. When he'd finished, they took pictures of each other to serve as reminders that they'd spent several enjoyable hours together. Simone was a sweetheart. Her family's wealth might have affected her demeanor, but it hadn't. She had a very sensible attitude toward her status and might well have been the daughter of shopkeeper or the like. It was unfortunate that this was probably Erich's last trip to Sydney because he'd have liked to spend more time with her. And practical Simone wasn't the type who'd fly off to New York on a lark. "Such is life," he thought. "It's a shame that we'll never know now our friendship might have grown." A different kind of woman, he liked Simone Dekker. But no point in dwelling on it. They'd have another hour or so together and then they'd most likely never see each other again.

At the airport, Erich checked in and got ready to board. With only a few minutes left before the flight would be called, he sensed that Simone wasn't ready to see him leave.

"I'd like to suppose that, given time, we might have grown close if the geography were different," she said. "But our lot is that we're worlds apart, and I'm truly sorry it's that way. You're the kind of man I could care for, I think, and be very happy in our relationship. As it is, you go back to your New York, and I live out my life here. Makes me feel sad. Life's lottery doesn't always work out the way you might like it to."

"Don't let it get you down, Simone. You're young and attractive, and I'm sure life will treat you well. If it doesn't, call me and I'll come back and help you put it right."

She smiled pleasantly.

"Have a good trip home, Erich. And thank you for being such splendid company during these last twenty-four hours or so. You've been an inspiration. I shall not forget you."

They held each other briefly and shared a quick but tender kiss.

"Until next time, if there is one, And many thanks for everything, Simone. Bye-bye."

Before Erich boarded, he turned and waved. Simone smiled, but she continued to show him a hint of sadness, he thought. That bothered him some. They'd only known each other for some thirty hours, but it was clear that they'd enjoyed each other's company and that he might have been someone who, at another time and in another place, could have made her happy. For some reason, he felt a curious need to be her protector and the light of her life. It was never to be.

Chapter Eleven

The flight into Fiji went smoothly and Erich was pleased to be on the ground again on the verdant island of Viti Levu—in spite of the fact that it was nearing midnight. Before he left for Sydney, he'd reserved a room at a motel not far from the airport so that it wouldn't take long to get situated once he'd arrived. His continuing flight to Hawaii didn't leave for another twenty-five hours, so he'd be able to finish his trip summary in the morning. It helped that he'd been able to write the lion's share of it on the flight into Nadi. His aim was to get it behind him so he could spend most of his day doing some shopping and simply taking it easy. He still had eight thousand miles and a good many hours to go before he got home to Seaford. Feeling mostly satisfied about what he'd already written, Erich went to bed thinking it wouldn't take long to finish it up in the morning. He'd quit about an hour before BOAC's Flight 592 landed, the reason being that he was getting into too many rewrites, always a sign that he'd lost his edge.

But something Erich discovered long before daylight was that being near the airport turned out to be something less than a smart move. It seemed to be busy all night long, and four engine jets were interfering with his plan to get a good night's rest. A few hours later, when Erich finally gave up on the idea of getting more sleep, he had breakfast and then came back to finish up his report. On rereading it, he decided that he should have quit even earlier than he did. There was a fair amount of repair work to do. At least the content was there. It was now a matter of turning it into something that made sense grammatically.

When he was finally finished, Erich stood up, stretched, and then decided it was time to do some shopping. Late as it had been when he arrived last night, his body was still on Sydney time, and he'd asked the cab driver to make the ten-minute drive into Nadi Town before dropping him at his motel. His aim was to see what the place was all about. His conclusion? Not much. But they did pass by a couple of shops that showed promise, and with the report behind him, he was now ready to do some poking around.

So before midday, Erich hired another taxi and had the driver drop him in front of a shop he'd seen on his tour several hours earlier. What he found on display were hand carved wooden masks. They'd do nicely on one of his living room walls, so he bought two, both with rather menacing looking faces. Then, after a short walk down Main Street, he came to a shop he hadn't seen earlier. It was called Jack's, and they were promoting something that looked very much like artwork. Inside, he found a middle-aged American couple eagerly pawing through a stack of whatever it was that was on sale. Given their enthusiasm, it was beginning to look as if they were going to wipe out the entire inventory. Erich cornered the owner and asked him what it was they were looking at.

"Tapa cloth," he said. "The best of it is made on Vatulele about twenty miles off the south coast. What those people are sorting through are placemats."

"Placemats? That's artwork. If they leave any behind, I'll pick out some with good designs and have them framed. Since the colors are mainly black, shades of brown, and tan, I'd mount the one the woman's holding on oatmeal linen and put a medium-size black frame around it. Be a conversation piece in my part of the world."

"You see something they never will." He smiled appreciatively. "It's an artistic idea that I might be able to use as well."

The couple, Texans as it turned out, bought a stack of the cloth, including one design that Erich really liked. But he found others that would do nicely. He decided that he'd keep two and give one to Brenna and another to Tina. "Shopping's done," he thought. "Well, maybe not. I should probably get something for Dawn, too. But what?" Then he saw the answer in a shop right next door. Coconut soap. It was a box of four bars with different colors and scents. It was also flat and would fit in what little space he had left in his overstuffed garment bag.

Back in his room, Erich dumped the things he'd bought on the bed and then made a halfhearted attempt to pack. But a beer and some lunch interested him more than the task at hand. His taste buds won, so he went off and found a place near the motel where he could have both. In the heat of the day, most of the customers were sitting at the bar tucked under a thatched overhang. Interesting that one of them looked like Hemingway. It might've fooled him except Erich knew that he'd blown his brains out earlier in the sixties. Most of the others also had beards, and he wondered if any of them were artists or writers. They certainly looked the part. The English they spoke was American made, so they could have been anything or anybody. But, no shade for Erich. It would be months before his body would be exposed to this kind of weather again, so he made every effort to bake his skin with the help of some Fiji beer. Lunch helped neutralize the alcohol. When the sun dropped behind a big tree and shaded the patio, it was time to call an end to the tanning season until probably late spring in the U.S. For a fleeting moment, he thought about becoming a beach bum and saying to hell with the corporate life that was all he'd known since the fall of '55. But there were responsibilities at home, and a woman who loved him. Whether or not she'd ever have him was still an unanswered question. If not, he'd be tempted to come back, grow a beard, and join those guys at the bar. Then, suddenly, he thought about Tina and the possibility of life without her. It sent an unwelcome shiver through his body. "What's going on?" he asked quietly. The disturbance carried with it an ominous feeling, one suggesting that their paths would never be parallel. The premonition was troubling. "Best I go for a walk," he thought.

That Erich was able to appreciate the beauty alongside the walkways helped him repress the disquieting emotions he felt. His personal defense mechanism also came to his aid, and it reminded him that in Brenna he had a caring friend. He also thought about his dreams, the voice that had urged patience, and the nameless face he'd seen—three times now. Patience and the face were linked, he thought. "It'll all work out, with or without Tina," he decided. "Much as I don't want to face it, I'm sure I'll survive if that's how it's to be."

Erich had a late dinner, finished his packing and was at Nadi International at about midnight to check in. His ongoing flight to Los Angeles would stop in Honolulu. An early arrival, an hour on the ground, and then it would be on to the U.S. mainland.

BOAC's VC-10 was full, and most of those aboard were clearly in a holiday mood. Erich had a double martini and then slept until breakfast was served about an hour before they were to land on Oahu. Everyone, including those going on beyond Honolulu, had to disembark so they could clear immigration and customs. With those formalities behind them, the flight continued to Los Angeles and arrived just before five o'clock. Erich was among a handful of people going still farther on. The airline put all of them up in a hotel near LAX until, in his case, he was to continue the last leg of his long trip at one minute after midnight. At this stage, he was beginning to feel travel worn, much like all of his eastbound flights back in October. But killing nearly seven hours wasn't nearly as tiring as it was when Roxane walked off and left him in San Francisco a little over seven weeks ago. Seemed liked ages, not less than two months.

Finally aboard, and on the last sector of his trip, Erich slept like a rock until, once again, breakfast was served when they were close to Kennedy. "Not much body heat in that," he groused.

On the ground, and with luggage in hand, Erich headed for the taxi queue and walked straight into seventeen degrees. He was absolutely freezing. It was more than a sixty-degree temperature change in about twenty-four hours, and he thought he'd die before he was dropped off at 4 New York Plaza. He didn't. When he got to his floor, Katie was just taking off her coat.

"Erich! Welcome home. You're back okay. I had a scary dream about you. Glad to see it was all wrong." She gave him a firm squeeze and a peck on the cheek.

"I needed that. It'll help me thaw out. I'm friggin' frozen."

"You have a gorgeous tan, and I'm jealous. Otherwise, you look like death warmed over again. So how was your trip?"

"Everything went fine, I think."

"The telex that Joel got said Malcolm was very pleased with all your help. But then there was something about your having been baited. Joel was furious about it. You should have seen his face. I gave him a wide berth that morning. Wow! Did I ever."

"I'll tell you about it when I'm back on the fifth. More important things to do now. Joel will be back before I am, so here's the trip report. I'll let you proof it and make corrections if you think any are needed. Give it to him unsigned. I'll do that after the fact. But, sit down. I've got something that'll rattle your cage, I think. Nothing sharp in your hands and you're not near water."

"You're madly in love with me and you're going to propose. Or I'm to spend the weekend with you."

"What're you on? Not quite. But you'll never guess who I ran into at the hotel in Sydney."

"Roxane?"

"Nope. Tina."

"Oh-my-God! You had to be in shock."

"Absolutely dumbfounded. But after all this time, she's still crazy about her ex-boss, and we had two of the most enjoyable days imaginable. Our affair will probably die eventually, for reasons we both understand, but for now we're two people in love. When time allows, we'll see each other. It won't be often, but she cares, as do I. So we're going to give ourselves time and see where it goes. Tina comes into New York once in a while, and she wants to meet you. Anyway, I guess it's obvious that I feel pretty good about things at the moment."

"For all your fatigue, it shows. I'm happy for you, Erich. It hurts some to say that, but I hope to meet the woman who owns your heart and mind."

"The problem will be the same one that's always been there. Tina wants children. In the end, that'll win out, I'm guessing. Still, I like what I'm feeling. And she told me in Sydney that what her parents think about our age difference isn't a factor anymore. So, that's the news I bring back from Down Under. But what I'm *not* going to do is cut any ties; that is, with Brenna. At this stage, and with my misgivings, there's no reason to."

"Okay. To business, then," Katie said. "I know you wanted to be brought up to date, but there really isn't much of anything that needs your attention. So go home, enjoy your vacation, and come back rested. You do look tired, but I have to say it again. You've got a great tan. It'll stop traffic."

"Not likely. I'm taking a taxi home to Seaford. Joel said before I left Sydney that he'd okay it. So would you dig into petty cash and give me enough to cover a cab? I'm about out of dollars, and my wallet will stay mostly flat until I can get to the bank later today. In the meantime, I'm going to call my good friend, Clayton."

"Oh, he left a message while you were away. He'll be up at the Cape and, like you, will be back on January 5. He also said he's changing jobs."

"Thanks, Tina. Oops! Sorry Katie. Whew. Tells you where my head is. That's a throwback. Like nothing has changed since last March. I apologize."

"Forget it. I understand, and I'm as envious as I can be. Now, I'll get you some cash and then throw you out."

When Katie came back with cab fare, and more, she gave Erich a hug. He tensed for a moment; she understood why.

"You're all sentimental and mushy inside, Erich Mauer. That's something about you I never knew. Now, get outta here. I called a cab, and it should be waiting down front. Have a Merry Christmas and a Happy New Year. I'll be here when you're back."

"Thanks, dear heart."

Erich gave Katie a caring hug, and then, as he turned to leave, she said, "You shouldn't do things like that. It's a cinch I'd get used to them and want more. Now, scram!"

"Most likely. Bye-bye, gal. Thanks for all your help, and happy holidays to you, too."

The taxi ride to Seaford cost an arm and a leg. The only interesting part of it was that the driver commented on his deep tan and insisted on knowing where he'd been. After Erich told him, and that he'd just come in overnight, he shut up. He assumed the guy could figure out that he was weary to the bone.

It was good to be home. He'd been away for sixteen days, had traveled almost twenty-one thousand miles, flown in and out of nine time zones in both directions, and had again crossed the International Date Line and the Equator twice. Erich was taken with all this, but it also struck him that, although wiped-out, he was still on his feet and couldn't decide which impressed him more, so he let it be. The fact remained that it was nearing 3:00 a.m. in his departure city, Sydney. Tired or not, he needed to call Dawn.

"Hi, babe. It's the travelin' feller."

"Hello, Erich. Good to know you survived the trip. The boys told me all about it. I don't know how you do it. You must be pooped."

"Something like that. Is it true that I'm invited for the evening?"

"It is. I really hate to admit it, but it'll be good to share a bed with you again. Guess I'm mellowing some. Maybe it's because I'm lonely at times. Not your fault. But you don't need to hear about that. Come over whenever you're ready."

"I'm grubby, have to partly unpack, wrap some things, get to the bank, and then I'll be along afterwards. But first, I'm going to feed myself. See you in two or three hours."

Erich found a burst of energy, did all the things he'd mentioned to Dawn, and then went off to her place on Soundview Heights. When he pulled up near the front door, a welcoming committee came out to greet him.

First words out of Dawn's mouth were, "God! Look at your tan. Disgusting." But to Erich's surprise, she gave him an warm hug, and then the boys joined the welcome home reception. His ego was full to the brim. It felt good!

"Hi, babe. Guys. Good to be home again."

"Let's get inside. It's freezing."

"Tell me about it. I stopped in Fiji for about twenty-four hours, and it was around eighty degrees. It was seventeen at JFK when I came in at about eight o'clock. Torture. Thought I'd die before I got inside a cab. I'm ready to go back. Fiji stole my heart."

"It's Christmas Eve, and late enough in the day, so would you like one of those dry martinis you used to drink?" Dawn asked. "I'll join you, but it'll be something less potent, like a glass of wine."

"I don't usually like beer unless it's hot outside, but I think I'd better take it easy, too. Maybe later on I'll have that Gibson over ice, but a beer for now would be fine. Thanks."

For the next hour, or a big chunk of it, Erich's audience wanted to know all about his trip. By the time he'd finished, he was ready for another beer.

"I'll get it," Rudi said. Both he and Kurt were happy to see their dad. They still couldn't get over his tan. He explained that he got a good start on it by just walking around Sydney, accelerated the process when he was out on Sydney Harbor last Sunday and then added a little more to it in Fiji. That was Tuesday there, Monday here. That got a blank stare from the boys, so he explained how it was possible to leave the Fiji Islands on the twenty-third and arrive in Honolulu on the twenty-second.

"We got a map out and looked at all the places you were," Kurt said. "It's a long way off. About half way around the world."

"You didn't do that for my October trip. On that one I went all the way around the world. I'll show you when we get home."

"Could we see it now?" Ryan asked.

"Sure. Get me a map of the world, if you've got one."

Ryan found their atlas, and Erich showed all four boys where he stopped on his way to and from Sydney. "My October trip was over twenty-eight thousand miles. The one I came in from this morning was about twenty-one thousand. But it's the time zones that get you. The West Coast is three hours earlier. Now multiply that by three. That's one way to look at it. Going the other way, we're about 4 p.m. here, a Wednesday, but in Sydney it's 7:00 a.m., and it's tomorrow, Christmas Day. So, the further east you go, the later it gets. It's 10:00 p.m. in Europe, and you keep adding hours until it gets to be morning on the other side of the world, like Sydney. My body is still on their time so I've been up all night, you might say."

The boys were impressed. It looked as if Dawn was, too.

"That's heavy," Greg said. "I want to know more about it. When I get back to school, I'll look it up. There's a map of the world that shows how the date line is fixed and how midnight comes around and starts a new day. I remember seeing it."

"I'm pleased that you want to know more about it. Well, I lost a day going west and gained a day coming east. If I were still in Sydney, I'd be about ready to open presents."

"We'll do that in the morning, like it used to be," Ryan said. His expression told Erich he was sorry that those days were gone.

"I brought a couple of things back with me. I'll slip 'em under the tree later. Now, Dawn, I'm ready for that Gibson on the rocks."

"Sure. I'll put it together for you. Glad you could make Christmas Eve with us. Makes it special. Thanks."

"You're welcome. And thanks for having me. Been pretty lonely by myself over at number 710. While you stir up my 'silver bullet', I'll go get the presents out of the car."

"Do me a favor? I have the makings for your mom's chili soup. Any chance I could talk you into stirring up a batch for us? We just love it, and it's been a long time since we've had any. It's really cold out and a perfect night for it."

"Sure, as long as I can stay awake. And you'll have to dice the onions. I'd probably chop a finger off. Get the stuff out. I'll go get the gifts and then come back and go to work. By the way, I forgot to mention what a pretty tree you have. Nicely decorated, too."

"You taught the boys how to do that. You're seeing a reflection of yourself in it."

Dinner was a hit. Afterwards, Erich kept his eyes open as long as he could and then fatigue finally did him in. Dawn went up to her bedroom with him. "Much as I'd like to jump your bones tonight, I'll leave you alone. You look completely beat. But in the morning you can give me a gift that isn't under the tree."

"A better idea. No fun making love to a corpse. And that's about one step away from where I am right now."

Erich got his clothes off and slipped into bed. Dawn stood close by and watched him fall sound asleep inside two minutes. It was one of those moments when she regretted that their marriage had failed. But inside, she knew that much of the blame for its collapse was hers. The love of vodka had not served her well. Its volatility in her system also helped explain why she was lonely. A single exposure to her explosive temper when she was under the influence was about all any man could be expected to stomach. But she was finally learning—and taking steps to deal with it.

A long night's rest was just what Erich's worn out body needed. Groggy, and slowly waking up, he felt Dawn's fingertips tracing patterns on his skin. That was followed by some serious probing to determine if everything was as it should be. Once the attack began, he didn't have long to wait for it to be mounted. The best part of it was that he didn't even have to move.

"I want to start this way for a couple of minutes. It's just to get the ball rolling." Dawn giggled.

"If it goes much beyond a couple of minutes, it'll be all over. Both ways."

"I'll slow down." And she did.

Two things Dawn hadn't lost. She could turn out a great meal, and she still knew how to make love. This Christmas morning was no exception. Settling down, they both enjoyed a union that would leave them contented. After the finale, she said, "Ahhh, you still know how to make me smile."

"You didn't do so bad yourself. But that's all there is. Anyway, I hear two legged mice rumbling around downstairs. Best we have Christmas. But not until after I shower."

Refreshed and into a change of clothes he'd brought in with the gifts last night, Erich felt better. It was a good guess that he'd live until sundown.

Before anything else happened, Dawn and Erich made coffee for themselves and hot chocolate for the boys. They were perfect starters. Then later, when they opened gifts, all four guys were pleased with their Australian sweatshirts. They were something they could wear at this time of year. And Erich got all the sizes about right. Dawn was thrilled with the coconut soap, although she asked him if the reason he'd bought a four-bar set was because he thought she "smelled ripe", as she put it.

"Sure, but you weren't supposed to think I thought that." They all laughed. "Nobody in all of Fairbanks County has genuine Fijian soap that was hand delivered."

Joking, she asked, "Then how come the bottom of the box says 'Made in Passaic, New Jersey'?" They had another laugh.

"That's where the box was glued together, dummy. The soap is Fijian. I watched it being made."

"Yeah, sure you did."

"Well, okay. I watched 'em wrap it up."

Dawn put together another delicious holiday meal and everyone, as always, ate too much. And like last year, she gave Erich and the boys a generous helping of the big bird to take home.

At the end of the afternoon, Erich offered Dawn money to cover the extra food she'd had to buy while Kurt and Rudi were there. She refused to take it.

"No, it isn't necessary. They're a pleasure to have around. Anytime, Erich. I'm trying to make up for all the things I might have done when we lived together. I didn't do a very good job of being a mother to them. I hope someday they'll forgive me, and maybe you'll forgive me, too."

"I don't know what to say, other than thank you for all you've done over the past year. I'm obliged and really appreciate all your help. But, please. Use the soap." Erich smiled. Dawn stuck her tongue out at him.

"I don't suppose we could ever reconcile. It's a little too late for that, so just love me once in a while, like this morning. That'll be thanks enough."

"We can work it out, especially when the guys go someplace together, like to the movies or a game."

"Appreciate your being part of our Christmas. I know you're jet lagged, so it was extra special."

"Guys. Get your stuff, and let's go."

Erich hugged Dawn and thanked her again. The expression on her face told him that she didn't want to see Christmas Day come to an end. After they'd gone, she took an empty feeling up to her bedroom. It had been a joyful day. But as she thought back over the past three years, she said to herself quietly, "You had a good thing going for you girl, but you blew it."

On their way home, Erich told the boys what Dawn had said about not being a good mother to them and that she hoped one day they'd forgive her.

"She's sure changed," Kurt said. "I think she's sorry about the way things turned out. We had a really good time. Don't you think so, Rudi?"

"If she could be like she was since Sunday, I'd go back and live there. We had a lot of fun, and she didn't drink hardly nothin'."

"Well, now for a big surprise."

"You and Lara are getting married," Rudi said. That took the edge off what Erich was going to tell them.

"No, Looks like she and I are headed in opposite directions. We'll talk more about it while we're on vacation. Maybe we could do it tomorrow. The shocker is that I ran into Tina in Sydney."

"What? I don't believe it. You gotta be kidding," Kurt said. "All the way over there? That's crazy."

"That's what we both said. But she saw me, said my name, and I knew whose voice it was. Immediately. One word. That's all it took. We spent two wonderful days together before she had to come back. She's with her parents and is coming up to see us on Monday. Could be she'll come back on the Sunday before she goes back to Washington."

"I still don't believe it."

"I don't either, Kurt. But it happened at the hotel where I was staying. I was looking at the headlines on the newspapers outside the hotel shop. From a distance I heard a voice: '*Erich?*' I froze, and then turned around. She held her hands out toward me, and I turned into Jell-O. We talked and talked and decided that we should've stayed in touch. Our feelings haven't changed since early in the year, so we're going to give it another chance. It'll be her decision, but if she'll have me, I'll have her. Tomorrow, if she wants. It's simple, guys. I still care about her. A bunch."

"What about Lara?" Rudi asked.

"It's confusing, guy. We have to talk about it. Now that I think about it further, let's make sure that we do it tomorrow. I'm not sure that I understand all of it yet. Give me a day, okay?"

"Sure, but you know how I feel."

"I know very well how you feel, but I'm not calling the shots on this one either. Lara drove me down to the station the day I left, and when she said goodbye the way she said it made it sound like we'd come to the end. Before that, she wouldn't tell me if we'd see each other when she's back from Worcester. The expression on her face left me with the feeling that I shouldn't count on it. Doesn't look good, but until her uncle is gone she's not thinking about much else. For sure, she was different that last night she was here."

"Yeah, really," Kurt said. "Not close like she always was. Did you do something to make her mad, or has she got somebody new?"

"Nothing that I can think of. And, no, there isn't anyone else. She has big plans for her business, and some wild ideas that I'll get into when we talk about it. Let it be for now. It's Christmas, and I don't want a cloud to hang over the rest of our evening."

The boys wanted to know even more about Erich's trip, and they talked until almost bedtime. Before he finished, he told them that Brenna would be around over the holidays and that he'd get into that tomorrow, too. "I'll try to explain what's going on."

"Sounds like we got a lot to talk about," Rudi said.

"We do, but let's leave it until tomorrow afternoon. I hope it'll make sense. There are times when I'm not sure any of it does, but I'll do my best."

"Glad you're home," Kurt said. Rudi concurred.

"Good to be home. Let's call it a day and get some rest. Thanks for your gifts. I appreciate it that you remembered your old man."

"Old man?" Kurt said. "Not hardly."

Erich's body clock was still well off Eastern Time, so he slept late. As he was coming to, the phone rang. It was Brenna.

"Hi, world traveler. How're you?"

"Mornin', babe. Good to hear your voice after all this time. How am I doing? My body clock is only part way home. Let's say I'm on Honolulu time, and it's not yet daylight. But I'm okay otherwise."

"I just wanted you to know that I'm so glad you're back and to tell you that you've been on my mind. A lot. Every day, in fact. I was going to call last night but there was too much going on here. And I guessed you'd probably go down early. Anyway, I want to see you. Any chance I could drop by this afternoon for a little while? There are people here who can take care of Alan and Scot."

"I'd love it. Only thing standing in the way is a summit meeting. Rudi wants to know about Lara. Wish I knew something more definite. The way she said goodbye at the station back on the ninth gave me the impression that she's decided we're history. It's almost like something snapped. Thing is, I'm not a mushroom, so I don't do very well in the dark."

"I know more about Lara than you do, so I'm not in the dark. Let me suggest that you bring up the subject while I'm there. Coming from me, Rudi will know that what I'm saying is true. I'm not out to kill a relationship, Erich, but you've got it right. It's over."

"*Ohh*, Brenna, that smarts. You don't know."

"Yes I do. I've been there, and it's the reason why I don't want to get involved again. I've got my boys and they're my life. I care for you more than I should, but we both understand the script. I'd hoped we could make this a joyful homecoming and that we could put this off until later, but it looks like Rudi has moved it up on your calendar. I can help, I think."

"I've sure had a tough year with my women. You're about the only one who's stable and you won't have me."

"Yes I will, but mostly as a lover and companion. With that comes a lot of caring about you. It's why I'm calling and asking if I can come over. And you also know that I'm looking forward to tomorrow night. That'll be your welcome home I mentioned before you left. But it'll be pleasant for me, too, you know."

"Maybe you can help repair the damage. I'm not surprised, I guess. It was when I was looking out of the hotel room window in Sydney that I came to grips with what I thought the truth was. I'm just not ready for it, especially after all the feelings we brought back to life about six weeks ago.

It was like what we had when we were new to each other. Then, suddenly, the flame went out."

"Lara and I grew up together. We've known each other since we were in kindergarten. At the beginning, she couldn't talk about anyone or anything but you. You've satisfied her with the one great love in a lifetime she wanted. But she fears death. Yours. Her uncle will be gone soon, if he isn't already. And her mother is next on her worry list. She's not at all well either, and her brother's cancer has made things worse. Lara's numb, Erich. It's like all the people she loves are dying right before her eyes. She's absolutely certain you're next. Fault her if you will, but she cares too much about you, loves you too much, to watch it happen. If it came about the way she sees it, losing you would destroy her. And she knows that. Let her hang onto the memories, love you from a distance, and have peace of mind, too."

"That's ridiculous. She's running away from life. I'll outlive her, Brenna. My people have a way of making it into their late eighties and early nineties, in spite of their awful diets."

"She has a whole list of things that could go wrong."

"Sounds like she's gone at least part way around the bend."

"When it comes to you, it's more than part way."

"Well, if I live until this afternoon, I'll give you a big hug to show you that I'm still very much alive. And assuming I make it all the way into tomorrow, I'll do it again."

"I have a feeling that you're going to survive being cut loose. And I'm selfish enough now that I don't want to share you with anyone else. But since I'm not marriage material, I know there'll be others. The boys need a woman, a good woman, to do all the things a man can't do. You've said the same thing. Several times over."

"I know, but their timetable says now. At least Rudi's does. Problem is that I keep losing candidates left and right. But if someday I'm able to hang onto one and it turns out to be a mistake, they don't have to live with it, or go through another divorce."

"We've talked much, much longer than I'd intended. I just wanted to let you know you that I was thinking about you, say welcome back, and invite myself over. All that's done, and a whole lot more. See you at about two o'clock. That okay?"

"Sure. And if you stick around long enough, it could be I'll buy you a glass of wine."

"I'm not sure I should have one. Being deprived, I might just put a move on you because I can't wait until tomorrow night. Not a good idea to give the boys a demonstration."

"We wouldn't be teaching Kurt anything he doesn't already know. At least that's my take on it."

"I figured as much. See you later in the day, love bug."

"Bye, gal."

"Love bug" sunk in after he hung up, and he chuckled.

Erich went to the kitchen and was followed by a sleepy-eyed Kurt who asked, "Who was that on the phone?"

"Brenna. She's coming over this afternoon and will be a part of the conversation about Lara. I was right. I've been dumped. Brenna worked for her the two Saturdays just before Christmas and has the whole story. Certainly more of it than I do, so it'll help Rudi understand. I hope. He's going to take it hard, and I'm worried that he'll get back into drugs. I'll need you to keep an eye on him. And Mr. Kaplan will be able to explain how you might help."

"Sure, but we aren't together at school. Best I can do is make sure we leave together and be with him until you're home."

"That's all I'm asking. He has some rough days ahead of him. I can feel it in my bones."

"Feel what?" Rudi asked, as he shuffled into the kitchen.

"Good morning, young man. Cold weather and old bones. Like mine. How about some breakfast?"

After they'd eaten, the guys went off to watch TV. Erich tried to figure out what they needed from the market, how much stuff to drop off at the cleaners, see what bills had to be paid, and generally bring his personal affairs up to date.

Chapter Twelve

Just after two o'clock, Brenna was at the entrance adjacent the visitor's parking lot, and Erich buzzed to let her in. He went to the elevator to meet her. "Hi, babe," he said. They hugged, and she could feel him tense for a moment. She understood that Lara was on his mind and let it go.

"It's *so* good to have you back. And, look at that tan. How about I drive you around town and show you off? You may be tired, but you look good."

"Thanks. You don't look bad yourself. Been messing around while I was gone?" Brenna punched him on the arm gently.

"What I've been doing is waiting until you got home so I could mess around with you. Not this afternoon, though, but I might be able to stay the night. Colleen's offered to look after the boys. She's been really good about things like that because she thinks I look better since we met. She's convinced that you're good for me. And I agree. But there's a more important reason to stay. I think it might help Rudi. My guess is, he'll need some support beyond this afternoon. And maybe you could use some, too."

"That's really sweet of you. And you're right. We'll both need a crutch. Mine will come to an end, maybe, when the lights are out, but that's a different kind of care. Your being able to stay over is something we hadn't planned on. Great. But let me pry the guys away from their little TV."

Summoned, they came out and gave Brenna a hug. "Been three weeks since you were here," Kurt remarked. "How're you?"

"Good. Did you have a good Christmas?" Both boys said they did and they made sure Brenna noticed their new sweatshirts.

Turning to Brenna, Erich said, "I have something for you. It's a day late, but there wasn't much I could do about that."

He brought out the Fijian tapa and showed it to her.

"What is it?"

Erich told her the whole story, including the avaricious Texas couple, and how he saw artwork in it.

"It's *so* different," Brenna said. "I love it. Since I'll be here tonight, maybe we could go out tomorrow morning, look at the setting for the opal, and then stop by a framing shop that just opened. Sis had some stuff done and said they're really creative. I'll bet this'll get their attention. Thank you, Erich. You always have such good ideas."

"You're on for tomorrow. I have to grocery shop and run some other errands, but let's work a jeweler and the framing shop into our schedule."

"I know you offered to pay for the setting, but I'm taking you off the hook because you've already done so many nice things for me. I did some shopping while you were gone and discovered that the sort of ring I want will be kind of expensive. The jeweler said the cost of the stone locally would have been, too. So I'm meeting you half way." Seeing that Erich was about to react, she said, "No arguments. Please? I've already seen what I like. If you agree, then it's done."

"Not what I promised to do, dear heart."

"No more discussion about it. I'm pleased to have the stone. It's gorgeous. There are so many colors in it. Sometimes it looks like it's on fire. Like me." They chuckled. Given her news about Lara, it felt good to begin the healing process.

As they were finishing up a midafternoon snack, Erich got onto the subject of Lara.

Turning to Rudi, he said, "I told you last night that I'd try to help you understand what's happened with Lara and me. It's time we talked it through and put it behind us."

"Sure you want Brenna here?" Rudi asked.

"Very sure. They grew up together, she worked at the shop the last two Saturdays, and she knows the story. I'd only be guessing. She has the facts and asked if she could help us understand. I said yes. You remember I told you that when Lara said goodbye at the station I thought it was for the last time. And I was right. No point in beating around the bush. I know how much you like her, but she's made the decision. There isn't another man. It's a case of wanting to spend more time with her business. That's the lover we've had to compete with. Brenna can tell you more about what's inside Lara's head."

"*Oh*, Dad." Rudi covered his face with his hands and was in tears. Kurt was upset, but he understood these things better. Much as he didn't want to, he accepted what he'd just heard.

After Rudi had settled down and wiped his eyes, Brenna said, "Let me see if I can help, Rudi. These are the hard lessons we learn about life. My husband walked out on me and it really hurt. Lara's husband did the same to her. It broke her heart. And something I'm sure you don't know is that she had a baby, a boy that was born dead. That was when her husband left her."

Brenna was right. It *was* something they'd never been told and all three Mauers straightened up in their chairs.

"After that, she went years without having any interest in men. But then your dad came along, and she cared about someone again. She told me he's been the one great love that a woman wants. But Lara has real problems. Her father had an accident and was killed at work about six years ago. Now, her favorite uncle is dying of cancer. Her mother isn't well, and she's certain that she'll be gone before long. But instead of coming here to get support from all of you, she's afraid of seeing more death. She's sure your dad is next. Like she said to him before he left, and then to me just a week ago, 'I couldn't watch him die. He means way too much to me. I'd be destroyed.' So, she's pulling back from personal relationships, and death, which she sees all around her, and making her businesses the only family that won't cause her any pain."

"That's super weird," Kurt said.

"Maybe so. But you have to be inside her mind to understand what she believes. It's that anyone she really, really cares about dies before their time. I don't agree with any of it, so I don't share her fear. It isn't rational."

"Maybe I could go see her," Rudi suggested.

"I think it'd be best if you leave her alone. When she says no to you face-to-face all it will do is hurt more. Lots more."

"Then maybe I could live with Dawn, or go back to California to my mom. You don't care anything about us. You already have your own family."

It was obvious that his words stung.

"Rudi, stop it! That's impolite and downright rude. You're upset, but don't strike out and try to hurt people who care about you. Apologize to Brenna, please. She's here to help us understand," Erich said.

He said he was sorry, then added, "But nothing can help because I don't understand."

"I told your dad I'd stay overnight just so I could be with you. But if you'd rather I didn't...."

"You're not Lara, so I don't care what you do."

"Rudi, you have nothing to say about it. Brenna's offering to sit and talk with you, alone, to be helpful, and you're treating her like dirt. I won't have it! You do *not* make decisions about my friends. Understood? Now, start acting like you're fourteen. And just remember, you aren't the only one in this house who cared about Lara. What about my feelings? This hurts me too, you know."

With that, Rudi got up from the table, went to the boys' bedroom and slammed the door.

"Guess I didn't do too good," Brenna said.

"You did just fine. We're dealing with the same kinds of emotions that any separation brings about. Hopefully, time will heal his wounds. But I need to call Nate. I can tell you now where this is going to lead and how Rudi will try to deal with what he feels. You can guess."

"It's real sad," Kurt said. "I'll miss her. But like Rudi, I don't understand either. Is she okay? She sure was different the night before you left for Australia."

"There's an expression about marching to a different drummer," Erich said. "She's found a new one and it's called ambition. It's the wall Lara's put up so she won't have to face the pain that comes with losing someone she loves. Money doesn't keep you warm at night, and you can't snuggle with it, but that seems to be what she wants. Anything I might say wouldn't help. And I'm sure she doesn't want to see me again because she'd have to rethink her decision. She's made hers, so we have to make ours. Lara's gone."

The three of them moved into the living room, talked on about Lara, and the baby that was a surprise. Then Brenna wanted to hear about Erich's trip.

"You should've been here last night. The guys had lots of questions. But I don't mind. It lets me think about it again. It was a successful trip." And he talked about Simone, something that he hadn't done with the boys.

"With the tan you got, it looks like you spent most of your time in the sun."

"No, it was just that I walked around Sydney in their sunny weather, had the whole afternoon on Sydney Harbor last Sunday, and then most of Tuesday afternoon in Fiji."

"That's like me. It doesn't take you long either. I'm envious."

About two hours later, Rudi came out of the bedroom and everyone looked up at him expecting more sass. They were wrong.

"I just came out to say I'm sorry. Especially you, Dad. What you said about Lara just before I went to our room made me think. You liked her a lot. So you've lost her, too. I remember the only time I ever saw you almost cry, she was here to help."

That just about got to Erich. Brenna saw it, knew what he felt, but offered no comment. None was needed.

"You know, Rudi, I tried to prepare you for this last night. Sorry I wasn't more specific."

"I know, but I didn't think it was real and that she'd do it."

Then Rudi went over and stood in front of Brenna.

"I'm sorry for what I said. You've been real nice to us. I hope we can still be friends." He reached down and took her hands. When Brenna was standing, Rudi gave her a hug that showed her how he felt. She had a show of tears well up but held on.

"Of course we can be friends. We always have been. And you know that I care about you. You're one of my boys, too." Rudi held on tightly, bit his lower lip but had tears on his cheeks.

"This has been a rough afternoon on all of us. We're going out tomorrow night, but maybe we could do something with the leftover turkey and dressing. We need to eat it or it'll go bad."

"I'll help," Brenna said. "I'm the leftover turkey queen." The boys smiled faintly and the spell was broken. At least partly.

Brenna made final arrangements with her sister, Colleen, so she could stay overnight. Erich was pleased, if for no other reason than he could thank her for the support she was giving them. After the boys had gone to bed, they sat for a while in the living room and talked about what had happened earlier. Erich also made what would be the last of his comments about Lara's stillborn. "I'm not especially upset that she never mentioned the baby, but during the year-plus that we were together I never saw any stretch marks. Considering that she's trim, and from what you said her pregnancy went nearly full term, I should think I'd have seen some indication of it. Lara always expected me to be honest with her, but she didn't play by the same rules. I'm still surprised by it all."

"Her post-delivery condition is something I don't know anything about," Brenna said.

"I thought as much. It's that I'm just puzzled. Now, something else that needs saying. I want you to know how much I appreciate what you did this afternoon. You weren't obliged to be any part of it, but you showed me that you care about us. What you said was brief, to the point, and it got the message across. It's at times like this that I'm sorry we don't have much hope of tying our two families together. You were good, and it's what the boys needed, or at least what Rudi needed. I'm grateful."

"It was a team effort, and it worked. You got tough at the right time, defended me, and in the end Rudi figured out that he wasn't alone. I feel bad about Lara's decision. As long as I've known her, it's the first time I've seen her go off the deep end like this. She's changed, and it's to the point that I have to believe she isn't the woman for you. Maybe earlier in the year, but not now."

"It's history and time to move on. Rudi is still fragile, but maybe I can help him get through the loss of the woman he wanted to be his mom. He loves Lara more than his own mother. Strange how things like this come about."

"Could I suggest that it's time to think about us now? I don't know what you've been up to, but I'm in bad need of some undivided attention. Any chance you could find a not-so-quick fix?"

"Follow me. I'm the guy with the solution. Ahhh, two of them if you think about it some."

"I'll have both and be doubly satisfied."

Brenna did need looking after and Erich found both solutions she wanted. At the end, there wasn't much doubt that she was satisfied. When they cuddled afterwards, she offered up a simple *"Mmmm."*

"You're contented, I take it?"

"For the moment, but tomorrow I'll be looking for more. You've kept me waiting for what, three weeks? Glad we have another night together. One wouldn't be enough, especially since I don't know when I'll see you next."

"Well, you can take over all of Lara's dates. She doesn't have any now, so I'm completely free.

"I don't know. After this afternoon, seeing the kind of guy you are, and the delights we just found, maybe I'll change my mind about us. Women are allowed to do that, you know."

"Always have, but how would you have me react to this sudden change of heart? The dilemma I can picture, if we got involved, is that I might find myself whipped into a frenzy, start making plans, and then maybe later on you'd decide it wasn't such a good idea after all. Then I'm right back at the starting gate. Two old friends dumping the same guy? Not a good deal for the three of us. Leaving it in a mostly casual mode is probably a better idea."

"Does that mean I couldn't have you if I decided you'd be good for me? I really missed you while you were gone."

"It doesn't mean anything of the kind, but you're sure humming a different tune than you did on the phone this morning. Quite a swing in your thinking."

"The way I've thought about us hasn't left much room for compromise. None really. But today has made a difference. I'd like us to give it a little room to breathe. You could be right, though. After a while, I might decide to let our relationship stay the way it is. On the other hand...."

"While you're shaping our future, I'd like to get some sleep. I'm at least a couple of days away from getting my body clock on Seaford time."

"I had plans on attacking you again, but that isn't fair. It'll keep, at least for a few hours."

"Leave me with enough energy so we can do our shopping. Nice part about your being here tonight is that we have two mornings ahead of us instead of just one. Now, if you'll turn away from me, we'll pretend we're spoons. I can also be a regular little furnace, so I'll keep you toasty warm all night long."

"Yumm. Sounds delicious. Night, love."

"Night, babe."

When morning came, Erich and Brenna generated enough heat to fog up the windows. He asked afterwards if their loving could be classified as a steamy event. They chuckled and decided it could be. And by the time they were ready to start their day, they agreed that they'd rather effectively reduced the backlog of what they'd missed since early December.

At breakfast, Rudi seemed to be functioning all right, even though he was the picture of gloom. Erich reminded him that what Lara decided hurt him in a different way, but that they'd eventually get over what had happened. They couldn't change what she believed, or how she felt, so they had to accept her decision and move on.

To keep the boys' minds occupied, even though it wasn't at all exciting, Erich asked them to look after the laundry while he and Brenna did the shopping. They agreed, both feeling that it would be best, probably, if they were busy doing something. That earned them a bump in their allowance and it was sufficient to get a feeble smile and a thank you from both of them.

"Just be around when we come back from shopping. There'll be a bunch of stuff to bring up."

"We'll be here," Kurt said, "and with the extra money we'll go to the movies this afternoon. The new James Bond film came out last week. Chris said he'd like to see it, too. You probably want to talk when we aren't into heavy stuff like we were yesterday."

"After we're done shopping," Brenna said, "I'll have to go home. Jordie is coming over to pick up the boys this afternoon. I'll need to be there."

"When we get done with the laundry and help with the groceries, we'll get a sandwich downtown," Kurt said. "You don't have to worry about lunch."

"Fine," Erich agreed, "We'll probably do the same after we drop off everything. Brenna and I have a couple of other things to do. One of them is to look at a ring."

"A ring? Like to be married? Rudi asked."

Erich chuckled. "No, guy. On my first trip to Australia, I brought back a semi-precious stone and gave it to Brenna. It's called an opal and it has to be put in a ring. While I was gone this time she found something that might be a good setting for it, but she wants me to see it first."

"If it was an engagement ring, that'd be okay."

Brenna turned and gave Rudi a hug. "That wasn't the way you felt last night. Thanks for letting me back into your heart."

"I'm sorry for what I said. I didn't mean it." Rudi hugged her back. Brenna looked at Erich and showed him a loving smile.

"Okay, let's clean up and get going," Erich said. "The Saturday two days after Christmas is no different than any of the others. Lots to do. We'll come straight home when we're done."

Kurt was glad he didn't have to get involved with shopping and added, "Have fun."

When they were on their way, Erich suggested that they see about the ring and then go to the framing shop. "We'll stop at the cleaners on our way to the market. And we should probably do the groceries last. I don't want anything freezing in the car. With the temperature where it is, it wouldn't take long."

"My guy, the lover—and excellent organizer."

"So, how do you feel about all the things you said last night?"

"The same way. Daylight doesn't change anything. You're not an easy catch. Too cautious. Me too. But there's a lot about you to like, and maybe love. I've seen that since yesterday. In some ways, it helped that you weren't around for three weeks. Plenty of time for me to think, especially when I was alone at night and it was quiet. There are problems that would come along with our living together. The two sets of boys, their age differences, and the negative influence that Rudi might be. But let's allow it to coast for a while. I want to keep you in my sights. You're important."

"And you are to me. We have a good relationship and the boys do care about you. The first time you came over, they cornered me in the kitchen and told me that you were a real mom. I got a kick out of it. You were a hit right from the start, and it's the reason why I wanted you to be part of what I had to deal with yesterday. They respect you. And the way you handled Rudi paid dividends this morning. Better results than I expected. But all he had to do was remember two things. How we both felt about Lara, and how you impressed him as a caring, loving mother the first time you met. And he did. Both."

"You're making me feel good. Like I said yesterday, I haven't been very flexible when it comes to a long-term relationship, but it's time to look at that differently, at least as far as you're concerned. Unless I'm missing something, the two divorces don't figure. We've known each other since early fall, and I've watched to see if there were any clues. I haven't found them, assuming they're there."

"I can be pretty feisty at times, and you'd need to keep a bar of soap handy to wash out my mouth. If things go wrong, really wrong, the air can get pretty blue. Major things I can handle. Frustration and impatience are my worst enemies and I can go ballistic without much prompting."

"Not much there that would suggest a trip to divorce court."

"You know the reasons behind the divorces. In Dawn's case, if her behavior eighteen months ago had been anywhere close to what it is today, I wouldn't be here now. The boys said she's eased off on the vodka, and that she was pleasant to be around. Christmas day, she even apologized for not being a good mother to my guys."

"No mystery to me why she's changed. It was a good man she drove off, and she's figured that out. At least that's what I think."

"Could be you're right."

"Sounds like you agree."

"I suppose so. Okay, is this the place you saw the ring you liked? If it is, or even if it isn't, maybe we should buy two. Any interest in one with a diamond in it for your left hand?"

Brenna stared at Erich for a moment, smiled playfully, and then said, "Not just yet, lover."

"I'm not sure how serious a question that was. I was mostly interested in how you'd react. Don't be put off." And she wasn't.

In the shop, the jeweler brought out the trays of rings that would be suitable for the size opal that was to be set. Brenna found the one she'd seen earlier and showed it to Erich. It was a simple white gold ring that would enhance the beauty of the mostly deep blue stone with splashes of fiery reds and yellows. Erich thought it was a pretty good choice.

"Looks great to me. But I'm no expert. I don't wear rings."

"Sir, this is a very high quality black opal you brought back. By the time I had it in my showcase, I'd have to charge a great deal of money for it. You're fortunate to have a friend like him, miss."

Brenna smiled and said, "Yes, I know."

Their business done, they went off to the framing shop that was nearby.

"*Good* morning. My name is Bruce. How may I help you?"

"Hi. We may have a framing job for you to tackle," Erich said.

When Brenna pulled out the twelve by eighteen inch placemat, Bruce was wide-eyed and asked, "What-have-we-here?"

Now an expert on such things, Brenna puffed up just a little and said, "It's Fijian tapa. A placemat."

"Placemat? Rubbish! That's first-rate primitive art."

Erich couldn't control himself and laughed. "Sorry Bruce, but that was just about what I said to the shopkeeper in Fiji this past Tuesday. I don't believe it. Be careful, though. It has over eight thousand miles on it already."

"You have any more? I could probably sell these like crazy. Really different from anything we ever see."

"I have two more," Erich said, "but they aren't for sale. Well, maybe. I might sell you one. Better yet, I have a card from the shop. You could contact them directly and make your own deal. No commission involved."

"So, you'd like me to frame this? *Ooooo*, I just love it!"

"What I had in mind," Erich said, "was to mount it on beige burlap, or similar. Something with fine texture that's lighter than the tapa colors."

"Lovely. You have a flair for this, my friend. But let me suggest something different. What I'd do is put it in a glass sandwich. For example, the back piece would be medium amber, or maybe light charcoal glass and the front would be clear matte."

"I like your idea," Brenna said. "Show me some examples."

After looking at mockups, Brenna settled on something that was eye-catching. The tapa was mounted on opaque medium brown glass. Bruce showed her how it would look, and she said, "Do it, and put a dark chocolate frame around it." That led to a whole new search, and after looking at maybe three-dozen possibilities, she picked one that Erich thought was just about perfect.

"You'll have yourself a piece of original Fijian artwork on your wall," Erich said. "And one thing for certain, you'll be the only person in Fairbanks County with something like this."

"You can surely say that again," Bruce added. "Simply lovely. I'm envious. This is *soooo* special." Brenna was thrilled.

"When we come back to pick it up, I'll bring you the card I got from the shop owner. If you're right, you'll make some money out of this. But remember, this is the original."

"Oh, I know!" Bruce took Brenna's address on Wisteria Drive and said he'd have it ready by late afternoon on Saturday. "This time of year we're *verrry* busy, but I'll move this up on our schedule for you lovely people. Happy New Year to both of you."

Erich dropped off his dry cleaning, picked up a suit that had been ready for over three weeks, and then headed for the market. Lots to buy, and they filled a big cart. "Good thing the guys are going to be around," he said to Brenna. "Looks like we bought out the store. I need a cart of some kind at home. That way, we might be able to get everything up to 710 in a couple of trips."

The guys had hung around, but as soon as everything was out of the car and put away, they took off. Erich reminded them that they'd be eating out tonight and to be thinking about where they wanted to go. He got an "okay" in reply.

"Lunch, here or there?" Erich asked.

"Meaning?"

"Either finish off the turkey or get a sandwich somewhere."

"Why don't we stop someplace between here and my house. I've had enough turkey. If we both drive, I can go on home afterwards, see the boys off, and then come back after they're gone."

"Let me give you an access card to get into the garage. I've got an extra one. It's supposed to be really cold tonight, so I think you'll be glad that your car is inside when you're ready to go home. Somebody told me the garage stays at about fifty-five degrees at this time of year. Beats trying to drive an icicle. If you stand behind the Mustang, the space on the right has always been open."

"What a sweetie. I'll be glad tomorrow that my car's inside."

"Keep the card. If you give it back, I'll know we're all done."

"Don't expect that to happen anytime soon. All right?"

"Okay. The other card's in the glove compartment. I'll give it to you when we get to wherever it is we're going. You lead the way."

Brenna stopped at a family restaurant on the Post Road called Frenley's. Since the place was in the town of DeRien, it was a little bit out of her way.

But it was a good choice. A grilled cheese sandwich and a bowl of steaming hot vegetable soup hit the spot. When they were ready to leave, Erich gave Brenna the access card for the garage. She thanked him, gave him a quick hug, and then left for home.

Chapter Thirteen

Erich hadn't been home very long when the phone rang.

"Hi, love. It's Miss Sydney."

"Tina! Good to hear your voice. How're you?"

"Now that I've heard yours, too, I'm fine. And I'm really excited about coming out on Monday. I just wanted to make sure it's okay."

"It's so okay that if you can get away late tomorrow afternoon, we could have two days together."

"I'd love to, but I'll have to see. My parents are having family in for dinner. It's early enough so that I might be able to come out on an evening train. Would it still be all right?"

"At three tomorrow morning if that's the way it has to be."

Giggling, Tina said, "It's good to know that I have my own limo service."

"You do that. I'm looking at my Penn Central schedule, and there's a Sunday-only express leaving at 8:10. Is that doable?"

"Might be a little tight, but I think so. We're eating at around five. Not the usual dinner hour, but that's the plan."

"If it's later, just call me. I'll come down to the station anytime you need me to show up."

"Sounds like you'll be glad to see me."

"More than glad. This is fantastic! Can't wait."

"Me either. I've thought about this ever since I left Sydney. Was it only a week ago? Can't believe it. Seems like ages."

"Unless you tell me something different, I'll see you at the station at 9:02. I was going to suggest that I bring the boys, but this is a you and me reunion. A private affair. You'll see them when we get home."

"That's a better idea. I want you all to myself for a few minutes. I need to look at you and hold you. Am I being selfish?"

"We both are. I'll see you tomorrow evening. Bye, sweetheart."

Late in the afternoon, Brenna came up from the garage and knocked softly on the door. Erich was puzzled for a split second until he remembered that Brenna didn't have to buzz to be let in now. He assumed it was her, and it was. When she came in, Erich said, "The next thing, I suppose, is to give you a key."

"No, my timing might be bad. For you, or maybe Kurt. If you'll let me keep your access card, that'll be enough."

"You can use it until management wants to charge me for the use of a second parking spot. But you won't be there every day, so they'll have to figure it out first."

Both Erich and Brenna had an idea about slipping into bed but decided it was late enough in the afternoon that it was neither necessary, nor should they risk it. If the boys came in and Erich said they were resting, both boys were old enough to figure out what was really going on. They agreed to wait. "We're not exactly starved," Erich said. Brenna agreed.

It wasn't long afterwards that the boys exploded through the door and went on about the Bond film. They couldn't have been more wound up. "I guess you liked it," Brenna remarked.

"It was great," Kurt said. "You gotta see it, especially when one of the bad guys skis down in front of a big snow blower. It grinds him up and there's blood all over the place."

"Sounds wonderful, Kurt. We'll talk about it over dinner."

"Oh, yuck," Brenna said.

"What did you decide about where to eat?" Erich asked.

"We don't want to go anyplace we've been lots of times with Lara," Rudi said. "We thought maybe the Half Shell House."

"Been a while. Sure. Why not? That okay with you, ma'am?"

"Fine. I'm ready for something other than turkey."

There were no ghosts of past attachments at the restaurant, although Rudi was obviously fighting with his memories of all the times he'd sat by Lara's side. The boys made an effort to keep her off their minds by talking about the Bond film, *On Her Majesty's Secret Service*. Other than the grisly snow blower scene, it sounded like it might be a pretty good movie. Plenty of action, for sure.

Dinner finished, they talked about Lara for a moment, mostly about the baby that she'd never mentioned. But they'd all had enough of the subject, and the boys got into how they planned to spend next week. There were outings and friends involved, and Erich thought it was a healthy sign. They were keeping themselves busy. Once school was back in session, that would help. Time was a healer. At least he hoped it would prove to be so.

At home, they continued to chat until the boys began to yawn. Before they got ready for bed, Brenna got a set of special hugs because she'd been there to lend the kind of support a mother would have. She was a woman of strong character and her help had been immeasurable.

Later on, Erich and Brenna shared a satisfying evening. They weren't in love, just lovers, they kept insisting. But what passed between the two of them were the requisites of a stable relationship, one on which they might build. Time would tell. Their evening was followed in the morning with a loving embrace that signaled an end to the agreeable hours they'd been able to string together.

Over breakfast, and for the balance of Brenna's visit, it seemed to Erich that she was a gentler, more relaxed partner, and he said so.

"I think you're right. I feel more at peace. Lara isn't in the picture, and I'm sorry about that. For you, I mean. Then what we went through with Rudi on Friday evening, it's drawn me closer to all of you as a family. I've felt like I've been a mother to them and that I've helped some. I liked the feeling. But there's more to it than that. I've seen another side of you during these past two days that's new to me. There's a lot about you to like, things that make me care more than I should, maybe. But it's happening anyway, like it or not. I'm going to be sorry that I have to leave this afternoon. That's also something different."

"Whatever happens, we won't be rushing into anything soon. But you know that I like spending time with you, especially the new, more relaxed Brenna. Where've you been hiding her all these months? It's a more lovable you. I like it."

"We have to be careful, though. There's a lot to think about. But you know that. You've been cautious for lots of reasons, and I understand why."

"Something's going on inside. Even your face has a softer look. We need to find out what your sister thinks. You've said she reads you pretty well."

"Colleen said she's coming down for a little while after I get home. I'll call you later and let you know what she says. You're right. She can see through me like I'm glass. I can't hide a thing. If you're right about what you see, she might say that I'm expecting."

"Well, we practice a lot. But wouldn't something like that bring the pot to a boil?" Erich asked. "Can you imagine?" He couldn't help but laugh at the thought—even though adding to the family would be disruptive.

Early in the afternoon, they had lunch and Brenna got ready to go. Rudi stayed close since she was the only stand-in mom he had now. And she made a special effort to let him know that he was important. An affectionate hug did wonders for his state of mind.

"Busy week coming up," Brenna said. "I don't suppose we can make any plans."

"I'll know more tomorrow. New Year's Eve is out."

"That's a shame. I'd like it if we could love in the new year. But it isn't possible anyway. Family again and, like you, it's only right that I'm there with Alan and Scot. They're old enough to stay up. Barely."

"Same with us. What about Tuesday night if you're free?"

"That's second best. Sure. I'll at least get to see you."

"We're getting into each other pretty snug-like," Erich said.

"If it's too much, tell me."

"Not at all. You know how I feel about you. I didn't mean it to sound like a negative comment. Sorry."

"No need to be. Remember, we have a date to see Bruce on Saturday. And the ring should be ready, too."

"Big day. I'm really interested in seeing how they turn out. Kind of exciting, isn't it?"

Saturday! Erich suddenly realized that he was overbooked. Tina might be coming out from the Bronx that morning. He'd have to see if he couldn't slip her schedule just a bit.

In the garage, Brenna said it again. "I'm glad you gave me the access card and that my car isn't outside in the cold." Erich gave her a quick hug and reminded her that she also had to use the card to get out.

"I want you to call me," Erich said. "You have to tell me what Colleen says. She has to see a change. I do. It's very becoming."

"You keep saying things like that and I *will* keep you around. Good for my ego. At thirty-five, it'll help me think I'm still young and sexy."

"You are. At least I think so."

She smiled, kissed Erich goodbye and then made her way to the exit door. Through the back window of her aging Dodge, he could see her wave.

Brenna hadn't been gone long when she called to give Erich her report.

"You were right. Sis doesn't know what we're doing, but she thinks I look better than I have for a long time. And she did ask if there was any chance I was expecting. I told her about your plumbing and then, using your words, I said we practiced a lot. We laughed about that. She said I have the same kind of serene look."

"I think it's that you're feeling good about what we share. You've been very much at peace since I got back. Could be it's because Lara isn't in the picture now. Whatever it is, Colleen and I both see a change."

"I said it a long time ago. You make me feel contented. Okay if I hang around for a while?"

"You bet. Now, something not very romantic. I've got to go feed the guys. We'll talk later in the week. Night, dear heart."

"Night, lover."

Dinner wasn't anything special, but it was adequate and the boys didn't gripe. After they'd eaten and cleaned up, Erich said he was going down to the station to pick up Tina.

Surprised, Kurt shook his head. "Wasn't she supposed to be coming out tomorrow morning?"

"Yeah, but she called yesterday and said she couldn't wait. Me neither. Try to understand how we feel about each other. The day will come when you will, if you don't already. If someone's special, you feel it. And it shows."

"There's a girl I like, so I know about that, I think. But you want somebody around. A lot. So do we, but it's different."

"My son, the thinker. You've just put your finger on something I didn't know was all that obvious. You and I need to talk, because I get the feeling that with the parade of women through here I'm not doing what I should to be a good father."

"I didn't mean that, Dad. But you are pretty busy."

"It's because I'm still kinda empty inside. I need someone I can care about, someone who cares about me and for the two of you. And whoever she is will have to give us the time we need to find out if there's a good chance it'll work out. Suppose Lara and I had gotten married. We've just found out that that would've been a disaster. And it's that kind of thing I've worried about all along. It isn't easy to put it all together. Tina is someone I would marry. But it's like I said before. In the end she'll most likely wait for a man who can make the babies she wants. But we've agreed to give ourselves another chance. I care about her, Kurt. A lot. I'm not uncomfortable saying that. Anyway, I have to leave in a few minutes, and we'll be back at about 9:15 or so. Maybe you'll be glad to see her, too. She's a sweetheart."

"Been a while. A lot's happened since she was here last. But we'll be okay. You know that. It's just that when we get to like somebody that's here a lot, they're gone. Like Lara. It's hard. You feel bad, and we don't like that either. Rudi feels that way, too."

"Thanks, Kurt. I appreciate knowing what's on your mind. I'm sorry Rudi isn't out here listening to what we had to say."

"He knows. We've talked about it since Roxane left last spring."

"Hang in there. That's what I'm trying to do. It'll all come together one of these days."

Erich grabbed his coat and got to the station just as the train was pulling in. Not many people on it, so Tina was easy to spot. As the most attractive looking passenger to get off, she would've been anyway. Tucking her little overnight bag under her arm, she walked quickly toward Erich. Their collision ended in a tight hug that lasted for nearly a full minute. Neither one said a word, but they did share humming sounds that expressed how they felt.

After a quick kiss, Tina said, "I'm so glad to see you. It's only been a week, but it felt like months. I've missed you like crazy. I'm beginning to think you're more important than babies."

"Let's not talk about that now. What I want to do is to pick up where we left off last weekend halfway around the world."

"That's why I'm here, Mr. Mauer." They laughed at the memory of the way Tina used to address her former boss. They hugged again briefly and then started for the parking lot.

"It's great that you could come out a day early."

"I had to do it this way and hoped that coming out tonight would be all right. Reason is, I've had to change my plans. My parents were really upset when I told them I was spending the last night of my vacation here. They know about you now, and our age difference, so this may be their way of putting up a small roadblock. But don't look so sad. I'm not going back now until late on Tuesday afternoon, so we'll have almost two full days together. Difference is, they're back-to-back instead of split. I tried to pull off another New Year's Eve with you, but when I told Papa where I spent the last one he made sure I understood there'd be none of that this year. They've invited a lot of people in, some I haven't seen for a long time. I might have objected, but what they won't know is that I'm going to make trips into New York and spend weekends with you when my schedule will let me do it. Feel better now?"

"We'll work it out. Yeah, and what you have in mind does make me feel better. So I promise not to look miserable. You've given me reasons to smile, at least for two days."

When they got to the lot at Eddie's Garage, Erich brought his Mustang to life and they were quickly on their way home. As they drove through town, and then up the hill toward Mianus Ridge, they chatted as if they hadn't seen each other for weeks.

"I was so keyed up about seeing you that I forgot to say anything about your new car. It's really neat. I also love your tan, but it's not fair that you have more color than me."

"The car was a fairly expensive and mostly ineffective way of trying to get over you. I took delivery two days before my birthday and exactly four weeks from the day that we said goodbye."

"I couldn't afford something this sexy, so I wound up buying a Falcon. Not a good idea because somebody said they're going to stop making them."

"Three days from now is what I read in the *Journal*. Not to worry. They'll be a collector's item someday. Okay, here we are again. Look familiar?"

"Garages don't change much in nine months." They chuckled.

Erich got on the intercom from the garage and told Kurt to get rid of their cigars and to make sure that all the chicks were dressed. Everyone laughed at that. Then, up the elevator and through the door that the boys had opened for them, they each gave Tina a hug and made her feel welcome. The guys had obviously talked about how much she meant to their dad, so it was a show of support for the parent in their life who was trying to keep things together.

Rudi took Tina's coat and her little bag and put them in Erich's bedroom.

"Thank you for such a nice welcome. I thought maybe after I left your dad behind that you might not like me very much."

Kurt then told her how things were as he saw them. "I know Dad likes you. That's what counts. When you left, he felt real bad. And some other things have happened that have been a bummer. If he's happy, we'll feel good, too."

"You're talking about Lara, I guess. Your dad told me in Australia that he thought it was probably all over."

"We just found out that we probably won't see her again."

"I liked her a lot," Rudi said. "I'm like Dad was when you left."

"Let's change the subject, guys. This is a happy house for the next couple of days. If we behave ourselves, maybe Tina will come back."

"And that's a promise. Your dad probably told you it wasn't a good idea that we decided not to see each other after I went to Washington. But a guardian angel was looking over us and gave us that one in a million chance to meet and to try again. There aren't many people who are as happy as I am that we can maybe fix the mistake we made. And it's good to see both of you again. You've grown, and you're handsome, just like your dad. Maybe I'll fall in love with all three of you." The boys smiled.

'I'd offer you a glass of good homemade Italian red, but it's long since gone. Lara was mostly responsible for that."

"You're not out. Look in my bag. About halfway down you'll find a new bottle. I'll have a glass with you for old time's sake. Remember the lessons last Christmas Eve?" That turned Kurt's head and the pieces started coming together, at least for him. He looked at his dad. They exchanged grins.

Erich got the wine out of Tina's bag and went to the kitchen to open it. Kurt followed and said, "She's even better looking than the last time she was here. I'd call her really beautiful now. Too bad you can't have kids. They would be, too."

"I've known for a long time how easy she is to look at. And that smile of hers. Still takes my breath away. But Tina's beautiful inside, too. Meaning, she's a sweet person and has a heart of gold. You'll find that out in time. Remember, we worked together for two years. I know her pretty well. That's important."

"Are you bringing me a glass of wine, or is there a summit meeting going on out there?" Tina asked. She wrapped a sweet giggle around her question.

As Erich walked in with their glasses, he said, "We were just agreeing on how much prettier you are compared to March."

"Let's not talk about that. There was too much stress then. We were getting ready to say goodbye. Forever we thought. If I look better, it's because all of that's behind us. I'm happy now. And I love you tons, mister. Even more than then." The boys were taking all this in, and they could see a different kind of expression on their dad's face.

Erich and Tina sat together and toasted. "Salute!"

It was getting late, but the boys had questions about Tina's job and where she lived. They also asked her to tell her version of the story about how she and their dad met in Australia. They were more than simply curious, and, because of their interest, they were showing her that she also mattered to them. Erich was glad to see that Rudi wasn't as blue as he'd been since last Friday evening.

When it got to be bedtime for all of them, the boys told Tina they were glad to see her again. They gave her another hug and then went off to their room feeling pleased with what had happened. More for their dad than for themselves. They hoped that after the bad news about Lara that this might work out. It wouldn't be fair for him to be hurt again.

After the boys were in bed, and Erich and Tina had finished their wine, he took her by the hand. Together in Seaford once again, they were both eager to share the warmth they felt and to continue building on the feelings that were reawakened in Australia just over a week earlier. She showed him a naughty smile. He responded, and it was with an intensity of feeling that surprised him, especially since his underlying hunger had been satiated the night before. But loving Tina went well beyond satisfying a biological appetite. There was a depth of feeling, of affection, that was confirmed by Erich's fervor and his eagerness to fully satisfy this woman he cared about. An unquestionably unique and very personal expression of the love that was theirs alone couldn't have been more fulfilling for either of them. For Erich, it was but one way to show Tina how much she mattered.

There was nothing left beyond this moment. They whispered words of love and then slept entangled. It wasn't often that two lovers were given a second chance. They were blessed, and just after first light they would give thanks that Sydney had happened.

"Since last night you've made a very convincing argument that I should say yes to the proposal you almost made in Sydney."

"Wasn't my objective. This morning, my body took over, and it wanted me to show you how important you are. Put another way, it was more like a desire, no, a need, to show you in a physical way how I feel about you. Thing is, I'm not sure there's a difference between what the mind and body want to do, or if what I'm trying to say makes any sense."

"It does, and I wanted to show you the same kind of feeling."

"Then we both gave and got what we intended. Loving as we have is only one part of a bigger picture, but it's important that we can say I love you and show it in ways that don't need words. Lara told me it was over that last morning she was here. She didn't say a word. Her body did. I guess that's my point. But what I have to acknowledge is that I've not cared enough about anyone to want what I do physically to express what's in my heart. I've just done that. Hard to explain."

"But easy to recognize. There are so many ways to show affection. A look, a gesture, a smile can say it all. Our giving to each other the way we have is just one part of it. The beauty of it is that we do it so well."

"While we're on the subject of giving, I have something for you. A little late for Christmas, but let me get it for you." Erich shifted, then reached over and opened the lower drawer in his nightstand. He pulled out a small box.

"You'll have to sit up now and pay attention."

Tina did and Erich handed her the box. When she opened it, her eyes lit up like a Christmas tree. It was the fiery opal he'd bought just a week ago.

"Ohhh, Erich. You're so thoughtful. It's just gorgeous. Thank you so much for being such a love."

"If we never go beyond tomorrow, maybe this will help you remember me. At least I hope so."

"We will go beyond tomorrow. I'm counting on it. But how could you know that I wanted a stone like this? I intended to shop for one, but then you came along and I forgot all about looking at anything but diamonds. Can't imagine why." She smiled. "I'm *so* pleased with it."

"Now, what goes with it is the setting. Gold, silver, white gold, whichever. You might want a pendant, or have it set in a ring."

"That's what I want. Maybe I could call it an engagement ring."

"Up to you. I tried doing that in Sydney but didn't get very far."

"Then I'll pretend for a while, or maybe even longer than that."

"What we can do is go look for a ring this morning, or you can see a jeweler when you're back in Georgetown. If you pick it out today, they might have it ready by tomorrow. If not, in fact probably not, I'd like to bring it with me when I see you off at Penn Station on Sunday."

"I thought you didn't want to say goodbye there again."

"No. The ghosts are gone, I decided. We are what we are now, and I've erased those painful old memories of last March and replaced them with brand new happy ones. What do you think of that, Miss Tina?"

"I think you're one in a million, and I'm going to attack you again because you're such a sweetheart!"

He agreed. And she did. It was captivating, and they smiled for hours afterwards.

With time running out before the boys got up, Erich said he'd go take a quick shower. For Tina's benefit: "You won't have time for a leisurely bubble bath, but there's no need for you to jump in and out at my pace."

"I won't be too long either. The guys might have an urgent call, so I don't want to be the cause of any accidents."

Erich did finish quickly. Then, feeling like an absolute scoundrel, he called Brenna while Tina was in the shower.

"Hi gal. I just wanted to find out about tomorrow evening."

"It's a bad time of year to get anybody in to stay with the boys. Could the three of you come over here for dinner? We won't be able to get friendly, but we can at least have some time together. I'm making lasagna, a green salad, and garlic bread. Interested?"

"Absolutely! And the boys will love it, too. They're really into your cooking. What time?"

"How about six o'clock, or maybe a little after? Okay?"

"Perfect," Erich said. "See you then, and we can talk about Saturday while we're at it."

"I've got problems with the weekend. I'll fill you in tomorrow evening."

"Fine. Bye, babe."

"Bye, lover."

After a late breakfast, the boys decided they'd go downtown and meet some of their friends. Erich told them that he and Tina would be going in the other direction to do some shopping.

"Remember, we're going out for dinner this evening. Make sure you're back and ready to go before seven."

"We'll be back way before that," Kurt said.

The boys took off, and Erich and Tina went in search of a jeweler. Not the same one Brenna had gone to. It wasn't until they were in a third store, this one in a local mall, that she found a fairly simple design in silver that she liked. Erich had to ask. "Any chance you could have it ready by tomorrow?"

The jeweler chuckled. "Not at this time of the year. Best I can do is Friday around four o'clock. At that, it'll be snug."

"Then that's it. I'll be here sometime after four."

Erich paid for the ring and said, "Happy New Year." He returned Erich's good wishes.

"Well, there it is, hon. Sunday at Penn Station, and I'll make a big deal out of slipping it on your left hand just as if we were going to add another ring to go with it." Tina had such an affectionate expression that Erich wished he could have photographed it. It just about melted his heart. "Don't say a word. It's one of those times you mentioned when nothing need be said. Your face says it all."

She took his hand and squeezed it. "Can't help saying something. You read me perfectly. That's what working together for two years has done."

"Like to take those two-plus years and trade them in for a lifetime of caring? Comes with a full guarantee that it'll work or your money will be cheerfully refunded."

Then two things happened. The first was that Tina laughed at Erich's trade-in offer. The second was that her laughter resonated, and it caused four or five people to look in their direction. From the corner of his eye, he saw that one of them, off at a distance, was Lara. Seeing the two of them together, she turned quickly and hurried away. It conclusively finalized their separation, and it would also be the last time Erich would ever see her.

"Your proposal's got my attention," Tina said. "You may just win me over. But for the moment, let's enjoy what we've found again. I feel good about us and never want any of it to end."

"You know the words, but I'm not pushy."

"Oh yes you are. You're just being subtle. Love it."

"And that, dear heart, is how I feel about you."

Tina put her arm around Erich's waist. He then put his around hers, and they walked through the mall as if they owned it.

"I just remembered. I dropped off film to be developed. It should be ready by now."

As they turned into another wing with several major stores, Erich pointed one out to Tina that was being remodeled. The sign above it read simply, "Lara's".

"That's part of Lara's big expansion plans. Her downtown shop is in a building that will be coming down soon. She has another one that'll open at about the same time as this one. Busy gal."

"Do you miss her?"

"If you weren't here, she'd be on my mind. But you know that she's got this crazy notion that everybody she cares about is dying. She thinks I'm next and couldn't deal with having to watch it happen. Even Kurt thinks she's gone around the bend."

"Another man—or some other reason to dump you?"

"I guess the answers are no and no. A lifelong friend of hers told me that Lara says I still matter, which is part of the problem. That's her nonsense of trying to avoid seeing a companion or a husband die. Makes absolutely no sense. And to prove her wrong, I'm going to outlive her. Anyway, I know where my future lies. If it isn't you, then I'd be starting over. But you're the one I care about. No pressure. It's just how I feel. No surprise there and no need to repeat myself. Now, let's go see if my pictures are ready."

"I like having you repeat yourself. Do it anytime you like." Tina smiled sweetly.

The prints were ready, and the photo shop got a pile of money for them. "Looks like I went overboard and took too many."

The two of them went to a snack bar and ordered coffee. Erich arranged the photos in sequence, then went through each of the envelopes and added commentary. When he got to a good picture of himself, Tina reached over and took it right out of his hands.

"This one's mine! Forever. It's a great picture, and I'll be able to show my parents what you look like. Finally. They'll see that at thirty-nine you aren't falling apart. I just love it. Get me an enlargement and I'll put it next to my bed. No. Make it two, and I can have one on my desk at work."

"Okay. We'll do it before we leave."

Looking at the remainder of the photos, Tina asked, "Who's the cute blonde? I'm jealous."

"That was the companion the search guy, Forsyth, had waiting at the marina last Sunday after you left. Her people are very wealthy, but for all of it she's lonely, I think. Part of it is that guys put a move on her not for the person she is, but for the family money. She was surprised that I didn't. My question was, 'why would I do a thing like that?' With me leaving in less than twenty-four hours, it was just a let's be friends thing."

"That's all? I'm still jealous."

"Tina. Given the condition you left me in, I couldn't have done a thing for her even if she'd been so inclined. We did have dinner, she dropped me off at the hotel, but before that asked if she could drive me to the airport on Monday. I said yes. That was all. The afternoon on the boat could have been it. But like I said, I got the feeling that she was lonely, and that I was the first guy she'd met recently who obviously wasn't after her money. Over dinner, she made a point of saying that she thought I was different."

"Can I at least be envious that you got to spend an afternoon on the harbor?"

"If you'd stayed over, we could've been out there together and then gone on to Fiji. I asked. Remember? *Verrry* romantic."

"At my company, a woman doesn't have those kinds of perks."

"Well, I've probably made the last of my IMCO trips, except for London. There are rumors that the company will revert to the way it was structured up until about a year ago. That was just before Warren and I, and some others, were hired. Going back to what you and I shared at Essex had its good and bad points. The plus side was that we were there to support each other. With IMCO, the news is all bad, I'm afraid. I expect to be out of a job and on the street again sometime next year. It's a situation that's been made even worse because there'll be no Tina there to lean on when needed."

"Oh, Erich, that's not right. It hasn't even been a year yet since you went down to New York Plaza. I'll worry about you. But I don't suppose that'll help very much."

"Let's get off the subject. It hasn't happened yet, and you and I have more than twenty-four hours together. So, first, let's go order your prints. You sure you want to see my face both at home and at the office? It might turn off any sexy admirers you have at work."

"That's two silly things you just said. Of course I want the pictures. If we order enough of them, I can have one in every room. And suitors? Might be some, but I'm not interested."

"So, how many more pictures do you want? Two?"

"Four if you count the bath. Order six. Two big ones and four medium size. Please? I'll leave one of them with my parents."

"You're too much," Erich said, smiling. "Six it is."

Before Erich and Tina left the mall, they did some window-shopping, which included looking at rings, and then they had a bite to eat. By the time they got home, the guys were already there and deeply immersed in watching an ancient movie on TV.

"What did you decide about dinner?" Erich asked.

Rudi spoke up and said he'd vote for Mazza's. Tina smiled at the thought of going back to the place where it had all begun with Erich a year ago.

"Any objections? Okay. Rudi has called it. Be ready to leave at about a quarter after seven."

Eating at Mazza's was exactly the right thing to do. It gave Erich and Tina a chance to flog another ghost. Lara's. The mood was light and it was a fun evening. Everyone around the table enjoyed the food and each other's company. It felt good. No. Better than good. Erich was feeling expansive and after two martinis, and with the Chianti about gone, he proposed a toast.

"To Tina, if she'll have me. If not, she pays for dinner."

The boys chuckled. Tina joined them.

"That puts me on the spot. Guess I'd better say that I'll have you, or at least give it some *verrry* serious thought now that I've been asked again."

The boys cheered softly. Erich was caught up in the fun they were having and had a happy blur in his eyes. No one knew that but him. He turned and gave Tina a quick, loving kiss. The boys cheered again.

"That's to seal your pledge. If you change your mind, I'll take it back."

"No. It's mine now. And I would have another one, please."

Erich delivered.

Since the bill was paid, the boys assumed they were ready to leave and went off to get all their coats.

"You going to be okay to drive?"

"Sure. It's a euphoric high, that's all. Who could've imagined when I left Seaford about three weeks ago that we'd all be here, together again, and enjoying the kind of evening we've just had. There is hope. I can't ask for more than that."

"There'll be other nights," Tina said. "I'm not letting go of you. So of course there's hope. I want to be a part of the dream, too. We're new to each other again, sort of. Just give me time. You know the questions. Really only one. But I may have my answer. It's you I need. More than anything else." She turned around, gave him a loving hug, and then whispered, "I love you, Erich. Almost more than life itself. Take me home. I want to show you, again, how much you mean to me."

On their way back to Mianus Ridge, Tina held Erich's right hand in both of hers. It gave them, she believed, a direct link to each other's hearts. She liked the thought of that, and it gave her a feeling of total contentment.

The boys said they weren't really sleepy and would watch TV in their room. Erich said that he and Tina would stay up for a while, and then be off to bed before long. He also reminded them that they were invited to have dinner at the Walsh's tomorrow at around six. They looked puzzled, said nothing, but took it in stride.

"I'll be taking Tina to the station at five, but I'll come back here first. Otherwise, we'd be too early."

They acknowledged what their dad had said, gave Tina a hug and went off to be entertained by their little TV.

"Friends?" Tina asked.

"She's Lara's friend, and the one who broke the news to me that it was over. Maybe I should say she confirmed it. We've become friends, and she invites us over once in a while."

"A romantic interest?"

"To be honest, I'm fond of Brenna. But her story is that she's divorced, has two boys a little younger than Kurt and Rudi, and they're her pride and joy. The way she sees it is that she's had her marriage and doesn't want another man in her life other than her two sons and her dad. She's a good mother. Runs a tight ship. Anyway, this is her way of saying Happy New

Year. It was sweet of her to invite us over. I'm not all that creative in the kitchen; she is, so I don't very often turn down an offer to eat free."

"Could I call you after I get home—or maybe later on?"

"I'm counting on it. We'll probably visit some after dinner, but we should be home by ten o'clock, half past ten at the latest. I know Lara will be on the agenda. Be interesting to see if there is anything new. Brenna works for Lara on Saturdays once in a while, so she's in a tough spot, sort of."

"Any chance that Lara might come back."

"Too late for that. Now that you and I are together again, my head is turned in just one direction. Yours. Even if you found someone to take my place, I couldn't have her back. She has this crazy fear of death, and I couldn't live with that. We have a lot of good memories, and they'll always be there. But she's gone."

"You shouldn't give much thought to being replaced," Tina said. "I told you at dinner that I don't want to let go. It was too hard getting you back. I'm fortunate beyond what I have any right to be."

"I share in that. It's still hard to believe. Yet here we are, just over a year later, sitting on the same sofa where it all began."

"Would you like to continue the lessons? It's *has* been a year, you know." They chuckled softly.

"I thought you'd never ask. Lean my way please."

After a few minutes of cuddling, they took their needs to Erich's bed.

Without much delay, they shared a stirring finale. Afterwards, it was minutes before either one said anything. It was just as it should have been. They wanted the time to appreciate the beauty of their union and the contentment they felt.

Finally, Tina said, "Just perfect. I can't believe what I'd have missed if I'd married poor Anthony. It's at times like this that I go back to the struggle I had last spring about whether I should stay in D.C. or come back to New York. I've about decided to come home. One of the reasons I went down there in the first place was to run away and not have to decide between you and a family. My choice is about made, I think. It wouldn't be easy giving you up now. Occasional weekends together won't be enough."

"But five years from now, or even late tomorrow when the fire isn't as hot, what then? Wouldn't the thought of babies, and what you'd have missed, be lingering in the back of your mind?"

"I want you, Erich. I've never felt this way before. But, it's more than a want. It's a need. You're the spirit that keeps me alive and moving. You're as important to me as my heartbeats."

"If you feel the same way in the morning, then I think it's time we did something about it."

"That won't be very objective. I'll have been after you again and feel then just as I do now. But when the passion has cooled later in the day, I'll still know what's in my heart. It'll prove that I want to be a part of your life."

"Then I suppose the true test would be to call me after you're back at work. Not much fervor associated with that."

"You've proposed. Twice. Are you having second thoughts?"

"Not at all. I just don't want your decision to be based on this alone, which is what we have going for us at the moment."

"If I say it again before I attack you in the morning, would that count?"

He chuckled. "Silly girl. I love you dearly. Yes, it would count."

Tina smiled warmly and gave Erich a hug. Then, abruptly, she said, "I want to be with you and have decided. I'm coming home. And I'll say the same thing tomorrow, and Sunday, and ten days from now. You're my future, and I pray that you'll want me to be a part of it for years to come. Until I move back, I'll be here as often as I can."

"You know I'm elated that you're giving us a chance." Tina kissed him goodnight, and then they both slept like logs—the snuggling kind.

Morning began with Erich and Tina looking into each other's eyes and smiling. They acknowledged the importance of their physical love, but they also knew that their relationship would be built on an even more substantial foundation. They truly cared about each other, were sensitive to each other's feelings and needs, had parallel interests, and shared similar goals. It wasn't perfect, but the nearly three years they'd known each other gave them a head start and would serve them well. Their loving now was less sensual and more of an avowal of what they meant to each other. Adding to the joy they felt was the fact that they now had an opportunity to pursue a common goal, one they hoped to achieve: a life together.

After the lovers were dressed, they went about putting together a big breakfast. It especially pleased the guys. For some reason, they were starved. Growing teenage boys probably explained most of it. Later on, Kurt and Rudi went off to meet some of their friends, and the lovers talked further over a second coffee.

Between sips, Tina said, "I don't want to do anything today except just be here with you. We'll have Penn Station on Sunday, but then it'll be a while. I don't look forward to that. If I had my way, I'd get my clothes together and move in with you over the weekend. But then reality takes hold, and I know it's the right thing to do to stay a full year with the company. After that...."

"What kind of effect do you think the three months apart will have on how you feel about us and our future?

"None at all. I can't imagine how anything would change. No. Nothing will. I won't let it. We're onto something so precious, and we will have weekends together. Last night, I said 'occasional', but in the shower I decided that it'll be at least once a month—more often if my travel schedule will allow it. Like I said, I want you in my future, just as I want to be in yours. We're at the beginning of a wonderful life together, the kind most people would envy. And I'll give you more than Lara could have."

"I don't doubt that for a moment. But if your travel schedule gets to be a problem, I could always come to Georgetown. My problem might be getting someone in to look after the guys. It isn't that Kurt needs it. Rudi does, and I'd want to be sure they have good meals and supervision. You understand."

"You're welcome to come down. I don't have to tell you that. Be wonderful. But assuming things work out the way we plan, I'd rather stay here and be around the boys. They'll need to get used to me, so the more exposure I have the better I think it'll be for all of us. What I'm trying to say is that if I'm to share parenting, then it's important that I spend as much time here as I can."

"I like the thought of that. But what we can't predict is what may happen to my job next year. We're into a terrible job market, at least for people like me. If the consulting firm has their way, there'll be a bunch of us out on the street. For sure, it'll affect all the people Joel brought in. I've been keeping an eye on Seaford's job openings, but there hasn't been anything for me here. Buildings in the run-down section of town just this side of I-95 will be coming down, new ones going up, and there'll be major companies moving in. But that's down the road and the timing is wrong if I do wind up having to look for a job again. I just did that a year ago. We'll see what happens. I don't want to be in a position where you'd have to support me."

"You know I would if it comes to that. It'd only be temporary. No matter what the market conditions are, you have too much going for you to be out of work for very long. I know. I worked for you, if you remember."

"What it says to me is that before we make firm plans, we'll need to get our lives stabilized first. You'll be looking for a job, and since it'll most likely be in the city, it raises a question about where you'll be living after you're back. And there'll be expenses, too. Moving isn't cheap, you know."

"I do, but to start with I could use my parent's place as a base during the week. I'd rather be here, and will be on weekends, but it is a good guess that my job would be in Manhattan. Be less expensive to come and go from home. But, I'd also want to look around here. That would mean I'd have long weekends with you, and then while I'm job hunting in Seaford I could divide my time between here and the Bronx. In the end, when I'm working, I'd be here, and we'd be living together, married or otherwise."

"Married and not 'otherwise'. It's been a hard year for you, I know, and making the decision you have wasn't easy. But I'm pleased that maybe children aren't an issue now. We're finally going to be a family of four, and you and I will have that chance now to spend a caring life together."

Tina smiled affectionately and took both of Erich's hands in hers. "And you know I share every one of your feelings about that." She turned and gave him a kiss. "What we have to do is to continue believing in us, as we always have, and show each other in simple ways how much we matter. That'll help our future turn out the way we want it to. There are some unanswered questions about jobs, so we'll have to be patient. But the strength of what we have, and what we feel, will help us get over whatever bumpy times we have. We did it together at Essex for two years."

"Nicely put. I get the impression that you really do believe in us, and that our outlook is bright in spite of what's ahead."

"And I'm beginning to get the impression that you haven't been paying any attention to what I just said."

They both chuckled softly, talked further about the unknowns they were facing and their possible courses of action. It was later on that Erich finally asked Tina what kind of job she hoped to find in either Seaford or New York.

She smiled when she thought about his question. "Following my mentor's lead, a certain Mr. Mauer, I'd like to get into recruiting and placement. One thing I'll do is call Seth McIvers at Ira North Associates. We worked well together. He left Essex about the time you got there. Anyway, he said at the time that I should call him if I ever thought about getting into placement. I could do that now, but it's premature. When I know what my schedule is, I'll call or write. Too bad you couldn't have gotten to know him better. He and his wife are lovely people and they adore each other. I see us as being a lot like the two of them."

Erich and Tina spent the balance of their day quietly. They simply enjoyed being in each other's company, and it was just as she had wanted it. Their hearts were filled with affection, and they had their first exposure to how living together might be. They'd have more time to find out about it when she came back from Washington in the spring. Undoubtedly their life wouldn't always be this tranquil, but Tina was a gentle woman with an even disposition, and Erich expected that heated disputes wouldn't ever be a part of their family life.

Late in the afternoon, the boys came home from their outing. Since it was just about time for Erich to take Tina to the station, she packed her little bag and got ready to leave. She told Erich and the boys that if it was all right she'd plan on coming back the weekend of the seventeenth. Three male voices said they'd like it if she could. She gave Kurt and Rudi a hug and then wished them a Happy New Year.

At the station, Tina reminded Erich that she'd call sometime after ten. "I want to say good night to you so I can dream about us all night long."

They shared an affectionate hug and a gentle kiss. Then as Erich was putting her on the 5:20 to Grand Central he added, "We'll share dreams and a good night even if we're not together,"

Tina easily found a seat, and they both waved as the train pulled out of the station. She blew a kiss and got one in return.

Back home, Erich said, "Okay guys, get yourselves ready. We've got about fifteen minutes. I want to be back by ten o'clock to take Tina's call."

"I really like her," Rudi said, "and I already miss her a little. Sure hope she can come back that weekend."

"You've liked most of my friends. Is Tina special, then? Sounds like it."

"Yeah, and so is Brenna. But I won't forget Lara."

"Nor will I. Sorry, but there's nothing we can do about that."

"You thought Tina was gone, and then look what happened. Maybe the same thing could happen with Lara."

"Different. Lara has cut us out of her life. As you just saw, Tina never really did that. She and I now have a chance. Lara and I have none. During that last week or so, she changed."

"She sure did," Kurt said. "I still don't understand it."

"What about Brenna?" Rudi asked.

"Like you said the other night, not at all politely, she has her family and really doesn't have much interest in me as her next husband. In fact, she says she really doesn't want one at all. I say that, but she's mellowed since she was here last week and is maybe having second thoughts about us. But don't hold your breath. You know how much Tina and I like each other. We've agreed to see if we can put it all together. We think it's possible, but I thought the same thing about Lara, and look at how that turned out."

"You should already know by now," Kurt said. "You've known her for almost three years."

"I don't have all that many doubts about us. But it's time to go. If we don't, we'll be late."

When they were on their way, Erich picked up where he'd left off. "Knowing Tina at work since April '67 isn't really the same as being together every day and living like a family. She's wanted babies. You know about that, but she's willing to put that on hold while she decides about us. It comes down to being sure that I'm more important than they are. Right now, she thinks so. Over the next few weeks, that could change."

"If it does, then you'd have to start all over again," Rudi said. "Why does it take so long to find a new mom for us and somebody you can like, too?"

"We've been through this how many times? Right now, you've got two moms who care about you. But you can't do the choosing because when you're out of school and gone, I still have to live with whatever choice I've made. If it's wrong, then maybe I've got a nasty wife on my hands again, or a Lara who's gone around the bend. I don't want another divorce, guys. Not ever. Anyway, one thing you can count on is that I'm not going to stop seeing Brenna. The reason is that we're good friends. At that, she isn't likely to be taking over Tina's place in our lives."

There was silence then until they pulled into Brenna's driveway at just after six o'clock. The guys were starved. So was Erich.

"Hello, hungry guys," Brenna said. "You're just in time to see the lasagna come out of the oven."

"Smells great," Kurt said. "And it looks yummy. Okay, that's my dinner. What are you guys having?" They all laughed.

"Salad, I suppose," Brenna said. "And garlic bread. Lots of it. But you don't get any."

"Then I guess I better share my lasagna with you."

It was a positive start to a meal that felt like family. There was something different about sitting at Brenna's table, and it gave Erich insight into how it would be if they were all together. There was a kind of familiarity that had considerable appeal.

Erich and Brenna talked about matters on their minds. The boys, sitting across from each other, had their own topics of interest despite their age differences. If Tina changes her mind, this might work. It was pleasant, but the young lady who boarded the 5:20 drifted in and out of his thoughts.

The meal finished, Kurt and Rudi helped clear the table then went off to watch TV with Alan and Scot.

As he and Brenna were cleaning up, Erich asked, "What do you hear from Lara?"

"Nothing, really. She's still up in Massachusetts, so I don't expect to hear from her until she's back."

"That's strange, because I'm positive I saw her at Ridgecrest yesterday morning. How could that be?"

"Might be it had something to do with the new shop she's opening. Or maybe she can't watch her uncle die. I'll find out next week. If you're right about seeing her, I'm curious, too. What were you doing at the mall?"

"Picking up all the pictures I took in Fiji and Sydney. I brought one for you to hang up someplace. It might help scare off the mice."

Erich went to the inside pocket of his jacket and gave Brenna one of the better photos taken while he was out on Edward's boat.

"Look at you. Your tan was gorgeous. Makes me sick," Brenna said, chuckling. "And you've still got some left. But not like this. Great picture. Thanks. I'll put it up on the fridge."

"It was taken on Sunday, the twenty-first. I did add a little more color in Fiji. That was two days later, just a week ago. Seems like a whole lot longer. I guess the length of the trip back makes it feel that way. Good to be home, even if the outlook at IMCO isn't all that clear."

Erich and Brenna had an amaretto, and talked on until about half past nine. By then Erich was yawning, and said, "It isn't the company, I'm just tired for some reason." Truth of the matter was that Tina had worked him over pretty thoroughly during the past two days.

"You've had a busy week. It's no wonder. Sorry we can't get closer tonight, but you understand."

"I do. Anyway, it's time I rounded up the guys so we can be on our way. Oh, you were going to tell me about Saturday. Has something changed?"

"Not Saturday, but Sunday. I'll have to come home after we've had breakfast. Jordie's got something going on, probably another woman, so I have to be back before noon. I didn't ask why. Not important. But I'll be over after lunch on Saturday."

"We have to go see Bruce and the jeweler, you remember."

"How could I forget? I'm really excited, especially about the ring."

"Would you go pry my two loose? It's time for me to think seriously about getting horizontal."

"Love to join you, but it sounds like you'd fall asleep on me. You look tired. Just be rested by Saturday."

"I'll be fine by then, and it'll be fun going off with you to pick up your loot from the Eastern Hemisphere."

Kurt and Rudi griped that their dad was interrupting a movie they'd been watching. They got ready quickly so they could see the end of it at home.

"I'll bet a nickel you've seen it before."

"Yeah, but it's good," Kurt said. "*Captain Blood*, with Errol Flynn."

"Okay, let's get going."

Erich gave Brenna a hug, thanked her for a great meal and then kissed her gently. Not one of the four boys missed it.

"Happy New Year, Erich. See you on Saturday afternoon." Then Brenna returned his good night kiss and said, "You're important to me, guy. Please take care of yourself."

"You too, babe. Thanks again, and Happy New Year. G'night."

Once home, the boys went straight to their little bedroom TV. Erich sat in the living room, troubled, and not seeing much of anything. Part of it was that he was plagued by the conviction that none of his relationships would go anywhere. Even Tina, for some reason. The thought made him ache. He was also convinced that his professional life would undergo a major transformation soon and that his days in corporate management would be gone, never to return. "You're tired, Erich," he thought. "Or maybe you had too much wine."

It was about ten minutes later that his reverie was interrupted by the harsh sound of the phone ringing. He thought it'd be Tina; it was Brenna.

"You okay? You seemed down, and it was why I said you're important. I thought it might help some."

"It did. But it's lots of travel, fatigue, Lara maybe, and then trying to find solutions to problems I see ahead. Some of them professional. And I need to stabilize our family life. Kurt's mostly okay, but Rudi...."

"You just need a good night's rest, sweetheart. My guess is you'll see things different in the morning."

"I went through this a year ago when Essex and my future were giving me reasons to be on edge. The whole thing is back again, but you don't need all this. We'll talk about it on Saturday. Sweet of you to be concerned and to call. It's what I needed. Now, I'm going to bed."

"Night, Erich. Try to have a pleasant dream or two."

"And you. G'night, babe."

Minutes later, Tina called.

"Hi, sweet. Tried to get through earlier but your line was busy."

"Brenna Walsh called. She thought I seemed depressed and wanted to know if I was okay. It was kind of her."

"Sounds like she cares about you."

"Guess so, but she's just being a good friend. Your having left, my fatigue, and then being concerned about where my career is headed were on my mind over dinner. Guess it showed. Don't worry about it."

"I don't want too much competition. If I have to do whatever's necessary to protect my interests."

Erich chuckled. "There aren't any challengers out there. Brenna is one of the people I mentioned to you in Sydney. And you knew that she'd invited us to have dinner with them this evening. She's not a threat because she isn't marriage material."

"Will you let me be a little bit jealous? I love you lots, you know."

"No need for that. But if it helps keep your love for me alive, sure."

"Have to tell you. I showed your picture to my parents. Papa couldn't believe that you're thirty-nine. He said you don't look much older than me. I guess he was expecting you to be gray haired and showing your age. And then I told him about how long people in your family lived. They really don't have any objections now to our seeing each other, but they both think it's sinful to spend nights together. I also mentioned that there wouldn't be any grandchildren. Not from us anyway. Since that's already taken care of by my brothers, that didn't bother them either. Papa asked about that. I just told him that you'd had your family and that at thirty-nine you felt like the time had passed for you to start over. I didn't give him the real reason. Anyway, now they know who you are and what you look like. What's important is that you've been accepted by two parents who've been very strict, at least with me. But I think they've mellowed. One thing they're glad of is that you came along and took Anthony out of the picture. It seems he can't decide if he likes girls or boys better. If I'd married him, Papa would have probably wrung his neck by now. He's strong enough to do it."

Erich laughed. It felt good. "You've lifted spirits that badly needed help after you left. You're the twinkle in my eye and the bubbles in my soda, but when you aren't around the light goes out and the fizz goes flat. Says I really care, I think it's fair to say."

"Sweet of you to say funny little things like that. Makes me feel all tingly."

"About Sunday, you said your train goes at four something?"

"Yes. It's the 4:15 Metroliner."

"Guess I'll have to take the 1:30 train, one that stops everywhere but Sydney, so I can be at Penn Station at three o'clock or so. With a gift, I should add."

"I can't wait. If that's when you'll be there, I'll do the same. We'll have time to talk. But I should tell you that Papa is driving me to the station so he can meet you. He promised not to stay very long, but maybe there'll be enough time for us to have a coffee."

"I'm all for it," Erich said. "Sure. But since I won't know where you're parking, or which entrance you'll be using, let's meet near the departures board at around three o'clock."

"Fine. Sunday's a ways off, though. We need to talk again before then. I'll want to hear you say you like me a little bit."

"Ahh, Tina, you know how much you mean to me. But I'll say it on Friday, and Sunday, too, if your papa doesn't object. Give me something hard to do. About the ring, call me on Saturday, say at about five thirty. I'll give you my opinion."

"Won't be needed. I know how beautiful it'll be."

"I have something else to give you on Sunday. Forgot all about it until now. It's from Fiji and different. Another little gift that'll show you, in a small way, how much I care about my Tina."

"You're a sweetheart. But it's late and as much as I want to keep listening to your voice, I'll let you go. Call you on Saturday. Pleasant dreams, my love."

"You too, sweetheart. Night."

Chapter Fourteen

When Erich was done with his Saturday chores, he decided to see if Tina's ring was ready. By the time he got through town, and to the jeweler, it was close to four o'clock.

"Hi, I'm here to pick up a ring with a pretty opal in it. Name's Mauer. Any chance it's ready?"

"Yes, Mr. Mauer. I remember you from earlier in the week. No, it was the stone. Exquisite. But to answer your question, yes, it's ready. I think you'll like it or, more precisely, your lady will." The jeweler took an envelope from a box Erich assumed was finished work. "Here it is. Turned out beautifully."

"I-guess-so! Tina will be thrilled. I'm giving it to her tomorrow before she goes back to Washington."

"So that's her name. I clearly remember her face and charming smile. You're a fortunate man, Mr. Mauer."

"Thank you. And she's very special, but we'll have to see how things go."

"The ring should help your cause, if I may call it that."

"Interesting that we were both in Sydney, and I bought the stone the morning I left. Just 10 days ago. Seems longer. Tina had left the day before."

"So you're new to each other?"

"No, we worked together for two years, and then went separate ways. A couple of weeks ago, she spotted me as I was scanning headlines at the hotel newsstand. We couldn't have been more astonished. Things like that just don't ever happen. But it did."

"Sounds as if it was meant to be. Well, I wish you all the best."

"Appreciate your good wishes. Thank you for turning out a gorgeous ring. I know she'll love it."

"You're indeed welcome. And a Happy New Year to you and your Tina."

"Thank you. I'll be sure to pass on your good wishes. Happy New Year to you, too."

While Erich was at the mall, he stopped at the photo shop and picked up the prints Tina wanted. "These ought to make her happy, too." he thought.

Back home, Tina called just before six. "Hi, my love. Happy New Year."

"And you, dear heart. I like the way we brought in 1969 better. Did you have a good party?"

"Yes, but it would have been so much better if I'd been in Seaford with you. We had a house full and some of them are still here. But, did you get the ring?"

"Nope, the jeweler sold it to someone else."

"*Ohh, Erich!*"

"No love, I have it. You'll like the way it turned out. The jeweler did a first-rate job. It's stunning."

"Don't do things like that to me. That wasn't nice at all. I nearly had heart failure. Shame on you."

"Sorry. I know you're excited about it, but I was full of mischief there for a moment. I apologize."

"If it wasn't so late, I'd come get it. But we still have a lot going on here, and for some reason I'm worn out. Anyway, I can hardly wait until Sunday."

"See you at Penn Station at about three, as planned. You have to figure out which finger you want me to slip it on."

"I already know, and so do you. But something I want to tell you is that I've been showing your picture around since Wednesday evening. Of course I had to tell everybody our whole story while I was doing it. You're a big hit. For sure, you are with me."

"I'm getting that impression. Maybe I should run for mayor. But that wouldn't work since I don't live in New York."

They exchanged news for several minutes more, and would have talked longer, but Erich heard a voice in the background that told him Tina was being summoned to help with something. She confirmed it.

"Got to go, hon. Mama's putting me to work in the kitchen. See you on Sunday. I'll need a big hug by then."

"Me too. Now that I'm a known quantity, say hello to all your family."

"I will. Tell the boys I said hi. Bye, sweetheart."

"I'll do it and will make sure that I bring a big hug with me down to Penn Station. Bye, love."

A Saturday evening free was unusual. The merry-go-round Erich had been on since he got back from Sydney hadn't given him much time to himself. That changed unexpectedly. Brenna called and wanted to know if she could bring the boys over so they could see where he lived—and maybe visit for a little while.

"Sure. But I was just about to ask my guys if they'd like to go out for a burger. I'm sure they will. After your two have finished their inspection, why don't we all go out together? We could make it a two-family affair."

"Love it. You sound better than you did on Monday night. I was worried about you. If we're not interrupting anything, we'll be over in about a half-hour."

"Anytime. We've just been hanging around and waiting for a sexy gal of Irish ancestry to call."

"You *are* better. See you at about six thirty."

"Hey, guys," Erich hollered, "any interest in a burger?"

They both came out of their cave and, as a duet, said, "Yeah!"

"Brenna just called and said that Alan and Scot want to see where we live and then visit for a little bit. I told her I was about to ask you if you'd like to go out to eat and was sure you'd say yes. See how smart I am? You did. Anyway, I suggested that we do it together, and she thinks it's a great idea."

The boys agreed with Brenna.

"First Tina and now Brenna. I don't believe you," Kurt said.

"Just trying to find a wife for me and a mom for you. It's extremely hard work." Kurt cackled. He saw through that comment immediately.

"I haven't mentioned it, but I'm going into New York on Sunday afternoon to see Tina off. Her dad wants to meet me, now that he seems to think I'm okay. I won't be gone all that long, so maybe you could go see a movie. There's a new one just out called *Airport*. I read the book. Be interesting to see how they handle it. Probably better than *Love Story*. Read that, too. It's a tearjerker. Two young people in love, but the girl, about Tina's age, dies. Best you see something else. How about the John Wayne movie, *Chisum*."

"We like his movies," Kurt said. "Be lots of action. Sounds better than the other two." Rudi agreed. With Lara gone, he had no interest in seeing a sad movie.

When the doorbell rang shortly after six thirty, Erich momentarily forgot, again, that Brenna had an access card to the garage and didn't need to be let into the building.

"Hi, babe. I can't seem to remember that you have your own access card now."

"Glad you gave it to me, especially at this time of year."

"You're looking good, ma'am. Hi, Alan. Scot," Erich said.

"So do you. Certainly better than you did Monday evening."

Kurt took coats. Rudi gave Brenna a hug.

"Thanks. I was touched that you called after we got home on Monday. The concerns are still there, but I'll survive."

"Don't want to beat the subject to death, but it sure was nice that we could pull into the garage. I'd like to keep the card, at least until spring, if that's all right with you."

"No problem. I can't use two of 'em."

Brenna took Alan and Scot on a quick tour of Erich's apartment. As pre-teen youngsters, they were mainly curious and details weren't important. That finished, they sat for a few minutes before they left for The Castle. It wasn't Erich's first choice, or even his third, but he was outvoted. He wasn't in the best frame of mind the last two times he'd eaten there. The place brought back memories of Lara, and then the evening he ate there alone right before his first trip to Australia. But it was time to move on. He couldn't continue to avoid places where he and Lara had been. No rational reason to do so.

When they were done, and the Mauers and the Walshes were about to start home, Erich asked, "We still on for tomorrow?"

"I'll be over after lunch. Be interesting to see how both things turned out. I'm really keyed up, especially about the ring."

"Any idea which finger you'll wear it on?"

"I haven't decided. We'll see how it looks first, and then I'll make up my mind. But the tapa ought to be neat, too. I already have a place picked out to hang it. You have such good ideas. Seems like I've said that before. Maybe I should keep you around." That got the attention of her two boys. They had long since found out where their mother was spending her overnights. It was part of the reason, Erich was sure, why they wanted to see where he lived.

"See you then." Erich gave her a quick hug, and they all said their goodbyes.

On their way home, Rudi said, "Brenna's nice, too, but I don't suppose that'll work out either. Sure would be nice to have a mom at home."

"I know, Rudi. Be good for me, too. Same person. All the time." But Erich still liked variety, so he wasn't quite sure how serious he was about what he'd just said.

On Saturday afternoon, Brenna showed up at about one o'clock and it was obvious that she was enthusiastic about picking up the framed tapa cloth and her opal ring. "I can hardly wait. This is like Christmas all over again. And I have you to thank. For all of it." She smiled warmly.

"I'd hate to see you get whipped into a frenzy too early in the day, so to help fill in the time until we pick up your stuff, you can come to the market with me. It's your lucky day."

"Oh, whoopee-doo! That's exactly the reason I came over early."

"Don't go getting feisty on me, or I'll take my opal back and give it to some really needy female person."

"That's describes me perfectly. It's too late for the ring though. The opal is already set. But I'll be glad to go with you. Just putting you on. After all you've done for me, how ungrateful could I possibly be?"

"That's better. Why don't we have a coffee first? I'll buy."

"You're full of charity. And you're right: it is my lucky day."

Having dispensed with their banter, Erich and Brenna went for their coffee, did the weekly shopping, and then went off to see Bruce at the framing shop.

"Hello, nice people. Happy New Year."

"Thanks. Same to you, Bruce. Do you have the tapa ready?"

"Yes, I do. And what a colossal hit it's been. I've had it in the window until about an hour ago, and all kinds of people have come in to ask about it. Did you bring the card with you?"

"Yep, have it right here. Name of the shop is Jack's Handicrafts. They just opened early last year. They're in Nandi, spelled N-a-d-i, which is where the international airport is."

Bruce took down all the contact information and then asked about the time difference.

"Let's see, it's seven hours earlier than Eastern Time," Erich told him. "It's morning down there."

"There's been enough interest in it during the nearly two days I had it in the window that I'm going to call the man. Lots of business potential judging from people's comments. Anyway, here it is, miss."

"Oh, Erich. I love it! Thank you. And thank you, Bruce, for the idea you had about matte glass over dark glass. It's perfect."

"Let me have the bill," Erich said.

"No, no. I'm paying for the framing," Brenna insisted. "You were so sweet to think of me, and to buy the tapa, so I'm not going to ask you to pay for the framing, too. I insist."

"Nope. You're picking up the tab on the other item, so this one's mine. Part of the deal."

"What else did you do for this pretty lady?" Bruce asked.

Brenna answered. "He brought back a black opal from Australia. It's spectacular, and we're on our way to pick it up from the jeweler, Brunning's, after we leave here. They've set for me."

"Not much doubt that he thinks you're special. Better reel him in while you can. He's a keeper, it sounds like."

"It's under review." Brenna turned to Erich, kissed him on the check, and added, "Thank you, Erich."

"You're welcome."

"I'd say it shows promise," Bruce observed. Erich and Brenna looked at each other and smiled.

"About the guy in Fiji, I was there a week ago Monday. If he doesn't remember the American who saw art in the tapa cloth, he'll sure as hell remember the Texans who walked out with a pile of these things. At least one I wanted went with them."

"I'll see if he remembers. Thank you so much for your help. To show you my appreciation, I've given you a discount. Think of it as your commission."

Erich paid Bruce and thanked him for the price reduction. Then he and Brenna left for Brunning's Jewelry.

The jeweler recognized Erich and Brenna and greeted them cordially.

"You're the gentleman who brought back the beautiful opal that I covet." He opened a drawer and pulled out a little box with the ring it. As he opened it, he asked, "What do you think, miss?"

"*Ohhh, Erich.* It's magnificent! How can I ever thank you?"

"Just be a good friend until you've had enough of me."

Happy tears welled up. "That's a long way off."

The jeweler smiled. "I'm pleased that you're happy with the setting and our work. Now, when it comes time for your diamond, we hope you'll keep Brunning's Jewelry in mind." Brenna returned his pleasant smile.

"Wouldn't consider anyone else," Erich said. "But that's a ways down the road yet. You'll still be here, I imagine."

"We're a family business that's been in the city since 1924, so we certainly expect to be."

When Brenna asked for the bill, the jeweler looked slightly puzzled. "It's our arrangement. This is one special guy. He bought the stone in

Australia and brought it all the way back with him last week. I'm paying to have it set. We share a lot, so it's fair."

"You're a rare couple. Unlike many of our customers, you seem to have things worked out. It's a good beginning in my opinion."

"Which finger?" Erich asked.

"We can talk about that on our way back to number 710."

Erich and Brenna thanked the jeweler, wished him a Happy New Year and then the two of them drove back to Mianus Ridge. In spite of what Brenna had said minutes earlier, she didn't have much to say and spent most of the time just looking at her new ring, still in the little box. As someone who liked nice jewelry, she mumbled about how beautiful it was and how proud she'd be to wear it. After they got up to 710, she said, "I didn't put the ring on at the jewelers because I wanted this to be a you and me thing."

"Which finger?" Erich asked.

"I thought about that on the way back. The sizing was done on my right ring finger, but they're both the same. Left ring finger, I decided. As a promise ring, it can mean either an engagement or that I'm monogamous. Since I'm not ready to be engaged, at least just yet, I'll settle for the other meaning. You're the only man in my life, other than Dad and the boys, so it applies. Whichever, I'd like you to do the honors."

Brenna handed Erich the box. He took the ring out and slipped it on her finger. What he'd just done touched her deep inside. When they hugged, she shivered for a instant.

"Tradition suggests that a kiss ought to accompany an important moment like this. Don't you agree?"

Misty eyed, she said yes, and they kissed gently. Afterwards, Brenna asked, "Whose tradition is that, by the way?"

"Mine. Is that okay?"

"Sure is. Could we do it again the same way?"

"Your servant, Miss Brenna."

"You remember I told you about the night I drove away from here when I was all warm and fluffy inside?" Erich nodded. "You've done it to me again. The time of day is all wrong, but I'd give anything if I could show you how I'd take those same feelings and turn them into something even more special. Until we get there, take my word for it. You're a sweetheart, and you've done so many nice things for me. I just want you to know how good I feel about having you as a lover and a lovable friend. No, you're more than that. Do you understand what I'm getting at?"

"I do. We're more than just friends, as you call it. You're so easy to be with, and every time we've been together, going back to late September, you've always left me with good feelings. And Rudi said just last night that he really likes you, but he guessed it wouldn't 'work out' for us either. He's hurting and is still looking for a mom."

"Sweet of him to say that, but he's on thin ice, I think, so I'll try to be here whenever I can."

"It isn't my intention that you share my problems, but your support is important. And I'll have to try extra hard to do what I can to keep Rudi from going bad. I agree. He's at risk; I sense it, too. But I didn't mean to get into this. Let me change direction and have a look at your ring again. Looks great from this angle. How do you like it so far?"

"You know I love it. And you too, I'm beginning to think. You've brought something into my life that I've never had before. Feels good."

"I want the guys to have the benefit of a woman's presence, but I'm still not convinced that I'm a very good candidate for marriage. And you aren't either, I think. So you and I need to start sorting things out. We talked about an overnight away. Remember? That could give us a little window in time to begin the process. Maybe we should pick a Saturday before long that we can sneak up to the Sturbridge area. Be fun to show you my little piece of land, too."

"I didn't forget. An overnight up there sounds like a great idea. Or anywhere else with you. I've been to the Village and know a little bit about the area. It's beautiful. Even in winter."

"My weekends coming up are mostly open," Erich said. "When I'm busy, I'll let you know. But I'm ready for a weekend when we can be off by ourselves. And maybe longer than that if we can figure out how to make it work. That tell you anything?"

"It does, and we see things the same way. But we're out on thin ice, too, you know."

"Meaning?"

"I'm getting more serious about us than I ever thought I would. You've been good for me, I'm finding out, and the boys like you, too. They don't say much to you directly, but they talk to me at home. And I thought you'd like their inspection report. They liked your apartment, even if there aren't any games around."

"Thanks for the report. Yeah, we've gotten beyond the toys and games stage. It's mostly wild music now. My tastes are different. As an example,

Mozart's music needs gentle treatment to be fully appreciated. Something to sooth the savage beast, as Mother has often said." Brenna smiled.

Suddenly the boys exploded through the door breathless and frozen to the bone. "Could we have chili tonight?" Kurt asked.

"We just had it not long ago. You want it again?"

"Yeah, it's freezin' out and snowing a little. Great night for it."

"What do you think, ma'am?"

"I agree with the guys. Sounds like a good idea."

"Hopefully the ground round we bought this afternoon hasn't turned into a rock already. Let me check." Erich went to the fridge, took out the meat and squeezed it. "Just in the nick of time. Okay, chili soup it is. Again."

Brenna helped and the end product got smiles all around the table. Even Erich decided it was a good suggestion. A couple of minutes out on the terrace was enough to convince him. He could see why the guys came in frozen. It had gotten bitter cold.

A quiet evening for Erich and Brenna ended with them steaming up his bedroom windows again. They took their pleasures to a new plateau and then slept like the satisfied lovers they were. Morning brought with it warm smiles and snuggling.

Later on, Brenna took her left hand from under the covers and stared at the elegant new ring she was wearing.

"It's just gorgeous. I can't thank you enough." She turned and gave him an affectionate hug. The look in her eyes was different from what he was used to seeing, and it told him everything he needed to know about what she was feeling.

"Glad you're happy with it. And I'm also pleased that you like the way the tapa framing turned out."

"It's so unique. But what can I say if anyone asks me about it? Do you know how it's made, or where it comes from in those islands you went to? You know what I mean."

"An early morning lesson of a different kind," Erich said.

Brenna giggled. "There *are* other things we can do in bed."

"Well, okay, let me see what I can remember. In Fijian, it's called Masi. Same name as the paper mulberry tree that the bark comes from. The best of it grows on an island called Vatulele, about twenty miles off the south coast of the main island, Viti Levu. That's where the international airport is, by the way. What the islanders do is strip the bark off the trees, soak it, and when it's soft, they beat on it. What happens is that it comes out as strips. They overlap them to come up with a single piece, one like you have, and then they beat on it again. I have no idea how it all stays together, but afterwards they let it dry in the sun. When it's cooked, they stencil designs on the cloth. Usually the colors are black and shades of tan and brown, but the interesting part is that the stencils are cut from banana leaves. It's a long process to get a piece of tapa the size of yours. Might take days. Now, you got all that?"

"If I forget any of it, I'll call you. That's some lesson. I'm impressed. You don't miss a thing."

"Be careful about calling me. You might interrupt something." Brenna punched him in the ribs and stuck out her tongue.

"That wasn't nice. Are you the same gal who's wearing my promise ring?"

"I am, I love it, and I'm keeping it right where it is. So there, hotshot." Then she leaned over and gave Erich a juicy kiss. "That's because you're special, just like my ring."

"Since you have to be outta here before noon, it's probably a good idea if we get going. The guys won't be up for a while, so we can be out of their way before they need to use the facilities."

"I'd really like to attack you again, but if I can work it out, I'll come back on Saturday and do it then."

"Best I check my calendar first to see if I'm free." That got Erich another punch in the ribs. This one harder than the first.

"Ouch, dammit!"

"Serves you right. You're being frisky," Brenna said. "No, you're being the same pain in the butt you were the day you left for Sydney. Please stop. It hurts. And after the nice things you've done, don't ruin it by saying stuff like that."

"Tell you what. To show you that my heart's in the right place after all, I'll initiate an attack, one that's gentler—assuming you're interested."

"Well, I don't know." That led to the two of them getting playful, at the end of which they settled down, kissed warmly, hugged affectionately, and held on.

"You're forgiven," Brenna said afterwards. "There couldn't be any better ending to our weekend than just holding each other close." She confirmed how she felt with another loving kiss.

After showers and breakfast, Brenna was on her way. Before she left, she promised to call and give Erich a report on the tapa hanging. "That's my excuse, but what I'll really want to do is just talk to you for a few minutes before I go to bed. You're getting to me, Erich Mauer, so maybe

I'd better cool it for a week or so. When I leave here, I'm going to feel a little empty. It's the end of the holidays, all the people around, you, and your wonderful gifts. I think you know what I mean."

"Sure do. Been a lot going on since December 9. Part of it is a pretty opal ring on the finger of a sweet lady who's special."

"Don't say any more. That's enough. I know how you feel."

"Let me go down with you."

Brenna said goodbye to the boys, and then she and Erich took the elevator to the garage.

When she was behind the wheel, she said, "This is another thing you've done for me. It's great getting into a car that isn't frozen solid. Thanks for everything. And Happy New Year, love."

"Tonight, maybe we can talk about that getaway weekend. Give you a few hours to think about it. And something else. If you're talking with Lara, find out what's up with her. I'm positive I saw her at the mall."

"I'll do it this week. Gotta run, sweetheart. Call you tonight."

"Bye, babe. Be careful." Erich kissed her tenderly, and she left for home.

Chapter Fifteen

Early on Sunday afternoon Erich got his affairs in order, picked up the tapa cloth, the little box with Tina's ring in it, and then got down to the station to board the train to Grand Central at half past one. It felt strange. He hadn't gone into Manhattan since he and Lara said goodbye outside the station in early December. Stranger still, it was a weekend. He realized on the way into Manhattan that it would all begin anew tomorrow, and a year with doubts about his future was facing him. He knew that saying goodbye wasn't going to be easy, but there would be no repeat of the trauma that both he and Tina suffered when she left for Washington last March. They were certain that it would be the last time they'd ever see each other. Life sure is unpredictable, he thought.

At Grand Central, Erich took the Forty-second Street Shuttle, and a Number 1 IRT train to Penn Station. He arrived just after three o'clock. When he got to the area near the departure board, Tina and her dad were waiting for him. She and Erich smiled, and she rushed to meet him. Tina was absolutely glowing. They hugged with a longing that clearly said they wanted to take their feelings to another level.

"Hi, sweet. Radiant as you look, one might think you're in a family way."

"It's just that it's wonderful to see you. And don't I wish we could make that happen, but we both know it won't. What I'm showing you is how good it feels to have you hold me. And I can tell you're stirred up a little."

"You weren't supposed to notice that."

"If I hadn't, I'd have to be at death's door. Oooh, I wish we could go off in a dark corner somewhere so I could look after you. But I'll be back in two weeks. Hope we can hold out that long."

"Seems we don't have much choice."

"Come on. Papa wants to meet you."

Tina took Erich by the hand and led him to the place where her father was waiting. He'd seen how the two of them had greeted each other and was smiling broadly as they walked toward him. Erich now knew where Tina got her captivating smile. Her dad was ruggedly handsome and had one of his own. In his day he wouldn't have had any shortage of young ladies chasing after him. Erich was sure of it.

"Papa, I'd like you to meet Erich, the most important man in my life, other than you. Erich, this is my papa, Aldo."

"Mr. Conti, this has been a long time coming, but I guess that up until now there wasn't any need for us to meet. I'm glad it's finally happened, and the reasons why it has." Erich looked at Tina and smiled warmly.

"Good to meet you, Erich. And call me Aldo. I use your first name because I saw your picture, and Tina has said lotsa nice things about you. I think I know you pretty good by now. You had a great tan in that picture she showed me. I guess New York water washed it off."

"It doesn't take long, either here or in Seaford. Why don't we go have a coffee and get to know each other a little better?"

They found a coffee shop, ordered, and made small talk until they were served.

"You know, what I can't believe is your age," Aldo said. "You don't look any older than Tina. You must come from good blood."

"A hardy bunch, pioneers, and I think you already know that my people live a long time. My father died young. He was only seventy-five, didn't look it, but as a young man he had a disease that weakened his heart. His brother, a doctor, was amazed that he lived as long as he did. I'll outlive him by a good many years. Count on it."

"That's no worry. But no kids, huh? Ahh, no big deal either. My boys have made sure there'll be Contis after me. The important thing is if Tina and you decide to get married that you treat her right. She's my baby and a good kid. I don't want to hear about any abuse. I'm a cop up in the Bronx 48th Precinct, and I won't stand still if anything happens to her. You follow? I see a lot of it up there, but I think you're okay so I won't spend a whole lotta time thinkin' about it."

"No reason to because I'm not made that way. Never happened in our family. That kind of behavior isn't acceptable, and no woman deserves it. If Tina misbehaved, then she'd be on her own. I wouldn't put up with it, but a beating doesn't fix the problem. It'd only make it worse. Anyway, I don't have it in me to do something like that. You hear what I'm saying? And it's a two way street; I wouldn't cheat on her. She wouldn't deserve that either."

"I like you, Erich. You talk straight from the head, and I think you and Tina would do good. You don't have to ask my permission to go ahead. You have it if the two of you think it would make you happy. She is already, I can tell you. I never seen her look so good. She didn't with that guy she was engaged to. I'm glad you drove him off."

"I didn't have much to do with that. Tina was the one who pulled the plug on him."

"You had everything to do with it. She told me about the nights she spent with you around the holidays last year. My missus, Maria, and me don't agree with what you did, but times have changed, and it's what young people do these days. We don't have much to say about what's right anymore, and we can't do nothin' about what's already been done. If you love each other, and marry, then it don't matter much anyway."

Tina blushed a little at the frank discussion that was going on. She smiled and squeezed Erich's arm to let him know that she was all right.

"Before you go, Aldo, I have something, a present, that I brought back from Australia. It's finished now and ready for delivery."

Erich pulled the pretty little box from his pocket and handed it to Tina. When she opened it, her eyes got as big as saucers.

"*Ohhh*. It's gorgeous. Thank you, Erich, thank you. Would you take it out and put it on my finger?"

"Which one? You hadn't made up your mind when we talked about it the other night."

"I'll let you guess. Do you know which one I had it sized on?"

"Sure do. Left hand, please." Erich slipped the opal on her ring finger and then looked up at Tina. She glanced at her father first. He smiled and nodded, so with his blessing they shared a quick kiss.

"One other thing. You remember my saying that I brought back something from Fiji? Well, here's the rest of your Christmas." He brought out the tapa and showed it to the two of them.

"It's really different. What is it?"

Erich told them the story and then suggested how it might be framed.

"Would you do it for me?"

"I know a guy in Seaford who'll be happy to turn it into something you'll be proud to hang on a wall."

"Since I'm coming home before too long, why don't you have it done and then just keep it for me. No point in my taking it down to Washington and then having to ship it back."

"Glad to. It'll be ready when you come home. Oh, there's one other thing. Here are the enlargements you asked for. Sure ought to be enough of 'em." Erich said, chuckling. "Want to give one to your dad? Before long, you won't need any of them. You'll have me to look at, assuming you're still interested."

Tina leaned over and gave Erich a kiss on his cheek.

"Well," Aldo said, "you kids need time to yourselves to say goodbye. I'm just in the way. Erich, I think you and Tina will be okay. You come across as a good man. In my job, I sometimes have to think fast and decide who is and who isn't. You're okay in my book. Thanks for the coffee. I hope you'll come see us and meet my Maria. Tina, you have a good trip back to D.C., and I want you to stay in touch. I'm real glad to know you're coming home. That's because of you, Erich, so I have you to thank. Be good to have my little girl back in the neighborhood. I never liked the idea of her being so far away."

"I'm really pleased that we could meet and have some time to get acquainted. Tina is one very special lady, and I hope it'll work out that we can spend the rest of our years together. Time will tell us more about that. Anyway, thanks for coming down, Aldo. That's special, too. I've enjoyed it." They shook hands, and then Tina walked with her father toward a Seventh Avenue exit. They talked for a couple of minutes, and then she came back to sit with Erich until it was time to board.

"You're a hit with Papa," Tina said. "He thinks you're right for me, that you're the kind of man I need in my life. Never mind the babies. My maternal instinct is still there, like you said it would be, but I have to agree with him. I do listen to Papa's advice. It's most always been good."

"Like I said a year ago, the final decision is yours. You know what I can be, what I can do, and what I can't. And you also know how I feel."

"I'm coming home, Erich. It's the first step, and that should tell you where my heart is. I'll be up in two weeks, unless there's something at work I have to deal with. The time has come to be the woman in your life. Every day."

"I like that. I'll plan on you coming up late on the sixteenth, but let me know for sure."

"I will. Now, I probably ought to get aboard. It's about time."

Erich took Tina's bag, found her coach, and then got her situated.

"How much different can this be from last March? You crying, me with tears welling up. God was that painful. But the ghosts are gone. We've got the chance now to spend our years together. What a change, and it feels good. And all of this because you saw me looking at newspaper headlines at a hotel in Australia. Isn't life full of surprises?"

"It is, but there should be fewer of them now," Tina said. "I truly believe that our meeting again was meant to be. We've got each other again, and the love we never lost. We've been given another chance. Let's build on it."

"We will, and more than anything I want us to have all of what we thought would never be."

"I hate to see you get off, my sweet, but if you don't you'll be going with me at least as far as Newark. You don't need that. I love you, mister. Very much. I'll call you when I'm home just so I can hear you say you love me."

"I can do that that now *and* again this evening. I love you, Tina. As I look back on our days at Essex, I guess I can say, deep down inside, that I probably always have."

They held each other for a moment, shared a tender goodbye kiss, and then Erich got off her car. As the Metroliner pulled out, they waved and mouthed, "I love you."

Train Number 109 was quickly gone from view. Then as Erich started his trip back to Seaford, he had that same empty feeling that was always there after having said goodbye to someone special. But starting tomorrow, his personal affairs and feelings would have to take a back seat to what was expected of him at IMCO. The first workday of the new decade would begin in less than eighteen hours. The holidays and his vacation were over.

When Erich got home, he stirred up a drink and then moved to his living room window to enjoy the view, a virtual carpet of twinkling lights all across town. The scene was mesmerizing and it caused him to reflect on all that had happened since he'd left this room with Lara nearly four weeks ago. Tina was on his mind now. And well she might be because of how they felt about each other and the possibility that they would marry. It would be up to her to decide, finally, if she could forever abandon the idea of having her own family. She'd just about gotten to that point. On the other hand, she might have second thoughts although that now seemed unlikely. But Brenna was the unknown quantity, the variable. She was beginning to feel, Erich thought, that their friendship had substance and that it might have the makings of a solid long-term union. He could neither dispute that nor ignore the fact that their fondness for each had grown. For his part, it wasn't the kind of feeling he had for Tina, but there was something unique about what he and Brenna had shared in recent weeks. If he were to define their relationship, he'd call it mature. Then in a rare moment of candor, he considered that it might very well make for a better marriage. Part of it had to do with the fact that they were closer to the same age, both had children, and clearly understood much of what parenting entailed. But before he could give more thought to the subject, the phone rang.

"Erich? Brenna."

"Hi, babe. What's up?"

"I just wanted you to know that the tapa looks great, and it adds so much to the far wall of the living room. Thanks for helping me redecorate at least one little part of the house. The other reason I'm calling is to tell you that you've been on my mind. A lot. I really enjoyed what we did yesterday—and this morning. I said I wasn't going to let myself get like this, but the truth is that you're under my skin. It's another way of saying that I think maybe I'm at least a little bit in love."

"I hear you, and I share some of those same feelings. But with both of us going back to work after the break, we won't have as much time together. What it means to me is that things will be back to normal and the matter of where we are today will have a chance to settle in some. A little breathing room will be helpful for both of us, I think. What I don't want you to do is misinterpret my meaning. I care about you, Brenna. Probably more than I should given what we've both said right from the start. You understand that because you said about the same thing."

"My problem, if I can call it that, is that I want to spend more time with you, not less. I like what we have when we're together, even when you're being frisky and a pain in the backside. That's because it's part of the whole picture and all of the things we do that make us different. With Jordie, I never had any of those fun moments. You're playful sometimes and that's new to me. It adds a lot to what we have going for us. You bring something to a relationship that I've never known before. It isn't news, but I have to say it again. I really like spending time with you."

"Those are lovely thoughts, Brenna. I'm beginning to understand what's in your heart."

"Me too, but what I've said about us is probably more than I should've. Well, almost. I'm looking at my new ring and starting to think of it as more than a symbol that says I'm monogamous. I don't want to call it an engagement ring, but I don't want to reject that as a possibility either. Whichever, I'm in love with it. Wait till I show the people I work. Maybe I'll tell them it's an engagement ring just to rattle their cages a little."

"Glad you were happy with your Christmas. Makes me feel good that you liked the things I gave you and that they've helped make you smile. But I'm fresh out of trips to Australia, I'm afraid, so you'll have to settle for domestic stuff from now on. Next trip, if I still have a job, is to London this spring. You'll have a birthday before then, so I'll have to see what I can bring back."

"You're still too much. And just because of it, I'm going to order up some good dreams about you tonight. Sure glad I invited you to my bed back in mid-October. I'd have missed out on a lot of special nights. On top of that, I couldn't have known then that you'd turn out to be the kind of sweetheart you are."

"Easy, babe. But mid-October? You remember the date, too?"

"Friday night, October 17. The time? Just after ten o'clock."

"And you say I'm too much? Guess I made a good impression."

"By now it should be pretty obvious. And my feelings have grown since we met and had that quickie dinner at The Ingleside."

"That was September 26. But you know I have good feelings for you, too. How 'bout we organize a repeat on Friday or Saturday night?"

"There you go again. You have to know I would. I'll work it out so I can stay over on Saturday night again. So much for coolin' it. I'd rather not. Seeing you on weekends is a much better idea than letting everything settle down.

"We'll talk again during the week," Erich said. "Call me when you can. You know I'm usually home by seven or a little after."

"Gotta make dinner for the boys. I'm late getting it started. Thanks again for all you've done and for being the kind of guy who makes me feel good."

"Nice to hear that, Brenna. It gives my inflatable ego a big boost. Let's make sure we talk again before the weekend."

"We will. Night, guy."

After Erich and the boys had eaten, he started getting himself organized to begin his first workday of the new year. At about nine o'clock, Tina called.

"Hi, sweet. I'm home and wanted you to know that I'm okay."

"I imagine you're tired, but I'm glad you didn't have any problems along the way."

"Not a one."

"Hard to believe that just two weeks ago you were on your way back to D.C., and I was hours away from picking out your opal."

"On the way down, I spent more time looking at it than reading or looking out the window. The colors are incredible. I'm so pleased with it."

"Looked great on your finger, too."

"Won't keep you too long, sweet. I know you'll be getting ready for bed soon, and there's a lot I still have to get done here before I can, too. Have to tell you that the three-hour ride gave me a chance to think about you, and me, and my job, and I decided that I'll wait until about the first of March to give notice. My last day would be April 3, so it would be a little more than thirty days. That ought to be enough time, don't you think?"

"Thirty days, or even half that, is generally acceptable. Depends on the company and how important the employee is. Their reaction to your notice could be anywhere from you can clean out your desk now to we'd like you to stay on for another month."

"I imagine it'll be the latter. I won't know until I've told them I'm leaving."

"Let me know how they react. But, a thought. Any chance they'd let you transfer up here? That way, you could stay on with the company."

"Two things. First is that what I do and what goes on in New York are completely different so I'd never fit any of their openings. The other is, I'd like my next move to be into what I know best. Placement. I learned an awful lot from you."

"It kinda grows on you. You'd be good at it. I was never much interested in what else goes on in personnel, so I understand. Completely. But back to us. See you in a couple of weeks?"

"I plan on being up the evening of the sixteenth, like we talked about, and then come back on the same Metroliner I took today. They might let me take the 4:30 train from here. That would put me into Penn Station at around seven thirty."

"And in Seaford at about nine o'clock. Late dinner."

"You remember that I do make trips to the New York office once in a while. I always tried to work it out so that it was a Friday. That way I could leave on Thursday evening or the really fast train early on Friday morning. I've done it before, and I'm in town at ten o'clock. It's been a way for me to visit the family on the weekend and have the trip paid for."

"Clever. But we have time. Just tell me what the plan is, and I'll be there."

"Not sure I mentioned it before, but with an office there we have a New York line. I'll be able to talk to you for a few minutes when it's free. It's just like the Pennsylvania line we had at Essex. If I remember right, you used to call the woman who'd been your high school sweetheart. Didn't you say she lived in Germantown?"

"You've got a mind like a steel trap. But you're not supposed to commit things like that to memory. It's ancient history."

"I really should get going, hon. I'll need to hear your voice, so expect me to call you sometime this week on our direct line. I miss you. Sweet dreams."

"Miss you, too, dear heart. Sleep well. Night."

"Love you, mister."

Erich had enjoyed the last twelve days off too much to be ready for an early alarm and then to be standing on the station platform in the freezing cold. His memories of Fiji were too fresh, and the lure was still there. The boys were grumpy, too, so all the Mauer guys were resisting getting back into their routines.

By the time Erich got to the office, Katie was at her desk and beaming.

"Happy New Year, Erich."

"And to you, gal. What's with the big smile?"

"Found me a man over the holidays. Knows how to keep me from starving, so you're off the hook. Partly."

"Love you dearly, Katie, but I was never on it. That was all in your head. We're a good couple, but only at 4 New York Plaza. I'm pleased for you if you think this is the right thing to do."

"Thanks, Erich. I just want to know at least some of the happiness you've found. You saw Tina over the holidays?"

"She was out for a couple of days right before New Year's Eve, and then I saw her off at Penn Station late yesterday afternoon. What a difference from last March 29. Her dad came with her."

"Sounds serious, then."

"Yes and no. He thought we should meet since all Tina did over the holidays was talk about me. She showed him a picture that was taken on Sydney Harbor. He couldn't believe I'll be forty in April and wanted to see for himself, I guess. You know about my vanity, so I have the same photo with me so I can show total strangers how good I looked in late December." Erich laughed. "Here. This is the same one Tina showed her dad."

"What a great picture. I can see why he said what he did."

"He thinks I look closer to her age. I'd show you why he said that, but I don't have one of her. It's an oversight that I'll fix when she comes up."

"Oh, I finally remembered your Christmas gift." Katie giggled. "It's on your desk."

Katie followed Erich into his office and sat down across from him while he opened his present. It was an English Leather set with aftershave, stick deodorant, and soap on a cord.

"Ahhh. Thanks, Katie. You know the aftershave is one of my favorites. And the soap is special. But I guess you think I must need a good scrub now and then."

"Wouldn't know. I'm not that close to you very often, and it looks like that won't change anytime soon."

"Shouldn't matter. You've got a new stud looking after you. Hopefully there's more to it than that."

"Longer term, I'm not really sure. He's a good-looking guy, Greek heritage, so I'm guessing there's competition. I like him, though. It all happened kinda fast. We'll see how it goes."

"You know I hope it works out. It's time you had some good news on the romance front."

"The same with you. Your path hasn't exactly been smooth, but things do sound better."

"By the way," Katie said, "you were going to tell me what it was that got Joel so worked up just before you came back. He's still not in a very good mood. Something's going on, and I can't find out what it is. Do you know?"

"I have a fairly good idea, but it isn't open for discussion. I've been told to keep my mouth shut, so I can't talk about it. Sorry."

"Sounds like it isn't good news, and with the way Joel's been acting, I'm guessing it'll affect our department in some way. Any chance at all that I'm gonna lose my partner?"

"Could be, Katie. But your question doesn't have an answer, so let it be. Next item on my travel agenda is London in April. Not much I have to do for that one. Trip's short anyway."

Erich started the new year with a call to Clayton "Great hearing from you." After they'd talked for a couple of minutes, Clayton said, "I'm off to a meeting. We need to get together. It's been a while. How about Friday at our old place, The Watering Hole?"

"Sure. I'll try to leave here at about five if that's okay. Got lots to tell you. If you're sitting down and don't have anything sharp in your hand, I have a bombshell to drop on you."

"You got married over the holidays."

"No, but it might happen one of these days. I ran into Tina in Sydney. Can you believe it? We're back together."

"No! Impossible. You *do* have news. I've got to hear the whole story. But I have to run. See you on Friday at about five thirty?"

"Perfect. I'll be there."

Then Erich called Nate Kaplan.

"Nate. It's Mauer. Remember me?"

"You bet, Erich. What's behind the call? Trouble?"

"Could be. Lara is history, I'm sorry to say. Her decision. Rudi was very fond of her, as you know, and he's taking it hard. I just wanted to alert you to the possibility of trouble brewing. He may have been on another downer recently, but there wasn't any way I could prove it, at least to my satisfaction. What I'm worried about is that he might try to fix whatever he's feeling with something really heavy. He's brittle, and at the snap of a finger I think he could break away from being mostly clean. A friend of Lara's, Brenna Walsh, told him to stay away from her because he'll only wind up being hurt more. Brenna's been a wonderful stand-in, and I'm grateful for all her support. She and Lara grew up together, but she can't figure out what's going on."

"We get all kinds of reports, and I can't figure it out either. Maybe you don't remember, but Lara, Brenna, and I were in school at the same time. Our network is pretty good, but I also hear a lot of things of a personal nature, talk that goes on outside my regular sources. The stories I've heard about Lara trouble me. She's changed somehow. Brenna's solid, and I'm glad to know that you're friends. Given your appeal, I assume there's more to it than that. At the same time, I'm awfully sorry to hear that Lara's turned her back on you and the boys. It might've been good for all of you."

"She has an uncle up in Worcester who has cancer, her mother isn't at all well, and she's convinced that she'll lose anybody who's important to her. Before my last trip to Australia about a month ago, Lara said she cared about me too much to watch me die. That's really off the wall. Doesn't matter. It's where her head is. I'll outlive her, but that's beside the point. The other part of it is, she's all caught up with her businesses now and they've become her lover. Anyway, we're way off the subject of why I called. Romance counseling isn't your department. What I need from you is input from your sources about what Rudi is up to should you hear anything. Second, I need a number where I can reach you in case I've got a crisis on my hands."

"Sure, Erich. You can call me at 323-3232 anytime, day or night. At times we're like the fire department. Call me right away if you have a problem."

"Thanks, Nate. I really appreciate having your help. You've got a worried dad on your hands, so I'd like to be wrong about what my gut feeling is telling me."

"Hope so, but I appreciate your call. I'll let you know if we turn up anything. I'd like you to do the same."

"You got it. Thanks again."

"You're welcome, Erich."

Erich and Katie got right back into their routine as they started the new year. It was business as usual and, like a finely crafted watch, things ran smoothly. Throughout the week the two of them were kept busy with projects and requests that had piled up while Erich was away. They worked long days with few interruptions, so it was a welcome break when Tina called late on Wednesday afternoon. They didn't talk long, but she wanted Erich to know that she missed her man and that she loved him dearly. He was pleased to hear from her. And then Friday was upon them almost before they knew it. After Erich and Katie wished each other a good weekend, he went uptown to meet Clayton.

When Erich walked into The Watering Hole, Clayton was waiting and he greeted him with, "You still have good color. Must've been a deep tan two weeks ago."

"You know about my extra-large ego, so I just happen to have a photo taken out on Sydney Harbor four days before Christmas."

"Nobody should look that healthy in December. It's obscene. But what's the story on Tina? There isn't any way two people could run into each other on the other side of the planet."

"I know, and we agree, completely, but it happened. She spotted me and I nearly collapsed from shock. And she looks terrific. Hasn't married, and doesn't even have anyone she's interested in. Except me. The love never died, and we're going to have another shot at it. She's maybe, repeat *maybe*, given up on the idea of having her own family. Our being together seems to be more important now. As you might expect, we had a couple of fabulous evenings in Sydney trying to make up for lost time. We're both hoping it'll work. She had her dad bring down her to Penn Station last Sunday. He wanted to meet me, and I guess he thinks I'm okay because he said he didn't have any objections if we decide to tie the knot. Could happen." Erich then told Clayton the whole story about the way they met, how they spent their two days together after they got back from Australia, and the general details about Tina's planned return to New York.

"It's a perfectly delightful story, Erich. Maybe when I get to TWN, we can do a human-interest piece. You have to be ecstatic. But what's happened to Miss Lara?"

"She's gone off the deep end." He explained to Clayton how that came about, and that he was still seeing Lara's friend, Brenna. "She says she isn't interested in a husband, so you understand the kind of relationship we have. How's your love life?"

"I'm onto the new lady, Nicole. I mentioned her just before you left for Sydney. She was with me on the Cape. Had a good time. It could be serious. Like you, we'll have to wait and see. I do go out with Judy once in a while, but it looks as if it's about to be a thing of the past."

"If I didn't have so much going on, I might chase after her. She's a cutie."

"She'd probably be pleased if you called. One night she told me she thought you were the cat's whiskers. Not exactly sure what that means, but it sounded positive." The two friends shared a chuckle about her comment.

"You have a new job, then, if I understand your comment about a human interest story."

"Last day in the retailing business is on the thirtieth. I start with TWN on February 9, after I've had a week in the Caribbean sun. It'll be your turn to be envious. I'm taken with the idea of being a part of the media business. Ought to be interesting. You'll have to drop by so I can take you on a tour."

"I'd like that. The one reminder I want you to stick on your 1970 calendar, now that you have one, is to have a drink with me on my fortieth coming up in April. It's a Tuesday, but maybe we can have a couple of 'em to get my evening off to a good start."

"It's a ways off, but it's a milestone and I'll buy."

"And I'll drink. I've got a trip to London coming up sometime in April, but I'll work it out so that I'm back before the twenty-eighth. Now, sorry to cut this short, but I've got to be on my way. There are two hungry mouths in Seaford that need to be fed. Late as it is, I'll probably have to spring for a pizza. I called to let them know that I wouldn't be in until about seven thirty. Been great seeing you again, Clayton. Now that the holidays are over, let's do this more often. We always have news of one kind or another, and I'll be interested in hearing more about you and your Nicole."

"Couldn't agree more. We've stayed in touch, and we'll keep it that way. Sorry to hear about Lara, but Tina is the best news I've heard in ages. You're happy, and it shows.

"Nearly forgot to mention that Tina said to give you her best. She wanted me to tell you that she comes up to her company's New York office once in a while and hopes that on one of her trips we could have dinner with you."

"Love to. Be wonderful to see her again. I always thought she was a very special young lady."

178

"Tell me about it. She'll be coming up to Seaford on weekends as often as she can arrange it, but I'm going to be selfish and keep her to myself."

"I understand completely and agree that it's exactly the way it should be. Any idea when she'll be moving back here?"

"Like I said earlier, about the beginning of April. At least that's the plan. She'll give notice somewhere around the first of March."

"I'd like to talk with her when she's back. It might be that I could help her get situated."

"You know she isn't a secretary any longer. She's gone into administration and it'll be hard, if not impossible, to roll her back."

"No, no. I'm going to need an executive assistant at TWN, and she'd be what I'm looking for to fill the job. She's bright, attractive, and good with people. A good match."

"I know she'd like to get into placement. Seth McIvers told her before he left Essex that she should contact him if she ever gave serious thought to doing that."

"There's time to work things out. Maybe when she's up, say sometime in March, I could come out to Seaford to talk with her. Wouldn't want to do that over dinner."

"Good idea, Clayton. Now, I've got to run. See you again soon?"

"I'll call you one of these days. Say hi to your guys."

"Thanks. I will. And you to your girls, too."

"Take care, Erich."

Chapter Sixteen

Brenna spent Saturday night at number 710, and it was as always enjoyable for both of them. It was also clear that her feelings continued to grow and that Erich and his sons had become an even more important part of her life.

Over Sunday morning coffee, Brenna said, "We can't be doing this every weekend; otherwise we might as well head for a church. But neither of us is ready for that."

"I wouldn't worry about things getting out of hand. There's too much up in the air for me to think about anything permanent. I'm concerned about Rudi, and my job at IMCO is decorated with question marks. Another snag is that we can't live together to find out if what we have would work. But it's obvious that I enjoy the time we spend together."

Brenna agreed. "You've gotten to be really important, and I see it as the same kind of problem Lara had. I heard too many of her stories not to recognize the similarity. You're special to me, just like you were to her. Thing is, she didn't have a family. So, like you said, what we can and can't do isn't the same. But if you want me here every weekend, I'll do all I can to make it happen. That may not be fair to Alan and Scot, though. They have a right to expect that I'll spend time with them on Saturdays and Sundays when they aren't with Jordie."

"One option is dinner out on Friday evenings. After we're back, and they're in bed, I could stay on for a while," Erich suggested.

"I like the idea, except that I'd want you all night. Still, it's a middle ground of sorts. And there would be our weekends when Jordie has the boys. Sure. It'd work, I think. Maybe we could start with dinner tomorrow evening." They both chuckled.

"Not much delay in checking it out. Love it." Erich smiled.

"I meant to tell you about Lara after I got here yesterday, but I had other things on my mind." Brenna showed him an impish smile. "I called Lara at her shop and found out what's going on. First, her uncle died. It was New Year's week. She and her mother stayed on and came back last Monday. Lara said her mother's taking her brother's death very hard and isn't at all well. She's certain she won't last long."

"Lara thinks the same thing about me, you know, but she shouldn't worry about my longevity. It's in the genes."

"By the way, you did see Lara at the mall. The contractors had some questions and they wanted her there to spell out exactly what she wanted done in the new shop. She came down and went back by train. All the same day, the way it sounded. But she said something troubling. It was that she saw you with someone and was sure it was your Tina from Essex. She also confirmed that she'd said her final goodbye at the station before you left for Australia. So she intentionally tried to avoid you at the mall. Was it Tina?"

"It was. I saw Lara out of the corner of my eye, and she wouldn't have known it. I never turned and looked at her directly. She did a quick about face and then vanished. But I knew that her having seen Tina wasn't something I could hide under a rug of any size."

"Well, that was the final nail in the coffin. In spite of it, she still cares about you but would never have you back. "

"Considering her obsession with the idea that anyone she cares about dies, we have no future. I couldn't live under a cloud like that. The end."

"I thought you told me Tina was gone and that you didn't know where she lived, or even the company she worked for."

"All I knew was that she'd been hired by the U.S. subsidiary of an Australian company and then moved to Washington last March. I saw her off at Penn Station. How it happened is unbelievable; we ran into each other in Sydney. I wouldn't have bet anything on the odds of something like that happening. But it did. I could've said Lara was wrong, and denied it, but you're entitled to the truth. You mean too much to me to lie about what happened and then have you eventually find out that's what I'd done."

"Thanks for being honest. But where does that leave me?"

"In exactly the same place you were last night, and this morning, and where you are at this moment. Tina's aim right along has been to have a family. You know I can't make that happen. She's back in Washington now, and I'm right here. With you for the moment. Longer, maybe, if you think that makes any sense for the two of us and our guys."

"You're serious."

"I am, to the extent I'm able to be given my relatively uncertain future at IMCO."

"And if I'm not?"

"Then life goes on. We could see each other, if you want, just as we have since last September. But if Tina gives up on her idea of having babies, then she and I have something that could work. I'm fifteen years older than she is. That doesn't seem to bother her, but I can't disregard it. In the meantime, she's there and I'm less than twenty minutes from your front door. If you need to know that you're important, I'm here to tell you that you are."

"That pretty much hits it head on," Brenna said. "You'd have to be blind not to know how much you mean to me, so I either have to accept the situation as it is or do what Roxane did and walk away."

Erich reached across the table and held Brenna's hands. "I meant what I just said. Please don't forget it."

"I'm not into tears very often, but you've got me close. What I need is for you to hold me. That'll help, I think."

"Can't do that sitting at the kitchen table." They stood and Erich took Brenna in his arms. The bonus that came with his affectionate hug was a warm kiss that confirmed how much he cared about her.

"You've given me a lot to think about, Erich Mauer. Tina is a surprise, and I don't like having her complicate things. Not one bit. But if you think it's possible that we might fit into each other's plans someday, then I'll try to manage." Brenna looked at her ring and added, "This opal says a lot about your feelings for me."

"It was more than just a simple gift because it came with an awful lot of affection attached. Think of it that way. Always."

"I know, and I do. It's special. Now, I really don't want to break this up, but I've got to get back to the house before Jordie brings the boys home. He must have something going on. This is the second Sunday he's wanted his afternoon free. One thing I'm going to do is make sure he sees my new ring. I'll let you know how he reacts."

"We'll talk later on. Better yet, tonight before we turn in."

Brenna said goodbye to Kurt and Rudi, and then Erich went with her to the garage.

"Thanks for another wonderful Saturday night and Sunday morning. They're so important to me. A repeat sometime soon?"

"You bet," Erich said. "We'll get into that and also our weekend away. It's never came up, but for sure it won't be in January. Maybe when the weather's warmer. Give it some thought."

With a wave, Brenna drove off and left Erich wondering what the hell he was doing, again, by caring about two lovable women at the same time. Outwardly, it might appear to be an unanswered question, but his subconscious knew exactly what was going on. Life's so uncertain, and he was keeping his options wide open.

Just after dinner, Tina called.

"I just had to hear your voice. I miss you and wish I could be there to share your night. But I also have to tell you that I'm being sent off to Atlanta on Thursday and won't be back in time to come up next Friday afternoon. I'm really upset because I'm overdue for a big bear hug. Would I be welcome next weekend?"

"You know the answer to that, dear heart. And I'm sorry, too. But just you wait. When we're together, we'll make it worthwhile."

"Easy, Erich. You're stirring things up, and I don't need any help with that. About the weekend of the twenty-fourth, I'm going to ask for Friday afternoon and will try to be on the Metroliner that gets into Penn Station at four. I'll come straight to your office and say hello to your Katie just so she can see who her competition is."

"No such thing. She's found herself a hot-blooded Greek who's looking after her. It may not last, but she seems to be enjoying herself while the bed's warm. Anyway, getting in earlier gives us a good start to our weekend. Makes it worth the wait."

"Got to go Erich. I haven't eaten yet, and for a change I'm hungry. For you, too, but this is different. I'll call you at the office before I go to Atlanta and then early next week. Hearing your voice helps keep me going. Take care of yourself and count the days. I'll be there before you know it."

"Night, sweet."

"Night, Erich. Love you."

Later in the evening, Brenna called to say good night and also to tell Erich that she got a rise out of Jordie about the new ring.

"He doesn't want me, but he acted like he doesn't want anybody else to have me either. Selfish S.O.B. And he really got irritated when I told him about us when the lights were out. I said you'd forgotten more about all the ways you could make me smile than he'd ever learn. He tried to peel rubber when he left, but all he did was kill the engine on that old Chevy he drives. Then he had trouble restarting it. I was so tickled that I was nearly on the floor."

Erich enjoyed Brenna's replay and got a good laugh out of it. But there was more to her story.

"The tapa, and all I could tell him about it, ticked him off, too. He doesn't know who you are, but he knows you travel all over the world, and I think he's feeling small town. I suppose one day he'll try to get your name out of either Alan or Scot. I've asked them to play dumb because it would only hurt me if he got on my case. I won't keep you, but I wanted you to know that I stuck it to him when he brought the boys back."

"Hope I don't ever get crossways with you. You can be ferocious when you want to be. But I'm glad you called. Now I can sleep in peace. Sweet dreams, babe. Call when you have the urge. I'd really like it if you did."

"Night, lover. And thanks again for a cuddly overnight."

The routine during the first weeks of the new year fell into a pattern. There was the usual activity in the office, then a wonderful weekend visit by Tina starting on January 23, another over the Valentine's Day weekend, and generally his Saturdays with Brenna.

Then on the first Monday in March, Tina called to say that she'd given notice and wanted Erich to know what had happened.

"It caught them by surprise," Tina said, "But they took it well, I thought. They countered with an offer to have me move to our headquarters in Sydney. It would be a big promotion, but they didn't seem willing or able to understand how important you are to me. Even if we didn't have each other, I couldn't do that to my parents. They think Washington is a long way off. As a compromise, I agreed to stay on until June 26. They want time to find a replacement, and then to have me handle most of the training afterwards. And I'm to be involved in the selection process. Right back into placement."

"My turn, babe. It's good to hear your voice, but it's been two and a half weeks, and I haven't heard a word from you. Sharing part of your time with somebody else?"

"Certainly not! You're jealous, Erich Mauer. And I'm of two minds about your question. It tells me you care enough to worry about something like that happening, but I'm also disappointed that you'd think that of me. I'm your girl, and you should know better than to let an idea like that cross your mind."

"Well it did because I don't deal with silence very well."

"It's totally out of character for you to be uncertain. Guess I'd better come up this weekend and help get you straightened out. And I know you'll like this, too. Part of the deal I made to stay on is that on the weekends I'm coming up to Seaford they'll let me take the afternoon so I can catch the one o'clock Metroliner. It means I can be at your office at a little after four. When we tried that back in January, and then again three weeks ago, it didn't work. This time it will, for sure, and I can finally meet your Katie. I hope you're not too upset about my decision to stay on."

"Not really, I guess. As your ex-boss, I can understand why they've asked for your help. And because you're the kind of person you are, it wouldn't be like you to turn your back on them. Looking at it selfishly, I'm sorry you won't be coming home sooner. The other part of it is that Clayton probably can't wait until early July to fill the job he wanted to talk over with you."

"I really want to get back into placement. I learned a lot from you, and it's what I'd like to do. We've talked about this before. I'll call McIvers one of these days and see if I can't meet with him sometime in May."

"Any interest in having an early dinner with Clayton on Friday?"

"Oh, yes. I'd like that. Be good to see him after almost a year."

"I know he's really looking forward to it, so I'll call him this afternoon to tell him it's a date."

"And just so you'll know, I've been given an okay to use the New York line whenever I want. I'll call you later in the week to find out what Clayton's dinner plans are. And I do want to meet Katie. Don't let her get away early."

"I'll tell her right after we're done. Like you said, the last two times you tried to come in on the earlier train, and then you couldn't make it, I know she was disappointed."

"This time I will. Promise. But thanks for not being grumpy about my having agreed to the extension."

"If things work out for us, thirty years from now we won't have missed the ninety days, unless between now and June 26 you find another man."

"There you go again. I'm not looking, and if anybody's looking for me, I can't be found. I have the guy I want. You're worrying too much. Please don't. No reason to."

"Okay, but it'll be reassuring to see you on Friday afternoon. And before you go, I had an idea. I'm going to London next month and will be flying back on the twenty-fourth. Why don't I come through Washington? It's the weekend before my fortieth, and we can celebrate together. You'll still be there. What do you think?"

"That'd be wonderful. I'll plan on it. We can talk about it this weekend."

"I'll nail down the flights by Friday so that you can have something firm to plug into your calendar."

"I don't need a calendar to remember something like that. Oops. Got to go, Erich. My manager is calling me. I'll tell him that my boss in New York has agreed to let me stay on and help out. He'll laugh about that. I'll also let him know that I won't be around on Friday afternoon. Talk to you on Wednesday or Thursday. And stop worrying. You're the only man in my life, and I couldn't love you more even if I tried. Remember that. Will you?

"Okay. I'm convinced."

"Good. Bye, my love."

"Bye, babe."

Erich passed the message along to Katie, and she was pleased to know that Tina would finally become a face she could attach to a name. He also talked with Clayton about an early dinner on Friday. "Wonderful! Be great to see her again. Will seven o'clock be okay? If so, I'll make a reservation at a restaurant near Grand Central. You'll want to get home at a reasonable hour so you can get reacquainted." Clayton chuckled.

"Appreciate it that you're concerned about our agenda. It'll have been three weeks, so you know I'm really looking forward to the weekend. But why don't we all have a drink first? You name the time and place."

"Why not The Watering Hole at around five thirty? Tina might like to see where we held some of our summit meetings."

"Done. She's to call later in the week. I'll let her know that we're all set for Friday evening. See you there at the appointed hour."

"Take care, Erich. Thanks for calling."

When Tina called on Wednesday, Erich told her that Clayton was expecting them to join him for an early dinner on Friday. They'd also agreed that he, and maybe a friend, would meet them for drinks before they went to eat. "The place we decided on was where we'd gone to hold our important after-work meetings during our Essex days." Tina was delighted. Erich also said Katie was really looking forward to finally meeting her.

"Exciting," Tina said. "All of it. Be there at a little after four the day after tomorrow. Be good to see you, mister, and to get a bear hug. I've really missed you this week."

"You shall have one, dear heart. Right in my office."

When Friday afternoon came, it all played out exactly as planned. Finally. Tina showed up at about four fifteen and Erich heard Katie say, "You have to be Tina."

"I am. And you're Katie. Erich said you remembered that I called you last year, so I'm glad we could finally meet. I've heard so much about you."

"And you. Since Erich came back from Sydney your name comes up every day. But you're not here to talk to me. Let's go find our boss."

"Hi, babe. I thought I heard another familiar voice out there. Come over here and let's have that bear hug." That was followed by a tender kiss. Katie smiled, and turned to go.

"Sure you don't want to stay and be a part of the audience? There are a couple of people in the building across the street who've been checking us out." They all chuckled and waved to the spectators. They waved back.

"I'll leave you two alone. When you're done hugging, maybe Tina and I could visit for a little while."

"Sure. In a few minutes," Erich said.

"She's a cutie," Tina said. "If I didn't know better, I'd be jealous. Hard to believe you haven't been tempted."

"Never more than that. If we bedded, she'd never let go. And you know as well as I do that you can't bring your personal life into the office. Let's change the subject. I haven't told you yet that you felt awfully good inside my bear hug. You've lost some weight, but you look good. Sure you aren't expecting?"

"You asked me the same thing at Penn Station in early January. No, not unless your plumbing system, or whatever, has been reconnected. But could I have another one of your hugs, please? You felt pretty good yourself. Having you hold me is the thing I miss the most when I'm there and you're here. Doesn't work very well over the phone."

They shared another hug, one they needed, and then Erich suggested, "Why don't you go have your girl talk with Katie. I've got a couple of things I need to finish up, and then I should be ready to go uptown at a little after five or so."

"Just as long as you're not trying to get rid of me."

"Not on your life. I've waited three weeks for this, and I've got you for the whole weekend."

"You sure have, because I'm not going back until Monday morning.

"Great! My kind of surprise."

"We'll talk about my schedule later. Now, I'm going visiting."

And visit they did until Katie said she had to go meet her Greek guy. And since it was nearly time for Erich and Tina to leave so they could keep their date with Clayton, it worked out perfectly. The girls said goodbye and Tina promised that she'd come back again soon.

On their way up to Grand Central, Tina said, "You know that Katie's crazy in love with you. I can relate to that. If she ever gets her claws into you, that'll be it. I'd never see you again."

"Takes two to tango, love. The light of my life is right beside me. And don't go promoting Katie, otherwise I might find out that she's something special, too, and there's no way I could handle two fiery ladies at the same time. And remember, I'll be forty at the end of next month. Almost over the hill."

"That'll be the day. You do very well for an antique." She attached a cute little giggle to her comment.

At Grand Central, they went through the tunnel to the Roosevelt Hotel entrance, then up the street and around a corner. When they got to The Watering Hole, Clayton was waiting.

"It's so good to see you, Tina," Clayton said as he gave her a quick hug. "You look wonderful. Should I assume this guy is responsible?"

"Entirely responsible, Clayton, and I'm so glad to see you, too. Who'd have ever thought this would happen?"

"No, who would have ever dreamed that the two of you would meet in Sydney? Talk about the odds. But it looks like it's the best thing that could've happened. I have to say that after you left Essex, you've never seen such a miserable looking guy as this one." He aimed a thumb in Erich's direction. "I was really worried about him. You both made a bad decision a year ago. I know the whole story. He laid it out for me right here at TWH. I assume he told you about it."

The three of them had drinks and then went on to dinner. One of the subjects that came up was Tina's ninety-day extension with her employer.

"I had hoped you'd be back sometime in April. Erich probably told you that I need an executive assistant, and I've been waiting for you to come back. But I can't put off a decision until early July. Too much that needs to be done. Any chance, Erich, that I could come out to your place and bother you for an hour or so tomorrow? I'd at least like to tell Tina what's involved. But not over dinner."

"Sure. But it's up to Tina. What do you think, dear heart?"

"It won't hurt to listen. What time do I have to be up?"

"Think you could be out of bed and dressed by two o'clock?" Clayton asked. That got a good laugh.

"I'll see what I can do. Might need Erich's help."

"*Ahhh.* Sounds as if you're going to take full advantage of your trip up," Clayton suggested.

"We don't share stories about our personal life. But, yes, I plan to enjoy the weekend with the only man on the planet."

"What time are you going home tonight?" Clayton asked.

"We'll be on the 9:57. The guys are staying overnight with Dawn, so there's no rush. It's been a long day for Tina. She was up at five. Even so, she's promised not to drift off until after we've said good night."

"I wouldn't touch that for anything."

After they'd eaten, and chatted for a while, Clayton picked up the check.

"Whoa. That's mine, Clayton," Erich said. "I didn't invite you to dinner to have you pay for it. Hardly civilized of me to let you do that."

"My treat. It's been a year since I last saw Tina, and it's a real treat. You could have opted to go home, but instead you made me a part of your first evening together in three weeks. That's special. No arguments. Glad to do it. Besides, I can charge this off as a business dinner because it will lead to an interview tomorrow, such as it is."

"Okay. Then I'm fresh out of arguments."

When they left the restaurant, Tina hugged Clayton, and Erich thanked him for dinner.

"See you tomorrow, shortly after we get out of bed," Erich said. Clayton responded with a hearty laugh.

"Behave yourselves. See you at two or thereabouts. Night."

On the train, Tina said, "Clayton told us to behave ourselves. We'll see about that. Just you wait until I get you home. We're going to review every one of the lessons going back to Christmas Eve of '68."

"Think someone who's on in years can handle it?"

"I'd bet my life on it."

"Not necessary. I'll do my best."

And Erich was in his prime. As was Tina. It was a night of intensely passionate loving. After a separation of three weeks, and given that the affection each had for the other was constant, they expressed their feelings in ways that had been unfamiliar to them before this night.

"You've won me over, Erich. Family couldn't make me any happier than I am right now. I just want this to go on forever, and maybe a day or two after that. The only thing that bothers me is the question you raised on Monday. I don't have anyone else but you, and for you to think I'm spending time with somebody else is, well, how to say it, disturbing. It isn't like you to be uncertain about me, but that's the way you sounded on the phone."

"You're there. I'm here. Then I don't hear from you for over two weeks and for whatever reason I can't reach you by phone. So a busy mind can imagine all kinds of scenarios. Remember, I have some awfully painful memories of what might have been."

"I've been covered up with work, but I promise that I won't let it happen again. You'll never have any reason to worry about me. I'm yours now. Now? I've been yours practically from the day you walked into my life nearly three years ago. I was in your office then. Now I'm in your bed. And my mind and body are for your touch and your eyes alone. I'm giving you all of what I have to give. Tonight and for the rest of my life if you'll have me."

"This life and maybe others that follow."

The weekend was all that any two people who cared about each other could've hoped for. And since it wasn't a distraction, Tina did set aside part of Saturday afternoon to talk with Clayton about his staff job. While he was there, Kurt and Rudi had a chance to visit with him for a few minutes before he started back to East Seventy-seventh Street. They were glad that they could at least say hello.

Erich and Tina had dinner at Mazza's on Saturday evening, a snuggling Sunday, and then early on Monday morning, she was on her way back to Washington. As they were taking the train into Grand Central, Erich asked her, "Should we set a date?"

"Late in the year. Around the holidays. I'd like that. I have an engagement ring, so I want a plain, burnished silver band to go with it. When I come back on Easter weekend, we can go shopping. All right?" Erich squeezed her hand to show her that he agreed.

"We never did talk about my trip back from London and my birthday party with you."

"It's a few weeks off. We'll talk, and I'll be back before then. Next time."

"What's firm is that I'm on the ground at BWI at 3:50 on the twenty-fourth. It isn't as convenient as Dulles, but maybe you could still pick me up in your sexy Falcon."

"Sexy Falcon is hardly the way to describe it, but I'll be there. And we'll celebrate like no other birthday you've had."

"I like your style. Would you consider marrying me?"

"Yesss! If we could find a JP at this hour, I'd do it now."

"Should I shout down the car and see if there's one aboard?"

"On second thought, we haven't had blood tests, don't have a license, or the wedding band. We'll wait until everything's in place. Unless you're in a hurry."

"Not really. We have time."

When they got to Grand Central, Erich went across to Penn Station with Tina to put her on the train to D.C. As she was getting ready to board, Erich asked, "Do you realize that when you're here on Easter weekend that it'll be exactly one year since we said that awful goodbye scene on track whatever?"

"Don't remind me. After the kind of weekend we've just had, this one's hard enough. I may call you every day until June 26."

"I'd love it. But come back on the eve of Good Friday, so we can have a good long weekend together. We'll need it by then."

"Let me try to work it out. But it's time to get aboard before this thing goes without me. I couldn't explain that to my boss."

"Bye, sweetheart. Call when you can."

"Love you, Erich. I'll call. Promise. Bye, hon."

The Metroliner eased out of Penn Station with the two lovers waving. Afterwards, they both felt empty, but they understood why.

At the office earlier than usual, Katie's first words when she finally came in were: "I can't compete with her, Erich. And good morning, by the way."

"Who are you talking about, dear heart?"

"Don't give me that. She's a sweetheart, and a rascal like you doesn't deserve someone that good. I tried to set her straight, but she's mesmerized and wasn't listening. You've put her in a trance."

"Tina thinks you're a doll and had trouble understanding why I haven't been receptive to your advances."

"That makes two of us."

"There's a reason, and you just met her on Friday."

"But you have Brenna. That doesn't seem to bother you."

"Not the same thing. She'd mostly interested in companionship. But we also have needs, so we look after them whenever. Call it an accommodation. Your aim is different. And on top of that, we work together. If you and I were to have each other just once, my guess is you'd want more of the same, and that would interfere with the year-end wedding plans Tina and I are working on."

"That's wonderful. But not even one overnight before then?"

"Katie, you're not listening. Anyway, you've got that sexy Greek god taking care of you. Right?"

"I think he's just using my body and will move on to someone else before long. I'd like to keep him around, but he's slippery. In some ways, he's like you; that is, until you told me about your wedding plans."

"If she'll have me," Erich said, "then I'm most likely hers."

Chapter Seventeen

The relatively smooth sailing that Erich had known during the early weeks of 1970 came to an abrupt end on Friday evening, March 20. It also marked the beginning of events that would alter the direction of his life. It was nearing eight o'clock and Rudi hadn't come home yet. Erich was waiting for him so he could put dinner on the table.

"Kurt, do you have any idea where Rudi is? He didn't say anything about being late."

"I saw him right after school, but it looked like he was headed downtown, not home."

"Not good. I don't want the police involved, at least not yet."

Suddenly the door burst open and Rudi staggered in. His face ashen, his eyes barely open; he'd obviously gotten into something heavyweight. Erich's worries had become reality. Rudi lurched toward the boy's bedroom, partially undressed himself on the way, and then collapsed face down. Erich checked his pulse, and for a few seconds monitored his breathing.

"Kurt. Here. See what you can do to wake him up. He's in deep trouble. I'm calling Kaplan."

"Nate? Erich Mauer. Rudi's done it, and I need an ambulance. He's bad off. Can you can get one here quick."

"Yep. And I'm on my way. Walk him if you can."

"He's collapsed, but we'll try. See you shortly."

The ambulance came within minutes and Nate Kaplan arrived right behind it. One of the medics inhaled sharply and said, "Hope we've got enough time to save him. His blood pressure and respiration are way down. Move him outta here. Go!"

"Kurt, stay here in case I need your help."

"What can I do?"

"Stick close to the phone."

Nate Kaplan and Erich Mauer rode in the ambulance to the hospital while two attendants looked after Rudi. Erich said a prayer to beg a caring God to spare the kid's life.

"I've let him down, Nate." Tears welled up.

"Stop it! This is no time for a guilt trip. He's had to meet you half way. Every day. He hasn't. And you couldn't have reacted any faster."

Erich guessed that Nate was probably trained to lend support to a troubled parent. His words helped some.

At the emergency room, the doctor and nurses on duty were in place to deal with this latest crisis of the evening. They moved swiftly to determine what had to be done to save Rudi Mauer.

After what seemed like hours later, the ER doctor came out and gave Erich and Nate his report.

"Well, Mr. Mauer, if you hadn't moved quickly, we might've lost your boy. We got close to running out of time, but I'm pleased to say that we didn't. He should make it now. Fortunately, what he did to induce his condition wasn't taken intravenously. It most likely would've been too late for us to do anything if that'd been the case. First indications are that the culprits were alcohol and Phenobarbital—a lot of it. And he still had some with him. Our preliminary opinion is that he may have taken it at intervals. Maybe he thought it wasn't working the way it should. Be useful to find out where he got his hands on that much of a supply. Someone should be put away if it's on the street."

"I think we have the answer, Dr. Gertler, and there's no dealer involved." Kaplan said. "Looks like Rudi broke into a doctor's office up on Tower Hill. I just got a message from the police. I think we can make the connection. There was someone with him. Two sets of footprints in the frost at the back of the building. We'll find out what the story is on that, too. You probably saw that Rudi's shoes were muddy. I'll want to talk to him when you say he's fit."

"I don't want him disturbed until at least Sunday afternoon. This is a very troubled lad. We may have an attempted suicide on our hands. He apparently knew what he was after, had at least a vague idea about the amount to take, and what the effects would be. In any case, consider it a possibility."

"Rudi and I will get to know each other again real good. He's ours now. If he wasn't going to be placed, he'd go to juvenile hall for breaking and entering and theft of a controlled substance. Mr. Mauer and I will be back on Sunday at midafternoon. If he's not ready by then, have somebody ring me at this number." Nate handed the doctor his card.

Erich asked the receptionist to call a taxi so he could get back home and Nate could pick up his car. On their way, Kaplan remarked, "When he's recovered, I hope Rudi recognizes that you saved his life. On the other hand, he may have tried to take himself out, as the doctor suggested. But his life was in your hands, and you saved it. Most parents would have thought he was just drunk. Given his history, you knew the difference."

"It was obvious that he was in trouble, but I also have to thank the late Roxane Bouchard for tips on how to recognize drug abuse."

"She's dead?"

"No, no. Wrong way to put it. We've been history since the beginning of November. She got tired of waiting. A few weeks later, Lara was gone. Sure do have problems with my love life."

"Our pipeline on your social affairs has pretty much dried up. I guess you talked to your guys about it."

"Sure did. I try to keep a low profile. They weren't helping."

Back at Mianus Ridge, Erich thanked Nate for his support and said he'd be at the hospital at about three o'clock on Sunday.

"You're welcome, Erich. That's what we're here for. And about Sunday, I'll be there a little earlier. I'll want Rudi one on one for a while, then I'll see you before you look in on him."

"Fair enough. Thanks again. See you on Sunday. G'night."

Up at number 710, Kurt told Erich that the police had been there. "Big dudes, and they said they wanted to talk to Rudi. I told 'em what happened and that you'd just left. They didn't tell me anything, but I guess Rudi's in big trouble. And Brenna called. I gave her the same story, and she said she's coming over as soon as she knows you're home. You're to call her back. But you've got to tell me what happened."

Erich told Kurt everything he knew up to the time they left the hospital. Kurt's expression showed nearly as much pain as his dad's. "He'll be a ward of the state, now. This weekend you might want to rearrange your bedroom for a single tenant. Rudi won't be coming home. Kaplan said the first step will be the juvenile detention facility in Bridgeton, then a school of some kind for troubled young people like your brother. I'll need to call your mom and give her the bad news. But before I get to that, I'll ring Brenna and then Tina. She may have second thoughts about becoming a part of our family. Meaning marriage. This may scare her off."

Kurt looked surprised. "I didn't know you'd decided on that."

"It's in the planning stage. I guess that's one way to put it. No. It's a little further along than that. She's trying to work it out so she can be here next Thursday evening, assuming she still wants to keep our date. It's Easter weekend, and she has four days off. I'll see how she feels about it."

Erich called Brenna to let her know he was back.

"It's late, but I'm on my way over. No argument. I've already made arrangements. There'll be no fun and games. I simply want to be there to give you my support and maybe talk about what this means for us."

"Okay, but I'm sure upset. I may not hold up very well."

"That won't bother me a bit. It'll say that you're a caring father and very human. I'll be there inside thirty minutes."

Erich decided not to call Tina until Sunday evening. She'd want to know more than he could tell her at this stage. He also had in mind that he couldn't handle talking to her just yet. No point in making a call when all she'd hear was an unsteady voice. It'd do more harm than good. She'd already phoned him at the office earlier in the day, and he didn't want to take the edge off all the good feelings she had when they talked. "Best to wait," he decided. "There's nothing she can do but worry. I'll spare her that until the doctor gives me his report. It's my load to bear, not hers."

With that decision made, Erich turned his attention toward Kurt. "Did you have anything to eat?" Erich asked.

"Yeah. The stuff you made is cold, so I heated up a can of soup and made a cheese sandwich. I'm okay. What're you gonna do?"

"I wasn't hungry when the clock said I should have been. No surprise, I guess. Brenna's on her way over. Maybe we can have a snack later on."

"It's kinda late, but I know how you feel. Whata bummer."

"Yep. Sure is."

It wasn't long before Brenna was at the door.

"Here's your support team: me and the good Lord. I'm here until Sunday afternoon."

She and Erich hugged. He inhaled sharply, had tears in his eyes, but held together fairly well given the emotional hit he'd just taken.

"I called Lara at home to tell her what happened. Bad idea. She screamed like she'd been stabbed and said, 'It's all my fault!' Then she broke down completely, wasn't able to say another word after that, and hung up on me. Any idea what she meant?"

"No, unless she was referring to the fact that she walked away in early December and took Rudi's heart with her. She sure as hell did that. You were here afterwards and saw how he reacted."

"I'll find out next weekend. She asked me earlier this week if I'd help her out in the shop for a little while on Saturday."

"Do I need to tell you how much I appreciate what you're doing? It's says a lot about you, and I'm touched. I haven't known this kind of support since I was a youngster on the farm. If anything went wrong, there were always people around to offer you a shoulder to lean on." Brenna gave Erich a hug. He was hurting.

"You didn't grow up in Seaford, so you wouldn't know that it isn't much different here, especially with people in our Irish community. The blood's pretty thick. Your heritage is different. Doesn't matter. You need help. I'm here." Then Erich lost it.

Recovering quickly, he said, "Sorry. Meant to do that in private."

"If you hadn't showed me emotions like that, I'd have been wrong about you. Your feelings run deep, and it's what I'd want to see in a man if I ever marry again. It's important."

"You're being kind."

"I'm being honest!"

"It's a shame we didn't meet years ago, love, marry, and that your two boys could've been ours. Kurt and Rudi were what Dawn wanted. She didn't figure into my plans, so I wasn't ready, as a returning veteran, to be a husband and a father in my first year at Ohio State. What I expected to do was date and eventually make a lasting commitment to a woman I really cared about. Despite the way things turned out, and in case it isn't obvious, I have a father's affection for Kurt and Rudi. But the idea I had was that I'd be head over heels in love with the woman of my choice, really want the babies as they came along, and not have to accept someone else's plan about parenthood. They were handed to me, and it was as if I was arguing with a voice that said, 'Here, take the child. You made it happen. No. She made it happen. Do I have to? Yes. You were a part of what you did.' If only I could've known the trap was set and that Dawn was the bait. She assured me that it was safe, but there were those wide-open eyes staring at me as we made love. She knew exactly what was about to take place. I had no chance to have what I wanted and in the way I wanted it to happen. But you and I were separated by age and geography. You were here; I was thousands of miles to the west, and older by nearly four years. That age difference meant that as you were planning a Halloween party, I was on a minesweeper sent to clear out North Korea's Wonsan harbor so the First Marines could land."

"I've never heard you say things like this before. You're bitter. It's a side of you I don't know at all. It sounds to me like you've lived with it all these years and kept everything inside. But I've been around you long enough to know that you're a loving father. You didn't let Rudi down. He let himself down. And he let you down. If you're willing to accept the blame for Rudi, then you also have to take credit for Kurt."

"He has his own problem. I've found out he likes his beer, more than he should at his age—or any age for that matter. That could be another issue I'll have to deal with someday. My two are reasons why you and I might have a hard time making it work, at least until Kurt is on his own. Rudi belongs to the state now, so he won't be in the picture for probably two or three years. Whatever, I wouldn't want either of them to be the wrong kind of influence on your two. We've talked about this before, so you know what my feelings are."

"You have a way of zeroing in on something. It's probably what makes you good at what you do. I can't disagree with you, though. Yet I feel that I'd like you to be a part of my life. Thinking about what you just said, what chance do you think we have?"

"I don't know. Wrong time to ask. Let's talk about it over coffee tomorrow. I'm worn out and would just like us to hold on to each other for a while. Would you take on being my prop tonight?"

"Maybe longer than just tonight.. Life hasn't treated you very fair. I'm beginning to see that now. I want to help, assuming you'd like me to."

"I would, and it begins in my room."

There'd be no loving this night. The reason was simple. There was too much emotional debris to deal with. Brenna snuggled up to Erich's back and they slept like spoons. She had to be near. Among her reasons was one that now stood out above all others. She'd come to terms with her feelings and had to acknowledge the truth: she cared very deeply about this man. In the early morning hours they changed positions, but throughout the night they stayed close.

By morning, they'd turned toward each other. Erich awakened and studied the pleasant face he saw before him. He wondered how her estranged husband could have walked away from such a compassionate woman. Eyes open, the serene face smiled. Erich smiled back. "Morning," Brenna said softly.

"Morning, dear heart. You brought good medicine with you. It's made me feel better. Thank you."

"Glad it did. I was worried and wanted to help. You needed it."

"You have helped." Erich said. "And what I'm asking myself is how could we possibly improve on what we've shared since last night? When we love, we find fulfillment. It's a desire, sure, but it's also a way of expressing, physically, what we mean to each other. That's one part of it. But what I'm feeling now is something that has a wider meaning. What you've shown me is the kind of compassion that's at the heart of a really durable relationship. It's the sort of bond that's important if two people are to hold onto the affection they have for each other all through their later years. It's there after the passions cool."

Brenna smiled and added, "I know exactly what you're saying."

"Best example that comes to mind is of a gray haired couple I saw walking through the park over off Lincoln Boulevard. They had to be in their seventies, but they were holding hands like they were still dating. Their physical needs have diminished, I'm sure, but the love they were still sharing was shining like a beacon. It's been there for probably a half-century, and it looked to me like it was as bright that day as it's ever been. That's what I mean. It's what I call the love and the beauty inside, and those two seniors know to this day exactly what it is and how important it's been during all of their years together. And I'll bet if you asked them, they'd say that younger people don't have any idea what it's all about. They're a different generation. My parents had the same kind of love, so it was easy for me to recognize what I was seeing."

"That's lovely, Erich. Now more than ever, I understand perfectly what you mean. We may never get to an altar, for the reasons we talked about last night, but it's time you knew that I'm in love with you. Those words haven't been in my vocabulary for a long time, and I never thought I'd say them again. But the sentiment's there. It's real."

Erich reached out, put his arms around Brenna, and then held her tightly. For a few minutes, neither one spoke. She'd said what was in her heart, and he needed time to let her words sink in.

"I thought something was going on inside that pretty head of yours, but you've caught me off guard," Erich said quietly.

"Question is, now that my feelings are out in the open, what am I going to do with them? You have a Tina in your life again, a problem son, maybe two of them, and an uncertain future with your company. I have to be crazy to feel what I do, but I can't change what's inside. Just as important, I don't want to try. It took a while for me to decide that I wanted you in my bed, and it's taken six months for me to let you inside my heart. But you're in there now. No more of just being under my skin. And I'm jealous, too. It's hard for me to think about sharing you with someone else, but I don't have any control over what you do." It was Brenna's turn to show a tear that wouldn't be denied. Erich wiped it away and then kissed her gently.

"When we met, I never wanted to do anything, ever, that would hurt you. It bothers me to think that I've done that. I give the appearance of loving the person I'm with or maybe that I can love two women. It can't be that way, so what I have to ask of you is to be patient. Much as I care for Tina, there are still some underlying questions, even if she's not willing to recognize them. The age difference isn't an issue with her, but it continues to bother me some. Why? I don't know. She's young and has a lot of spirit, and I'm closing in on being middle-aged. I haven't told her about Rudi yet. I called you, and I find that interesting. Why you, and just you so far? It tells me something, but I'm not sure what it is. Still, I agree. Even if there were no Tina, the odds of your getting an engagement ring are probably slim."

"I already have one. It came from Australia, or at least part of it did." Brenna smiled. Erich was pleased to see her do that.

"For the time being, things may not happen the way you want them to. But don't throw me away just yet. Give us time. No, give me time. Your life and your routine are relatively stable. Mine has been turned upside down, and I have an uneasy feeling it'll be even more chaotic before long. Rudi's a part of it. IMCO is another. If I'm on the street, we're going to have some rough sledding until I wind up with whoever will have me."

"Throw you away? Not very likely. You're inside. Remember?"

"You're being better about this than I have any right to hope for. But by being here when I needed a prop, you've changed the way I look at the order of things. Meaning us."

"Let's talk about tomorrow afternoon. I want to go with you to see Rudi. I'll get Dad to come to the house for a little while if need be. And I'd like the two of you to meet sometime soon. You'll like each other. You both have your heads screwed on straight."

"Not sure mine is. Would you take a look and see if it's okay?"

"It's just the way it should be."

"I don't have any objections to your coming with me to see Rudi. In fact, it's probably a good idea. He still needs to feel a woman's touch, and you have the designated hand. It'll also give you a chance to see Kaplan."

"I haven't seen Nate in ages. Be interesting to hear what he has to say about Rudi. This is serious. He might have died last night. God! I don't want to think about it." Erich took Brenna in his arms. She shivered. The thought of what might've been got to her. "I put it into the perspective of having lost Alan or Scot. I can maybe understand some of what you feel."

"We were lucky. I might have had dinner with Clayton, or you, or I could've been out. We talked about Friday nights. If that had been the case, we'd be down to Kurt and burying Rudi."

"We need to change the subject because I'm having trouble dealing with what's happened. Some pillar I am. But it's finally hit me. The timing, the odds, and what might have been. It's scary."

"You've been solid as a rock, and I'm grateful that you insisted on being here last night. I had so many different kinds of feelings. Anger, fear, frustration, distress; you name it. But having you up against me helped in a way that I think we both understand. Maybe there's a book about the healing power of hugs and nightlong body contact. It was wonderful. So are you."

After breakfast, Kurt said he'd take care of the laundry, and Brenna offered to help Erich with his weekly shopping. She was following through on a commitment she'd made during the holidays. So they shared part of their day giving the impression that they were a couple keeping a household up and running. A casual observer wouldn't have seen anything much different from any of the other families in the store. The fact remained that they'd been married an average of one and a half times, had two sons each, and had been to a market and shopped before. Probably thousands of times. A familiar picture. But Brenna stayed close to Erich and smiled at him occasionally. It might have suggested that they were newlyweds. And he enjoyed having her by his side. A bonus was that she was good at offering shopping and product advice as they pushed their cart around the store. Erich was still something of a novice, so her suggestions were helpful.

"Never thought I'd be so caught up with doing the Saturday shopping," Erich said. "It's great having your help. Makes me think we've already tied the knot. It's a good feeling."

"Strange. Me, too. Maybe we should think about it. Really."

At home, Erich called Dawn to tell her what had happened. She was clearly upset and said if Erich needed anything that he should let her know. Kind of her. Next he phoned Rudi's mother, Erich's first ex, with the news. She wasn't exactly charitable and nagged at him for not maintaining tight enough control and a heap of other rubbish that she knew nothing about. The New York metro area, and what went with it, was foreign to her and Erich chose not to get into a row with someone so ill informed.

"Aren't you going to call Tina?" Brenna asked.

"Eventually. Probably tomorrow evening. Until then, you get 100 percent of my attention. I'm glad you're here. It's a special thing you're doing, and I won't forget it."

"It's because I care. You're important to me. You know that."

Erich gave her an affectionate hug to express how he felt.

"That said something words couldn't have."

"It was intended to." They shared smiles.

"Have you told anybody at work about Rudi?" Brenna asked.

"I'll call Katie at home tomorrow to let her know that I probably won't be in on Monday. Depends on what the doctor says. Since he was on duty in the emergency room, I'm not sure if he'll stay with this or if he'll hand it over to our GP. I suppose our doctor will get involved at some point."

"I'm pleased I can go with you tomorrow. If we ever get to be an item in the Sunday paper, it'll help to know what's been said."

"One thing we haven't thought about is dinner. I'm in favor of going out. Let me go interrupt Kurt. He's been changing their den into a single room. You willing to do seafood or would you prefer something else."

"Doesn't matter. Ask Kurt."

They decided on Chinese, had dinner, and a quiet remainder of their evening at home. Since it had been a stressful twenty-four hours, they all went to bed early. Erich fell asleep quickly but had disturbing dreams. Then, for some reason, his Massachusetts land and the face of the nameless young woman with long brown hair came into view. This was now her fourth appearance, the first since December, and he continued to wonder about her visits. Whatever the reasons, he slept peacefully afterwards.

Chapter Eighteen

On Sunday afternoon, Erich and Brenna got to the hospital just before three o'clock. They stopped at reception and got Rudi's room number. Erich knocked softly and walked in. Nate Kaplan was there. He turned and said, "A few more minutes, Erich. I'll meet you in the lounge when I'm done. It's just down the corridor."

"Fine." When Nate was finished with Rudi, he came and sat with Erich and Brenna.

"Hi, Brenna. How long has it been since our paths crossed?"

"Ages. I can't remember either."

"You look great. This guy a part of it?"

"Yeah. More than I'm willing to admit. Even to myself." Nate Kaplan chuckled softly.

"I won't ask any awkward questions. But I have to say it, Erich, you sure do get around for not having lived in Seaford very long. Anyway, Brenna I'm glad you're here. If there's a chance you're serious about each other, then you should know what's going on."

"There's always that possibility, but I asked to be involved."

"Before we go on," Erich said, "there's something I want to add. Brenna helped me through some very difficult hours. I don't know what I'd have done without her. When she heard there was trouble, she was right there to prop me up. This is an extraordinary woman, let me tell you." Brenna blushed just a little. Nate smiled.

"I've known that for a long time. Glad you've found that out, too. But, let's get to the matter at hand."

"What did you find out?" Erich asked.

"I don't know that we have a suicide attempt on our hands. Let's leave it at his having misjudged the amount and potency of the drug he took. He had some other options; that is, other drugs, or combinations of them. We were lucky. You're having moved on it as fast as you did saved his life. No question about it. He may level with you as to his intentions. I'm not his father. And maybe he won't tell you either. Could be we'll never know. Anyway at the center of it is how much he cares about Lara. He went to her downtown shop on Friday and tried to talk to her. She gave him the cold shoulder. Stonewalled him. He didn't understand, and frankly neither do I."

"God! What's happened to her?" Brenna asked. "Adolescence is hard enough. You don't do that to a youngster. She knows how Rudi feels. That's downright cruel."

"He's carried this around inside since December," Kaplan continued, "misses her, and simply wanted to say hello. She broke his heart, and it drove him to do what he did. Much as anything, I put the blame at Lara's doorstep. No need for that kind of treatment. It was malicious and damned hard to understand."

"I called her at home to let her know what had happened," Brenna said. "She screamed like she was being tortured. Before she started to sob, she said, 'It's all my fault', couldn't talk after that and hung up on me. I'm supposed to help her out next Saturday. Guess I better do it. Maybe I can find out what her thinking was."

"She's not exactly my problem," Nate remarked, "but I'd be interested in knowing what she says. Call it personal."

"So, what's next?" Erich asked.

"Rudi will be released to our custody tomorrow morning. I'll need you to get a few of his clothes together and then meet me here. We'll be taking him to Bridgeton, like I told you on Friday night, and he'll be there until we can place him in a school run by a foundation. They have a string of them from central Massachusetts to eastern Pennsylvania. There are other schools, but these are the ones we work with. He will get an education. If he behaves himself you may get him back in a couple of years. In between, there'll be summer camp, probably in Maine. It may be too late to get him situated for the coming summer. If so, we'll have to make other arrangements. But that doesn't mean he'll be with you. No reflection at all, but you're out of it."

"Nate, I've been around Erich off and on since last September, and I can tell you that he's been a good father. I'd have no trouble having him as a stepfather for my two if that day comes."

"I don't doubt that for a minute, Brenna. The fact that Erich came to us when he first found out what Rudi was up to says a lot about his concern for the welfare of his guys. But being a single parent commuting into the city leaves a lot of holes in his day. Ones that give curious youngsters, like Rudi, time to get into trouble."

"Getting somebody to come in for forty-five minutes in the morning, and maybe up to three hours late in the afternoon, every day during the week, is next to impossible I found out. But it doesn't make much sense to close the barn door now. The horse has already run off. Kurt's headed toward seventeen, so I don't need a watchdog for him—assuming he mostly behaves himself."

"Your Ohio farm boy background is showing," Brenna observed. She smiled at Erich.

"What time tomorrow do you want me here with Rudi's stuff?" Erich asked.

"We're scheduled to leave at about ten o'clock. We'll talk then about days and times that you can see him."

"I'll be here before ten. Now, are we allowed to see the patient?"

"Of course. It's expected. Let me know what comes out of your conversation. We need all the information we can get."

"We've stayed close on this long enough for you to know I'll share whatever I find out. We may be covering the same ground but there might be something new. We'll talk tomorrow before you go to Bridgeton. Appreciate all your help, Nate."

"You're welcome. Brenna, awfully good to see you again. Look after this guy. In my opinion, he's a good man."

"Couldn't agree with you more, and it'll be a pleasure to do that. I may come back with him again tomorrow." Erich glanced at Brenna and showed her with a thin smile that he liked her idea.

When they walked into Rudi's room, Erich stopped and stared at him for a moment before saying anything. Rudi was sitting on the edge of his bed and looked away. Erich then walked over and hugged his troubled son.

"Well, young man, you gave us quite a scare Friday night. How're you doing?"

"Crummy. The doctor and Kaplan said you saved my life. It'd been okay if you hadn't. Don't know how I got home."

"Sounds like you intended to take yourself out."

"Yep."

"Rudi, that's a permanent solution to a temporary problem. Not a good choice. Not even close to one. There's no coming back to reconsider what you did. When you're gone, you're gone for a long time. Like forever."

"It's a crappy life, so it doesn't matter."

"That's being really selfish, don't you think? You know how much love we have for you, and what you did hurt. Real bad. If I'd taken myself out and left you alone, how 'bout them apples? Maybe I've had a crummy life, too. You're not the only person who's had setbacks, or disappointments. You're looking at another one. But I haven't thrown myself off the terrace, or taken drugs, just because someone said no, or gave me a hard time. Life can't always be exactly the way you want it. There are good times and bad times, and you deal with each one of them as they come along."

"It's my life, so I can do what I want to."

"Sorry. Wrong. That says you don't care about anyone else and their feelings for you. That's not right, and you know it. Any idea how many people would've cried over your grave had you finished what you started? Two of 'em are here. Think about your family and your friends. You count the tears. When I told Brenna what you'd done, she came over to be with Kurt and me to show us that she loves you, too. I lost it, not because I wasn't able to stop you from getting into drugs again, but because I was so relieved to know that you were going to make it. What you did tells me that I'm a lousy father. You hurt me in ways you'll never know."

"You're not a lousy dad. It's Lara. She wouldn't even talk to me. Treated me like I was dog poop. After all the times we sat together, she put her arms around me, pretended she was a mom, and . . . ohhh, Dad." He reached over, held on to Erich, and cried his heart out. Brenna was in tears.

"It's all right, Rudi. We're starting over," Erich said gently. "You've been given another chance. We'll work side by side and try to put a life together that isn't crummy. I won't have much to say about it for a while, but you have to be willing to see if, together, we can make it work."

"I can try. And I'm glad Brenna's here. It's good to have at least one friend."

"You made peace with her the day we told you about Lara. I thought you'd like to know how important she thinks you are."

Brenna went to Rudi and held him tightly. "You're one of my boys, too. Please remember that." He cried in her arms.

When he'd recovered, he said, "Guess I messed up."

"You're still with us," Brenna said. "There's time now to undo the mess. I'll help, too, because I like you and your dad. A lot."

For the first time in a good many days, Rudi Mauer smiled, albeit faintly. It brightened a gloomy, overcast March day.

"We have to talk about tomorrow," Erich said. "Tell me what clothes you want, and not just one each of something. You won't be coming home for a while, so to get you started let me have some idea of what you want to take with you to Bridgeton. I'll bring the rest of your things after I'm told when I can come up to visit."

Rudi gave Erich an idea of what clothes he wanted. Then he said, "I'm sure gonna miss my own bed, and TV, and your chili soup, and eating out. Stuff like that."

"That's somewhere down the road. That didn't cross your mind on Friday evening. A shame. If you'd stopped to think about those things, we wouldn't be here. Tomorrow is the beginning of a whole new chapter in your life, Rudi. We've already gone over it, so you know what's ahead."

"Yeah. What I did was dumb."

"That's one way to put it. It's something you'll remember for the rest of your life. Hopefully you'll learn from your mistake. Next time you want to pull off something like Friday night, stop and think about it first. You'll probably decide it isn't worth it. Anyway, Connecticut Juvenile is in charge now. So, like you just said, you'll be missing out on all the things you've had at home. And whether or not you come out of their program early depends entirely on you. Good behavior could mean that you can come home sooner. I'll leave you with that to think about. Now, we'll be back in the morning to see you off." Erich gave him a hug and said, "We still love you, and are on your team. Friday night didn't change a thing, so let's see what we can do to fix the problem." Rudi hugged his dad, and then hung onto Brenna for nearly a full minute. When he finally released her from the hug he badly needed, Erich and Brenna both said, "Bye, Rudi."

"Bye, Dad. Bye, Brenna."

In the corridor, Erich had to stop and get control of his emotions. "This is one of the more painful moments in my life, Brenna. I'm glad you were here. It was terribly important. Rudi knows there's a mom who cares about him. He doesn't feel abandoned. You showed him that. With all my heart, I thank you."

"You said something yesterday about being sorry that my boys weren't ours. After having been with you just now, I'm sorry, too. Jordie's never been confronted with anything like this, but there isn't any way he could have handled himself like you just did."

"I wasn't totally pleased with it, but since we ended up with a smile and hugs, it turned out all right, I guess."

"Very all right, Erich. The more I'm around you the more I think you're one very special guy."

"And you're one helluva woman, Brenna Walsh." The two of them finally had a reason to smile.

When they got back to Mianus Ridge, Erich called Katie at home. He told her what had happened and said he wouldn't be in tomorrow. "I'd appreciate it if you'd let Joel know."

"I'm sorry about your boy. It has to hurt. I'll tell Joel. He might want you to take more time."

"Can't do that. I've got London coming up shortly, and some other things that need to be finished before then. I'll be in on Tuesday morning. And thanks."

"You're welcome. If you need anything else, just let me know."

Erich called Clayton because he thought that as the father of two young girls he'd want to know. He appreciated the call but was shocked by the news. "In a situation like this, I don't know how much help I can be."

"Thanks, Clayton, but the ball's in my end of the court. I'll keep you posted."

Brenna said she was serious about taking the day off. "Your support system is still in place, and I'm going back to the hospital with you to say goodbye to Rudi. It's going to be hard for him. His life will be totally different starting tomorrow morning. I'm so sorry about what's happened, and I want to help in every way I can. Damn Lara, anyway."

"I can't ask you to take the day, but if you do I'll be pleased that you have. It'll be good for Rudi, like you said."

"Let me go feed the boys, spend some time with them, and then ask Colleen to stay over. Under the circumstances, I know she'll help me out and then get the boys off to school in the morning. You can call your Tina while I'm gone. She has every right to know."

"You're precious." Erich hugged her warmly.

After Brenna had gone, Erich called Washington.

"Tina. It's me."

"Erich! What a nice surprise. What's the occasion?"

"Rudi. We damn near lost him to an OD on Friday night. Luckily we were able to get him to the emergency room in time, and the doctors pulled him through. It was a close call, they said."

"*Ohh, Erich.* That's horrible news. Poor kid. Why?"

"Lara. He misses her, just wanted to say hello, and she turned her back on him. Broke his heart. He got into a doctor's office and downed a heap of Phenobarbital—which he downed with booze. The combination nearly killed him. Doctor said that if I hadn't reacted quickly, we'd have lost him."

Erich could hear her unsteady voice. "I love that kid. Oh, Erich."

"Rudi's a ward of the state now, but before he leaves the hospital tomorrow morning, I have to make sure he has some clothes to take with him. He'll be in detention up in Bridgeton until he can be placed in a school for kids with his kind of problem."

"With everything going on, would it be better if I changed the plans we made to have me come up?"

"Tina! Why would you suggest something like that?" Erich asked crisply. "If nothing else, *I'd* like to have your support."

"You're unhappy with me, and it hurts."

"And you don't seem to understand know much I've been through since Friday night."

"I just thought I might be in the way. But, you're right. I'm being insensitive, and I apologize. What I should have said first is that my parents are insisting that I spend the entire Easter weekend with them. And they want me at mass on Sunday, too. I don't go very often, so I buckled. It's like Christmas all over again. Papa can be pretty demanding at times. I know you and I had planned on the long weekend, so what I have in mind is to tell them that I'll be spending at least one night with you. With what's happened, I thought maybe you'd rather have me come back so that we could have all of the following weekend together instead. But since you want me there, and I really want to see you sooner, not later, I'll explain why I'll also want to be with you on Thursday night. They'll accept it, I'm sure. If not, too bad. I have a life, too. It'll help that Papa likes you."

"You're starting to sound like an organized and strong-minded business woman. But now I understand the reasons for your question about coming out to Seaford. Glad you explained it. Two nights here and two in the Bronx is fair, I think."

"I just had another idea. My manager is all soft inside when it comes to things like this so I'm going to ask him to let me come up on the one o'clock Metroliner on Thursday. I'll come to your office, say hello to Katie, give you a hug, and we can be on our way. Two nights together and a little extra time I can give you my support."

"Now that sounds like my girl. Good idea. Would you call me on Tuesday, and let me know what kind of reaction you got?"

"I don't know how he can turn me down. I'm close to working on my time now, because I'd have been gone a week from Friday if I hadn't agreed to the extension."

"I'll make sure we roll out the red carpet on Thursday." Tina chuckled.

"I miss you tons, mister. It'll be wonderful to give you a hug. I want to be there for you."

"I'll be ready for one. Probably two. They'll be most welcome. But I'm not sure how much fire there is in the furnace. These last two days have taken a lot out of me emotionally."

"I understand, and if that's the way it is we'll have other weekends, and a lifetime of being able to look after those things. I just want to be near you now so I can show you that I'm your girl and that I'm there to help. If possible, I'd like to see Rudi."

"I'm not sure what the visitation schedule is, but I'll have that tomorrow. If it's only on weekends, that could wipe out my swing through Washington on my way back from London. I'll want to see Rudi on a regular basis."

"In that case, I'll come to Seaford and we'll see him together."

"You're being the sweetheart I've known since day one at Essex. And that's real support. Rudi will love it. He'll want to see us whenever possible."

"I'll be ready. And I'll call you on Tuesday because I'll want you to know what's going on."

"I should be in the office at the usual time. Got to run, love. Kurt and I have to eat sometime this evening."

"Thanks for calling, Erich. I'm so sorry to hear about Rudi, but I'll be up in a few days and will bring a shoulder for you to lean on. It was there all through the weeks your divorce was going on."

"I remember. Give you a bear hug on Thursday, hopefully."

"I'm past ready for one of those, too. Night, love."

"G'night."

After they hung up, Erich had a fleeting thought that maybe this was too much for Tina and that she really did want to keep it at arm's length until everything had settled down. He dismissed the idea as probably being unfair.

A few minutes later, Brenna called.

"I've got some leftover lasagna. It's going in the freezer or on your table. Hungry?"

"Not very. Bring it with you, would you please? I haven't done anything about dinner yet."

"I'll be there before you know it."

Brenna came with food. Kurt wolfed it down. Erich toyed with his. He was still upset by the events of the past forty-eight hours.

"Don't you like my lasagna?"

"I don't need to tell you what the problem is. Food's great, like always. My thoughts are elsewhere. I'm having a hard time dealing with what's happened."

"I know, but you have to start eating."

"I'll get my appetite back. But thanks for being concerned. Another night together will help." And it did.

On Monday morning, they all had breakfast; afterwards Kurt left for school. At a little before ten, Erich and Brenna were at the hospital with the things Rudi had asked for. Among them was a little Essex Steel radio. The story accompanying that was painful to recall. Erich was reminded of a much happier time: the party at Rubino's when Rudi celebrated his thirteenth birthday. The radio had been a part of it. Lara was there, and she'd helped make becoming a teenager the kind of celebration they both thought it deserved. But he guessed he'd never go back. Maybe someday Lara would tell Mario why.

When the state's van came, Rudi hugged Brenna and then turned toward Erich. They were both fighting tears. "You've just about broken our hearts. Can you imagine what we'd be like if you hadn't made it."

"Alone last night, I had time to think. I'm sorry for what I did. I hurt a lot of people. I hurt me, too. I need help. Maybe this is the best thing for me."

Rudi and Erich held on to each other until Nate Kaplan, who had just joined them, said it was time to go.

"Bye, Rudi. I'll see you on Saturday. Count on it."

"Bye, Dad."

Nate told Erich that he could visit most anytime during the day on weekends, but only in the evening during the week. "We won't make the rules too tough for you. With you going into New York every day, we'll be flexible up to a point."

"Thanks, Nate. I appreciate it. By the way, I never did see the doctor after Friday night. Was I supposed to?"

"It isn't necessary, unless there's something you want to talk over. What I told you yesterday was pretty much what he gave me. You know who he is, so you can call him if you want."

"I'd like him to give our GP a rundown on what's happened. It should probably be in Rudi's record."

"Good idea. I've got to go, Erich, I'm driving up separately so I can get back to the office."

"Before you leave, Rudi said he did try to take himself out."

"Since you're at home, I want to talk to you about it. Drop by after lunch."

"I'll be there at about two if that's okay."

"Fine. I'll work you in somehow. It's important."

"See you then."

As the van pulled out, Erich saw a feeble goodbye wave and a forlorn young face looking out the window. Brenna knew Erich needed help, so she stood by his side and held him tightly.

"I feel like I've just been kicked in the stomach. Let's go for a drive. I need a change of scenery. I'm glad you're here, dear heart. Means the world to me."

"Want me to drive? You're preoccupied."

"It's probably a good idea. Would you mind?"

They took their drive, had a light lunch, and then met with Nate Kaplan. By nightfall, Erich felt completely drained. It was evident.

"Wish I could stay," Brenna said, "but I've got to get back to Alan and Scot. They've been orphans since Friday night."

"You've been wonderful, and I'm grateful to you beyond words. If someone could show me how to erase what happened on Friday night, I'd sure do it. But having you by my side these past three days is something I wouldn't change for any reason. It's been so supportive to have you share all this and to offer your help. And thank everyone who's made it possible for you to be here. I owe 'em."

Erich went to the garage with Brenna. Before she drove off, he held her in a way that expressed, without any doubt, how much she meant to him.

"That says a lot to me. I get the message. I'll call you tonight to see how you're doing. And maybe sometime soon we can talk about that overnight away that we've never had. It really is time now to start sorting things out if only to get some idea about what our future looks like."

"I'll need to make sure Rudi is settled in first. But, sure, I agree. And I'd like you to call if you can."

"Before I go to bed. Bye, love."

"Bye, dear heart. Thanks a million for all you've done."

Chapter Nineteen

When Erich got to the office on Tuesday morning, he sat with Joel to tell him where his personal life stood and also ask for Friday off.

"There won't be that many people around since it's Good Friday, so I don't have any problem with your taking the day. You have a good reason for it. A damn good reason. I'm sorry to hear about your guy. Every responsible parent worries about the possibility of having to deal with what you just did. It's obvious that it's affected you some. I'm not surprised, but, while we're at it, do you want to cancel your London trip?"

"No reason to. Rudi will be into his routine by then, and we have everything pretty much set up for me to arrive on the twentieth. Bill Drake says the forsythia will be out by the third week of April, so there isn't any way I can afford to miss that."

Joel chuckled softly. "Seems the healing process has already begun."

"Not many options. Life goes on and time's a great healer. We'll make it."

Tina came up on Thursday as planned, and she and Erich had their early weekend together. When she came into his office, and they'd hugged, he said, "You've lost more weight. You're thinner."

"A little. Blame it on the workload and not having much of an appetite." Erich let it pass, even though he felt she wasn't her usual bubbly self and that she'd also lost some of her glow. It worried him. Yet they had an affectionate couple of days together and their two nights were fulfilling. It was special that they could spend a little time together. They had hoped to see Rudi, but Tina said she was extremely tired, so they made plans to do it during her next visit. On Saturday morning, Erich took her to the station so she could spend the balance of the Easter weekend with her parents. As he was putting her on the train, Erich said he'd changed his mind and would try to come through Washington on the twenty-fourth after all. That lifted her spirits and she gave him an especially loving hug.

Since Tina had gone home to the Bronx and wouldn't be going with them on their trip up to Bridgeton, Erich and Kurt moved their visit with Rudi over to a later time on Saturday afternoon. As expected, he was glad to see them. They were able to spend more than two hours with him and left only because it was time for him to eat.

"They sure do feed you early," Kurt said.

"Yeah. By the time we go to bed, I'm a little hungry again. But we can usually have a snack. It isn't all that bad."

"Kurt and I are having Easter dinner with Dawn. She and the guys may want to come up for a visit. I'll suggest a Sunday."

"I'd like that. Ask them if they would."

"I'll do it. See you next week."

The following day, Erich mentioned over an Easter ham that Rudi hoped the three of them, Dawn, and Ryan and Greg, would come see him. They promised they would. And they did.

The long Easter weekend behind them, Brenna and Erich continued to talk when they didn't have a date of some kind. But Erich still had his own agenda. If he was busy he simply told her that he had other plans. Brenna understood that she couldn't expect to occupy 100 percent of his free time, and she didn't ask questions. But their relationship was on a solid footing, so she knew that he was hers when they got together. She usually spent Saturday evenings at number 710, and their time together was always fulfilling for both of them. Then Erich was at her house frequently, sometimes until late in the evening, and he and Kurt continued to be occasional dinner guests. Erich and Brenna had been on a path to form a close mutual attachment; their having shared Rudi's brush with death accelerated the process. Their feelings, in another context, might have been called love, but it went beyond that. It was a common bond they shared that lay closer to the soul. Once more, Erich saw beauty inside and Brenna's was indeed elegant.

During the three weeks before Erich made his trip to London, he and Tina also talked often during the week. Hearing each other's voices helped them manage their separation. Plans for a wedding late in the year were part of what they talked about. And Erich's upcoming visit also got its share of attention. It was the nearest event on their calendars and they were both excited about it. "I just can't wait to see you, and for you to share *my* bed," Tina said just before Erich was ready to leave for England. "I've missed you so much this past week. Be good to have you hold me. I'm in need and very much in love, mister"

"We share in that. It won't be much longer. I'll see you on the twenty-fourth, love."

"You know I'll be at BWI way before you land." Tina laughed sweetly.

In mid-April, Erich took Kurt and Brenna to Bridgeton for their usual Saturday visit with Rudi. He always looked forward to seeing them, and it seemed to help him adjust to his environment, one that Erich and Brenna found depressing. Before they left, Erich told Rudi, "I'm leaving for London tomorrow and want to bring you something. What do you think?"

"If you can find one of those hats the British cops wear, that'd be really neat."

"What size?"

"If it's going to fit over all my hair, maybe a seven and a half or whatever the English size is. Maybe it's different."

"See what I can find in the souvenir shops. But I won't see you now until the morning of May 2. And then Brenna and I may be going on to Sturbridge from here for belated birthday celebrations. Both of 'em, even though hers is in late February. It wasn't the time of year to do it then."

Brenna looked at Erich and smiled brightly. "News to me, lover."

"Better get your plans in order. This is the overnight away that we've had in mind for months now."

"Wonderful! I'll get it organized next week while you're gone."

"Sorry I can't buy you a gift, Dad. I do have a little money, but I can't shop for anything here. Kurt, could you buy something if I give you the money?'

"Sure."

"Keep your money, Rudi. You need it for odds and ends. It's not important. What *is* important is that you get yourself back on track and be my guy."

"You know I am. I'll make it up to you someday. Everything."

"We've got to be on our way. I have to stop by the cleaners, and also get some food in for when I'm back on the twenty-sixth."

"Don't worry about it," Brenna said. "You and Kurt can eat with me that night, and I'll go with you to help with shopping on the Monday evening after you're back."

"What do you think guys? Is this gal special, or what?"

Their smiles confirmed that they agreed.

The three of them gave Rudi a hug and said goodbye. On their way back to Seaford, Brenna asked, "Why are you coming back on the twenty-sixth? That's a week from tomorrow. Sunday."

"You never ask what I'm up to, and I don't volunteer much. I'm generally not very far away from you, in person or on the phone, but I'm coming back through Washington."

"I see."

"No, I'm afraid you don't. Tina isn't well, I think. She's lost weight, looks washed out, and suddenly the livewire I've known for nearly three years doesn't have much energy. She's way too young for all of these things to happen. If I remember the warning signs correctly, she may be facing a serious medical problem. She says it's her heavy workload and pooh-poohs my concerns. I'm going to look in on her. I think she's a sick girl. But don't be worried about me. I'll be back and be your guy if you'd like to have me around."

"You know the answer to that. But you care about her."

"I do that. But you changed the way I look at us when Rudi went down and you were there hour after hour for three days. And you've been by my side in person, or spiritually, ever since. So I'm asking you. Be patient with me. Please? You've reached a special place inside that hasn't gotten much attention, at least until recently. What you gave of yourself changed my perspective. But yes, I love her dearly. Even if I didn't, I certainly care enough about Tina to be concerned about her well-being. I'm uneasy about how a diagnosis will turn out. I've seen almost identical symptoms before. It was in the fall of '52 when I was in my first semester at Ohio State. A distant cousin, Marie, didn't make it. And she went fast. I'm not saying it's the same thing, but I'm going to write down what my gut feel is telling me and put it away until a doctor has determined what it is that's wrong. It isn't her workload. We'll see if my suspicions are right."

"Dad, you said, 'my first semester at Ohio State'. I thought you and mother were already married by then."

"No, Kurt." Then Erich fell silent.

"Then I came a little early; a surprise."

"Someday you can ask your mother to explain it. Maybe this summer. Rudi will be away, so you might as well spend July and August in California again. But back to Tina. I want to check on her and also call her family if need be. I don't know her mother, but I've met her dad. That goes back a ways. And now that I think about it, it'll be three years on Monday that Tina and I first started working together at Essex. At the heart of it is that we've always been close, and it isn't a time to ignore what I think she's facing."

"God, what else can go wrong in your life?"

"Hopefully it won't be Miss Brenna. You've been my backbone for the past month. I've needed you more than you know. And for more reasons than that, I've discovered." She reached over and squeezed Erich's right hand. It was her way of sending him a message that he was important.

"Well, if you're going to look in on her, I'll pick up Kurt next Saturday and we'll surprise Rudi. What do you think?" Kurt approved of it instantly.

"You're somethin' else, dear heart. Rudi will really appreciate it, I know. Me too. It'll help him forget about Lara. By the way, you worked for her three weeks ago and you were going to tell me what she had to say. Never thought it would slip my mind, but it has."

"Mine, too. What she said was that getting close to Rudi again would lead her back to you, and she didn't want that. It's still that idea of hers that if she loves you, keeps seeing you, it's the kiss of death. Maybe she got the vision wrong. It was Rudi who almost died. She's not wrapped too tight emotionally, at least not at the moment. I'm really worried about her. And I'll call Nate this week, now that you've reminded me of it. Anyway, Lara was on a severe guilt trip when I was there for a little while the day before Easter. It's a terrible thing to say, but I'm glad she's moved aside so I can have you all to myself."

Kurt agreed with her. It was Erich's turn to squeeze Brenna's hand. "There may be more to the story, but I've heard enough."

"Oh, and I have a news flash for you."

"You're expecting." They laughed. Kurt joined them.

"Hmmm. Not a bad thought at that. No, I'm driving you to Kennedy tomorrow evening and will pick you up when you come back on the twenty-sixth. I suppose that'll be at LaGuardia."

"I've said it before. You're a very special gal. The flight out is on TWA, but it doesn't leave until eight o'clock. That a problem?"

"Nope. I can feed Alan and Scot first and then be home in time to put them to bed. Any idea when you'll be back next Sunday? If it's at a reasonable hour, I'll feed you, like I said before. Or maybe we could have dinner out. Then if you have any energy left, I might just stay over, assuming I'm invited."

"You're invited," Erich said. "I have the feeling there won't be anything going on down in Washington. Not to worry. I'll be fine."

"Glad I'll be at Dawn's," Kurt said. "Might get rowdy." They all chuckled.

"What makes you think something like that? You an old hand at it going on seventeen?"

"We've talked about that before, Dad."

"Change of subject. My flight from Heathrow comes into BWI, Baltimore-Washington. Not convenient at all, but I wasn't given a choice.

The one coming back into New York is with Eastern, I think. I'll take a look at my itinerary when we get home."

Late in the afternoon, Erich poured drinks and then got out his schedule to check on the Sunday return. "Yep," he said, "the flight up from Washington National is on Eastern and it gets into LaGuardia at 2:45 if it's on time."

"That'll make it easy. I can have lunch with the boys before I leave. Will you let me keep the Mustang while you're gone?"

"Sure, as long as I get it back in one piece and with no dings in it."

"My insurer, The Metro Agency, says I'm a certified safe driver." Brenna chuckled at the fact that her employer carried her policy. "Your 'horse' will be in good hands. Trust me."

"I do, or I wouldn't let you drive it. But I know you're a good driver. I agree with your insurance company. Now, what about dinner? I'm spending zero time in the kitchen until breakfast."

"How about Rubino's" Kurt asked.

"Sorry Kurt, but that's off limits now. Forever. Maybe you can go down and tell Mario why I'm not coming back."

"He and I grew up together," Brenna said. "I'll get around to telling him why someday. Lara won't, for sure."

"Pick another place, Kurt."

"How about La Taniére? We haven't been there for quite a while. Any problem with that?"

"What do you think, love?" Erich asked.

"Mazza's is better."

"Kurt?"

"Sure. But that's Tina's place. Someone in her family owns it."

"It's a distant cousin, I believe. Not a problem for me. Brenna?"

"Me either. I feel like I'm getting to know Tina. Got a picture of her so I can see what she looks like?"

Erich went to his album and pulled out a photo Tina had finally given him.

"She's an absolute doll, Erich. Sweet and innocent looking. What a lovely face. And that smile. Beautiful. I can see how she stole your heart."

"This was taken fairly recently, but the glow is gone now. She's thinner and looks pale. It's happened too fast, and this shows me just how much she's changed. I hope she'll be all right. She needs medical attention, at least a complete physical exam. But she says it's all work related, stress, and to stop bothering her about it. I know better, I think. But, let's go eat.

Otherwise I'm going to get upset. She's such a good person and, like you, she has great beauty where it counts. In her heart."

They had their dinner, and later in the evening they loved gently. It was one of the few times in recent weeks they'd taken their feelings for each other to a place that gave them comfort. Afterwards, they held each other close. It lasted throughout the night. At first light, they awakened, shared a quick kiss, and then dozed for another hour.

After their catnap, Brenna said, "I'm going to miss you. The hardest part will be Saturday night, but then you'll be back and I'll have you to hold onto again. That's the good part. I understand what you have to do and it's right, I suppose. It'll bother me, but I have to agree. I'm starting to get the impression that if Tina doesn't get medical attention soon, you think her life's at risk."

"I'm not a doctor. But like I said, I recognize some of the same warning signs that I saw in late '52. She needs to start by seeing her GP down there, and then getting blood work done. I have some clout with Aldo, her father, and he'll listen to me. He's a cop in the Bronx, a bull of a man, tough. If I tell him what I suspect, he'll see that she does it. I had hoped Tina would hear me out, but she thinks I'm overreacting. I'm not. To put it simply, I'm worried. We need to get off the subject. It's a short night going over and a long day when I get there. I'll be on the ground at Heathrow around two forty tomorrow morning, Seaford time. I'll send you a message while you're in bed and turn you on."

"Don't you dare. It'll be hard enough. You leave me alone, Erich Mauer!"

"I'm just trying to stir up a little excitement in your life."

"You've done that, but I'll count the hours until you're back next Sunday. Then the following weekend, maybe we can make up for lost time."

When it was time to leave, Erich let Brenna drive. They first dropped Kurt off at Dawn's before they went on to JFK.

"You're a good driver," he said. "Maybe you should be certified as one." Brenna stuck her tongue out at him.

"That wasn't very nice, unless I can nibble on it."

"Don't you go stirring up images like that, or I'll run off the expressway."

The plan was that when they got to Kennedy, they'd have dinner before Erich boarded. He remembered his last overnight into Europe the previous

October—and all the other eastbound flights he'd taken. The lesson he'd learned was that he'd get precious little sleep if his snooze didn't begin shortly after takeoff. They had their dinner, held each other for a moment before he boarded, and then he was on his way. Brenna felt lost on her drive back to Seaford. She was especially glad, though, that Erich had let her keep his Mustang. He was with her, in a way, and it helped fill a small part of the empty space she had inside.

On the ride into London from Heathrow Airport, Erich saw that Bill Drake was right. The forsythia was out in its yellow splendor. He really didn't want to make the trip, but he was here and would do what had to be done, little as it was—or so he thought.

When Erich got to the Mayfair Hotel, he showered and changed. Looking at his watch, and subtracting the five-hour time difference, he saw that it was a little after six o'clock in Seaford. Feeling playful, he decided to call Brenna. A voice that wasn't quite awake said, "Hello."

"This is a horny old goat calling from London. Could I slip into bed with you for a few minutes before you get up?"

"Oh you crazy, lovable man. What a sweet thing for you to do. I was all hollow inside after you left. Your 'horse' kept me company and it did make me feel better. Then I had warm and fluffy dreams about you all night long. If I had you here, I'd attack you. Does that answer your question?"

"Ease up, girl. I've got to walk through the lobby shortly, so I can't have anything obvious on display. If I were to walk over to Berkeley Square, I'd probably attract all kinds of ladies interested in a heavy equipment operator."

"There you go again being a pain. Just keep yourself in check. I'll look after you on Sunday night. Do good while you're there, and I'll be waiting to see you on the weekend. It's really sweet of you to call. Love you, guy."

"You too, babe. See you at LaGuardia around three on Sunday. Now, don't forget. Bye."

"Not possible. Bye, lover."

Both Erich and Brenna felt better after they'd talked. She was deeply touched and had a lump in her throat. "He didn't have to do that, but it shows he was thinking about me and cares enough to call. What am I going to do with all these good feelings I have inside?

Erich began his London visit with afternoon meetings that ran longer than he thought they should. The subject matter was pretty thin, but he considered that maybe it was the way things were done here. In between sessions, he looked out the window for a couple of minutes at the roundabout adjacent Lambeth Bridge. He decided that he couldn't drive here and go clockwise around the circle. "I'd probably go the other way and kill somebody."

It was then that a friendly voice said hello and welcomed Erich to London. The man was a retired Royal Navy Commander who took Erich under his wing and served as his host during whatever free time he had. But most of the week was taken up with meetings, and, as they'd already agreed, the emphasis was on matters related to personnel recruitment, placement, and training. When he met with Bill Drake, he told Erich he'd be over in a couple of weeks to attend the "train the trainers" workshop that Warren Lambros had organized. "I understand you'll be chairing a session on recruiting techniques and practices."

"I'd forgotten all about it, Bill. Guess instead of hitting the pubs I'd better start drafting something. Be interested in hearing what it is I'll have to say."

Drake laughed. "Get away, Erich! You've been at this for years, and in three industries, I'm told. You can walk up to the lectern and let it flow."

"My knowledge base is first, last, and always U.S. oriented. Every foreign location has a different approach to staffing."

"You chaps are well ahead of us in that regard. I'll surely benefit from your know-how and over time will make adjustments to *our* placement methods. I'll bring you a bottle of Glenlivet as an incentive."

"You've twisted my arm just enough to get my attention." They shared a friendly chuckle.

Friday morning came, and Erich said goodbye to his British counterparts. He singled out Bill Drake and said that he looked forward to seeing him in New York. Just after midmorning, Erich left for Heathrow to board what would turn out to be his last flight home from an overseas location.

It was on his way into Washington that Erich began to worry about Tina. With all the meetings, and lunches, and dinners, he hadn't had time to think about much of anything beyond company matters. He was far busier than he'd expected to be.

Tina met Erich at the gate. He was *not* happy to see her looking so thin. Her color was a little better, but something was wrong. He was convinced of it.

They smiled, held each other tightly, and kissed in a way that said their feelings, and the accompanying fire, were still very much alive. Tina was more animated than she was at Easter, so maybe he was wrong. God, he hoped so.

"For your birthday, I'm taking you to dinner, then I'm going to love you all night long. What do you think about that, mister?"

"I'm your slave. But remember that my body clock is five hours different from yours."

"In that case, we'll love first, and then have dinner. Maybe we can sneak something in afterwards. Dessert at home, maybe? I need you. It's been one day short of four weeks. I'm overdue for some serious attention. Then I'm going to hold onto you all night. I need that, too."

"I like the program you've laid out. You're okay, then?"

"I keep telling you that I work long hours and don't eat much. Not a lot of interest in food because sometimes it doesn't agree with me. Stop worrying. I'm all right."

When they got to Tina's delightful little Georgetown apartment, she went straight to her plan of loving first and having dinner later. There was no question that she was deprived and that an inferno was raging inside. It was the Tina he knew from sixteen months ago and then again just before Christmas when they'd met in Sydney. She finally reached the place she wanted to find, and Erich joined her when she asked.

While they were resting, Erich noticed a couple of ugly purple bruises. "Looks like your other lover is pretty hard on you," he said, pointing to her upper thigh.

"Yeah, he's with the Redskins and plays rough." Then she laughed. "I don't have time for anyone else. Besides there's only one man in my life, and he's right here beside me."

"The bruises?"

"I don't know. Must have bumped into a file drawer or something."

"Had any headaches or sore joints lately?"

"What are you trying to do, Erich, play doctor?"

"That's exactly what I'm trying to do, but I'm not playing."

"To answer your questions, yes."

"I want you to call your doctor tomorrow and tell him, don't ask him, to arrange a whole set of blood tests. You're not going to ignore the weight loss, and some of these other symptoms any longer. I'm cross with you."

"I guess you are. But do you still love me anyway?"

"Silly girl. When have I not loved you?"

"I love you too, my worried husband-to-be. We still haven't set a date, but maybe we can talk about that over dinner. I'm not very hungry, but you probably are."

They had what was billed as Erich's birthday dinner, but he was worried about his Tina. There were now more reasons why she needed to see her doctor. She toyed with her food. Erich's appetite was less than robust. Not a way to remember a milestone, his fortieth, coming up on Tuesday.

After they'd had an after dinner drink, and Erich was beginning to feel the effects of the five-hour time change, Tina drove back to her apartment. When they got to bed, Tina complained that her little bit of dinner had upset her stomach.

"Can you wait until morning to be attacked? I had big plans, but now I'm not up to it."

"Better that you rest. Then we're going to go see your doctor tomorrow. No call. We're going to show up, and he *will* see you."

"It'll have to wait until Monday. He doesn't have office hours over the weekend. Do you think I'll live until then, Dr. Mauer?"

"You better, or I'll never speak to you again." Tina giggled. Erich didn't. "After you've seen him, I want you to call me. It won't be necessary to ask him for blood work. He's going to look you over, ask some questions, and then he'll order it done. Count on it."

"I've never seen you like this before. You're frightened, or angry, or something else."

"Both, and more."

"Well, in the meantime, it's time to snuggle." She gave him a loving kiss and said, "G'night, my love."

"Night, sweet."

They spent part of Saturday walking around Georgetown. A charming area, Erich thought. Tina tired fairly quickly, so they went back to her apartment and spent the remainder of the afternoon simply enjoying each other's company.

"We didn't set a firm wedding date last night," Tina said. "In fact, we never even got around to talking about it. I said weeks ago that I liked the idea of having the ceremony around the holidays. What do you think, love?"

Erich's heart sank. He was overwhelmed by the feeling that Tina would never see another Christmas. He said a silent prayer that he was wrong. His face showed something that Tina couldn't quite read.

"Looks like that wouldn't be your first choice. Well, if I'm to have blood tests, that'll take care of me, and we can do it anytime. But you'll need to get yours done, too."

"It'll be sometime after I get back. I have a physical coming up anyway, so those blood results will do, I'm sure."

"Why the physical? Something wrong?"

"No, no. My employers have always arranged annual checkups, so that's what this'll be. A stress test is part of the process. Since I'll be forty on Tuesday, and on my way to becoming a bona fide antique, it's important. Just like your car, it's good to keep track of what's going on. But about a date, I'll leave that with you. After you decide, just tell me and I'll show up."

"Good idea. I'd look pretty silly standing in front of a priest or a minister all by myself. I'll plan on you being there." She smiled.

Tina fixed a light evening meal. For different reasons, neither of them had much of an appetite. In bed early, and with her energy restored somewhat, Tina loved her man with all the passion she felt. In the process, she found that special place that left her totally satisfied, and she murmured softly afterwards.

"I needed that. Now, you've worn me out, or I did it to myself, so would you just hold me until you leave tomorrow? I'm starting to think that maybe you're right about me. It's time I followed your advice and got a checkup."

They slept entangled, and shared the feelings of affection that were uniquely theirs. When morning came, they stayed close and talked quietly about their past, and the future that would be theirs. There was no loving other than what passed between them as they looked into each other's eyes. Tina's face was still handsome, even if it was noticeably thinner. And the beauty inside continued to shine like a beacon—one that drew him inside her heart and soul.

With Erich scheduled to leave National Airport at 1:20 p.m., Tina got a light breakfast together. After they ate, they made small talk until it was time to go.

"You going to be okay, or should I take a taxi?"

"No, I'll take you. I'm not dead yet."

"Please don't say things like that."

Tina laughed and said, "It's just an expression. Easy, my love."

At the airport, Erich asked, "When can you come up next?"

"In a couple of weeks. If not, Memorial Day weekend. We'd have three days together that way. I don't know. Maybe both.

"Good. And I want daily reports. The first one tomorrow after you've seen your doctor—and then the results of your blood work."

"I promise, Mr. Worrywart. Say hello to the boys for me. Give them my love, and tell Rudi I'll come visit the next time I'm up."

"He'll like that. Okay, love. Time for me to get aboard. Talk to you tomorrow."

They held each other close, and then kissed affectionately. Tina felt Erich tense for a moment, but she let it go. She didn't need another message from him to know that he was apprehensive.

"Bye, sweetheart. I'll try to come up in a couple of weeks. Promise. Be good to be back."

"Bye, hon. Take care of yourself. And call me. Please?"

Erich turned at the mouth of the jet way, waved and blew a kiss.

Tina smiled and waved back. After he'd disappeared from view, she suddenly felt terribly, terribly alone. Maybe Erich was right. Now was a time when she badly needed his support, but he was gone.

Chapter Twenty

At LaGuardia, Brenna was happier to see Erich than he was to see her. Caught in the "love the one you're with" syndrome, Tina was very much on his mind when Brenna came down the concourse to meet him. She smiled. He made the attempt.

"Hello, lover." Brenna gave him a welcome home hug. "Glad to have you back." She hugged him again and added a tender kiss to her greeting.

"Good to be home, and to see you and your smiling face."

"You look depressed. Tina?"

"Yep. Tina. She's facing a serious problem. I'm even more convinced of it now. She'll find that out within a few days. Take me home, would you? I need a friendlier environment and to be around someone who's healthy. My mind is begging for a fresh air cure and a reason to smile about something."

"Your support team is still in place, sweet. Only thing is, I can't stay after tonight. But we'll have your birthday dinner on Tuesday and part of next weekend to ourselves."

"I'm looking forward to getting away with you. It'll do me a world of good. I need it."

"Is she that bad off?"

"I'm fairly sure of it, but she doesn't agree. We'll know soon enough. You remember that not long ago I wrote down what my sixth sense was telling me. Hope I'm wrong. But let's change the subject. How are your guys?"

"Fine. They're covered up with school work and grumbling about it some. But they're okay otherwise. They asked about you. I told them you were in London, and they asked me to show them where it is. They were impressed."

"And Rudi?"

"He was *so* excited to see Kurt and me. It took him by complete surprise. He gave me a hug and wouldn't let go. Nearly got to me. He's a good kid; I love him like he's mine. He just needs a woman around. Someone to straighten him up once in a while, and bake his birthday cake. Those kinds of things. You know what I mean."

"It's probably why you got the long hug. You've helped him take a big step toward blurring his memories of Lara. I really appreciate what you did. It was sweet of you."

"I didn't think it was anything out of the ordinary, but he thought it was. So do you. Glad I could help."

"Another subject. How do you like the Mustang now that you've had a chance to drive it for a week?"

"Love it. Great car and it kept me company while you were in England and D.C. Made me feel closer to you when I was sitting behind the wheel."

"Glad you're driving."

"I understand why. And it's a treat, because I really do like your horse. I'll be your chauffeur anytime you'll let me. In exchange, I'm feeding you tonight, if you'd like. Or we could eat out, and then I'll make dinner for you on your birthday. Your choice. You remember I offered to do that before you left me all by myself."

"You aren't alone now. But let me think about it."

"Should we go get Kurt?"

"He said on the way down from Bridgeton last weekend that he was glad to be at Dawn's. Remember what he said about things getting rowdy?"

"Yeah." Brenna smiled at the recollection of it.

"Why don't we eat out. And you know what I'd like to do?"

"Let me guess," Brenna said. "Go back to The Ingleside?"

"Yeah. I need to be there with you tonight. It'll help shelter me from the real world. That's our place. It's where this good thing of ours got its start."

"I know. I was at the same table. You *do* recall?" She chuckled.

"Vividly."

"But I never imagined then that my heart would be where it is today. I agree. Let's do it. It's been a while and it'll be fun. And maybe it'll help you forget about Washington, at least until tomorrow. I'd like you and your head to be here with me tonight."

"It's all right, Brenna. I'm here, and I brought my head with me." Erich showed her a smile. "I'll be fine, but we'll have to see about later on."

"It's all right. You're still the same guy I saw off to London."

Erich and Brenna had a fine, intimate dinner. They talked about Rudi, about Tina briefly, and about where their lives were headed. Small talk filled the gaps, and it was another pleasant night at The Ingleside. Eating there was a good idea, and they went back to number 710 filled with good feelings for each other.

When they were in bed, Brenna told Erich, "I'm going to show you just how much I like having you back."

"I'm guessing you're in need, but I've got too much on my mind tonight to be a good partner." Erich knew he was needed far more in Georgetown than in Seaford. And, much as he didn't want to think about it, he was sure the day was coming when Tina would be little more than a collection of precious memories. Loving Brenna tonight would surely trouble him then.

"Your body clock is still in charge, and I know it's telling you it's late. Maybe it'll be better adjusted in the morning."

"We'll have to see," Erich said.

Brenna, satisfied that it was a possibility, snuggled close and stayed that way much of the night.

By early morning, Erich was able to suppress enough of his anxieties to help Brenna start her day with a smile.

"What a nice way to start the week," Brenna said. "I'd like to do this on your birthday, but since we're eating at my house it won't happen. Doesn't matter. I'll be all smiles for the rest of the week anyway. If anybody asks me if I'm expecting, I'll tell them I hope so. That ought to shake 'em up. Some of my co-workers saw your Mustang, so they know something's going on. I told them about you and where you were. They were all eyes and ears. I loved it."

"And you talk about me being a pain. Looks like it takes one to know one. But, dear heart, this isn't the weekend, and we've got to get going. Join me in the shower?"

"Yeah. I'm all for that."

Before they left, Brenna reminded Erich that she'd promised to go to the market with him after work.

"I'd forgotten all about it. Entirely. Thanks for reminding me. We don't have much in the fridge—or anywhere else. I was about to say I'll need to spend a ton of money on Saturday, but we won't be here. It'll have to be tonight."

"Let me feed Alan and Scot first, then I'll come over sometime after six."

"That's fine. I'd like to take Kurt with us; that is, if he wants to come along. He's not into shopping, but I'll at least ask."

"Sure. Good idea. He may want to spend the time with you."

Later, when Erich put the question to Kurt, he opted to stay home and watch TV. He also had some studying to do for a test that was coming up.

On the train to begin the new week, Erich's mind wouldn't focus on the morning *Times*. His thoughts were with Tina, and what this day would mean for her. He'd be impatient to hear what her doctor had to say. Blood results wouldn't be in until tomorrow, or maybe not until Wednesday. In the office, Katie agreed that Tina had changed between the two times she'd seen her. "I'm scared stiff," Erich had to admit. "And I can't shake this awful feeling that she doesn't have long to live. I've had premonitions like this before."

"You're just upset. She'll be okay."

"I'm expecting her to call sometime today. Whatever it is I'm doing, interrupt me."

When Tina's call came in, she was cheerful enough and started off by saying, "My doctor is concerned, but he's not showing me any alarm. They took a lot of blood, but I won't know until late tomorrow, or more likely midweek, what the results are. Don't worry about me, my love."

"Get back to me tomorrow if you know anything. That's your ex-boss talking. Clayton is buying me a birthday drink, so if for some reason we don't connect, call me on Wednesday. Promise?"

"Yes, Mr. Mauer. Sir!" They shared a laugh. "I have to tell you that when your flight took off yesterday, I don't know when I've ever felt so alone. It was the strangest sensation. I need to have you around me permanently. It's the only time I feel whole."

"Come home, Tina."

"I still have another two months on my extension. We've hired my replacement, but I can't leave unless there's a compelling reason to do it."

"Am I not a compelling enough reason?"

"Yes, but we've been around each other long enough for you to know that I keep my word. They've been good to me, so I'll see it through. You've got me for a lifetime after I'm done here."

"I know about your dedication. That's what made you such a good partner at Essex. We were good. Among the best. Then the idea of a long life together? You're melting my heart. How does it feel? Wonderful."

"We've been good since then, too. And your words? They're touching. You sure know how to get to me. Wait a minute. Uh-oh, Erich. It's my boss. I have to go. I love you tons. See you in about ten days. That's my plan."

"Hope it'll work out that way. We'll talk again tomorrow or on Wednesday. Take care of yourself."

"You know I'll do that. Especially for you. If I don't catch up with you tomorrow, have a very happy fortieth, Erich. And many more. I'm just sorry I can't be there, but we'll celebrate all the rest of them together. Give my love to the boys. Bye, sweet."

"I'll do it. Bye, babe."

Erich felt relieved. At least a little bit. Tina was in good spirits, and what her doctor had to say offered some hope that her condition wasn't one that should lead him to believe it was life threatening. Still he couldn't curb the ominous feeling that sat in the pit of his stomach.

Tina didn't have any further news on Tuesday, so her call was mainly to wish Erich a happy birthday. Again. At the end of the afternoon, Erich went uptown to meet Clayton for that birthday drink they'd put on their calendars a good many weeks ago. When Clayton offered Erich his best wishes for good health and happiness, Erich had to say that apart from his concerns about Tina, he felt great. "On my thirty-third birthday, I thought my life was about over, and I was depressed. At forty, my attitude is that I'm not anywhere close to it. Now I'm expecting to live well past eighty and die in a house of ill repute fighting over some cute blonde a third my age."

"That's funny," Clayton said. "But the not so funny part is your concern about Tina. Your romance on the rocks?"

"More serious than that, Clayton. She's ill. Seriously so, I've convinced myself. About eighteen years ago, my mother had a distant cousin with identical symptoms and it took her life in a couple of months. I'm desperately hoping that it isn't a repeat of that. Tina's only twenty-five. Marie wasn't much older than that. If I lose my girl, I'll be shattered. We'll have test results in a day or two. They may turn out all right; something inside me is saying they won't. But this isn't the way to celebrate a milestone birthday. Sorry for all the gloom."

Erich shook his mood, and he and Clayton had a good visit. It was an enjoyable little party between good friends. At the end of it, Clayton asked Erich to let him know how Tina was doing. In his own way, he loved her, too. Anyone who knew her did. She was that kind of person.

When Erich got home he changed clothes, and then he and Kurt went to Brenna's for dinner. She had a knack for turning a simple celebration into a festive event. There were little touches here and there, and a small banner that proclaimed this to be a special day. Erich was moved. The dinner was exceptional and the hour or so he and Brenna shared afterwards was filled with good feelings. He was glad to be insulated from his fears about Tina. And since Brenna didn't bring up the subject, deliberately Erich thought, he didn't offer any comments. There'd be time enough for that after their evening together was a distant memory.

"Sorry we couldn't be alone for a little while," Brenna said, "but we understand as parents that once we have youngsters around our time isn't always our own."

"It would have been a fitting end to the day, but we had yesterday morning, the pleasant shower, our shopping spree last night, and we have our weekend escape coming up. We do all right for ourselves, and we certainly make the most of it when we're together. That applies to the daylight hours, too."

Erich and Brenna shared more of themselves on her sofa by sitting close together and making small talk. It felt good, and it kept Erich's mind occupied.

"If you can arrange to leave fairly early on Saturday," Erich said, "I'd like to see Rudi in the morning, have lunch along the way, and generally slow the pace of our outing. We've waited months for it, so I'd like it if we could squeeze everything we possibly can out of our time away from your house and mine."

"I'm so looking forward to going away with you, so I'll be ready whenever you say. It's been years since I've done anything like what we have planned. Sharing it with you makes it special."

"What a sweet thing to say."

"You know I mean it."

"Before we get all caught up with our plans, I have to remember to bring the Bobby hat that Rudi wanted. When I was over, one of the guys in our London office said the name came from a Sir Robert somebody or other who was the Minister that set up the police force. I think he said it was in the early 1800's. The stuff you learn, even trivia, when you travel. I'll tell Rudi about it. And he was right about the size. British take an eighth of an inch off our sizes. Hope it'll fit. If not, he'll have to get rid of some of that mop. He's got enough hair for the whole family."

"Get used to it, Erich. It's the style and it's not likely to go away anytime soon. I'm holding on as long as I can with Alan and Scot."

"Good luck. Now, it's time for Kurt and me to go. Forgot to mention how much I like where you put the tapa. Looks great."

"I don't know how many times I've told the story about it. It's an attention getter. Dad thinks you must be all right. I told him you are. You two still have to meet."

"We'll get to it. There are some other things to deal with first."

"I know."

"Thanks for a great dinner. I really enjoyed it. And I appreciate the billfold. You know that mine is worn out. Be nice if I had some money to put in it." They chuckled over Erich's feigned poverty.

Erich held Brenna close and then kissed her affectionately. She understood the reasons behind the especially firm hug but made no mention of it. She hoped he'd be all right over the weekend.

"I'll call you on Friday, and we'll set a time that I can pick you up on Saturday morning."

"Like I said. Anytime. Take care of yourself, Erich. And, again, happy birthday."

"It was a wonderful party. Thanks so much. You're a love."

"So are you. Night, sweetheart."

"G'night."

Brenna went to bed worried about her man and the emotional load he was carrying. Before she slept, she said a prayer for him.

On Wednesday morning, Erich found a gift sitting on his desk. Considering its shape, he had a pretty good idea what it was.

"I never can remember to be on time," Katie said. "It's a day late, but I'll bet it doesn't matter."

Erich opened his gift. It was a bottle of Beefeater's.

"This stuff makes absolutely the best dry Gibson on the face of the earth. Thank you so much, Katie." Erich gave her a big hug.

"You're welcome. 'Enjoy', as we say out on Long Island."

At midafternoon, Tina called. "I've been with the doctor, and he's seen something in the blood results that troubles him. He wants me to go back for additional tests tomorrow. I'll have those results on Monday, he says."

"Did he say anything to you about what he's seen?"

"No. I guess he just wants to make certain that his diagnosis is correct. Who knows? Maybe they got my blood mixed up with somebody else's. Best I can do is pray that it isn't real serious and we can deal with it."

"Amen to that, sweetheart. When you know something, you'll tell me right away won't you?"

"You'll be the first to know. But we'll talk tomorrow and again on Friday."

"I'll be seeing Rudi on Saturday morning. Then I'm going on to walk my lots in central Massachusetts. I want to make sure they haven't been stolen."

Tina laughed softly. "I hope not. That's our weekend retreat. You've never taken me up there, and I'd love to go. Your pictures of the area showed me how pretty it is. Maybe when we get on top of this medical thing, we can do that later in the spring."

"We'll map out a plan when you're here in a week or two."

"I need to get back to work, Erich. Call you tomorrow. Until I can say it again, I love you, mister. It feels good."

"Love you, too, babe."

"Bye, Erich."

Tina seemed to be in reasonably good spirits. A positive sign. Maybe.

Late on Friday afternoon, Erich met Clayton for a drink at their old haunt, The Watering Hole. "I'm as concerned about Tina as you are, Erich. Any news?"

"Not much. There were further tests yesterday. Tina and I talked afterward, and then again early this afternoon. I know she's worried but, bless her heart, she's putting on a good front and still plans to come up at mid-month."

"If there's any chance I can see her, let me know."

"It'll be up to her. She complains of being washed-out most of the time, so we'll have to see."

Erich wanted to be on the 5:09, so he and Clayton finished their drinks, wished each other a good weekend, and then said their goodbyes.

When Erich got home, he made dinner. Then after he and Kurt had eaten, he called Brenna. The timing of their overnight away couldn't have been worse. But until the test results were in, he'd try to minimize his concerns about Tina's condition.

"Hi, ma'am. How are things down near the Sound?" Erich asked.

"No complaints. Especially since my guy is taking me across the state line for immoral purposes and a wonderfully good time. Can any of it be called white slavery?"

"Part of the Mann Act, if I remember right. It won't apply if you're going to enjoy being enslaved as much as it sounds like you are. And I need the break, too. I'm going to try running away from myself with you in tow."

"I'm willing to tow or be towed," Brenna said, "and I'll help keep you focused. But you'll need to give me a chance."

"What time can you be ready in the morning? I've got to run Kurt up to the Engel's before we go. Chris has invited him up to spend the day, and then stay overnight."

"Like I said before. Anytime. But if you're here by about nine, we could spend a couple of hours with Rudi and then stop for lunch before we go on to Massachusetts."

"Sounds good. Gotta go. It's time to go clean up the mess in the kitchen. I'll pick you up at around nine."

"You sound better. We'll be okay. See you in the morning. Night, love."

"Night, gal."

After a night of conflicting and sometimes painful dreams, Erich rousted Kurt at seven thirty and saw that he was fed. When they got to the Engel's, Chris greeted Erich with his customary, "How's it goin', XM?" so named because of the vanity plate on his Mustang. Erich also saw Matt and asked him how he was doing. His response was a little frosty.

"Somebody was a fink and talked about my problems. I didn't much appreciate it." The way he said it made Erich think he was being accused of leaking his confession.

"Don't look at me, Matt. I don't talk to anybody in this town except Arch Radford, Maurie down at the station parking lot, Nate Kaplan, my ex, and the young lady I date. Even if I did, you took me into your confidence so what you said some time back stayed right here." Erich tapped his forehead with an index finger. "I don't abuse someone's trust. Never have."

"Sorry, Erich. I'm pretty edgy. It's led to some problems, as you can guess."

"Given my track record, I'm the last guy to give advice, but who was at the center of what happened? You told somebody else after me. Look there for your answer."

"You're being hard on me, but I deserve what I got. We've made peace at home, but it's left a scar. Maybe over time I can put it right. But you've got problems of your own, according to Chris. I'm sorry to hear about it. Kurt told him you saved Rudi's life."

"And something else has been added to the heap. The gal I'd marry is pretty sick, I think. She's only twenty-five. If I have to take many more hits, maybe I'll OD. It's been a bitch of a year so far."

"I hope you're not serious."

"Not really. I've just hurt a lot inside since March. Got to run, Matt. Thanks for having Kurt up. He always enjoys being here."

"Chris's idea. They're pals. It's good to have friends. And we enjoy having him around."

Erich and Brenna got everything in order and were ready to leave at a little after nine. She was pleased to be going on an outing and her warm smile closely rivaled Tina's. And for the first time, Alan and Scot confirmed what Brenna had been saying right along. By their actions and their words, they showed Erich that they liked their mother's friend, Mr.

Mauer, and even said they hoped that he and their mom had a good time. Suddenly, Erich felt like a stepfather. But the prospect of having added responsibilities, at least at the moment, troubled him some.

In Bridgeton, they had a good visit with Rudi, and he was tickled to get the "Bobby" hat. It fit. They all said, "Whew!"

Rudi's news was that he would be going to summer camp after all. It was on a lake in Maine called Embden Pond. He was excited about being accepted and talked at length about all the things he'd be doing over the summer. Erich was pleased to see how upbeat he was. But then, almost anything would be an improvement over where he was now. The other news was that after summer camp, he'd be assigned to a Ducheneaux Foundation school in north central Massachusetts.

"I go away for a week and look what happens," Erich said. "Next thing I know, you'll be home. But being in Massachusetts means you'll be close to where I'm going to put up our little cottage someday. Maybe they'll let you come help me out, assuming the timing is right."

"I don't know about that," Rudi said. "There are a lot of things what they want me to do. I guess it'll be two years. Sounds like a long time. But I screwed up, so I gotta do 'em."

"Don't suppose there's any point in saying that you should have listened to us and stayed away from Lara."

"I don't listen very good. By the time I get out of the program, I'll be older and maybe I'll know enough to pay attention. Hope so. Being at home sure beats this."

"On that thought, and since you're about to have lunch, it's time we got on our way up to Sturbridge. Take care of yourself. We'll see you next week, probably in the afternoon."

"Thanks for the hat, Dad. It's great."

"You're welcome. Glad to do it. For sure, nobody else here has one like it. Just don't let anybody steal it."

Erich and Brenna hugged Rudi, said goodbye, and then left to find a place to have lunch. There weren't a whole lot of choices along I-95, so it wasn't until they got east of Hartford that they saw a restaurant near the highway that looked decent.

"Rudi seems okay," Brenna said. "He still doesn't have a mom, unless I'm it now, but he gets regular meals and has structure to his life that he hasn't had for probably two years. That's no reflection on you because there wasn't anything you could do short of sending the boys back to California."

"I'd like to have him at home," Erich said, "but you're right. All I have to do is look back at what he's been into since the end of '68 to know that he's better off in a well-ordered situation. We'll see what effect it has later on—say two or three years from now."

After they'd eaten and driven further east, Erich came off I-86 at an exit where a sign pointed toward Stevens Springs. He drove north until they crossed into Massachusetts.

"There's the state line. The naughty stuff is now in effect," Erich said. Brenna laughed.

"After a week of being alone, you don't know how ready I am for that. Only thing is, it's the wrong time of the month. We didn't plan very well."

"Not to worry. There's always next week."

Driving further into Massachusetts, they went through Monon, and then came to Pelham on U.S. 20. Erich had looked at a map and found that if they turned east they'd drive through the little town of Bromfield where that beautiful white church was. He'd mentioned it to Brenna, and she wanted to see what it was he'd been talking about. It wasn't long before they were in front of it. He parked across the street.

"Beautiful. Suppose it's open? I'd sure like to see inside."

"I have no idea. Let's give it a try."

They walked up the knoll and found to their disappointment that the door was locked. They could hear someone practicing on the organ but decided not to press their need to check out the interior.

"Best we don't disturb whoever it is that's getting ready for tomorrow's services. I saw on the sign we just passed that it's called First Congregational Church. Sure is lovely. And old, too. We'll try again on our next trip up."

Brenna smiled. "Is that a promise?"

"Sure."

She looked at Erich and showed him a sweet smile.

While they were there, and parked near the entrance of a restaurant called the Woodside, they decided to go in for a coffee. What they didn't count on was that it was served in white, industrial strength mugs. Good, though. They both agreed on that.

"I'm guessing that most of their regular customers are muscular folks like truck drivers, bulldozer operators and the like. You could kill somebody with one of these. Maybe I should take one back to New York. I'll bet Katie would get a kick out of having one."

It was late afternoon, so they drove on to Sturbridge and the Liberty Cap Motel. It was colonial charm in a number of low-rise buildings near the entrance to Old Sturbridge Village. After they'd checked in and their overnight bags were unpacked, they were both about ready to eat. The two of them spent some time going over the motel-supplied magazine about the Sturbridge area. Afterwards, they talked some about their situation and how good it was to get away by themselves even if, for at least two reasons, it was the worst possible weekend to do it.

When they were ready to leave for dinner, the young man at the registration desk suggested that they try the Oxen Pub located west on Route 20. A graduate student, he was doing some historical research on this part of Massachusetts. Drawing on his knowledge, he was in his glory telling them that the building dated from 1820. "It was a meeting house in Bromfield, after which it was moved to its current location in 1834 and used as a Catholic church. From 1860, it was a shoe factory; then in 1940 it was turned into a restaurant that's become popular."

"We would've passed by the place on the way into town," Erich said. "Guess we missed it."

"It's plain looking and shows its age, so you probably wouldn't have noticed it. The food's good, and on Saturdays there's entertainment. It's a local guy, Skip Kendrick. He plays guitar and has a decent voice. Most of his music is aimed at a mature crowd. I think you'd enjoy yourselves. The building is a piece of local history; Skip is part of the local color."

"Okay, we'll give it a try. Thanks for the suggestion."

And Erich and Brenna did enjoy themselves. It had been months since they'd spent so much time over cocktails, good food, and liqueurs afterwards. It was a delightful evening.

Back at the Liberty Cap, they both had to admit they were tired. Even so, they talked for a while. "It's good that we could get away," Brenna said. "Makes it easier to appreciate what we have."

"Right from the beginning, you've been a joy to be with. I've told you that any number of times. The plus is that you've been tremendous support. I don't know. It might be that someday we could be an item in the social column. But like I said before we went out to eat, there are questions that need answers first. Let's put them aside for now and enjoy the rest of our weekend."

With that thought in mind, Erich and Brenna went to bed, stayed close, and quickly fell asleep.

At first light, Erich woke up feeling a bit guilty about enjoying a weekend away with someone other than Tina—especially given all the uncertainties she was facing. But the fact that she was in his thoughts let him rationalize that it wasn't completely shameful.

"Where are you?" Brenna asked.

"For a moment, I was thinking about Tina."

"I understand, but this is *our* weekend, so why don't we add to it by having some breakfast. Any ideas?"

"I know a place off on a side street near Route 20. It's called Smokey's. Only thing is, I went there with Lara."

"Not a problem. In fact, I'll be happy to chase her ghost out of the place. I owe you that."

"It's a deal. They have some very tasty homemade sausage, assuming you'd be interested."

"Oh, yumm! You've just said the magic words and they made my stomach growl. Could we get started?"

Their late breakfast was scrumptious. After a second coffee, Erich and Brenna drove off to Bass Lake so she could see his lots. At the last minute, Erich decided to go by the real estate office to see if it was open. As they pulled around back, they saw a couple of cars, so he assumed it was.

Once inside, the only person there was Owen Laird.

"Hey, Erich. How you doin'?"

"Okay, mostly. You?"

"Good. You about ready to have me put up a cottage?" While Owen was asking his question, he looked Brenna over very thoroughly. She cringed.

"Got to put the money together first. My younger boy got into drugs and the state has him now. I'm not sure yet what kind of money they'll be looking for. That comes first. And my job has some uncertainties written all over it. I'd love to do it, but let's see how everything gets sorted out."

"We work with a bank over in Monon, and I know they'd be willing to give you a construction loan. Once the cottage is finished, we could roll your loan over into a permanent mortgage. Wouldn't take much cash. The equity you have in your lots would probably cover it."

"You're a skillful salesman, Owen, and going ahead with it is tempting. But I have to wait. I'll be back. You know that."

"Well, you know that I've got a job for you here if you want it."

"There's that carrot again," Erich said. "New York and I aren't as friendly as we once were. I may come back to you one of these days and ask you to tell me what you have in mind."

"My offer's open, you know. When the day comes, I'll be ready. Someday you'll work for me, I have a feeling, even if it's only on weekends after your cottage is up."

"Could be. It might be fun. Different, for sure. By the way, I thought you had a customer. I saw another car out there."

"No, no. We just opened for the season this morning. The car belongs to one of my tenants, Abbie Knox. She's a teacher over in Bromfield and rents from me. I have three big bedrooms upstairs, and a teacher in each one of 'em. It's a little extra income. But you haven't introduced me to your friend."

"Oh, sorry. This is Brandi Galliano, my stepmother." They laughed. Brenna knew exactly what Erich was doing.

"Ahh. Named after two drinks. Tasty sounding."

"Sorry. The Brandi has poison in it," Brenna said.

"Snappy comeback. I like that. Sharp."

"I discovered that some time ago. But times up, and we've got to be on our way. If my corporate world collapses, you might hear from me."

"Let me know, Erich. Bye, Miss Brandi."

On their way over to the lots, Brenna asked, "Are you serious about his offer? I wouldn't work for that S.O.B. if he had the last job on the planet. He might put a move on you. He surely did it to me. Those eyes. I feel violated."

"I've known Owen for about three years now, so I ignore him. But I don't want you to lose what you've had since yesterday. Focus on that."

After a couple of minutes, Brenna said, "I did what you suggested, and I'm fine now. Thanks."

When they got up on the lots, Brenna said, "What a beautiful setting. Be great if you could build something here. The leaves aren't out yet, so you can see the pond below, and the lake, too. I love it. Hope I can see it happen."

"Probably will, if my instincts are right. By the way, when I've been up here during the summer, I've discovered that you can always see the pond. It's the lake that'll disappear in three or four weeks. The trees across the street turn into a wall of deep green by the end of May. And something I haven't mentioned is that all these offshore lots have deeded rights to beaches and docks, so I'd be able to use the lake when the time comes. Maybe you'd like to come up for a swim sometime."

"No need to ask. Just say when. I'd love it."

Erich and Brenna walked the land, and then headed back to Seaford. As they drove, she said, "I was surprised to see the laurel coming out already."

"I'm not sure when it's in bloom. It was out in May last year, but it was about three weeks later than this."

"With it growing in that big granite outcrop, it really sets off the building site. You made a good choice. I'm as excited about it as you are. Will you have a fireplace?"

"A local expression answers a question this way: 'Is a clam's butt watertight?' It's another way of saying that I wouldn't be without one. It's part of the dream. Laird has a half-dozen basic floor plans, but they can be customized. I pretty much know what I'll be doing with my little place, right down to the interior details."

"Any chance you'd move up here?"

"The idea does have some appeal. If my career goes to hell in New York, I might take Owen up on his offer. I wouldn't make the kind of money I'm used to, but I sure could live a lot cheaper. I figured out that mortgage payments wouldn't be much more than what I pay Penn Central for my Forty-Six Ride commuter ticket to Grand Central."

"My uncle Fergus, Dad's brother, makes a good living in real estate. I'll bet you'd be good at it, too. You have lots of business experience that would help. Only thing is that you'd be leaving me behind. Seaford's home, and I'm a city girl, so there isn't any way I could live here."

Erich chuckled. "The cottage is still in the future plans stage, and my idea is that it would be used on weekends and summer vacations. You could bring the boys, and we'd have a fun time. A boat is also on my covet list."

"I like your plan. Be fun for the boys. They've never been to camp or had a chance to stay at a place out in the country."

"It won't happen this year for sure, so you'll have to put up with circumstances the way they are. You know the reasons why."

"Let things come about as they will. I know what's on your mind. Whatever happens, you know I'll be there for as long as you want me."

"I do, and you know how much I appreciate it."

They drove in silence for several miles. Erich was wondering what Tina's blood results would be, decided that his courage had abandoned him, and that he really didn't want to know. Brenna was thinking about the cottage, and how much fun it would be to spend part of her vacation there with Erich and the boys.

"Hungry, babe?" Erich asked.

"Not really. We don't have far to go, and maybe we can find something to snack on when we get to your place. No problem. I'm just enjoying the scenery and all the signs of spring out there. After our long, gray winter, it's wonderful to see color again. Makes me feel upbeat."

"And that rubs off on me. My boy-girl relationships have rarely been this good, so maybe I'm learning how to get it right. As we've been driving, I spent a few minutes thinking about Tina and the differences about the way I see the two of you. With her, there has always been something intense about my feelings. Being too possessive is part of it . . . not much different than the way I behaved in high school. Not very mature. Tina's something of a trophy. You've seen her photo, so you know what I'm saying. If someone stared at her the wrong way, like Owen did to you, I'd probably take on someone twice my size and half my age to defend my territory."

The thought of that made Brenna chuckle. "There's a streak of feistiness in you. But I guess I've known that right along."

"And Brenna Walsh? An entirely different set of emotions. We're closer to the same age, have sons, been tested, survived, and now we're as comfortable together as a pair of fleece slippers. Instead of it being intense, there's warmth and a wonderful mushy feeling that certifies what's inside is pure contentment. Because I know where our hearts are, I don't have to think about doing battle. It isn't that we're over the hill, or past caring, it's as simple as knowing where we stand. Owen's leer bothered you. It didn't me. If he'd done that to Tina, I'd have had sharp words for him. What we have is something settled, something mature. It's absolute harmony. And after struggling with how to say what I feel, I'm not sure the difference came out the way I'd hoped."

"Everyone has probably had a romance that's made them ache a little," Brenna said. "Intensity of feeling *is* maybe a better way to put it. Then a good thing like us comes along. I decided not long ago that people ought to mature first and maybe wait until about thirty before they try to put a life together with someone they care about. By then, they should've had time to grow out of their adolescent silliness which could damage a relationship that might otherwise work. I followed what you were getting at. Pretty easily."

"I think you put it better than I did. For sure, you understood the point I was trying to make. But before we get too deeply immersed in the subject, I want to give you a little something when we get home. It's the birthday present I mentioned when I left for London. Nothing like being a couple of months late. Meant to bring it along, but I forgot. Too many things going on, I guess."

Once back at 710, Erich said, "Let's get to your gift. What you have to do is imagine that it's Monday, February 23 and not Sunday, May 3. It's hand crafted, so it took a while." Erich turned, took a small box from the upper drawer of his nightstand, and handed it to Brenna. She opened it. Inside was a simple white gold bracelet to match her ring with the opal set in it.

"Ahhh, you've done it again. Another great idea and it's so chic. I have to show Colleen when I get home. She'll probably want to steal it. Thank you so much. I love it." She gave him a hug to confirm that she was happy with her present.

"Now, sweetheart, I hate to see a good thing come to an end, but I've got to get you home so I can pick up Kurt. If I leave him there much longer, the Engels will start to think he's part of their family."

At the little brick Cape on Wisteria Drive, Erich walked Brenna to the door and gave her an affectionate hug.

"I'll call you tonight if for no other reason than I want to," Brenna said. "Give me a chance to say thank you again. Especially for the bracelet."

"We'll talk later. Say hi to the boys—and thank your sister."

"I'll do it. Bye, hon."

"Bye, babe."

Chapter Twenty-One

The first Monday in May was a day as painful for Erich Mauer as the two preceding days had been pleasant. Early in the afternoon, Tina called.

"Hi, love. The blood results are back, and I've seen the doctor."

"And?"

"Bad news, Erich. Really bad news. The diagnosis is leukemia, and he doesn't give me much hope or very long to live."

"No, Tina. NO!"

In the relative quiet of the seventeenth floor, Erich's voice carried well beyond Katie's nearby desk. She easily heard him and bolted into his office, her eyes as big as saucers. Tina continued talking, but as she did Katie waited while Erich wrote something on a notepad. Finished, he turned it so she could read the single word he'd written in bold letters: LEUKEMIA! She covered her open mouth with the fingertips of both hands and exclaimed, "Oh, my God! *Oh, no.*" He signaled her to leave and to close the door.

"I should have mentioned some of my symptoms to you when I left to come back after New Year's. I thought it was just the long hours, and I still might not have gone to the doctor if you hadn't been for you. I'm sorry, Erich. This sure puts an end to our wedding plans. I never dreamed I had something that could be fatal. But I do, according to my test results."

Hard as it was, Erich had to keep his emotions under control. He felt it was vital.

"Is your doctor saying that nothing can be done? I can't believe he's already given up. There must be something he can do."

"I'm being admitted to Georgetown University Hospital and will be going in this afternoon. They have a new cancer center and he wants me to undergo treatment there. I'd like you to be here with me, but it looks like I'm going to be pretty busy for a while. Best I can do is take my big picture of you with me."

That just about undid Erich, but he hung on. He had to.

"Somehow, you'll have to let me know what's going on. I want you to get better, love. After all we've been through, we've earned the right to have a life together."

"We have, but I'm not holding up my end. I'll try. You know I'll do the best I can."

"I'll be saying lots of prayers for you. Do your folks know yet?"

"No. I don't want to call until Papa's home. It'll be hard on Mama. He needs to be there. We should be able to talk before I leave for the hospital."

"Where are you now?"

"At work."

"Why?"

"I had to give my boss the news. He's released me from the extension, of course, and has said he'll see that I'm paid through the end of the month. After that, I'll be on medical leave. The company will carry my group insurance so that I have coverage. I couldn't afford treatment otherwise. I told my doctor here that I really want to be back in the New York area as soon as it can be arranged. He's going to call a classmate who's at Kettering. But if the treatments don't work, I'll be going home, I suppose. Will you come see me?"

"Ohh, Tina. Nothing could keep me away. Even if it costs me my job. And you have to let me know if I can see you before that."

"I will as soon as I know something. Papa will have your phone numbers in case you're needed. I wanted to come spend a weekend with you and see Rudi, but it won't happen, at least now. He's got enough to deal with. I don't want to be another worry."

"The way you sound, it's hard for me to believe how well you're taking this. I hurt like hell."

"I don't have much choice, my love. It'll probably hit me later on. If I feel anything, it's that I don't like the idea of being alone. But that won't last. I'll have lots of company starting later today."

"You know I'll be with you in spirit."

"I know. I can feel it, and it helps. Your picture will, too. But I've got to go, sweetheart. I need to get home and pack a few things that I can take with me to the hospital. I'll make sure I have a phone and will call you when I can. I love you, Erich, and I'm sorry to put you through this."

"I love you, too, Tina. But don't worry about me. Just get well."

"I'll do the best I can. Bye, my love."

"Bye, sweetheart."

Katie saw the light go out under the line Erich had been on, but she decided not to disturb him even though a shoulder would surely be helpful at a time like this. He'd come out when he was ready. In the meantime, she intercepted calls and turned anyone away who wanted to see him. Even Joel. She explained what had happened. He understood. "When he's ready, have him come see me."

After Erich hung up, he turned his chair around and stared out the window. There were no tears. What he felt was shock and a refusal to accept the fact that Tina could be gone from his life before long. The odds that she'd survive were astronomical, but he refused to give up hope. Miracles did happen, like their chance meeting. But life, he thought, was certainly being unfair. Maybe it was the price he was paying for having been a rogue. Then he reflected on what the Kennedy family had endured over the years, and the entertainer, Roy Orbison, who'd lost his young sons in a house fire. "I'm not alone, but it doesn't offset the pain one bit."

After nearly a half-hour, Katie knocked softly and asked, "Is there something I can get you or anything I can do?"

He turned around and said, "Yes, Katie. Find someone who has a cure for leukemia."

"Joel was here. I told him about your bad news. He says when you're ready he'd like to see you."

"Maybe this is the day of reckoning. Might as well see him now and get it over with. I couldn't possibly feel any more torture than I do right now."

Katie got misty eyed when she said, "You don't know how sorry I am, Erich. I've known since the first day you were here how much Tina meant to you. And when she called to tell me about you, it said so much about the kind of person she is. Then to meet her...." Katie got some tissues and went to the ladies room.

"You wanted to see me, Joel?"

"Compared to what Katie just told me, it's pretty unimportant. She says your fiancée has leukemia."

"That's what the test results show. She'll be on her way to the hospital before much longer. Her doctors don't seem to be offering her much hope. I'm devastated."

"Was she the attractive dark-haired girl who was here a couple of months ago? It was late on a Friday, as I remember. There was something about her that reminded me of Katherine Ross who played Mrs. Robinson's daughter in *The Graduate*. What got my attention was her smile. It was radiant."

"You could hardly miss it. Not much question that you saw her. It was the first weekend in March. But when she came back on the eve of Good Friday, I could see the change. Her face had lost a lot of its glow. The part of the story you don't know is that Tina and I worked together at Essex. When the company was taken over, she went to Washington and it was over, or so we thought. Then we ran into each other in Sydney last December, the afternoon after Forsyth's Christmas party, and we got everything back that we'd given up early last year. Now this."

"You're right," Joel said. "I didn't know the details. She was a striking young woman. I'm terribly sorry, Erich, and I understand what you feel. If you need time, take it. The company will still be here when she's gone—if that's the way it's headed."

"Looks that way, I'm afraid."

"I don't know, Erich. You sure have taken more than your share of hits lately. If you want the rest of the day, you can go. I can imagine what you're going through."

"Thanks, but I need to be around people as much as I can for as long as I can. There isn't anything I can do for Tina. She'll be busy, under the care of doctors, and in the hands of Providence. There's a chance that she'll be moved up here soon. That'll help."

"This is a difficult time for you, I know, so we're here to lend support in whatever way we can. And if you'd rather not make your presentation at Warren's meeting on Friday, I won't object."

"Thanks, Joel. I appreciate your understanding, but Warren is counting on me, and my part of the program is set. I can't back out now. Besides, it'll keep my mind occupied."

After Erich had settled down some, he called Clayton

"Sorry to get your month off to a bad start, but I've heard from Tina."

"What's the news?"

"As bad as it can get. Leukemia."

"My God, Erich! And she's only twenty-five? How unfair can life be?" His voice was unsteady.

"It really, really hurts. We were working on plans for a year-end wedding. I said a long time ago that Tina was the one woman I'd marry, and now it's almost inevitable that she's going to be taken from me. She's at Georgetown University Hospital, but it's possible that she'll be hospitalized locally."

"If that happens, I'll want to go with you some evening to see her. Please let me know."

"I will. Got to go. I have another call waiting."

"Erich. It's Aldo. You heard from my Tina?"

"I have. Knocked the wind out of me."

"Same here. Mama's taking it real hard, but we have to stick together and do what has to be done. I want her in a hospital up here until she gets real bad, then we'll bring her home. I know you got an important job, but she'll want you around whenever it's possible. We'd like that, too. And you can stay here if you want."

"Thanks, Aldo. My Rudi's in detention, but I still have Kurt at home. I'll do whatever you ask. You know that. Tina means everything to me, and I'll be available."

"We gotta move her stuff outta her place down there. I'm gonna rent me a truck on Memorial Day weekend, and me and my boys are gonna do the move. What I want you to do is drive her car back here. She's finished with it. Would you do that? She wanted me to ask you to."

"You know I will. Maybe I can help you load the truck, too. Just let me know what the plans are, and I'll show up."

"When we met back in January I figured you for a good man, and I was right. I'm real sorry you won't be a part of the family. You two were good for each other. I could see it."

"What you're saying is that you think she won't make it."

"That's what I'm telling you. She's already given up."

"I'm not ready to hear that. You won't object if I try to change her mind? She's my future, at least the biggest part of it."

"No. I want you to try. Be rough on all of us if we lose her."

"You know how to reach me here and at home, so stay in touch."

"Sure. Appreciate it that you'll help out. We'll talk before long."

"Good. It's important. Say hello to Mrs. Conti. Bye, Aldo."

Not long after Erich got home that evening, Brenna called.

"What did you find out today?"

"It's leukemia, babe. She won't be with us long, I'm afraid. The family wants me on call, and of course I've promised to be available whenever they need me. It's the least I can do. Tina's papa and her two brothers are going to empty out her apartment on the Saturday of Memorial Day weekend. I'm to drive her car back. Tina's request that I do it."

"Any objections if I come over for a little while? Sounds like you need a shoulder again. You've had a horrible year."

"Yeah, the decade's off to a bad start. I hate to keep bothering you, but it'd be good to have you here. I'm absolutely stunned. You already know she's only twenty-five. Not fair, even if I didn't care about her the way I do."

Brenna wasted no time getting organized and then leaving for number 710 at 17 Mianus Ridge. While Erich was waiting, he turned on the TV and for a few minutes and watched a news report about four students that had been killed at the Kent State campus out in Ohio. Unable to deal with more grief, he turned it off. "Isn't there any good news today?" he asked quietly.

When Brenna got to Erich's building, she parked in a visitor's space and then buzzed to be let in. Once at this door, she gave him a caring hug. He welcomed the comfort that came with it.

"The way things are going, I might as well move in so you can have a permanent shoulder handy. I'm not trying to be funny. This is a very sad day for you, I know. Your character's being tested, and I'm amazed that you're holding up as well as you are."

"I said the same thing to Tina this morning. Her papa says she's given up and is resigned to her fate. I'm sorry you never knew her. She's attractive, you know that, full of life, even-tempered, and a pleasure to be around. It helps, I suppose, that she's in love with me—and I with her. But that still doesn't change what I've said about you. We talked about that yesterday. I worry now that something will happen to Brenna Walsh. I seem to have a curse of some kind."

"That doesn't sound like the Erich Mauer I know, and I want no more of it. Maybe you aren't holding up that good."

"Doing my best, dear heart. It's the emotional drain talking. I'll be okay. Have to be, because I'm making a presentation on Friday. Same thing when Tina's brought up to a hospital in New York, or they take her home. I can't show her a sad face."

"Like with Rudi, I'll be here for you. That's a given. There are some hard days ahead, and I accept that fact. It's either that, or I walk, but I couldn't do that to you. Or me. You're too important. So what you have to do in return is meet me half way. I'm not going to let you mourn forever. Life will go on, and Rudi, and Kurt, and I, will all need you, as will Alan and Scot. You've gotten to be important to them, too. If you carry on too long, it won't be fair to us, and you certainly won't be treating yourself right. You have lots of years ahead, and we'll want you to share at least some of them with us."

"I hear you. Thanks for the sermon. I'll do my part, but I expect to be hurting for a while."

"But you can't let it ruin your life. I'll help you get on with it if you'll let me inside."

"Not to worry. I'll need you there. And I don't have to tell you how much your being here again means to me."

On Friday afternoon, Erich made his presentation on recruitment and employment practices to the IMCO personnel representatives who had come in from subsidiary facilities worldwide. When he'd finished, Warren Lambros took him aside and congratulated him on a job well done.

"For a guy who doesn't like to do these kinds of things, I could see that you got caught up in the give and take. You should take pride in what you've just done. You're good at it. Way better than I guessed you'd be. Considering your terrible news about Tina, I know it took something extra to be up for this. You hurt, and it shows. But you did a really first-rate job. We'll talk more about your situation later. In the meantime, Bill Drake brought a couple of bottles of Glenlivet with him, so it's time to have a sample."

Erich agreed, and it was a good way to end Warren's three-day "train-the-trainers" workshop.

The weeks immediately following were taken up with fairly routine workdays and then driving with Kurt and Brenna to see Rudi on Saturday afternoons. Dawn, and Ryan and Greg, would also drop in on him, generally on Sundays, so he was far from forgotten. Brenna made plans to stay over on Saturday nights whenever she could. Her support was unwavering, but whenever they loved, infrequent as it was, it was based more on physical needs than anything else. They understood the reasons and were patient. Important to both of them, though, was the fact that from time to time they were able to spend a night close together.

It wasn't until the end of the month that Erich's routine finally settled into a new pattern. It was then that the other shoe dropped. On the Friday that led into the long Memorial Day weekend, Joel called Erich to his office and asked him to sit down. He was certain that he knew what was coming.

"You've had a tough year, Erich, and I hate adding to your troubles. That out of the way, I'm fully-grown, over fifty, and have to carry out what I've been instructed to do. So, effective May 31, a week from Sunday, your recruitment and employment unit will be abolished. We'll cover your salary through the end of August, but our insurer won't allow us to continue your group coverage. You can use your office anytime you like, come and go as you please, but your termination will also be effective at the end of the day on the thirty-first. As such, you'll have no further responsibilities after that. Katie will work for me but will be available to you until September 1. And in case you're wondering, all your colleagues are in the same boat. No one is unhappier about this than I am. It's been a good team, and all of you have done good work, but the consultants won. After my call to you in Sydney, I promised you then that I'd bitch to executive management about what you had to go through—and then later on fight to save our department. I did that, but my arguments were mostly ignored. End of story."

Erich paused, stared at his boss briefly, without really seeing him, and allowing the words he was expecting to hear sink in. Then he said, "That's about as painless as you can make it. Guess I better update my resume. But before that, I have to go down to Washington tomorrow to help empty out Tina's apartment and then drive her car back to the Bronx. The new decade is off to an awfully rough start, I guess it's fair to say."

"Considering the personal hits you've taken since late March, I'd have given anything to spare you this. What's happened is equally unpleasant for me. But everybody's got a boss."

"Maybe the answer is to be your own boss."

"That's what Warren's doing. He and a couple of other guys are starting a consulting firm. If you want to stay in placement, here's a list of people who'll be told about our situation. It's possible they could have an opening. At minimum, they might be able to give you some leads. There are both corporate employers and executive placement firms on the list. You've dealt with Reuben Merrill in the past, and a while back I heard that he's had an ongoing interest in talking with you."

"Having always been a corporate guy, it might be an interesting change to work on the supply side. Problem is, the market for people like me is stone cold, and there are a bunch of candidates out there for any management opening that's come up. Merrill? He's a loose cannon, but effective."

"Your son, your fiancée, and now this. Hard to believe you're handling it so well."

"My mother likes to say, 'And this too shall pass'. We'll survive; Tina won't. But we're committed to meet on the other side. I like the thought. Maybe that's the equivalent of smokin' opium, but I'll use whatever props I can invent."

"From what I understand, your Tina had an awful lot to offer. I heard that from Seth McIvers. They worked together, and he thinks well of her. There sure are inequities in life. Just think about all of the really rotten people out there who'll outlive her. It makes me wonder if the God we know is fair. In Tina's case, I think not."

Before he left for the weekend, Erich sat with Katie and told her that their recruiting and employment function had been wiped out and that he'd been given notice. She was in tears. "You have to know that Joel's upset," Erich added, "and rightly so, because the human resources department he worked so hard to staff has been dismantled. That's what was bothering me, and what I couldn't talk about, after I came back from Sydney. But if it's any consolation, the downsizing is reaching into departments all over the building. At least I can still use my office until the end of August, and Joel says I can lean on you for help. Will that be all right, partner?"

Katie wiped away her tears and said, "I don't know what to say, Erich. Yes I do. Of course you can lean on me, as you call it, in more ways than one—and anytime even after the end of August. I told you a long time ago that I'm another partner who cares. I still do. You already know that. I'm fairly young, but I've never known anyone who's had as many things go wrong as you have. And it's all happened within a few months. I don't know how you're able to handle it. I'd have slit my wrists by now. It says a lot about your fortitude."

"Let's see how well I hold up. There are still plenty of dark days ahead. Looks like I'll have to reach down inside and find some farm boy grit. Maybe all my sins have come back to haunt me. Brenna's been great support, and I'm grateful that I can count on you, too."

"Anytime you need me, Erich. Remember that."

Parallel with Erich's having been given his termination notice, the medical staff in Washington concluded earlier in the week that they'd done all they could for Tina Conti. It was too little, too late. Most important, there was no known cure for leukemia. They recommended to the family that they make her as comfortable as possible in her own bed. There was no need for her to be hospitalized in New York. Her cancer was now beyond further treatment. There was no slowing its inexorable advance, and there was no hope of remission.

With plans set to move Tina's things out of her apartment, Erich thought he might be able to visit her at the hospital. It was not to be.

On the Saturday of the long weekend, Erich caught an early train into Grand Central, took the Forty-second Street Shuttle, a Number 3 IRT train to Penn Station, and the 8:30 Metroliner into Washington's Union Station. He then took a cab to Tina's little Georgetown apartment—not far from the university. He hadn't seen Tina for a month, but her image and the rich memories of four weeks ago came flooding back. Aldo had given Erich a spare key in case he got there first. He had. To be here now, alone, in this place she'd lived for the past year, tested his strength. The little things that were hers, the photos he'd given her, a glass she'd touched, the bed they'd loved in. There was too much pain to bear. It finally got to him, but for a time it would be the last of his tears.

When Aldo and his two sons, Raul and Luca, arrived, and after they'd been introduced, they went right to work. It was a job to get done. But they were rearranging Erich's images of Tina's home, and also blurring some of his memories of what they'd shared only twenty-eight days earlier. How could he have known this day would even happen? And it had all came about so quickly. But to salvage something of what had been, he took a glass with Tina's pale lipstick and smudged fingerprints on it, carefully wrapped it in a paper towel, and put it in her Falcon. Erich Mauer would live for nearly another half-century, and until his dying day that simple olive water glass would be among his most cherished possessions.

Before Tina vacated her East Eighty-third Street apartment in Manhattan, Erich had helped her dispose of a good many things, so there wasn't all that much to move back. What was left in the apartment belonged to the landlord. When the truck was loaded, and the keys returned, the Contis led the way as they started their 240-mile drive to Holland Avenue in the Bronx. While he drove, Erich reflected on all that had happened during the more than three years he and Tina had known each other. Then his thoughts turned to their loading the truck up ahead of him now on I-95. "The funny things that come to mind," he said quietly. When they'd checked what was in the chest of drawers in Tina's bedroom, it was the pair of undies with tiny pink flowers all over them that he remembered from Sydney. It was by chance that he saw them, and the fact that he did would leave him with a memory that he'd never forget. Erich's eyes blurred momentarily, but he held on. It helped to be sitting behind the wheel of Tina's little red Falcon simply because it made him feel closer to her.

When they got to the Bronx, it was late. Aldo invited him to stay over.

"We got lotsa room, Erich."

"After today, I think I need to sleep in my own bed. Call it an emotional thing. You hadn't seen Tina's apartment, but you probably know that I stayed there just four weeks ago when I came back from London. It was hard watching my memories being loaded on the truck. I'll come back in the morning to help you unload it if you'd like."

"Nah, no more than there is, me and the boys can take care of it. Thanks anyway for the offer. Late as it is, you ought to take the Falcon. Make the trip easier for you."

"I'm exhausted, Aldo. Best if I ride the train. The Burke Avenue stop on the Number 5 line ought to be close by, and there's still time for me to catch the 9:57 to Seaford. I really need to be with my Kurt and make sure he's okay. But before I go, do you know when Tina's coming home? I've only been able to talk to her a couple of times a week after she gave me her bad news on the fourth. The last time she called was at midweek. Since we were going to be close by I thought maybe I could work in a quick visit. She liked the idea but discouraged me from trying to fit it into what she knew would be a busy day. Another reason could've been that she doesn't look all that well and didn't want me to see her that way."

"Meant to tell you about that earlier," Aldo said. "We had a call yesterday to tell us they're bringing her up next Wednesday. Should be here sometime in the afternoon. Tina wouldn't have known that when you talked to her."

"I'll come back then if it's all right. What I haven't told you is that my job has been wiped out. I don't have to go to work after the thirty-first, so you can expect to see a lot of me."

Incredulità! Tina, a kid in detention, and no job now. Gesù, you got a lot to deal with. Well, you're welcome anytime. And I gotta say it again. Working with you today makes me real sorry that you won't be part of the family. Tina's been right about you all along. Maybe we'll adopt ya anyway."

"It goes both ways, Aldo. I'd have been proud to be your son-in-law," then turning toward Raul and Luca, "and a brother-in-law to you guys. That won't happen now, but I'd be pleased to be an honorary member of your family. Thank you. And when I come back, I want to meet your Maria. I'd do it tonight, but I should probably get going if I'm to make my train."

"The Burke Avenue stop is close," Aldo said. "Can't miss it. Just go straight up the street. First one you come to is Burke. You can see it from here. Look. Anyway, turn left and it's two blocks over. You'll be able to see it once you're around the corner. Take the number 2 train and change to the number 5 at 180th. It's the fourth stop down. The Number 5 goes under Grand Central. You know the subway system, so you won't have any problems."

"Thanks. G'night, Aldo. Raul. Luca." They shook hands. "See you on Wednesday."

Erich made the 9:57 with time to spare. And then when he walked in the door at home, Brenna was waiting for him.

"You're too much, babe. I didn't see your car in the garage, but I'm awfully glad you're here. It's been a long day." They held each snugly for nearly a full minute. They both needed it.

"You look awful, Erich Mauer. I'm here to keep you company and to make you look better, too. It's late, but it begins with a drink. I'm staying over until Monday, and since the weather's supposed to be good you're coming to our family cookout. You're not going to be alone."

"I feel bad about your guys, though."

"Dad is with them until Colleen takes over. They always enjoy having him around."

"Where's Kurt?"

"He played baseball all afternoon and then ate with the Engels. He's also been invited to stay over for their barbeque on Monday.

"Good that you had Rudi's key. How long have you been here?"

"A couple of hours. I knew you'd be late. And just so you'll know, I took Kurt and my two and went up to see Rudi for a little while this morning. He loved it. Until he asked about Tina. I told him she was very sick and it broke his heart. He was in tears. So like a caring mom would do, I held him. His tears were for you, too. He asked me, 'What else can go wrong for my dad?'"

"Well, I've got his answer. My department at IMCO has been wiped out. It's effective a week from tomorrow. I'll be unemployed as of June 1. Just because of that, I'll have another drink."

"God! I can't believe what you've had to go through since March. What's left? It's a miracle you haven't lost your mind."

"That comes later. Mother thinks things run in threes, so maybe this is it for a while. I hope so. I'm near the end of my string."

"What are you going to do now?"

"Start hunting for a new job. Only thing is, I look awful, like you said, so no company will give me serious consideration until I shape up. And that will depend a lot on Tina. I wanted to see her today, not knowing until this evening that she's being brought up on Wednesday. When I asked about seeing her at the hospital, she turned me down. By now, I don't suppose there's much left of her. Could be that's the reason why. She can't last long. The fact that they're not admitting her to a local hospital tells me that. I'll try to see her every day until she doesn't recognize me any longer. If it's like Marie, she'll say her last words and close her eyes a few days before she's gone. That'll tell us that it's all over."

"Some time ago, you wrote down what you thought it was."

"Yep, I did." Erich went to the nightstand by his bed and took a folded sheet of paper from the lower drawer. He handed it to her.

She opened it and read the single word he'd written down. "How on earth did you know?"

"It was Marie Robertson all over again. The same signs. One right after the other. It was the only conclusion I could come to. I didn't want to alarm Tina, but I had to lean on her to see her doctor. Even if she'd gone to him immediately, the end result wouldn't have been any different from what it is now. Medical science doesn't have a cure. It was most likely too late when we ran into each other in Sydney. But there weren't any symptoms then."

"Sorry to find out that you were right. I'd have rather lost you to her than to see her die. I know it's hard, but I've already said it. I'll be right here."

"You don't have to do this, you know. But I'm grateful that you are. I'm also exhausted. It's time for bed."

"May I join you?"

"I was hoping you'd ask. Yes. I'd like it if you did."

Brenna slept snuggled up to Erich both nights. It was comforting. Then after they'd had a light breakfast on Monday, she took him by the ear and made him help with their afternoon barbeque. He wasn't especially hungry, but it was good to be busy and around people.

On Tuesday, Erich went to the office and made calls to several people he knew personally to find out if they had any interest in talking with him. He also worked through part of Joel's list of companies to see if they had openings or if they knew of anything that might be available.

When Erich took a break from getting nothing but negative answers, Katie came in, sat down, and showed him a sad face. "I can't believe what's going on. They're asking people like me to stay, but the cuts are deep for senior managers like you. What do they expect to do, run the company with administrative assistants and executive secretaries?"

"Our mainstream stuff will shrivel up and die before long, so they don't need me. Saves 'em money. Anyway, you can finish off whatever's left. If you need help, I'll be around. One thing for sure, nobody on the executive floor will wind up on the street. Doesn't matter if the corporate philosophy is centralized or decentralized, which is what it's reverting to."

"By the time you're gone, I'll probably have a job out on Long Island that's closer to home. Before that happens, I'd love to put a move on you, but that would be thoughtless beyond words. Anything new with Tina?"

"She's coming home tomorrow. No hospitalization. It's over. She'll spend whatever days she has left in her own bed up in the Bronx. I'd give you that number, but there's no need to. I'll either be here or you'll be able to reach me at home."

"When you see her, give her my love."

"That's sweet of you. I will."

By the end of the afternoon, Erich had done all his interest in job hunting would allow. His attention span was understandably short because tomorrow was a day he dreaded. He hadn't seen Tina since two days before his birthday. "She'll have changed by now," Erich thought. "I have a feeling it's going to be hard to take." And since Saturday, April 25 was surely the last night they'd ever spend together, he wanted to preserve every detail of it. That fixation stole time from his search efforts.

Katie came back into his office to say she was going home, but first she asked how the rest of his calls went.

"It's a dead market. There was an article in the *Journal* last week saying that even the airlines are complaining that business is way down. Anyway, I didn't turn up a thing, other than Reuben Merrill said he'd like to see me next Monday at his place on West End Avenue. He's sure he can use me, but it'll be hard to stay afloat until I make some placements. Whatever, it isn't your problem, so go home. I'll probably be in later in the week."

Chapter Twenty-Two

On Wednesday afternoon, Erich drove to the Bronx and was there when the van pulled up in front of what had been Tina's home for most of her life. Surprisingly, she hadn't lost much more weight, but her color wasn't at all good. He went out, and when Tina saw him, she gave him the best of what was left of her captivating smile. She greeted her mother and father first, and they each kissed her on the cheek.

Then she turned to Erich and said, "Hi, my love. It's so good to see you. I've missed you terribly. When I wasn't completely wiped out, you were about the only thing I wanted to think about. Helped me through some bad times. And I'm sorry about last Saturday. Much as I wanted to see you, I was having the last of my therapy and it's always flattened me for a couple of days. Then Papa said you probably wouldn't have time anyway."

"He was right. But I've really missed you, too. It's been over a month. I've been worried about you."

"You won't have to do that much longer."

"Shhh. You shouldn't talk that way."

Erich took her little hand and held it while the aides moved Tina toward her bedroom.

"The doctors have told me what's ahead, so I want you to come see me whenever you can."

"That'll be just about every day. I still need to see Rudi on Saturdays. But instead of looking too far ahead, let's just enjoy each other's company."

"You're right. Like all of our times together."

"I'm sorry we didn't get to talk much while you were in the hospital, but I understood what you were going through."

"There was so much fatigue, and then I was *so* depressed. I didn't think it was a good idea to call then. And I knew that with Rudi in detention it would've been nearly impossible for you to come down. Didn't matter. I wouldn't have been good company anyway. I'll try to do better here."

Once in her bed, Tina was propped up and wanted to talk. After all she'd been through, she looked reasonably good. Not healthy at all, but better than Erich had imagined.

"The first thing I want you to do," Tina said, "is to give me a welcome home kiss and then hold me for a minute. Not too tight. I might break." They shared their affection just as they had so many times before. She was still fairly strong; Erich hadn't expected that.

In the background, her parents smiled approvingly. Tina was glad to see Erich, and he was obviously bringing her some overdue happiness. And there was even a hint of color in her cheeks.

"You feel wonderful. It's what I've needed. I'm better already. You're good medicine," she said softly. "If they hadn't put out my fire in Georgetown, I might even let you attack me. But that would take energy I don't have now. Just stay close."

"You know I'll do that. Only thing is, I'll have to get home and feed Kurt at some point."

"I probably won't hold you up because I've been falling asleep for a while late in the afternoon. That way you can sneak off, and I won't know you're gone. Until that happens, I'd like you to hold my hand."

"Maybe I could give you another little hug first." They held each other briefly and kissed again. Very gently.

"I've needed that kind of medication. Tomorrow, you'll have to tell me about the last month, what you've been doing, and anything we didn't get into when we talked."

"One thing I can tell you now is that both my unit and my job at IMCO are history. I'm unemployed starting Monday."

"*Ohhh*, Erich. When things go bad, they come in a bunch. Makes me sad to hear that. Last year all over again. I'm just sorry that I can't be here to prop you up like I did before. But you'll be all right. I know my boss pretty well." She smiled weakly.

"I'll do my best not to let you down. Some friendly news is that Katie sends her love."

"That's sweet of her. Thank her for me. Before long, she'll be free to chase after you."

"Not likely. She has a lot going on, so she'll be just fine."

As they talked on, Tina did fall asleep. Erich slipped his hand out of hers and then kissed her softly on her forehead. She still had a sweet face. All the therapy hadn't changed that. He told Aldo and Maria Conti that he'd be back tomorrow, said goodbye, and then started home to feed Kurt. On the drive back to Seaford, Erich felt completely hollow. "With all of Brenna's support, why am I feeling like this?" he wondered. Not wanting to face the truth, he suggested aloud, "Maybe I need some counseling."

Since Erich didn't have to show up at his office any longer, he decided there wasn't any reason not to shop on Friday morning and then do the laundry before he left for the Bronx. That left him free on Saturday morning to take Kurt and Brenna to see Rudi. And committed as he was to spending every hour that he could with Tina, he dropped them off before going on to the Bronx. Brenna told him she'd be at his place by the time he got back. "I'll be there to check your mental health. Just as important, you matter to me in case you've forgotten."

"I haven't. And I won't."

The Friday, Saturday schedule would get to be regular pattern in the weeks just ahead.

Then on the last Sunday in May, Kurt said he wanted to go along so he could see Tina. At first, Erich wasn't sure if it was a good idea, but the longer he thought about it the more sense it made. And it was a good decision. It had been two months since she'd been out to Seaford and they were pleased to see each other again. Without question, it brightened Tina's day. That Kurt came with his dad confirmed how much she meant to him, too.

They had a good visit, and then when they were on their way home, Kurt said, "It's still Tina, especially the smile, but she's changed even more since I saw her just before Easter. Once is enough, though. Don't think I could handle another visit. Knowing her the way you have, you gotta hurt inside."

"Worse than it was with my dad, your granddad. He came in from being out at our big barn, said he didn't feel well, and within an hour he was gone. I wasn't there. But to care about this woman the way I do, and to watch it happen, one day at a time, is about the hardest thing I've ever had to do."

"One thing I'm finding out is that life sure isn't fair. She's such a good person." Kurt wiped tears from his cheeks.

The next afternoon, Erich saw Reuben Merrill and had an informal meeting to talk about the possibility of his getting into the executive search business. When they'd finished, Erich explained what was going on in his personal life and told Merrill he needed a little time to consider his offer to join the firm. He was sympathetic and said he totally understood.

And, without fail, Erich made his afternoon trips to the Bronx to be at Tina's side. By mid-June, her condition had deteriorated. Noticeably so. On Friday of the third week in June, Erich couldn't have been sure, but she apparently sensed that the end of her life was at hand. Difficult as it was for her, she wanted to talk. As she did, Erich held her frail hand in his.

"When I sleep," she said in a weakened voice, "I see this bright light and someone in white with arms out toward me." Erich thought about how Tina had approached him last December in Sydney. "I feel so much peace, so much comfort. I'm not afraid any longer. I'm ready. But, no babies. No Erich. Not even a life. I want you to be all right. Worries me to leave you behind. And with a broken heart. Like last year. Mistake to go away. Would've had all that time together. If we hadn't met again . . . could've spared you this. You wouldn't have known what happened. Treasure what we had . . . glad we could sha . . ." She was drifting in and out of consciousness.

"You need to rest, my sweet."

Then in a failing voice, "I'm so tired . . . so tired . . . you've meant so much. Everything. Wait for you . . . share our lives then. Love you so, Erich . . . 'member your Tina...."

"Always, my love."

Her eyes closed, and she slept. There was the trace of a smile on her lips. Erich squeezed Tina's hand ever so gently, kissed her on the cheek, and then said goodbye to the Contis as he left her bedroom. Alone with his anguish, it was a very difficult ride home.

During Erich's Saturday afternoon visit, Tina didn't awaken. He kept his vigil, but she never spoke again. Erich Mauer and her parents had heard the last of her words. He went home tormented with the thought that he might have done something more to save her life. It wasn't rational to think that way because leukemia had no known cure.

When Erich got to Holland Avenue just before one o'clock on Sunday, Aldo met him outside their front door.

"It's good you got here early. Tina's doctor and our priest are with my baby." When they walked into the room, Erich could sense death. The priest anointed Tina on her forehead and administered last rites: "Through this holy unction may the Lord pardon thee for whatever sins or faults thou hast committed." Maria and Aldo each held one of her hands.

At about one fifteen on June 21, Tina Conti drew her last breath and left behind those who loved her. The woman Erich Mauer thought would share his future was taken from him. He had no tears. On this day, at this hour, he had no feeling. His face was ashen, and he was numb to the core of his being. Maria Conti dropped her head on the body of the last child she bore and sobbed with grief. Aldo, who had seen death so many times as a police officer, gritted his teeth and held on. But his contorted face plainly showed the pain he felt.

Before Erich left Tina's bedside, he stroked her hair and then gently kissed her lips. "Goodbye, my love. The time will come when we're together again. Until then, you'll always have a place in my heart and in my thoughts."

Aware that Tina's family had seen him, he said, "I . . . I hope you don't mind that I did that. We had a bright future; now we have none. And the love we'd have shared is gone."

"No," Aldo said. "Mama and I know that she was your girl, and that you had a wedding planned. You had good reason to say goodbye to her the way you did. It says how much you loved her. Tina knows. I know she's smiling. It's all right, Erich."

Maria made coffee, and those who survived Tina were obliged to talk about what would follow. Aldo had already made calls and said the funeral would be on Wednesday morning. "I'll have the rest of the details for you tomorrow. Calling hours will be on Tuesday. Tina wanted you and your friend Clayton to carry the casket. You, yes, but if Clayton is a pallbearer, it cuts out Maria's brother. I know you and Clayton worked together, so he's invited. I want you to take care of that. The six will be you, Raul, Luca, my brother, Maria's brother, and me."

"You couldn't keep Clayton away. He'd come even if he wasn't invited. We were all close; in his own way he loved her, too."

"Good to have a friend like him. Now, there was a picture you brought back from an island. Tina told me you should keep it."

"You saw it when we met back in January. I was to have it ready for her when she moved back. That would've been next Saturday. She asked me to have it framed. It's done and still at home. I'll be glad to keep it. She liked it, so it'll be a part of our memories."

"Tina asked to be buried with the ID bracelet you gave her because it was something special you did. She told me the story, and I read the words on the back. They got to me. She also wants one of those little pictures of you from Australia to go with her. I thought that was kinda strange, but she was crazy about you, Erich, so why not? She had 'em in every room at her place down in Washington. Tells me a lot about what was in her heart and the kind of love she'd have given you—had she lived."

"Much more of this and I'm going to come unhinged, Aldo."

"I know. I know. But hang in there. It's tough on us, too. Last thing is the ring with the opal in it that you gave her when we were down at Penn Station. Tina forgot that she'd told me it was her engagement ring. Real pretty. She was going to have you take it off her finger since you put it there, but she couldn't handle that. Anyway, she wrote a note to the wife of Erich Mauer and put it in an envelope along with the ring. She said you'd eventually accept the fact that she was gone and would get on with your life. She was sure that someday you'd meet somebody who'll make you happy and will want to marry. She wants that woman, your wife, to have it. The envelope isn't for you, so you're not to open it."

"I won't. You have my word." Tears welled up. "God, you've got me on the edge. She did the same thing when I went down to New York Plaza. Before she left for Washington, she called my secretary and told her about me—what I liked, didn't like, and things like that. Your daughter was one in a million. This is very hard on a busted heart. Is that all? Please?"

"For now. Erich, you have to remember that we knew Tina longer than you did. Your memories are different, but you don't have any corner on the hurting."

"I know, and I need to be reminded of that. We're all having to face the same thing. It's just that my feelings are so intense. Maybe that's why I think I'm the only one with an ache the size of Manhattan Island. But there's something I can't figure out. When I think about all the hours I was here with Tina, she never mentioned what she wanted me to do with the tapa cloth, or about Clayton, or the bracelet, or the ring. That hurts right here." Erich put a hand over his heart.

"Tina said you had lots of good times together, but that she'd also given you a lot of pain going back to early last year. She knew what you'd go through after she was gone. So she wanted you to enjoy your visits, like she was down with the flu or something and that you'd still have your years together. She just wanted to stay away from anything that would remind you that she wouldn't be around long."

"That was my Tina. When I was going through my divorce two years ago, she worked really hard to keep everything light and cheerful around the office. But before she left for D. C., she wrote a memo, which I still have, and put it in the office mail. I got it the first morning after she was gone and it just about destroyed me. If I could've opened a window in my seventh floor office, I might have been tempted to jump. She was trying to say thank you. It was sweet of her, but it hurt something awful. I hope she didn't do that again. I couldn't handle it. As it is, the ring is a trauma waiting to happen maybe two or three, or even five years from now. It'll be a reminder of all we meant to each other and what we finally had to look forward to."

"No. About two weeks ago, Tina told me the story about the memo and she said she wouldn't do anything like that again. This time, she thought the pain would be too much."

"God bless her."

"Let's get on to other things. We don't need you here later today or tomorrow. Luca's called for the hearse. It'll be here soon, and we'll take care of all the arrangements. I want you to be at the funeral home by noon on Tuesday, and stay all afternoon."

"You know I'll do it—and anything else you ask."

"I thought you'd say something like that."

"Now, I've got to get home to my guy, give him the news, and then make some calls to people who mattered to both of us."

"Okay, Erich. See you on Tuesday. Take care of yourself." Erich hugged Maria, and then said goodbye all around.

Part of Erich's haste was that he didn't want to be around when Tina was taken from her bedroom. She would always be there, at least in Erich's memory. He'd walked in with her, held her hand when she was brought home in late May, and that was as far as his fortitude and his sanity would allow him to go.

As he was driving home, Erich remembered that today was the summer solstice, the longest day. He couldn't help but think back to the last one, December 21, when it marked the beginning of Australia's summer. It was also the last of the three days in Sydney when their love was reborn and a new chapter in their lives had begun. The recollection was so clear, that of seeing Tina off at Kingsford Smith airport, the happiness they felt, and the possibility, finally, of their having a life together. But he guessed that the deadly cancer in her system had no doubt already begun its long, unremitting march toward this day six months later. He wanted to cry, but there were no tears. At least not yet.

When Erich got home, he called Brenna. "I thought you'd want to know that Tina's gone. She died at about a quarter after one. We were all there with her. I haven't told Kurt yet. What I'm going to do is take him with me to Bridgeton and break the news to both boys at the same time."

"I'm terribly, terribly sorry, Erich. You don't know how sad I am about it. So young and so much to look forward to. It's a tragic end. If you don't mind, I'd like to go along. Maybe it'll help some."

"You don't have to, you know that, but it's sweet of you to offer. I'll come by and pick you up."

Erich pried Kurt away from the TV and said they were going to see Rudi.

"Why? We never go up on Sunday."

"I couldn't get there yesterday, so I know he'd like to see us. We're picking Brenna up on the way. Get your things together." Kurt didn't ask any other questions. Erich assumed that he was afraid to.

Rudi was really pleased to see them. "Super! I thought maybe you couldn't get here this weekend."

"Part of the reason I couldn't come up until today had to do with Tina. And I wanted both of you to know it at the same time. Tina's gone. She died early this afternoon. I was with her, even though she didn't know I was there."

"*Ohhh, Dad.*" Rudi held his dad and sobbed. Kurt put his arms around both of them and said it wasn't fair. Tears were running down his cheeks. Erich held on. He was still in shock and felt very little other than a severe ache in his chest.

"I thought there was a reason for this," Kurt said. "It's about time we had some good news. The last few months have been the pits."

Brenna interrupted and said, "Guys. All three of you. I want you to know this makes me sad, too, and I'll be as much help as I can."

"You've done a lot for us already," Kurt said.

"It'll take a while for the wounds to heal, so we'll spend as much time together as we can. This is hard on a family. I know that from when my mother died. It tests our strength, but we'll survive. And I also want you to know that I'll be there if you need me." Erich gave her a hug. His sons did the same, and all three of them thanked her.

"Tina will be buried on Wednesday, probably in the morning. I'm one of the pallbearers. Tina wanted it that way. So does Aldo, her dad. Rudi, I can't spring you from here, but Kurt you can go if you want to."

"I wouldn't want to go," Rudi said. "I want to remember her the way she was, not what she's like now. Anyway, we leave for the camp up in Maine tomorrow morning, so I couldn't go."

"Kurt?"

"I feel the same way. Seeing her after what she went through? I don't know. Let me hang onto the picture I have of her when you both got back from Australia. She looked real healthy, but she'd changed a lot when I went with you to see her that last time. I guess you never know. If it's okay I'd like to stay home."

"I can't argue with you, guy. It's been hard on me watching her waste away after working together for two years, and then what we had afterwards. But I don't have any choice. Fact is, I wouldn't want to have the option of being someplace else on Wednesday."

"You didn't forget that I go to L.A. on Saturday?" Kurt asked.

"Nearly had. Good thing I bought your ticket when I did. But, okay, I'm on my own come Wednesday."

Erich said goodbye to Rudi and wished him a good summer. "If you can find a stamp, be good to get a card from you."

"I can do that. It's real sad about Tina. She was super nice. I'm even sorrier now that I gave you so many problems."

"One thing I won't be doing is taking drugs to deal with them. You guys are still counting on me to be around—and I will be."

Rudi hugged his dad, then Brenna, said thanks for her help, and then did a fancy handshake with Kurt, something that was inappropriate considering the reason they were all together.

When the three of them were on their way back to Seaford, Brenna said, "You two are eating with me tonight. Nothing fancy, just good food. After a day like this, it's the least I can do."

"Appreciate it," Erich said, "but my appetite's gone."

"I know, but give it time. That'll change. I'll see to it. I'm the best medicine you've got." And, over time, she proved to be.

After they'd had dinner, and were ready to leave, Brenna made sure Erich had a caring hug and a gentle kiss. They were intended to remind him that his support team was still in place. It made him feel a little better, but there were dark days ahead. So he said, "I'll need more medication like that if I'm to be cured." He was far more serious than he made it sound.

"I have a full supply on hand. Just call on me. Anytime."

"Be prepared." They held each other and she kissed him again.

Kurt gave Brenna a hug and thanked her for all she was doing. When Erich started for the car, Kurt turned and said, "Dad needs your help. He's having a real bad time."

"I know, Kurt. And he'll get it. G'night."

Erich waved, and they were on their way home. Brenna stood at the end the driveway, waved back, and said quietly, "I feel so sorry for that good man. What a trial he's had. It's a wonder he hasn't lost his mind or buckled." She had a feeling of heartfelt sympathy, and it showed in her eyes.

On Monday, Aldo called to see how Erich was doing and also to give him the address of the funeral home in the Bronx. It was on Allerton Avenue, not far from their home. Then, armed with the details, Erich called Clayton to give him the sad news. It came as no surprise, but he was unquestionably upset.

"I've been expecting your call. I just couldn't know when it would come. I'll be there. You must be starting to think that your life is cursed. My condolences, Erich. I know how dearly you loved her. It's got to be painful."

"It is that. There are no words. But losing my job gave me the freedom I needed so I could spend time with Tina. A small blessing, in a way."

"Maybe we can talk for a few minutes on Wednesday. I can't make the service, but I'll see you at the cemetery."

Then Erich called Katie. She was in tears immediately. When she recovered, they talked for a few minutes, and then said, "Life is so unfair, and I just hate it that you have to face something like this. But you remember, I've said several times that I'm another partner who cares. It still goes. See you on Wednesday."

"Thanks, Katie."

Tuesday turned out to be a very long day. Erich expected that it would be. But he met so many genuinely kind people. He had their sympathies. And the Contis were very fortunate to have such compassionate support. And it would always be there. He envied them. Erich had but three or four people he could look to for help, foremost among them, Brenna Walsh.

Throughout the day, he circulated among the visitors, but he was never far from Tina's casket. What the mortician had done was remarkable. She looked healthy, almost the way she did in Sydney. And he had restored her features to that sweet face he had seen so many mornings just before she opened her eyes. He couldn't stop looking at this striking young woman who had been taken from him. God, did he hurt inside!

And then on Wednesday morning, the time arrived to say goodbye to the daughter, and sister, and sweetheart, and niece, and aunt they'd all loved dearly. Erich was so caught up in his own thoughts and profound sorrow that he barely heard the words the priest spoke. The service over, he rode in the limousine with the Contis. Aldo confirmed that he'd been informally adopted and that he would ride with them as family. Erich felt honored.

At the cemetery, he saw Katie. She gave him a hug and showed him tears. "Thank you for coming," Erich said. "I'll be in the office maybe late this week, more likely sometime early next."

"Just let me know. By the way, you had a message yesterday from Peter Fitzhugh in Sydney. Here's what I copied from it. Given the timing, I'm not sure how you want to reply." Erich shoved it in his suit pocket.

"Thanks again for being here. Tina really liked you. You had a common bond: Erich Mauer."

Then Clayton arrived. "Who was the pretty little redhead?"

"My teammate at IMCO. Warren hired her for me. She's been great, and she's also been after me. Too bad she doesn't fit into my plans. Katie would be a keeper. She's fairly young, though. But that's not why we're here."

"I'll stand with you," Clayton said.

The number of mourners had dwindled from those Erich had seen at Mass. It was now primarily immediate family the way it looked. He and Clayton stood near the coffin and listened to the final words Father Marzetti offered. He concluded by imploring a caring God to accept Tina Conti as a member of his flock. Just as the coffin was being lowered into its final resting place for all time, Erich reached out with his right hand and touched the cover. The words Erich whispered were: "Our day will come, my love." It was a gesture that touched Aldo and Maria Conti, but his intent was to signify that he and Tina had come full circle. It was the same hand he had used exactly eighteen months ago to begin the process of introducing her to the unique beauty of physical love. It was the hand she took when they walked across the lobby of the Wentworth Hotel in Sydney last December 19. And it was also the hand Erich had used in early January to slip the opal ring on her finger. He never talked with the Contis about any of his reasons for doing what he did. It was between Erich and Tina alone. Then, as he began to straighten up, he reached out as if to find support. Extreme grief had finally punctured Erich Mauer's shell, and he felt lightheaded. Clayton and Raul Conti were quick to react, and they held him until he was steady again. Maria and Aldo saw what happened. They now fully understood how deeply this never to be son-in-law loved their daughter. It was a poignant footnote to a brutally painful day. Erich apologized. Neither Clayton nor Raul would hear of it. "We feel your pain," Raul said. Clayton, with a grim and worried look, nodded to show his concurrence.

There was the customary meal after the interment, and Erich invited Clayton to come with them. He was hesitant, but Raul and Luca, now knowing his relationship with both Tina and Erich, insisted that he join the family. He finally agreed and would never regret that he'd accepted their invitation. The Contis made Clayton feel welcome, and they went out of their way to see that he was comfortable among so many strangers. He was introduced as the boss of Tina's boss, Erich, at Essex Steel—the man who would've been part of their family, had she lived.

"Had she lived." Those three words, now etched in Erich's memory, would torment him for months to come.

At the end of the meal, Clayton said, "Erich, I've got to get back to the office. I'm so terribly sorry that we've lost Tina. There aren't words. She was one of the finest people I've ever known, and it's a loss for all of us. In my own way, I loved her, too. The two of you were a perfect match, and that your future won't be what you'd hoped for saddens me very deeply. I'll be as much support as I can for as long as you need it, so I want you to stay in touch."

"Thanks, Clayton I'll be in and out my office for the next couple of months. Maybe some Friday evening soon we can have dinner. I won't be a stranger. It's at a time like this that close friends take on even greater importance. I'll call you sometime during the next few days to find out how your schedule looks."

"Please do. I'll also want to know how you're getting on."

Before the number of guests began to thin, Erich was pleased that nearly everyone made a point of echoing their expressions of profound sympathy. Later, as they were leaving, each of them said goodbye to this man they'd never met and would most likely never see again. When it was just the five of them, Erich got his things together and made ready to start a new chapter in his life.

"Erich," Aldo said, "we want you to feel welcome to come see us whenever you can. It was because of Tina that we know each other, so you're part of our family. She's gone, but our door will always be open to you."

"Thank you for your kindness. I will come see you. My future has question marks, but I'll let you know how things work out."

Maria came to Erich and gave him an affectionate hug. Raul and Luca shook his hand and wished him well.

At the door, Aldo put his hands on Erich's shoulders and said, "I've gotta thank you for giving our little girl so much happiness in her last months. She'll be waiting for you. Count on it. That's my Tina." Then tears welled up.

Erich gave him a firm hug, turned and said goodbye to everyone. It was with a heavy heart that he started the lonely drive back to Seaford. It gave him time to reflect on his situation, but he didn't need any reminders that with a son in drug rehab, his fiancée dead, and his career adrift, that he had reasons enough to wonder about his future.

But as he drove, Erich remembered the words of philosopher Jean-Paul Sartre. They were so fitting at this heartbreaking time in his life: "*Life begins on the other side of despair.*"

That simple expression of hope was about all this shattered man had to sustain him.

And it would.

Lightning Source UK Ltd.
Milton Keynes UK
UKHW020109220219
337759UK00010B/1059/P